Michelle Vernal loves a hap
husband and their two boys
It's a city that is slowing rebuilding its happy ending. She's partial to a glass of wine, loves a cheese scone and has recently taken up yoga—a sight to behold indeed. Her books are written with humour and warmth and she hopes you enjoy reading them.

@MichelleVernal
www.facebook.com/michellevernalnovelist
www.michellevernalbooks.com

Also by Michelle Vernal

The Traveller's Daughter

Sweet Home Summer

MICHELLE VERNAL

A division of HarperCollins*Publishers*
www.harpercollins.co.uk

Harper*Impulse*
An imprint of HarperCollins*Publishers*
The News Building
1 London Bridge Street
London SE1 9GF

www.harpercollins.co.uk

This paperback edition 2018

First published in Great Britain in ebook format
by HarperCollins*Publishers* 2018

Copyright © Michelle Vernal 2018

Michelle Vernal asserts the moral right to
be identified as the author of this work

A catalogue record for this book
is available from the British Library

ISBN: 9780008226541

This novel is entirely a work of fiction.
The names, characters and incidents portrayed in it are
the work of the author's imagination. Any resemblance to
actual persons, living or dead, events or localities is
entirely coincidental.

Typeset in Birka by Palimpsest Book Production Ltd,
Falkirk, Stirlingshire

Printed and bound in Great Britain

All rights reserved. No part of this publication may be
reproduced, stored in a retrieval system, or transmitted,
in any form or by any means, electronic, mechanical,
photocopying, recording or otherwise, without the prior
permission of the publishers.

An Introduction of Sorts

I am a Matchmaker, and I'm a long way from what was once my family's home. Us Sullivans were put on this earth to bring together two halves of a pair and make a whole. I've been here drifting through these brutal but beautiful Badlands for a long time now, and I'm half a world away from where my great-grandfather once roamed the equally rugged lands of West Cork.

He rode the seas before you or your parents; even your grandparents were born to the Land of the Long White Cloud, Aotearoa. He came to New Zealand on a ship with billowing sails and a cargo of Irish folk seeking a better future and a sniff of gold. Only he knew that some wouldn't get either without his help. You see, we know something, us Sullivans, something I'll share with you now. It's not a fortune having been made that makes the world continue to go round – oh no, it's love, and that's our business.

The years have gone by, and the book we carry has been passed down with many a successful match made between its pages. You, yourself, might be a product of a Sullivan's meddling, you just never know. It's all there, inscribed in our book if you care to take a look.

This last wee while, I've been keeping my eye on a right pair; young Isla Brookes and her grandmother Bridget, the two most stubborn women I've ever witnessed walk the West Coast. They've both got it wrong along the way but it's not too late, it's never too late to call the Matchmaker, and when they do, I will come.

That's enough about me and mine though; now it's time I told you their story.

Chapter 1

Two weeks or thereabouts earlier…

Isla Brookes was a woman on the edge of a nervous breakdown. The fact she was teetering on the brink of something terrifying was not common knowledge, and she intended to keep it that way. She'd told anybody who'd asked or needed to know that in a couple of days she'd be off-grid for a few weeks. She was taking a much-needed sabbatical from her job as an Interior Design Consultant for Upscale Development, a high-end London property development company. The reason? Stress – she needed to step off the corporate ladder and take some time to heal, because the collapse of her relationship with Tim was still so very raw.

Maura and Henry, whose flat she'd fled to when she'd found the strength to finish things with Tim, or Toad as she now thought of him, had made her very welcome. However, she had no wish to become a permanent fixture on their couch. It was a couch upon which she'd spent too many afternoons pondering what she was supposed to do next. What did you do when you were told you were on the verge of a breakdown?

She wondered, fingering the packet of anti-depressants she'd been prescribed, it was all new to her. She needed to remove what was causing the stress from her life – that's what the harried NHS doctor had told her. Well, she'd done that by finishing things with Toad and taking an extended leave of absence from work. There was more to it than that though, Isla knew. Toad and her job were symptoms, neither were the full-blown illness.

If she were honest, she wasn't sure she even wanted to be here in England anymore and, putting the pills back in her handbag, she picked up the telly remote. Dr Phil loomed large on the screen. She knew she wasn't ready to go home to New Zealand either. What was it she'd read once? Oh yes, that was it; in times of stress or upheaval, you shouldn't make any life-changing decisions. So, that meant she shouldn't throw the towel in on her life in London and head off to an Ashram in India just yet. Maybe therapy was the answer then? But she didn't want to go to some stuffy Harley Street specialist. No, she wanted something more holistic than that. And that was where Google came in. It was a marvellous thing, Google, she thought while tapping in the words holistic therapy.

As soon as Break-Free Haven Lodge popped up, Isla knew she'd found her answer. She gazed longingly at the red barn-style buildings set in rural acreage. She'd go to the States to seek help. Isla explored the website feeling more and more certain she was on the right track as she read about the various hands-on treatment programmes and counselling sessions on offer. The rustic exterior of the complex belied the calming oasis housed inside. Oh yes, she thought, her fingers tip-tapping her name into the contact form provided. This was a place where she could regain her mojo.

The British were far too 'closed mouths' and 'stiff upper lips', the Americans were much more into 'talking about things.' Look at the way they all managed to work their problems out on Dr Phil, she thought, glancing over to the telly where there was a lot of smiling and clapping going on. Isla knew she'd gotten to the point where she needed to talk, or she'd go under. She was lucky in so much as she'd been given a warning that something had to give. Now it was up to her to heed that warning. That didn't mean she had to tell anyone she was going to a mental health retreat, though.

So, the word she *was* putting about on the street was that, to try and get some perspective back on what she was doing with her life, she was going to float like a free spirit around California for a fortnight. Yes, she knew it sounded very *Eat, Pray, Love* but this was her story and if it stopped people asking too many questions, then she was sticking to it.

Unfortunately, as she sat cradling the phone between her ear and her shoulder, it was a story that was not going down well with her mum, Mary. Isla had taken a deep breath knowing she could no longer put off the inevitable and had called her to tell her mum she would be incommunicado as of Friday. The conversation was going pretty much as expected.

'I don't like this Isla,' Mary muttered. 'And this connection isn't very good. You sound odd like you're a long way away.'

'I'm in London Mum; you're in Bibury. It's the other side of the world. I *am* a long way away.' It was an understatement. Her hometown of Bibury on New Zealand's West Coast, and

London, her home for the past ten years, weren't just hemispheres apart; they were an entire universe apart.

Bibury was named for a Cotswolds village in Britain. Not just any Cotswolds village, oh no – Bibury was purported to be the loveliest of them all. Isla had heard that it boasted centuries-old stone cottages, their steeply slanting roofs giving the much-visited village its chocolate box quality. All this waxing lyrical had captured her imagination, and she'd had to go and see it for herself. It was top of her 'places to tick off' list while in the UK, and she'd spent a very enjoyable three-day break in the Cotswolds not long after she first arrived in London. She'd reported back to her family that yes, the British village of Bibury lived up to its good press. It was, she told them, very pretty, unlike its New Zealand counterpart which, in Isla's opinion, would never win any beautiful town awards. Rugged and run down, yes, but beautiful? No. Isla reckoned the only thing the two places had in common was a river.

Her gran, Bridget, had harrumphed down the phone upon hearing this, wittering on that she was willing to bet gold had never been found in the River Colne as it had in the mighty Ahaura River of her birthplace. Isla had rolled her eyes. Much like she was doing now as she realized that the slow hissing down the phone line was nothing to do with a dodgy connection. It was a sound she knew well. Her mother was sighing in that hard done by, heartfelt way she always did when her daughter's actions perturbed her.

'Don't get smart Isla; you know what I mean. What's going on with you? One minute you have a high-flying job and you're living with a man whose arse you think the sun shines out of, and the next you're chucking the lot in to go and look for yourself in California of all places.'

'The saying is find yourself Mum, and I've just taken an extended leave of absence from work, that's all. For your information, I'm feeling really sad about being single again too. I mean you had Ryan and me by the time you were thirty, and this isn't where I saw myself at this point in my life. I need a rest, some time to think and take stock. I want to figure out what's next for me, but apart from that Mum, I'm fine,' Isla lied. She knew she sounded completely self-obsessed and she hated herself for it.

Her mother snorted. 'So you say, and you think far too much if you ask me. I'm telling you though, Isla it's not normal being uncontactable in this day and age. How will we know where you are while you're busy swanning around doing your floaty, find yourself bit? And, I don't know what your gran's going to have to say about it all.'

Isla knew exactly what her gran would have to say about it. It would go something like this: '*What are you on about Isla? Trying to find yourself?*' There would be the same snorting noise her mother had just made (it was hereditary), followed by: '*In my day we didn't have time to think about anything other than how we were going to put food on the table. You young people seem to think it's your God-given right to be happy all the time.*' Gran hated self-indulgence and so did Isla, usually. West Coasters didn't analyse life. It wasn't in their DNA. They were programmed to tough it out and get on with it. They were of mining stock, and it made them hard.

'Oh Mum, don't make me call her please! And anyway, it's not so strange what I'm doing. Nobody even knew what a cell phone was when you were my age. Facebook was far, far away in a distant galaxy and people somehow survived without knowing what everyone was up to every single minute of the day.'

'Yes, but that was in the dark ages when our fingers did the dialling, and we didn't know any better. As for your gran, well I'll let you off that one this time. I don't want her getting all worked up about what you're up to because I'm worried about her to be honest, Isla. She hasn't been herself lately, not since she had that fall, but you know what she's like. She keeps telling me she's a box of birds for a woman of her years with a dicky hip and to stop fussing. No, I think it might be wise just to say that you need a spot of sunshine and that the cell phone reception isn't very good where you've gone. I'll tell her I'm not expecting to hear from you while you're in America.'

'Well you won't so it's not a lie, but thanks Mum. I just want a bit of peace that's all.' It was the wrong thing to say.

'Oh dear God! Now you've got me worried Isla. You sound like you're about to take up religion. Don't you go joining any of those strange sects they have over there in the United States. You won't find yourself by sitting cross-legged and making "mmm" noises my girl.'

In the background, she heard her father yell out. 'Ask her how she lost herself in the first place, Mary.' A huge guffaw followed; he was a right card, her dad, Isla thought.

'Mum, you had to twist my arm just to get me to go to

Sunday school, remember? So I'm not about to turn my back on my worldly possessions indefinitely, sit around meditating under the stars and then having group sex, or anything like that.'

'Isla! Watch your mouth please, remember who it is you're talking to. Oh, and I do recall your Sunday school career because the only peace your dad and I ever got when you and Ryan were kids was on a Sunday morning. The Andersons were angels letting you join their family for church.'

The Andersons, Isla recalled were a zealous family who had lived at the end of their street. They had four kids of their own but still felt it was their duty to take two extra little lambs, Isla and Ryan, to the Lord's house each Sunday. They'd given up on trying to bring Mary and Joe into the fold. Despite this being a normal telephone call and not Skype, Isla just knew her mum was elbowing and winking at her dad as she recalled what it was they used to get up to on their child-free Sunday mornings. She was spared from having to dwell on the sordid scene further by her mother's next question.

'But what about serial killers?' Mary was a huge *NCIS: Los Angeles* fan who held her hand up to fancying the trousers off Chris O'Donnell.

'I won't talk to any strangers, Mum.'

'Promise not to help any disabled men to their cars too. Think Ted Bundy, Isla.'

'I promise.'

Her dad got on the phone next to ask her to buy him a Stetson hat and some cowboy boots. He had, he told her, always hankered after both. It was Isla's turn to seek reassurance. 'Dad promise me you're not taking up line dancing or' – and she shuddered at the image that flashed to mind – 'planning on posing for a Mills and Boons cover targeting the octogenarian cowboy romance market.' He assured her he was just wanting to fulfil his boyhood dream of looking like Clint Eastwood as he cruised around the mean streets of Bibury.

'Not on a horse surely?' she gasped.

'No, in my new Ute and when I get the Harley done up, I'll need to look the part at the Brass Monkey.' Joe's latest garage project was a Harley Davidson he was restoring. He lived for the day he could ride it down to the Brass Monkey Motorcycle Rally in chilly Central Otago, Mary on the back. Although, from what Isla could gather her mother wasn't so enamoured with the idea of riding pillion. Her exact words were, 'Blow that, I couldn't be doing with helmet hair, and who wants to stand about all day in sub-zero temperatures drinking beer in a muddy field with a bunch of petrol heads talking about bikes?'

Isla decided she could live with her dad parading around in his Stetson and boots so long as Billy Ray Cyrus never graced his radio waves.

Two days later she sat with her head resting on the back of her aisle seat pretending to watch the air hostess do her demonstration. She was about to wing her way far, far away from the scene of her almost nervous breakdown. It gave her a profound sense of relief to know that in approximately eleven hours she would be in Los Angeles.

A few days after that, she'd be stretched out on a couch in a lovely, peaceful white room with one of those expensively yummy diffuser thing-a-me-bobs scenting the room with vanilla. No, scratch that, it would make her hungry. The smell of vanilla always conjured up images of her gran's homemade custard squares. Vanilla was the secret ingredient. Gran was fond of secret ingredients. Lilies then. Lilies signified peace. Yes, there she'd be, talking about herself and inhaling the scent of lilies while whale's sung softly in the background. Her therapist would be an older woman called Anne, a wise woman with a serious steel hair-do who nodded a lot and said, 'I see.' Wisely of course. After a fortnight's worth of these daily couch visits, Isla would feel well-rested and clear-headed. She would have both direction and focus and be able to get on with the rest of her life.

Now, smiling to herself she re-read the brochure she'd printed off on to what to expect during her fortnight's stay at Break-Free. She'd already read the most important bits, like what she should pack. It was comforting to know that in her carry-on bag she'd managed to squeeze two leisure suits and a ten-pack of Marks and Sparks knickers. Gran always reckoned you couldn't go wrong in life if you had a clean pair of knickers with you at all times.

Chapter 2

Around about now...

The town was dying, Bridget Collins thought as she rubbed the condensation from her front room window with a tea towel and peered outside to the stretch of road that was Bibury's High Street. The heavens had opened last night and despite it being February she'd had to get the fire going, hence this morning's unseasonal condensation. People said it was global warming, but she knew better, most Coasters did. It wasn't a new thing, this unpredictable weather; she'd known it to snow in February more than once. Still, at least the sun was trying to make a reappearance today.

Bridget had lived here her entire life and had seen the town through its boom times when the mines' money had flowed, and the town was prosperous. She smiled recalling how she used to mince off to her first job in the offices of the Farmer's building each morning, full of the joy of being young and pretty. What a pity one didn't understand then that youth was fleeting and try to bottle some of that wonderful joie de vivre to bring out and sniff now and again in one's golden years.

That wasn't the way life worked though, and this only became clear when time had faded every year, stretching them long and thin until they become worn and tired. A bit like knicker elastic, she thought.

The store where she'd once worked had long since departed, just like the money from the mines. These days the Four Square Supermarket operated out of the old Farmer's building, and if you wanted a decent pair of pantyhose, a person had to go all the way into Greymouth. Today, the High Street was deserted apart from the campervan parked outside the Kea Tearooms. Mind you, Noeline had told her just the other day that most of the tourists only bought a pot of tea between them so they could use the loo.

'Bloody cheek,' she'd muttered in strident tones, her ample bosom puffing out in indignation.

Bridget had been assailed with a waft of Noeline's perfume. She was heavy-handed with it, whatever it was. It was a shame she wasn't so heavy-handed when it came to the amount of filling she put in her mince pies.

'None of them want an egg and ham sarnie on white bread anymore. Oh no, it's all bagels with smoked salmon and cream cheese or goat's cheese tarts. And don't get me started on the Gluten Free Brigade. I don't mind telling you Bridget; I'm about ready to hang up my apron.'

Bridget had been tempted to say that with Noeline's niece, or whatever a second cousin's daughter was called, installed in the café these days it had been awhile since she'd seen her don an apron and *do* any work. Annie was the girl's name, and she'd arrived on the scene with the foreign fellow who'd taken the teaching post at the High School for the start of the new school year. She was determined to introduce some new 'modern' ideas to the tearoom. Thus far, Noeline was holding firm.

Bridget sympathized; she couldn't be doing with all that fandangled food the cafés served in Christchurch and Greymouth for that matter either. As far as she was concerned those pumpkin seed thing-a-me-bobs that were sprinkled on the top of everything these days were for the birds and cream cheese gave her indigestion. She was with Noeline when it came to a good old ham and egg sarnie, although she was partial to cheese and onion herself. Cheese made from cow's milk, thank you very much. And as for all these new so-called food intolerances, well ... she shook her head. In her day if you had a square meal put in front of you once a day then you were grateful.

Bridget looked out at the lifeless street and sighed; the town had been like a tyre with a slow puncture in the years since the Barker's Ridge mine had closed down. On one side of the tearoom across the street was Bibury Arts & Crafts, where local people could display and sell their wares. In competition with Noeline on the other side of her business, but with enough breathing space between the two thanks to a grassy Council owned strip of land, was everybody's favourite Friday night takeaway, the fish & chippy. The Cutting Room hair salon was next to that.

The corner block was taken up by the Four Square's brick building and gave the town's kids the opportunity of an after school job. It was where Isla had worked as a teenager. Bridget could still see her in her blue zip-up smock sitting behind the till when she closed her eyes. Oh, how she'd moaned about wearing that uniform. It was ugly, she'd cried. Her granddaughter was nothing if not determined though and Bridget had nearly dropped her eggs in the aisle spying her one Saturday afternoon in a blue zip up mini. Isla had taken it upon herself to fold the hem up several inches before loosely stitching it. The memory made her smile as her gaze travelled on towards the butcher's. It was owned by the Stewart brothers and competed with the supermarket for business. A narrow side street separated it from Mitchell's Pharmacy.

The Valentine's Day window display in the pharmacy urged the romantics of Bibury to pop on in and treat their sweetheart to something special. It was where Bridget's daughter Mary worked as a Revlon Consultant, and the pharmacy's only floor staff. Next to Mitchell's was the two-pump Shell garage. The Robson family had owned it under one conglomerate's umbrella or another for as long as Bridget could remember. From her front room vantage point, she could see Ben Robson's broad, overall-clad back bent over the engine of a Ute. She'd been at school with his grandfather. Poor old Raymond had gone a bit dotty in the last few years and was now in permanent residence at a care facility over in Greymouth. The garage's tow truck that Ben took out now and again was parked off to the side of the forecourt with a beaten up looking farm truck still hooked to its boom.

Ben had recently taken over the family business and his parents, Bridget knew, had swanned off last Friday on a month-long cruise to celebrate their newfound freedom. 'Not everybody's on struggle street in Bibury then,' she'd said, pursing her lips when her friend Margaret had relayed the news.

Ben had been at school with her grandson Ryan. They were great mates, the two of them, and still kept in touch. He was a lovely lad, and she'd been pleased when Isla had begun to step out with him. She'd glowed with her first love and in her, Bridget had seen herself as a young girl once more. She'd never understood why Isla had given him the heave-ho the way she had. He'd moped around the town for months after she moved to Christchurch. He'd kept asking her and Mary when Isla was coming home for a weekend, but the times she had, she'd kept him dangling by keeping her distance. The pair of them had been so smitten with each other too, or that was the way it had seemed from the outside looking in. Then out of the blue Isla had broken things off with Ben by saying their long-distance relationship wasn't working.

There was more to it, Bridget was sure, and she'd been hurt when Isla hadn't confided in her. She'd always had a special relationship with her granddaughter. Right from when she was a little girl who'd pop in on her way home from school for one of her gran's freshly baked scones or, if it was a special occasion, Isla's favourite, a custard square. Bridget could still see the pigtailed girl she'd been, perched up at the kitchen table earnestly telling her about her day.

Bridget understood her granddaughter's need to broaden her mind, and she knew it was all the fashion to put your career first and stay single well into your thirties these days. Women should have a career if that was what they wanted.

Of course they should, and nobody could say Isla hadn't done that. The thing that seemed to have been forgotten along the way though was that being a wife and mother was a worthwhile career too.

When had staying home to raise your children become a foreign concept? You didn't need a flat screen television and a new car for heaven's sake! But your children needed you, and they grew up so very fast. Bridget had to listen to Margaret prattle on about how the grandchildren were coming to stay for the holidays. 'Melanie works you know,' she'd state self-righteously. 'She has to with the cost of living these days.' Bridget would bite back the retort, 'and did she have to have a ridiculously big house in a posh suburb too?'

Times had changed and not for the better in her opinion. People didn't want to save for anything anymore or make do until they could afford to buy it. She remembered how she and Tom had eaten mince for a month back in the day, to buy their lounge suite. They'd bought it in Greymouth and had kept the plastic wrapping on the cushions for weeks after they got it home for fear of Mary or Jack putting their dirty feet on it.

She watched now as Ben straightened, missing smacking his head on the Ute's bonnet with the practised manoeuvring of a seasoned mechanic. He disappeared from her line of sight into the garage's workshop. She'd heard that he was seeing the pretty blonde girl who had taken over from Violet McDougall as the school's new secretary. From what her hairdresser, Marie, had been saying as she snipped at Bridget's hair last week at The Cutting Room, things were getting serious between them too.

Isla had made a mistake in breaking things off with Ben in Bridget's opinion. Yes, she knew it was all over years ago, but her granddaughter had not met anyone else worthwhile in the ensuing years. Certainly not the unmanly Tim she'd been shacked up with over in London – Mary had told her he used moisturiser for heaven's sake and that he had gotten very excited when he'd thought she might be able to ship him Revlon products over at cost. She'd seen the light, thank goodness, and called that relationship a day. But while Ben's life was moving forward, it seemed to Bridget that Isla's was floundering once more. It was all well and good having a high-powered job, but it would not keep a woman warm at night.

Bridget became aware that the postman was at the letterbox waving at her. He must think her a right old Nosy Nelly, she thought, giving him a nod of acknowledgement. She let the net curtain fall back into place but not before she saw him slotting an envelope into the box.

Her heart began to thud alarmingly as she left the front room and moved to the hallway with its long reaching shadows. She stood there twiddling her thumbs and telling herself to calm down. If she hadn't known that this sudden agitation was down to the possible contents of her letterbox, she might have taken herself off to the Medical Centre. A visit there was enough to induce a cardiac arrest in itself. It was another anomaly about getting older that a person was expected to discuss one's intimate body ailments with a chap who looked as if he had only just waved goodbye to puberty. She waited for a few beats longer to ensure the postman would have cycled further on up the street before stepping outside her front door. She wasn't in the mood to exchange banal pleasantries.

'No, I'm not interested in selling.' she muttered upon opening her letterbox and being greeted with a real estate flyer. 'And if I were I wouldn't employ you.' She pushed the flyer aside – the agent looked like Donald Trump for goodness' sake – and retrieved the plain white envelope with its Australian postmark tucked beneath it. She was about to disappear back inside the house when she heard a familiar voice. It made her jump, and she hoped she didn't look as furtive as she felt.

'Morning Mum. I was going to get some morning tea and then pop in on you. It's nice to see the sun again after last night, isn't it?'

Bridget waved across the road to Mary. Good grief, that orange face of hers was like a beacon sitting atop her white pharmacy smock. If she were to stand still by the roadside vehicles would slow and come to a stop thinking they'd reached a pedestrian crossing. When Bridget had asked her why it was she was getting about looking like an Oompa-Loompa lately, her daughter had shot her a withering look and told her it was down to the latest innovation in facial bronzing. 'It gives my face a healthy, sun-kissed glow Mum, without inflicting the damaging rays of the sun on my skin. Sun damage causes premature ageing as well as skin cancer you know.' Mary had her sales pitch down pat.

Bridget had snorted but bit back the retort hovering on the tip of her tongue. She'd given up arguing with her daughter years ago. Mary was a grown woman in her fifties and if she wanted to look like Mr Wonka's helper so be it. Still, it was annoying how the tune kept getting stuck in her head – *Oompa-Loompa doom-p-dee-do* – whenever she saw her.

She was one of a kind, Mary, definitely not a chip off the old block. There's a saying; the apple doesn't fall far from the tree. Well, it certainly had with Mary, Bridget often thought. Her daughter had never been much of a cook, despite her best efforts to teach her. She'd given up in the end and resorted to buying her a copy of the trusty *Edmonds Cookery Book* when she got married. Mary, she knew, wielded it with almost biblical fervour. It had become Ryan's and Isla's inside joke growing up, to try and guess the page number for the evening's meal, some of which they knew by heart so often had their mother made them. Still, Mary was a good mum and a good daughter, and Joe by all accounts was pleased with his choice of bride given his penchant for grabbing her bottom whenever the opportunity presented itself. Even if she was orange.

'Yes, it's going to be a lovely day, and you can see I'm fine Mary, you don't need to pop in. Besides I'm off to bowls shortly. Any word from Isla?' Bridget called back across the street.

'No, but I'm not expecting to hear from her while she's in California, she said the cell phone coverage isn't very good.'

'Ah right.' Bridget mentally shooed her daughter on her way, feeling as though the envelope she was holding was a hot potato.

'The warm weather will do her good, Mum,' Mary said

giving her a final wave before opening the door of the Kea. Bridget watched her go inside the café before turning and making her way back up to the house. A needle-like pain in her hip made her wince as she ascended the steps to the front porch. 'Sodding arthritis,' she said to no one in particular before closing the door behind her.

It was last night's rain and the ensuing damp air it had left in its wake that had set it off again. The tumble she'd taken a few weeks back hadn't helped matters either. Mary had begun making noises about Bridget selling up and coming to live with her and Joe ever since. She'd offered to turn Joe's workshop into a granny flat for her. Tripping over the lip on the backdoor step wouldn't have been a big deal had she not found herself unable to get up. At the time she thought she might have broken her hip but had found out later it was just badly bruised along with her pride. She'd felt, lying in a heap on the kitchen floor, old. Properly old for the first time and she didn't like it. Nor did she much like the idea of moving in with Mary and Joe. She was fairly certain Joe didn't think it was a bright idea either. She wouldn't want to put him in the position of choosing between his beloved Harley Davidson motorcycle and his mother-in-law.

Her son, Jack who was high up in mining and had a flashy house over in Greymouth had made noises too, about her coming to live with him and that wife of his, Ruth. He was just paying lip service to the idea though. Bridget knew she wouldn't last five minutes under the same roof as Ruth, who was far too bossy for her boots and insufferable when it came to singing the praises of their children, Thomas and Theresa.

No, while there was breath in her body she was staying put thank you very much. She hadn't spent the last fifty-five years creating memories in her home only to leave it when the going got a little tough.

Oh, they weren't all happy memories, but then that was the stuff of life. She'd learned to compartmentalize and shut herself off from what she didn't want to know, mainly thanks to Tom's philandering a long time ago. She wasn't called Bridget for nothing she thought, heading towards the sound of the radio emanating from her kitchen. Her mother used to tell her not to cry when she'd run in howling with a grazed knee or some such grievous injury. 'Don't you know Bridget means power and strength in Irish?' she'd say.

Bridget would've liked to have gone to Ireland. She'd always thought she and Tom might visit one day, but then he'd gotten sick, and the thought of going on her own after he passed away had been a daunting one. Her mind had been in turmoil for such a long time after his death. All she'd thought she'd known had been proven a lie in the hours before he'd passed and she'd clung white-knuckled, to the familiar. Sometimes she was secretly glad she'd never made the long trip to the other side of the world. That way she couldn't be disappointed if the colourful picture her mother had painted of the country in which her grandmother had grown up didn't quite live up to her expectations.

Besides, as she thought of the weatherboard sitting on its quarter acre section that she and Tom had purchased when they were married, she couldn't imagine leaving the old girl for any great chunk of time. It would be like leaving a sinking ship. It would be like leaving Bibury for that matter, and that was incomprehensible because it was all she'd ever known. Bridget flicked the switch on the kettle and set about making herself a brew. Only when it was strong enough to stand a spoon up in did she feel ready to sit down and open the envelope.

Chapter 3

Bridget's hands trembled as she stared at the Valentine's Day card in her hand. A white love heart on a red background inside which the words, *For Someone Special,* were inscribed. It was two days early, and she didn't need to open it to know who it was from. Nevertheless, she did.

Her fingers traced his handwriting, and she closed her eyes to see if she could conjure up a picture of what Charlie must look like now. It was the sixth Valentine's Day card she'd received from him. He'd heard through the miners' long reaching grapevine that Tom had passed away and had waited a full year after his death before sending her the first card. What a shock that had been! Sixty years had fallen away as she'd opened the card and read his condolences. The verse he'd chosen brought tears to her eyes but it was his request to come and visit her that had made her legs turn to jelly and her stomach begin to churn. She hadn't replied to that card or the ones that had followed annually since. How could she? Not when there was so much water under the bridge. She couldn't revisit the past with him; it was simply too painful.

Bridget donned her glasses and read the verse in this year's card out loud.

'There is a special place within my heart
That only you can fill
For you had my love right from the start
And you always will.'

He'd written beneath this that he would dearly love to visit her and that all she had to do was call and tell him yes and he'd book a flight. Bridget felt the familiar roiling in her stomach at this request. 'Oh Charlie, how did I get it so wrong?' she asked the empty kitchen. The phone began to ring making her jump at the sudden intrusion, and she swore softly as she got up from where she was sitting. A split-second later, Bridget winced for the second time that morning upon hearing Margaret's not so dulcet tones informing her she'd collect her in five minutes. 'Good-oh,' she said hanging up and retrieving her cup from the table. She tipped the dregs down the sink before picking the card up once more. She would tuck it away in the top drawer of her dresser where she put all of her life's flotsam and jetsam, and try to forget about it.

It was a victorious Bridget who was dropped home from bowls by a po-faced Margaret. She didn't even toot as she reversed back down the driveway in her cobalt blue Suzuki Swift. She'd always been a sore loser, Bridget thought, giving her a cheery wave before letting herself in the front door. She'd better rattle her dags and get the dinner on because Joe would be calling in soon on his way home from the wood-processing plant where he worked in Greymouth, hoping to be fed.

The packet of beef sausages were where she'd left them defrosting on the bench in the kitchen. Back in the days when Max had still prowled the premises, she wouldn't have dared leave meat out on the bench; she'd have come home to find the greedy old tomcat had mauled their dinner.

Joe enjoyed bangers and mash; he was a good man her son-in-law and Bridget liked a man who enjoyed his food. What was that phrase? Salt of the earth. She always thought it suited Joe down to the ground. He came to have his tea with her on a Thursday night when Mary swanned off to her dance in the dark session at Barker's Creek Hall. He'd tuck into the meal she'd put down in front of him with relish, reckoning it was slim pickings on the home front with Mary not wanting a full stomach for all that dancing.

Bridget shook her head, as she unhooked her apron from the back of the kitchen door and slipped it over her head before tying it around her waist. A brief search for the vegetable peeler ensued and after locating it in the compost bucket along with last night's carrot peel, she set about scraping the spuds. She didn't know what a woman past her prime was doing jiggling about in the dark with a group of other women who should know better! What was wrong with a brisk morning stroll?

Bridget had been doing the same circuit each morning for years unless it was wet or the frost was particularly hard. Off she'd march, what was the point in dawdling? Down the High

Street and passing by Banbridge Park, she'd always be sure to pause by the Cenotaph. It was her way of showing respect for the young men listed on the monument. The Great War was before her time, and she'd been too young to feel the effects of the Second World War. She'd known heartbreak in her time though. Her gaze would drift past the stone edifice and over the tops of the swings to the back of the park as she remembered stolen kisses under the Punga trees.

She'd continue on her way, the Coalminer's Tavern looming on her left. It always made her grimace when people referred to the old pub as the Pit even if it had seen better days. Then she'd get to School Road. It was the road on which she'd grown up, and it pleased her to see a swing and slide set in the front garden of what had been her family home. The house, long since sold, was rented to a family, which was nice even if they didn't keep it to the standard her parents once had. Her eyes would inevitably flit to the upstairs window above the thorny rose bushes that needed a jolly good prune, and she'd feel a pang for the girl who'd once occupied that room.

So many hopes and dreams but life hadn't turned out how she thought it would. She'd stand there on the pavement of her youth lost in her thoughts knowing the woman with the unruly tribe of under-fives who lived in the house these days probably thought she was potty. She'd caught her peeping through the Venetian blind slats once, and had tried to imagine how she must look to her but had found she didn't care. She'd stopped caring what people thought of her a long time ago and as the wind began to blow and the leaves to swirl, her mind would return to the night she'd met Charlie. She was once more that young girl twirling with joy.

1957

Bridget spun around and around, her arms flung wide. She was young and free, and in half an hour she would be off to dance the night away at Barker's Creek Hall. The evening that stretched ahead was full of new possibilities and lots and lots of fun. She enjoyed the way the powder blue, poodle skirt she'd sewn for herself, under her mum's helpful guidance, swung out high around her thighs. She'd spent the morning dipping her petticoat in sugar water, before ironing it over a low heat to give her skirt the fullness that was all the rage. Her mother had thought she was mad! Bridget was surprised, after all she should be used to such carry on from her older sister, Jean.

She had teamed her skirt with a crisp white blouse that suited her dark colouring, a blue scarf knotted jauntily around her neck to tie her outfit together, and on her feet, she had a pair of white kitten heels borrowed from Jean. They made her feel ever so grown up. They'd come at a cost, mind; she'd had to loan her sister her brand new Bill Haley and His Comets record to take around to her friend Edith's house, before she'd even had the chance to listen to it herself.

She did have her new stole, though. She'd saved hard to buy it from the shillings her mother handed back from the wage packet she brought home once a week. She had worked since leaving school six months ago, as a secretary in the administration area of the Farmer's Department Store on the High Street, and as such was entitled to a small instore discount. She'd put this to good use with the purchase of her first lipstick. It was tucked away inside her purse ready to be applied when she was a safe distance away from the house and her father's eagle eye.

Speaking of whom, he rattled his papers just then and her mother poked her head around the kitchen door. 'Bridget, don't you be throwing yourself about like that on the dance-floor tonight young lady; I saw your knickers then.' She tried to look fierce, but her mouth was twitching. Dad looked over the top of his paper, a plume of pipe smoke rising above him and filling the room with its distinctive aroma. He shot her a disapproving look before raising his paper once more. Bridget decided it would be wise to take herself off before he changed his mind about letting her go.

It had been touch and go as to whether his youngest daughter would be allowed to attend the Valentine's Day Dance at Barker's Creek Hall. He was convinced young people were being led astray by that music they were all going silly for. 'Rock'n'Roll has a lot to answer for.' He'd been heard to mutter more than once. He'd only agreed to Bridget going to the dance tonight because their parish church was organizing it as a fundraiser and Jean had said, under duress, that she would keep an eye on her. Jean could twist their father around her little finger; she could do no wrong in his eyes with her nice young man who had good prospects in the office at the mine where both men worked.

Mum, Bridget knew, was putting a dollop of jam and cream on to each of the pikelets she'd made for the girls to take to the dance as an offering for supper to be held later in the evening. She didn't want to run the risk of marking her blouse or skirt by helping, but she would go and keep her company while she waited. So picking up her stole from where she'd draped it theatrically across the back of the settee, she pulled it around her shoulders and went through to the kitchen and sat down at the table, safely out of her father's line of sight.

Jean's boyfriend Colin was calling for them both shortly, but Jean was still upstairs in the bathroom fiddling about with her hair. Normally Jean would sit on the handlebars of his bike risking life and limb on the gravel roads, but Colin had managed to borrow his dad's car. Jean had only consented to take her sister and friend because Bridget had threatened to tell their parents that she had seen her parked up with Colin last week when she'd told them she was going to the pictures at the Town Hall with him.

Mum chattered on about what the dances had been like in her day when 'swing' had been all the rage and Glen Miller the star of the day. She was about to demonstrate her jitterbug moves, jammy spoon still in hand, when they heard a toot, followed a moment later by a knock at the front door. Bridget looked on with amusement as her father folded the paper, leaving his pipe to smoulder in the ashtray as he got up from his seat to open the front door. She knew he would shake Colin's hand with a vigour that left no doubt that he had high hopes his eldest daughter would have a ring on her finger by the year's end.

Jean came skipping down the stairs in a cloud of Arpege perfume, an expensive gift from Colin for her birthday, and Bridget, carefully holding the supper plate her mum had placed in her hands, followed her out the front door. She barely heard the instructions her mother was reeling off for how she should conduct herself with decorum or her father's watch-tapping instructions for curfew, as she settled herself into the back seat of the Holden FJ, arranging her skirt just so. She did not want it crushed by the time she got to the hall! Colin, she knew would have to hose the car down in the morning because it would be covered in dust by the time they navigated the shingle road leading to Barker's Creek Hall.

They picked Bridget's best friend Clara up on the way, and the two girls sat giggling in the back as they bounced along, their conversation full of excited chatter over who they thought would be there tonight and who they'd like to dance with and who they most definitely would not! Their hands nervously smoothed the folds of fabric in their skirts in anticipation. Jean shot them both the odd, 'oh grow up' look over her shoulder before rolling her eyes and saying, 'Kids,' to Colin. He'd reached over and patted her knee with a smile. Bridget suspected it was just an excuse for him to touch her sister's knee.

Present day

A toot and a wave from someone she knew driving past would invariably drag her back from her remembrances.

'You're a nostalgic old fool, Bridget,' she'd tell herself before carrying on down the road and coming to the local school. Mary and Jack, then Isla and Ryan had all gone to Bibury Area School. She'd gone there too but in her day, there'd been a wooden schoolhouse plonked in the middle of what was now the sports field. It was long gone, cleared away to make room for the new like so many other pockets of Bibury's past.

The pavement forked a short way past the school, and she had the choice of following the path by the Ahaura River or the roadside footpath. She always walked down by the river remembering how she'd sat on the banks, hidden from view as she kissed Charlie. The memories of those kisses would fade as the path forked once more and she found herself almost reluctantly following the footpath that looped around back to High Street. She'd inevitably also find herself wishing that she'd been brave enough to choose a different path back when it had mattered.

It was a walk filled with memories and ghosts, but Bridget was sure it was the only thing that kept her hip from seizing up completely, and it gave her the edge she needed to beat Margaret at bowls.

The potatoes were bubbling in the pot, and her eyes were beginning to smart as she chopped the onion. She didn't know if it was the onion that was making her want to cry or the memories evoked from the card she'd received that morning. She blinked them away upon hearing the front door bang shut.

'You can't beat the smell of frying onions,' Joe called out

from the hall, and she smiled. He said the same thing every Thursday, bless him.

They'd settled into an agreeable routine of a Thursday evening with Joe always washing the dishes after they'd eaten. He'd moan and groan about how full he was while Bridget dried and put away.

'Pudding, Joe?' she'd ask when the last of the dishes were cleared.

'Ooh, I don't know if I can.'

'Are you sure? I'm having some.'

'Ah go on then, I might be able to make a bit of room.'

Tonight, she'd found a bag of stewed black boy peaches from Margaret's tree in the freezer, and so she'd whipped up a crumble. Having dished two bowls up with a dollop of ice-cream, they went through to the living room to eat off their laps while they watched Seven Sharp. Mary had harrumphed upon hearing of this arrangement.

'You always made me and Jack sit up at the table, Mum.'

'Seven Sharp wasn't on when you and Jack lived at home, Mary,' Bridget replied. She didn't like to miss an episode. It was the show's host Mike Hosking she was fond of, having listened and argued with him for years on talkback radio. It was like letting an old friend into her living room each evening.

Joe, however, was on the fence. 'He wouldn't last five minutes in a real job,' he'd say. 'Look at all that crap he puts in his hair.'

Bridget would tell him to pipe down and eat his pudding.

Joe would head home at half past seven when the current affairs programme had finished. He would get home just as

Mary was heading off to her dance class. They were ships passing in the night which suited him fine once a week. 'It means I can work on the bike in peace without Mary going on about how I spend more time with it than I do her.' He'd kiss Bridget on the cheek and thank her for looking after him before revving the engine of his ridiculously oversized motorized beast, and heading home in a cloud of exhaust fumes. Bridget would close the door thinking her daughter was right, she had married a petrol head but a petrol head with a heart of gold.

This evening however before the credits rolled on Seven Sharp, Joe and Bridget looked at each other startled as they heard the front door open and Mary call out.

'Is everything alright?' Bridget looked at her daughter seeking reassurance as she barrelled into the living room.

'Everything's fantastic, Mum. Guess what?'

'What?' Joe and Bridget chimed.

'Isla arrives home in two days. Isn't that just the best Valentine's Day present ever?'

Chapter 4

'You're not cold are you love after all that Californian sunshine? It gets a few degrees warmer there in the summertime than it does here, I dare say.' Mary swung her gaze from the road in her daughter's direction, and the car swerved accordingly.

'I'm fine Mum, keep your eyes on the road, and it was winter over there. Well, as close to winter as California gets.' Isla had been heartened when she'd stepped outside Christchurch Airport's terminal building to see the cloudless blue sky. It was a perfect Canterbury summer's day, and it felt like she was being welcomed home. She opened the shoulder bag resting on her lap and felt around inside it until her hand settled on the book of affirmations that her counsellor at Break-Free, Rita, had given her when it was time to leave. It was comforting to know it was there and she knew too, thanks to her time at the lodge, that whatever happened next, she would be okay.

The drive to Bibury was long, and she sat listening as her mum told her she was worried about Bridget living on her own especially since she'd had that fall a month back. 'If your dad hadn't called in on her – well, it doesn't bear thinking about. You know what your gran's like though, she refuses to admit she's getting old and she was back taking her morning constitutional, as she calls her walk within the week.'

Isla did know what her gran was like, tough and stubborn being the first two words that sprang to mind.

'It'll be strange not having you at home now you're back, but it'll be a relief to know you're keeping an eye on Mum for a bit too. She always seems invincible and then to realize she's not, well it scared me.'

Isla nodded, she struggled to think of her gran as anything other than a force of nature too. Mother and daughter knew only too well that were Isla to move back in under her parents' roof there would be fireworks before long. So, staying with her gran was the perfect solution. Isla and Mary got along like a house on fire in small doses, but both were secretly relieved when Bridget diplomatically suggested Isla stay with her. 'If Isla's there with me, it'll mean you'll stop running across the road like a headless chook on your tea breaks Mary, to check up on me.' Yes, it was a win-win situation for all.

'It's not like it used to be, Bibury you know,' Mary announced, her orange face earnest. She'd been keeping up a steady monologue since they'd exited Christchurch. Isla felt a sense of sadness that her old stomping ground of the Garden City would be one she'd no longer recognize when she returned to explore Christchurch beyond the airport. She'd kept track of the post-earthquake rebuild online and had been amazed at the change to the cityscape. Over the ensuing years since the ground had shaken with an unfamiliar wrath, the familiar had been cleared to make way for the new, not because of progress but because of necessity.

They'd been driving for over an hour now, having passed Castle Hill with its otherworldly moonscape, and the road they were on was nearly empty as the car began to wind through Talbots Pass. Isla tried to fight off the fatigue that hovered after the flight and look lively as her mother's voice intoned.

'You only have to read the police report in the *Bibury Times* to know crime's on the up.' Mary's sigh was heavy with the weight of it all.

'Did Sheree Davies get her knickers pinched off the washing line again then?' Isla asked with a smirk to lighten the sombre mood Bibury's crime spree had evoked.

Mary shot her a sideways glance through suspiciously thick eyelashes, and the car veered over the centre line.

'Mum! Keep your eyes on the road.' The hairpin bends of the mountain pass had always made her nervous. 'Have you got false eyelashes on? And what's with the tan?' she asked to distract herself.

'They're both the latest thing from Revlon,' Mary said batting her lashes.

She took her position as a Revlon Consultant very seriously. Isla wished the same could be said of her driving.

'And you're as bad as your father telling me how to drive. Trust you to bring up Sheree's knickers, Isla. That was years ago and anyway I don't know why she was so bothered, she still has trouble keeping the bloody things on according to my hairdresser, Marie.' Her face grew pensive. 'I wonder if

Sheree was the one Marie's ex-hubby was up to no good with, she'd never say if she was. What do you reckon on the cut she did me? I thought it was on the short side and your dad said I looked like one of those sheep that shed their wool sporadically of their accord.' She frowned and her hand flew up to the back of her newly shorn head to pat it.

Isla bit back a giggle; her dad could never be called a charmer. It was embarrassing the way he'd squeeze Mum's bum in public, but that he was also kind and generous and loved the bones off his wife, there could be no doubt. Besides, she thought looking at her mum properly, the back was indeed a little short. The top bit was still as full and curly as ever. Isla's earliest memory was of her mother looking like an alien, porcupine with a headful of heated rollers. Looking at her now, she reminded her of someone, *who was it?*'

'Mum! I've got it you look like—'

'Like Olivia Newton-John when she sang *Physical*. That was the photo I took in to show Marie.' Mary's face was alight with hope. 'That was one of Olivia's timeless looks, in my opinion. It never gets old.'

'Um ... oh yeah.' That hadn't been what she had been about to say. God help her, her mother had been a fan of Olivia's since her Grease days. There was no chance of her ageing as gracefully as her idol though, Isla thought with a fond sideways glance. She wouldn't put it past her to start wearing a headband and leotard to that dancing in the dark thing she reckoned was the new Zumba.

Nothing ever changed in Bibury, and where once it had irritated Isla, now she found the idea of returning to all that sameness comforting. Marie had been cutting hair in Bibury since she was a baby and Sheree must be well into her sixties by now. Age, it would seem, hadn't managed to slow down Shag-around Sheree, as she was known at the Pit, or her free and easy ways.

'The garage was broken into last month.'

Ben's garage? Isla was suddenly wide awake.

'They made off with cigarettes. The police caught the little buggers, apparently just kids passing through from Greymouth.' She made a tut-tutting 'what are the youth of today coming to' sort of noise.

Isla's shoulders relaxed on hearing no one was hurt. The memory of the time Ben had broken his ankle attempting to rollerblade around Bibury High's netball courts at her insistence flitted before her. He'd been stoic not wanting her to worry as he sat where he'd crashed to the ground. She'd seen the pain in his eyes though. It had hurt her as much as him while she sat squeezing his hand waiting for the O'Regan kid who'd been kicking a ball about nearby to fetch Ben's dad. A trip to Greymouth hospital had followed, and he'd wound up in surgery, a plate and screws being placed along the back of his shin bone to hold the shattered bones together. He'd said it was worth it to have her at his beck and call for the weeks after as he sat propped up on his bed, foot elevated. She'd tossed a grape at him when he said that and he'd reached out and pulled her to him for a kiss. They'd only broken apart upon hearing his mother's exaggerated throat clearing from the doorway. Isla shooed the image away; had she really once been that young and carefree?

She closed her eyes, ignoring her mum's questions as to what her plan was now she was back. The simple answer was she didn't have one. She felt like the prodigal child. The Andersons would be pleased to know she'd remembered at least one parable from all those Sunday school classes they'd taken her to. Giving up on getting a reply, Mary moved on to other topics, and Isla found herself drifting off despite her mum's chatter. She was woken with a sharp elbow to the ribs.

'Isla, we're home, and your dad's going to dislocate his shoulder if you don't give him a wave back. He finished early so he could be home to greet you.'

Isla waved back at the burly man in the t-shirt and stubby shorts who stepped forward to wrap his daughter in a bear hug the instant she got out of the car. And when he boomed. 'You found yourself then,' she was too knackered to say anything but, 'Yup Dad I did.'

Mum had been busy redecorating, Isla noticed as she stepped through the front door. The three-bedroomed house had been built when Isla and Ryan were small, and it had a brick exterior with dormer windows upstairs. It sat on a sloping large part of a quiet street with her dad's workshop off to the side.

'Do you like the colour scheme?'

It was black and white and blingy but it suited her mum down to the ground, she thought, glancing over at her dad who looked a little at odds standing under the chandelier in the living room.

'I told her we don't live in a high-class brothel, but she wouldn't listen.'

'I don't know how you'd know what the inside of a high-class brothel looks like and you've nothing against bling when it comes to that bike of yours. Honestly, Isla, make sure you put your sunglasses on when he drags you out to look at it. He's been pimping it up.' She wagged a finger at her husband. 'Your dad here thinks he's the star of *Easy Rider*.'

Isla smiled listening to the banter; it was good to be home.

She managed to have a few bites of the bacon and egg pie (that she knew fell on page ninety-four of *Edmonds Cookery Book*) that her mum put on the table for lunch before pushing her plate away. Mary made coffee and then plonked a big heart-shaped box of chocolates down on the table.

'My Valentine's Day present,' she said, smiling at Joe before jumping and slapping his hand away when he reached towards her. 'You got yours this morning; you can go and tie a knot in it thank you very much.'

Isla told them to cut it out when there were children present, slipping easily back into a long-forgotten role as she helped herself to a chocolate. Hopefully, it would give her enough of a sugar hit to get through the afternoon. She'd forgotten Valentine's Day had just been, not that the day held any significance for her this year. Her body clock was up the wop, and she stifled a yawn as her dad moved on to his three favourite topics, his new Toyota Hilux Ute, his Harley and his veggie patch. She would dearly love to crawl into her old bed, seeing the shape of the spiky cabbage tree leaves through the curtains as she'd done as a kid and sleep for the next twelve hours solid. Isla knew she'd be wide awake in the middle of the night if she did that, though. Besides, she couldn't take herself off to bed as much as she might want to because she had someone important to go and see.

Isla was perched in the passenger seat of her dad's Hilux with a bunch of carrots in a plastic bag on her lap. Apparently, Joe had had a bumper crop this year. She refused to look in the direction of the Robsons' garage as her dad drove past and wanted to slap his hand like her mother had done earlier when he waved over to Ben.

'He's a worker that Ben, you could've done a lot worse than him Isla. He's been stepping out with the new school secretary, a pretty lass she is too. I have to say, it came as a bit of a shock to hear Violet McDougall was retiring though. We thought she'd be carried out of the school in a box. She wants more time to devote to her Scottish dancing while she can still kick her legs up, apparently. Your gran reckons she's finally given up on snagging Principal Bishop. Yep, sorry to say you missed the boat with Ben there, love,' he finished helpfully.

'Thanks for that, Dad.' She could almost feel Ben's eyes burning into her willing her to look at him, as she kept her eyes fixed on the road ahead. Or perhaps she was being fanciful. Either way, she had no doubt he'd known she was arriving home today thanks to the Bibury bush telegraph. She wondered if he'd changed much, it had been years since she'd last seen him. The last time had been when she'd flown home for her grandfather's funeral. Isla, already grieving, had felt like she was talking to a stranger as he passed on his condolences.

Maybe his hair was thinning, and he'd gotten paunchy.

What would he think of her when he saw her properly? She didn't think she'd changed much apart from wearing her hair shorter these days, so it sat on her shoulders and not halfway down her back. It was darker too thanks to the tint her hairdresser had put through it, telling her it would off-set her olive skin tone. She hadn't put on weight though, no chance of that with Toad's constant passive aggressive remarks.

'That Tim was bloody useless. I told you that time and time again, but would you listen? Nope, you take after your Gran in that respect. She never listens either,' her dad said, as though reading her mind. 'I could never trust a man who uses moisturiser and puts more crap in his hair than your mother.' His tone softened. 'I can't pretend that I'm not happy you broke things off with him and to have our girl home of course.' He patted Isla's knee, and she gave him a watery smile, relieved that they'd reached Gran's.

'It's been painted!' The last time she'd seen the weatherboard house where, growing up, she'd spent as much time as her own home, it was beginning to show the telltale signs of the harsh coastal climate. Now it stood out like a gleaming pearl amongst the street full of other weatherboards that had all lost their lustre.

'Ryan and I got stuck in when he was home last. We thought if the old girl sees sense and decides to sell, then it's one less thing to worry about. Your mum and I tried to talk her into putting it on the market after she had that fall but I never met anyone as pig-headed as Bridget Collins. She'll miss the boat I reckon. Property prices have gone down enough since the mine closed.' He turned into the drive and sounded the horn. Isla couldn't help but grin, as the Dukes of Hazzard, General Lee's Dixie tune announced their arrival. He was such a petrol head, her dad.

'Gran! It's me,' Isla called, pushing open the door. Joe brought up the rear carrying her cases. She shook her head at the foreignness of leaving your front door unlocked as she stepped inside. It was shadowy in the hall despite it being high summer. This was thanks to the rich Rimu wood panelling that adorned the walls. Her dad deposited her worldly possessions (at least, until the rest of her belongings that Maura had kindly agreed to box up and ship arrived) in the spare room before kissing her.

'I'll leave you to have a catch up with the old girl. It's good to have you home Isla.'

'It's good to be home, and the hat and boots look great Dad.'

'Why thank you, lil' lady,' he drawled tipping his new Stetson before strutting out the door in his cowboy boots.

She wondered if he'd sleep with them on recalling how she'd felt like the perfect daughter, being the one to bring his boyhood dream to life.

Before she'd left the States, she'd walked into the LA stockists of the Stetson brand. Her jaw was agape as she'd stood gazing at the different designs. A cowboy hat was a cowboy hat, wasn't it? Except for when it happened to be a Stetson, it would seem. She'd gravitated towards a traditionally styled hat called the Rustler. Lifting it off the wall, she'd inspected the hat for a price and spotting it; Isla truly did feel as if she was having an out of body experience. She whistled between her teeth, a cool two hundred and seventy dollars for a flipping hat! Dad had better remember which one of his two offsprings it was who'd fulfilled his dreams when he sat down to write his will, she'd thought, marching over to inspect the boots.

Isla would have loved to have blamed the state of her nerves on the price of the Stetson hat and the matching cowboy boots (which, by the way, had cost her the grand total of five hundred and fifty dollars, a sum she still hadn't quite come to terms with) but she couldn't. The trigger had in fact been a conversation with Toad that had been so ridiculous she'd nicknamed it Banana Gate. The screenplay of their exchange ran through her mind once again like a scratched DVD as she stood in the doorway:

'Hey, hun, did you know bananas are fattening?' Tim was leaning against the doorway, watching her with a faintly amused expression playing across his handsome face.

Isla jumped. 'Oh hi, you frightened me! I didn't hear you come in.'

'I'm on target for this month, so I thought I'd knock off early and head down to the gym.' His brown eyes flickered towards the fruit she was holding, and a smile twitched at the corner of his mouth. He was a cat playing with a mouse.

Isla stared at the banana recalling those horrible flickering ads that popped up on the internet unbidden. The ones that featured a banana and a fat belly and tempted you to click to find the holy-grail to losing that wobbly belly. 'I, uh, I assumed being fruit it was good for me.' Why was she explaining herself? It was just a banana for goodness' sake, hardly a king-size block of chocolate and so what if it was? She was a grown woman, not a naughty kid pilfering food before dinner. He couldn't tell her what she should and shouldn't eat, and she was hardly overweight, so why did she feel like she was doing something wrong? 'It's going soft, it needs to be eaten.' The words continued to burst forth, an unstoppable explanation like popcorn from its kernel.

Tim shrugged. 'Hey, it's your call. It's just that I thought we'd agreed on you wearing the red dress to the awards dinner this Friday night.'

Isla knew the red dress didn't leave much room for movement. She also knew that the last time his advertising firm had been up for an award he'd had Tori on his arm. Tall, skinny, beautiful Tori, who'd turned heads. He'd dropped his ex into the conversation when he'd asked her what she was going to wear, adding that he thought her red dress was a show stopper. The awards mattered to him. She would be the trophy on his arm, not the fat cow that showed him up. Tori had always made an effort when things mattered to Tim and so should she, she decided, putting the banana back in the bowl. She wasn't hungry anymore anyway. She had that horrible sick, bloated feeling again that always assailed her after conversations like this. Now, he looked like the cat that got the cream as he turned away.

The sun was streaming in through the window as she watched him disappear down the street, gym bag slung casually over his shoulder, oblivious to the fact that tears were running down her cheeks.

Now, she shook her head. Toad was the past and this was

her present. She focussed on her dad swaggering to his Ute and grinned involuntarily. The cowboy ensemble was money well spent. Her hand hovered over the lock. What was the point? She knew she wouldn't be the one to change the habit of a lifetime. Gran was as stubborn as a toddler who refused to stop sucking her thumb. Isla's mum had often told Isla in exasperation that this was a trait that had skipped a generation bouncing directly from grandmother to granddaughter. 'You two are peas in a pod,' she'd say, shaking her head. 'I might as well bang my head against a wall when it comes to trying to make the pair of you see sense.' Isla and Bridget would grin at each, co-conspirators.

She stood in the hallway with its dust motes and red Axminster carpet that did nothing to lighten the hall. Gran was fond of saying it had cost a fortune but would see her out. Isla let the familiar surrounds wash over her. It was like stepping inside a time capsule and she knew, were she to push open the door to the living room, she'd find it just as it had been the day she'd told her Gran that she was leaving New Zealand.

It would be the same with her gran's bedroom, she thought, unable to resist a peek. She pushed the door to her left open and blinked at the sudden light. Her eyes settled on the colourful quilt spread neatly over the bed. Her gran's mother had stitched it for her and Grandad as a wedding present. For the sake of her gran's seventy-something back, she hoped the mattress wasn't the same one that had serviced their forty-odd years of marriage. Isla frowned, something was missing. The black and white photo of her grandparents on their wedding day was no longer hanging on the wall above the bed. In its place was a watercolour of what looked like Arthur's Pass. Perhaps it had been too painful a reminder to have it there after Grandad passed, Isla mused.

On the wall to the right of the old dresser drawers were the silver framed baby portraits of her mum and Uncle Jack. As a child, Isla had found it so hard to equate the bonny baby in her frilly dress with her ever unpractical and bossy mum. She supposed that was normal; it was hard to imagine one's parents having ever been small and vulnerable.

Isla's nose twitched as she tiptoed out of the room. Freshly baked scones! Gran could be a bite at times, and she wasn't one for public displays of affection. Her way of showing she loved you was not with grand gestures or declarations, but with her home-baking. As a child, Isla had loved those afternoons spent perched at the old Formica-topped table, with a plate of hot buttery scones between them. It was Gran who had taught her to bake too. Those times had been their special times. She'd been able to talk to her about everything until the day she decided to leave Bibury.

Chapter 5

Isla followed her nose to the kitchen, feeling like that child who'd popped in on her way home from school all over again. She called over the top of the radio talkback discussion being broadcast on the old transistor radio on the kitchen windowsill, 'Gran, it's me. And I haven't come empty-handed. I bring you the last of the carrots from Dad's garden.'

The old woman's back was to her as she busied herself up at the bench buttering the scones. Isla could see steam rising and blobs of golden butter melting into them, and her stomach involuntarily rumbled, despite not long having had lunch.

'We don't have any of that plastic rubbish they call spread in this house,' Bridget was fond of saying. Now, she stopped what she was doing and, turning around, wiped her hands on her apron. The Union Jack was emblazoned on the front of it, a Christmas present from Isla's first year in London. It looked at odds with her blouse and slacks.

Looking at the lovely, lived-in face, Isla couldn't stop the smarting of tears or herself from dropping the bag of carrots and rushing forward. She nearly knocked Bridget down as she threw her arms around her. 'Oh, Gran! I've missed you so much.' The surprisingly fit figure yielded to the hug and patted her on the back.

'Me, or my baking?' She disentangled herself from the embrace. 'Enough of that carry on now, go and sit down before these get cold.' She turned away but not before Isla saw that she too was blinking back tears. Isla picked the plate up off the bench, and carried it over to the table that had been laid for afternoon tea. It would fetch a pretty penny these days that table, she thought as she rubbed her hand over its lemon-yellow top. Formica was classed as retro, and therefore it was cool.

Bridget pushed the plate towards her and not needing to be offered twice, Isla reached forward and took a scone. The butter dripped down her chin as she took a bite and Bridget got up to fetch the roll of paper towel. 'Still a messy Miss I see.' She ripped a piece of the towel off and handed it to her granddaughter, pleased to see her baking being enjoyed.

'Gran you make the best scones in the world.'

Bridget sat up a little straighter and helped herself to one before adding, 'Isla don't talk with your mouth full. It's the secret ingredient that makes them so light. Margaret's always on at me to tell her what it is.'

It was over the second cup of tea that Bridget cut to the chase, 'Right, enough of the pussy-footing around. What is it that has brought you home?'

Isla's hand froze with the half-eaten scone midway to her mouth. She'd never been able to pull the wool over Gran's eyes. 'I'm home because I've missed getting the third degree from you.'

'Humph, well your mother said that after you had broken up with that Tim you went off to America and had some sort of epiphany that you wanted to come home. I told her she needed to stop reading those self-help books she's addicted to and talk sense.'

Gosh, she had a way with words, Isla thought, her mouth twitching. 'To be fair Gran, Mum *was* right in a way. My time in California helped me realize that I had no work-life balance in London. I'd gone as far as I could go in my career over there, I'm single again and what's that saying?' She frowned casting around for it. 'Oh, you know – you can take a girl out of the country, but you can't take the country out of a girl.' Isla wiped the crumbs from her mouth; she was quite pleased with that analogy. 'So, ta-dah! Here I am.'

'Who do you think you are? Dolly Parton,' Bridget said with a snort helping herself to another scone. 'They're lonely places, big cities.'

How her gran would know, given she'd never been out of New Zealand, Isla couldn't fathom, but she did know better than to argue.

'So my girl, what're you going to do with yourself now that you're back?' Bridget was not a woman who'd sit back and rest on her laurels and Isla was well aware there'd be no swanning about in her dressing gown for a few days to get over her jet lag. Not while she was living under Gran's roof.

'I'm not sure. It's all been a bit of a whirlwind since I decided to come home.' Isla felt bad for not having given Upscale Developments notice of her intention to leave. Her extended leave of absence had just turned into a permanent leave of absence. Then again, they'd had their pound of flesh from her over the last seven years. Besides, it was such a competitive industry she knew there'd be plenty of fresh, bright young things, chomping at the bit to step into her shoes.

Sitting there in her gran's kitchen where she'd always been right at home with a full tummy, she felt like she could breathe properly for the first time in a long while. Of course, knowing she had a nice little nest egg sitting in the bank was a comfort. It meant she didn't have to panic about what her next step would be. She hadn't come back from London completely bereft. 'I was thinking while I was on the plane about setting up an online design business. That way I can base myself here.'

Bridget's pleased expression didn't escape her granddaughter.

It was seven o'clock that evening when Isla's second wind began to wane. She wiped the kitchen bench down and hung the tea towel over the oven door before popping her head around the living room door to announce she was done in. Her gran had just settled herself into her recliner for her daily current affairs fix, and Isla kissed her on the cheek goodnight. Her room was still a shrine to the sixties, right down to the orange Candlewick bedspread neatly covering the single bed. It'd been a long time since she'd slept in a single bed, Isla thought, as her eyes settled on what was leaning up against the pillow.

The sight of Caroline, the pretty porcelain doll she'd itched to get her hands on as a child, made her smile. An ice maiden who'd been out of bounds, she had sat in her yellow crinoline dress on top of the chest of drawers in this room for as long as Isla could remember. She'd belonged to her great-grandmother, and Gran had always told Isla that one day, when she was old enough to look after the doll properly, it would be hers. Ownership of the family heirloom was skipping a generation as Gran said she didn't trust Mary not to try and make her over.

Isla picked the doll up. 'Hello Caroline, I guess I'm finally old enough to look after you.' She stroked the dainty, delicately painted face peeping out from beneath her bonnet, before carefully placing her back where she lived on top of the chest of drawers. Peeling back the bedspread, she climbed into bed and still feeling the floating motion of the plane, her last conscious thought was that she'd unpack in the morning.

Isla was hanging up the last of her clothes and trying to shake off the fuddle-headed feeling of having slept solidly when Gran knocked on the door. The smell of fresh scones once more tickled Isla's nose. 'You've been busy this morning, Gran. You never stop.'

'Margaret's picking me up in five minutes for Bingo and the Bingo ladies love my scones.'

Bridget had never driven, she'd never felt the need living in Bibury. Tom had always taken her where she wanted to go if she couldn't walk there herself, and now Margaret was more than happy to have a little bit of petrol money tucked away in her glove box.

'Margaret, with the insufferably superior attitude who goes

on and on about how well her daughter is doing in banking up in Auckland?'

'That's her, and do you remember Elsie Graham? She lived opposite the school and used to have the pesky terrier; it's a Jack Russell these days, horrible thing, but that terrier played merry hell with you children on your way home of an afternoon.'

Isla nodded, she remembered the ankle-biter well.

'Well, she drives Margaret mad going on and on about how light my scones are. Margaret's scones could be used as a permanent building material,' Bridget sniffed. 'Elsie's got an ulterior motive, though. I'm the current President of the Bibury Women's Bowls Association, and she's determined to be made Vice President. The only thing is, I wish she wouldn't talk with her mouth full. It's a very unattractive trait of hers.'

Isla bit her lip to stop the grin that threatened, as they heard a horn toot Margaret's arrival. Oh, how she'd missed her gran! There was no one quite like her.

'Hold your horses, I'm coming,' Bridget muttered. 'What've you got planned today then my girl?'

'Well, I think I might pop over to the Kea for a coffee now that I've unpacked. I'll have a bit of a wander around. You know, reacquaint myself with the town.' The instant stuff Gran was fond of had not given her a sufficient caffeine hit. 'Enjoy Bingo. Wipe the floor with Margaret.'

Isla got her competitive streak from her grandmother.

Sometimes you meet somebody and know instinctively that this person is someone you're going to be friends with. It might be a certain light in their eyes that hints at a kindred spirit, or it could be the way they smile that lets you know there will be a shared sense of humour. That's how Isla felt as the redheaded vision who looked to be of a similar age to her, standing behind the coffee shop counter, greeted her cheerily.

It wasn't just down to her warm welcome, though – it was more than that. Later, when she mulled their meeting over, she'd tell Caroline that it was because of the woman's mane of curly, red hair. Isla could imagine how many hours she would have spent agonizing over it when she was younger. Kids could be cruel, latching onto any point of difference. For Isla, the point of difference had been her name. She'd had a lifetime of explaining it was pronounced like 'island' but without the n and the d. The fact that her name did, in fact, mean 'island' in Irish was neither here nor there. Every time she repeated this mantra she would send a silent, 'Thanks very bloody much,' to her parents. It was alright for them with the ordinary, if slightly biblical, names of Joe and Mary.

Isla had been her mother's nod to her Irish ancestry as had Ryan. 'It's not fair,' she'd wail on occasion to Mary. 'Why couldn't you call him something unpronounceable too?' In protest, she'd taken to calling her brother Ennis after coming across the Irish town's name in a book and deciding it sounded suitably rude. He'd retaliated by calling her turd face. Ennis had stuck, turd face had not.

Isla could imagine the redhead sending silent, aggrieved messages to her parents for the genetics that had blessed her with Little Orphan Annie hair as a child. Yes, she thought, the parents probably both had mouse brown, boringly straight hair. Now, this woman probably loved those red curls. She imagined the woman's hair would be part of who she was just as she quite liked the fact her name was different these days. Of course, the Shopaholic actress, Isla Fisher had helped both their causes!

'The savoury pinwheels are really good, if I do say so myself.' The redhead indicated the cloche covered goodies, next to the till. 'I baked them an hour ago.'

Mm, they did look yummy and accounted for the delicious smell hovering in the air, and Isla noted that she hadn't been stingy on the cheese. 'Why not? I could do with a bit of comfort stodge. Ih and I'll have a double-shot latte too, please.'

The woman who looked to be around Isla's age giggled. 'Sorry, I'm trying to drag my aunt out of the stone-age but its plunger coffee or nothing.'

'Really?' Isla didn't know why she was surprised; she was back in Bibury now after all. Not wanting to sound obnoxious, she quickly covered up her reaction. 'Ah, I wondered what I could smell along with the baking, you can't beat the aroma of plunger coffee. Blue Mountain?'

'Liar,' the redhead laughed. 'And yes, it is, I'll put an extra spoonful in if you like?'

'Yes, please. I feel like I've been hit by a bus.'

'Big night?' The woman took the note Isla fished from her purse and after ringing up the order, she handed her a couple of coins back. Isla watched as she lifted the cloche, removed the biggest pinwheel with a pair of tongs and placed it on a plate. A woman after her own heart. 'Heated and served with relish?'

'Ooh yes please.' She was right; this woman was indeed a member of the comfort food sisterhood. 'And it's jet lag. I arrived home from Los Angeles yesterday.'

'L.A., that sounds very glam. What brings you to Bibury then?'

'I grew up here, but I've been away working in London for the last ten years, and I lived in Christchurch before that. I had a bit of a sunshine stop in California to break up the trip home.'

'Ten years, that's a long time to be away, has the place changed much?'

'I haven't had a chance to have much of a look around, but from what I saw yesterday, no it hasn't changed a bit.'

'Small towns are like that. That's what makes them special I think.'

Isla hadn't thought about it like that before. She'd always been on intent as making as much change as possible.

'Why did you decide to come home?' The woman looked over her shoulder from where she was setting the microwave timer. 'Sorry, you can tell me to mind my own business if you like.'

'It's fine,' Isla said before reeling off her new catchphrase. 'I finally realized that I had no work-life balance and I was missing my family. It was just time to come home that's all. What about you, you said Noeline's your aunt?'

'Mum's second cousin actually. I just call her aunty, it's a habit from when I was a kid, and it's a long story, but I've only been here a month myself. I'm from Christchurch, but I've been living over in Crete for the last couple of years.'

Isla was intrigued. It was a big leap from Crete to Bibury, but then again so was London to Bibury. It was kind of nice to know she wasn't the only new arrival back in town too. 'That's an interesting choice of place to go and live. I wouldn't think there'd be much chance of stuffing up your work-life balance in the Greek Islands.'

She laughed. 'Yup, stress isn't a word that's in their vocabulary. I went over on holiday initially but wound up staying. I met someone—' The smile turned to a frown. 'Oh crap! I forgot the ginger crunch; it'll be ginger bloody crisp by now. Sorry, I'll be back with you in a tick. Grab a seat.'

Isla watched her disappear out the back and went and sat down. She was spoilt for choice; the place wasn't exactly buzzing. Her designer's eye took in the worn décor. The café felt like it had given up hope. It was serviceable, a truck stop and nothing more. She caught sight of a sepia photograph on the wall. It was the only point of interest in the room. It was a group of hardened miners, frozen in time, the picks they were holding in front of them denoting the era.

That was what she would focus on were she to give the place a facelift – the mining history of the town. She would give it a rustic and welcoming vibe as befitted the Coast. That was what this part of the world was famous for after all, that and its storytellers. So busy was she making over the café in her mind's eye that she barely noticed the door to the café jangle open.

It was only when she felt a warm breeze that she realized she was no longer the only customer. She glanced over in the direction of the door, and her expression froze. She'd know that back anywhere, she thought, her heart thudding. She suddenly wished she wasn't feeling like such a crumpled wreck, as he turned and saw her.

Chapter 6

'Isla? Hi, wow, it's been a while. I heard you were back.'

'Ben, hey. How's it going?' *Awkward, awkward, awkward and not just because this man had seen her naked.* She knew he'd seen her yesterday when she'd sat with her nose in the air in the passenger seat of her dad's Ute. Isla squirmed in her seat wishing she could press a button on her phone and transport herself anywhere but here. Instead, she began rearranging the little packets of sweetener and sugar in the pot on the table for want of something to do with her twitchy hands.

'Yeah, pretty good actually. I don't know if you heard, but I took over the garage last year.'

He was in his overalls, and his strong, familiar hands were resting on the back of the chair opposite her. His face had thinned out with age, and a light stubble decorated his jawline. He looked good, far too bloody good. *Don't go there, Isla Brookes.* 'Mm yes, Dad told me that your parents have retired. They've become cruising fanatics I hear. Good for them and you. It's what you always wanted, so I hope business is booming.'

'I can't complain. There's never any shortage of cars to fix, and people always need petrol. And yeah, the folks are hardly ever home these days. When they are, Dad's started to talk in "cruise" speak, and Mum dresses for dinner.'

Isla forgot to be uncomfortable as she laughed at the image of Mrs Robson in formal attire, serving up steak, egg, and chips. 'What's cruise speak?'

'Oh, things like "shall we have a cocktail or head up to the buffet for a bite?" I have to remind Dad that in Bibury its head up to the Pit for a pint of beer and a pie. They're probably in Indonesian waters now as we speak, having High Tea or something.'

'Good for them.' She sounded like a jolly-them-along Girl Guides Leader.

'Yeah, they've earned it.'

'Do you still live at home then?'

'God no!' He laughed, and Isla was suddenly very aware that she was a thirty-year-old woman who'd just moved in with her grandmother.

'I bought a house a few years back; it's an old villa tucked down a back section off River Road. She's a labour of love, but she's home. So are you back for a holiday?'

'No, I'm home for good.'

'Really? I had you down as a big city girl these days.'

'I'd had enough of big,' she said shrugging. She wasn't giving away any more than that. Or at least she hadn't planned to. He was waiting for her to elaborate, and she couldn't be doing with an awkward silence. 'It was just time to come home and do something different and, well, Gran's not getting any younger.'

'I heard about her fall. That would've been a bit of a scare for her and you all. She's a tough old bird though, nothing broken. So you're staying with her?'

'Yes, for the time being. It seemed like a good idea for me to be around to make sure there's no repeat performance of her lying on the kitchen floor for hours in pain.' She shuddered at the thought of her poor, dear grandmother helpless like that. 'Besides Gran and I rub along well together whereas Mum, and I are great for the first couple of days and then it's as if I revert to being a teenager, and she reverts to being a menopausal maniac. It's not fair on Dad to put him through that again.'

Ben laughed. 'I remember you and your mum used to have some real ding dongs.'

'Oh yeah, our house was hormonal hell for a few years there.'

'Hiya Ben, the usual?'

'Hey Annie, yes ta.'

Isla felt a sharp pang of something she couldn't quite pinpoint as his gaze flickered over to the counter. Once upon a time she'd have known what his usual was, now she wouldn't have a clue.

'What are you going to do with yourself then? I wouldn't have thought there'd be much call for a high-flying interior decorator in Bibury.'

'Oh I don't know about that, people's houses always need redecorating at some point.'

He smiled at her.

Annie popped the ginormous savoury scroll, cheese oozing out of its sides, down on the table.

'Peckish then?' Ben raised an eyebrow, and Isla felt her face flush. 'How's Kris settling in at the school, Annie?' Ben was looking back at Annie.

'Great, he's enjoying it. A country school like Bibury Area is a big change to teaching at an urban Athens high school, but so far it's all good. He says teenagers are the same the world over!' She turned her attention to Isla. 'Kristofr, or Kris as he likes to be called now he's living in New Zealand, is my boyfriend.' She frowned. 'No that doesn't sound right, I'm too old to call him that. Um, partner ... ugh I hate that term.'

'At least you didn't say life partner that's the most cringe-worthy term of them all.'

The two women grinned at each other in silent understanding as Ben filled in the blanks. 'How about just calling him by his name? You women always have to over complicate everything.'

'Thank you, Ben. Yes, Kris.' Annie sniggered. 'My man friend teaches history at the high school.'

'He's a good bloke, your man friend.' Ben winked at Annie as he gave her 'man friend' the seal of approval.

'I think so.' A silly look drifted over her face.

'They met in Greece,' Ben said. 'It was front page news in the *Bibury Times* that the school was employing a foreign senior history teacher.'

'I can imagine it would've been, just like Violet McDougall retiring.' She couldn't help herself.

Ben didn't take the bait to mention his new girlfriend, though. 'Miss Seastrand's gone too, a bloke called Callum Packer's replaced her.'

'Not before time.' Isla recalled the Deputy Head, a grey-haired harridan. She was convinced the woman had it in for her. 'I caught her smoking cigarettes on the school field again,' Miss Seastrand announce to Principal Bishop as though she had just collared a criminal mastermind and was awaiting her reward.

'She was a holy terror that woman.'

Ben laughed. 'Yeah, she was. I remember the time she caught Ryan and me down the Four Square trying to buy cigarettes when we were supposed to be in Science class.'

'Oh, I remember that! Gosh, I would've been about twelve, and you guys were fourteen. Dad brought home a pack of Benson and Hedges and made Ryan smoke the lot. He was green; it was more entertaining than watching The Sopranos.'

'Ah, they don't do good TV like that anymore.' They smiled at each other until Isla became aware of Annie's hovering presence.

'So how did you meet Kris, Annie?'

'We met at the Acropolis in Athens. He was on a day trip with some of his students.'

'Oh, how romantic! I was in Athens a few years ago. The Acropolis blew me away. To be able to walk amongst all that history was amazing. He's Greek then, your man friend?' She smiled.

'Yes, he's from Naxos, and it was romantic apart from my friend Carl who I was travelling with coming down with the traveller's trots. He's a bit of a drama queen at the best of times. Anyway, it's a long story, and I'll tell you it when we know each other better, but the gist of it is that Carl had stampeded off to find a loo and I was sitting admiring the view when Kris left his students and came over to say hi. I'm Annie Rivers by the way. It's nice to meet you.'

'Isla Brookes and it's nice to meet you too.' They smiled at each other before Annie headed back behind the counter to fill the coffee plunger.

Isla was pleased Annie thought that they would get to know each other better, and she watched her potential new friend as she busied herself filling Ben's order. He was staring at her, she realized, and she felt the need to babble bubbling up in her throat. She swallowed it back down when he broke the silence.

'You don't want to let that get cold.'

'No,' she said picking up her knife. 'Yum, it looks good.'

'Here you go Ben, coffee to go, white with one sugar and a sausage roll.'

'Cheers Annie.' He took the takeaway cup and the paper bag through which the grease from his sausage roll was already seeping and hovered, watching as Isla cut into the pinwheel. 'It's good to see you again Isla; I'll see you around then.'

'Yeah, it was good to see you too. See you around.' She kept her gaze fixed on her plate until she heard the door bang shut behind him.

'Well, that last goodbye was like a scene from a Nicholas Sparks movie. All the two of you needed to look the part was a cowboy hat each.'

Isla looked up at Annie, startled.

'You obviously have a history.'

'You could say that, yes and I know where I can get hold of a cowboy hat.'

Annie grinned, pulling the chair out opposite Isla, where a few seconds ago Ben's hands had been resting. 'So come on then, spill.'

'I will when I know you better,' Isla said smiling before she stuffed in as much scroll as she could fit in her mouth.

'Touché.'

'Yum.' Isla could hear her gran telling her not to talk with her mouthful. 'What's in this? It's divine.'

Annie was only too pleased to share her recipe secret, it was all in the relish apparently, and the two women whiled away an uninterrupted half an hour chatting about food. Annie told Isla how she'd fallen in love with cooking while staying with a Greek family who ran a guest house in Crete. 'All the produce they cooked with was picked fresh straight from their garden.'

Just then, a middle-aged man who looked like he'd just crawled out of the bush after a week-long tramp barrelled into the tearooms, and greeted Annie cheerily nodding in Isla's direction. Annie excused herself, taking herself around to the business side of the counter as he inquired loudly as to whether the toasted cheese rolls were any good. Left to her own devices, Isla found her mind drifting back as she recalled the pleasure she got from gardening during her stay at Break-Free Haven. She could almost feel the arable soil running through her fingers and the Californian sun warming her back.

Chapter 7

Break-Free Haven Lodge

The last of the morning mist was hanging like a thin vapour stream over the meadow by the time Isla donned a floppy hat and ventured outside. She was a week into her stay at Break-Free and knew it wouldn't be long before the sun broke through the mist – and then it would be *hot*. She'd inherited her gran's olive skin, and dark eyes which Bridget always reckoned was a nod to her Irish Celtic ancestry. And, although she tanned easily, she was part of the Kiwi slip-slop-slap sunscreen generation and was wary of too much sun. This colouring had bypassed her mum much to Mary's chagrin; she was a fair-skinned blonde with a penchant for spray tans.

As a moody teen, every time Isla had fallen out with her mum, she'd be sure to go and look at an old school photo that still hung in the halls of Bibury Area School. Gran had told her the story of how her mother, as a know it all fifteen-year-old had basted herself in cooking oil before lying out in the sun despite being told not to, to be tanned for her class photo. The sight of Mary Collins as she had been back then, lobster-like in the front row of the class of seventy-five, always made Isla snigger and put her life back into perspective.

Now, she pulled on the pair of gardening gloves she'd been given and headed over to the greenhouse. The first time she'd taken part in the vegetable garden therapy session, she'd felt vaguely resentful at the situation she found herself in. She'd been perched on the wooden side of one of six raised boxes in a sunny spot behind the main red barn building, half-heartedly thinning out a row of carrots. Why should she have to get her hands dirty when she was paying a small fortune to be here? It wasn't as if she'd get to eat the fruits of her labour either because by the time these spindly baby carrot thingies grew to an edible length she'd be long gone.

Her father was a gardener; his veggie patch was his pride and joy. She started to understand what drove him as she planted out the beetroot seedlings. There was something satisfying in knowing that by doing what she was doing she'd be providing nourishing, organic food for future women in need passing through Break-Free. She'd been rostered on for last night's meal too and had been surprised by how much she'd enjoyed the process of preparing food for others. She'd forgotten how much she loved cooking. Proper cooking, not the ripping open of a packet or opening a jar of sauce cooking that she'd been used to in the latter years of life in London. There'd never been enough time to prepare anything from scratch.

Today, she was working alongside Betsy who hailed from Texas; she was planting out baby lettuce. They made great companion plants, Betsy informed her, while setting about her task. She looked to be around the same age as Isla, but she already had the haunted, bruised look of someone who'd packed in a lot over the years and led a hard life.

Isla was enjoying the peaceful setting as she settled into a pluck-from-the-pot and pop-into-the-soil rhythm. It was beautiful here, she thought. There were only twelve women in residence at Break-Free at any given time. She'd been lucky that there'd been a cancellation, otherwise, she'd have had to go on a waiting list. Twelve women here as guests, or inmates as they liked to joke, and four staff who were also all women. The only male she'd seen since leaving L.A. was the driver, who'd met her at her hotel.

Perhaps that was the answer, she mused watching a bee buzz lazily past in search of nectar. Maybe she should set up an all-women Amazonian style sanctuary deep in the heart of New Zealand's West Coast. They could be self-sufficient. She warmed to her theme. If anybody felt the need for any of that other business she'd sworn off for the foreseeable future, they could always pop into town and drag some young buck back from a local bar. She grinned. Where on earth did the word buck come from? It was like something her gran would say.

'My mom's boyfriend raped me when I was twelve.'

Isla's grin was wiped from her face, and her hand froze over the little hole she'd been about to drop the beetroot seedling into. Betsy didn't look at Isla as she continued her story in her soft Texan drawl, carrying on with her planting while she talked. Her mother hadn't believed her when she'd gone to her and told her what happened. She hadn't believed her or hadn't wanted to believe, Betsy said, but either way she'd left home by the time she was fifteen as a result. By twenty-one, she'd had three kids to three different fathers and had lurched from one bad relationship straight into another until this year when she'd told herself, enough was enough. The only good things that had happened in her life to date were her kids, and that was why she'd come to Break-Free.

'I've made some bad choices along the way, and I want to start making the right ones. I don't want what that bastard did to me to shape the rest of our lives. He doesn't deserve that kind of power.'

Isla wondered how as a single mum she could afford it here and Betsy must have sensed her curiosity.

'My mom saw the light one day, and when she died last year, she left me her house. I sold it, bought a place for my kids and me, and here I am. I've gotta do my best here for their sake because they're my world you know?'

Isla nodded. She didn't know, but she could imagine. 'Who's looking after them? You must be missing them.'

'Oh yeah, I am, but they're fine. My friend Joanne, the kids call her Aunty Jo, she's staying with them. She's been like a sister to me. They're in good hands. What about you, you're a long way from home with that funny accent of yours. Why're you here?'

'Um, I'm kind of a work in progress, but I suppose the trigger point for me coming here was my last relationship. It wasn't healthy. He didn't abuse me or anything, well not physically anyway but he had this knack of making me feel like

I wasn't good enough without actually ever saying so.' Isla glanced at her nails; they'd been chewed down to the quick when she left Toad but were starting to grow again now. 'And since I've been here, listening to you and the other girls as well as talking to Rita, I've realized that he was very good at it.'

'He was a bully.'

'More of a control freak with manipulative tendencies.' The two women smiled in mutual understanding at the counselor lingo. 'He chipped away at my confidence in such a subtle way that I used to wonder if I was being overly sensitive and imagining it.' Isla had realized while she'd been at Break-Free that she'd been on eggshells trying to please Tim. To be skinny enough, bright enough, funny enough for him, but never quite measuring up. All the while her work commitments were pushing and pulling at her until she'd reached snapping point.

'Yeah, I know the type. I've been there, done that, and got three kids to prove it,' Betsy said. 'You don't need to hit to hurt.'

Isla nodded her agreement with the sentiment before realizing it was time for her one-on-one session.

Half an hour later, Rita, the White Feather Programme Co-ordinator, was listening to Isla in her therapy session. 'The wrong kind of man and career burnout are what pushed you to the edge sweetie-pie. I'm thinking you're suffering from this thing called Rushing Woman's Syndrome. It's not something we normally see in a woman your age with no kids, but from what you've told me about your lifestyle, it fits.'

They were seated opposite each other, enveloped in the squidgy bean bags that you had to roll out of onto your hands and knees to stand up. From Isla's vantage point she could see out of the open window to the sequoia forest. The room was not at all clinical, with a Navajo rug dominating the wooden floor space between the orange coloured bean bags. The walls were painted a neutral taupe colour, and a massive artwork dominated one of them. Rita told her it had been donated by a former guest

It depicted a peace lily with the giant Californian redwoods, or sequoia as was their first given name, that formed a backdrop to the land on which Break-Free sat illuminated in the background by an orange sunset. It was almost half past three, Isla saw, glancing at her watch. She'd never worn a wristwatch before but had purchased one in LA, as cell phones were banned at Break-Free. She'd handed hers in after a quick call to Maura to let her know she was doing okay. Isla liked to know what the time was. It gave her a modicum of control over her days.

It had been a light bulb moment sitting on that beanbag, to hear a label that did not involve the word nerves or breakdown. She didn't get the Russian connection though. 'Russian Woman's Syndrome?' The mind boggled.

Rita smiled, and Isla thought she had the kindest blue eyes. She also noticed that there wasn't a single grey hair in amongst her blonde mane. So much for a steel grey smart haircut stereotype.

'R-U-S-H-I-N-G honey, Rushing Woman's Syndrome. Dr. Libby Weaver, she's a Nutritional Biochemist who hails from your part of the world and has written a book on the subject. She believes it's a modern-day scourge for women, and so do I.'

Isla listened as Rita filled her in on the ins and outs of the condition, mentally ticking off all the things she could relate to. Yes, she was always in a mad rush to get the job done whatever it may be. Yes, there were never enough hours in the day. Yes, she'd gone off sex in the latter months of her relationship with Tim and had to keep pretending he was Hugh Jackman to get the job done. Yes, she did feel wired most of the time but strangely fatigued too. Yes, she felt bloated and sick on occasion. Yes, around that time of the month she could happily wreak havoc on anyone who crossed her path. Yes, she'd lie in bed at night finding herself unable to switch off. The list went on, but Rita was ready to summarise. 'Basically honey, your body has been running on adrenaline and not much else. It's telling you it's had enough.'

Okay, so now that she knew what was wrong with her, Isla wanted to know how she was going to make it all better? It was time for Rita to produce her magic counseling wand and fix everything. The next thing Rita said, however, was not, 'Abracadabra, so this is what you're going to do now Isla,' but rather:

'So what're you going to do now Isla?'

Isla looked at her, startled. That wasn't in the contract. 'I don't know. That's why I'm here. I want you to tell me what I should do next.'

Rita laughed. 'Oh, that's not for me to say, sweetie, but I think it might be time for you to re-evaluate exactly what it is you want from life. The pace hasn't always been that hectic for you so why don't you start by telling me about the town you grew up in?' Rita looked at her in that counselor way of hers, inviting her to elaborate without actually asking out loud, and so Isla did.

For Isla, at eighteen Bibury had become unbearably claustrophobic. It was a town so tiny it didn't even get a mention on most maps. The closest thing to a cultural experience it offered was karaoke at the Pit on the first Saturday of the month. So as soon as she finished school, she broke things off with her boyfriend Ben, packed her bags and left town so fast she wouldn't have been surprised if there had been smoke coming off her heels.

Her mum and dad had thought they understood her need to go and broaden her horizons. The world, Mary had said wisely upon hearing her daughter's news, was a wonderful place. Her parents had just come back from visiting Isla's older brother, Ryan. He'd gone to work in the mining industry just outside of Emerald in Queensland, and Mary was feeling not only worldly after visiting Australia but magnanimous too.

It was her gran who'd been hit hardest by the news that Isla was leaving to set up home two and a half hours away in Christchurch . Poor Gran, she couldn't relate to her granddaughter's burning need for more. She tried to placate her by telling her she was only going to the big smoke to study and that she'd be home every other weekend. Looking into those wily dark eyes reminiscent of her own though, she'd felt uncomfortable. They both knew she was lying. Gran had always known when she wasn't telling the truth.

Bridget had some grandmotherly super-power, Isla was sure of it.

Christchurch was small so far as cities on the world stage go but after Bibury, population two hundred thousand, it had been a culture shock. Isla had stuck it out though and completed a design course at Polytech while living in a draughty, old weatherboard house in the student suburb of Riccarton with three others. It was a stone's throw from the city centre, and despite lean student times, there'd been plenty of good times too. It had been hard breaking things off with Ben, though.

'Why don't you tell me about this Ben?' Rita interrupted. 'You sound like you were fond of him.'

Isla smiled, she always smiled when she thought about Ben. 'I was yes. He was a friend of my brother's. I'd known him most of my life, and I'd never thought of him in any other way than as just another of Ryan's annoying mates. But then one day he put a packet of potato chips down on the conveyor when I was working on the till at the local Four Square supermarket and asked me out. I could tell he was nervous as he stood waiting for me to scan the chips through, but I was still hesitant about saying yes.'

'Why?'

Isla shrugged. 'I knew I'd be leaving Bibury at the end of the year when I finished school, and I knew Ben wouldn't.'

'But you said yes?'

'I didn't want to embarrass him by saying no,' she said smiling. 'And besides, so far as Ryan's annoying mates went, he was one of the nicer ones and definitely the cutest.' She thought back to their first date, it had been to the movies over in Greymouth, and he'd taken her to a pizza restaurant afterward. The movie had been rubbish but later, as his hand reached over to wipe the dangle of mozzarella from her chin, she felt a fluttering in her stomach. He was good-looking with his gentle blue-green eyes and shock of blond hair, and she wondered why she'd never noticed him in that way before.

'We went out together for the rest of the year, and I fell for him hard. I still broke things off when I moved to Christchurch to study, though.' Her eyes welled up, even now all these years later at the painful memory. 'We were just too young, and I wasn't right for him.'

'Why not, Isla?'

'Because I was scared of my feelings for him. I loved him too much.'

'Earth to Isla, earth to Isla.' Annie waved a hand in front of Isla's face.

'Sorry I was somewhere else.' Isla blinked, becoming aware that she was sitting at a table in the Kea Tearooms and not on a beanbag at Break-Free. She flashed an apologetic grin at Annie. 'Where you stayed in Crete sounds wonderful, and home-grown vegetables do taste different to store bought. I love to cook, I'd forgotten how much until recently. I'm not a bad baker either if I do say so myself, but then I was taught by the best.' She wriggled her fingers. 'She taught me to tell by touch what the mix needed.'

Annie raised an eyebrow. 'And who would that be?'

'My gran, Bridget Collins. I'm staying with her.'

'Oh, I've met Bridget! She's lovely, her and Aunty Noeline are good friends. So, that must mean your mum is Mary from the pharmacy?'

Isla nodded.

'Mary pops in most mornings for a coffee and something to eat. She always brightens my morning up.'

'Uh-huh, I bet she does, with that glowing face of hers.'

Annie laughed. 'She does have a good tan. But honestly, I look forward to my morning chat with your mum because it's so dead in here a lot of the time. I think Aunty Noeline's just given up on this place. She pretty much leaves the running of it to me,' she said gesturing around her. 'It frustrates me because Bibury is such a thoroughfare through to Greymouth and the rest of the Coast. This place could be a real goldmine if it was done up and the menu was brought up to date.'

Isla's mind began to whir at the mention of goldmine; it was the mine bit that got her going. 'I'm an interior designer, and an unemployed one for the minute so maybe I could put some ideas together for you to show Noeline? I think you're right that this place could be a real goldmine given the right makeover.' She held her breath hoping she wasn't pushing in and overstepping the mark but it would be a way to check she still had her design mojo. She needn't have worried.

Annie clapped her hands. 'Really? That'd be amazing.'

'I'd love to,' Isla said without hesitation. She left the Kea with a spring in her step. She'd made a new friend, and she had work to be getting on with. It felt good to have a purpose.

Chapter 8

'Isla, I'm fed up with looking at the face on you tonight. Skipping the Light Fan-Tango is coming on the telly in half an hour, and I don't want to have to listen to you huffing and puffing your way through it. Why don't you go with your mum to that thing she loves so much? It will get you out of the house for a bit.'

Isla looked at her gran blankly. What was she on about?

Bridget flapped her hand in frustration. 'Oh, you know that thing where they prance around in the dark to music. Tell her Joe.'

'Your mother's keep fit class,' Joe said. He was settled into Bridget's other recliner with his hands clasped around a belly full of bangers and mash.

'Oh, I'm with you. No Lights, No Lycra you mean?'

'Yes, that's it. Give her a call; it'll do you good to get out for a bit. A girl your age shouldn't be sitting at home with her grandmother night after night. Should she Joe?'

Joe nodded, he'd agree with Bridget on anything if there was a bowl of her creamy rice pudding in it for him.

'It's only been four nights Gran,' Isla said feeling ganged

up upon, but she was feeling fidgety too. Oh God, she frowned, was this what her life had come to? Was she seriously considering shaking her groove thing in the dark, with her mum and a bunch of other middle-aged women? It would appear so because she was fed up. She'd mooched around the house on her own for the best part of the day waiting for the internet to be connected. It was rural broadband only in Bibury and nowhere near as high speed as she was used to, but at least as of three o'clock that afternoon, she was in touch with the outside world once more. The first thing she'd done was message Maura to tell her how she was getting on and then she'd hit Pinterest for some ideas for the Kea. That had kept her busy until Gran had got home. Joe had popped in not long after looking for his dinner.

Bridget, it would seem had a pretty hectic social life. There had been bowls in the morning and then she'd invited Isla to join her for afternoon tea at Margaret's house. She was heading over to discuss the coup she suspected was being plotted by Elsie.

Isla had heard all about it over lunch. Gran reckoned Elsie was no longer content to wait to see if she was made Vice President of the Bibury Women's Bowls Club. Oh no, she was planning to overthrow Bridget and push her out of the role of top dog. It was like listening to a geriatric episode of Wentworth. The whole business was serious enough, Gran said, for her to contemplate telling Margaret her closely guarded secret; the secret as to what it was that gave her scones that extra light, airiness in exchange for insider information.

It was all very intriguing, but Isla had declined the invitation. Instead, she found herself peering out the front window of the living room from time to time in the hope of catching a glimpse of Ben. Why? She didn't know. Ben was such ancient history that their relationship could be classed as early Jurassic. However, she did see him. It was as if he'd felt her eyes on him because he'd looked up from the car he was working on and his gaze had swung her way. She'd let the curtain drop quickly, feeling as though it had burned her fingers, and sent up a prayer that he hadn't seen her. To her shame she realized that since arriving back in Bibury, she was not only a thirty-year-old woman, living with her grandmother, she was also a curtain-twitcher.

The current affairs programme on the telly went to an ad break. To Isla's alarm, Gran began stabbing at the screen and getting very hot under the collar as the shorts for Skipping the Light Fan-Tango appeared.

'Look at her there in her sparkly ... well you could hardly call it a dress, there's not enough fabric for that. A sparkly belt, maybe. She's a floozy, that one, and she's only got as far as she has in the competition because she slept with Javier Franco. Look, he's the judge in the middle.' She gave a particularly virulent jab towards the television. 'You can tell by the way they look at each other.'

Okay, Isla thought, it would seem her options were staying here and listening to Gran's slanderous character assassination of the stars of SLF or she could ring her mum and cadge a ride to a dancing in the dark session. Best ring her, she thought hauling herself out of her chair.

'Good girl,' Joe mumbled.

'Mum's picking me up in five minutes, do I look the part Dad? Gran?' she asked a few minutes later from where she stood in the living room doorway. She'd changed into her trusty leisure suit and a pair of running shoes that were in for a shock because they never usually did anything remotely sporty. She'd pulled her hair back into a ponytail.

'Why are you asking us that? I thought the whole point of having the lights off when you dance is that it's dark. Nobody can see what you look like. Your mother says it's very liberating,' Bridget said with a grimace. 'I'd hate to think what get up she goes along in. She always has to take things one step too far, your mother. She has done since she was a child.'

Joe caught Isla's eye, and they both grinned in silent agreement.

'Right well, I'll leave you both to your show.' Isla planted a kiss on top of her gran's silver head and one on her father's bristly cheek.

'I'm off in a minute too,' he said.

'Working on the bike?'

'Too right, only peace I get to tinker on it is when your mother's out dancing.'

'Oh Isla, before I forget, when the lights are on have a look around the hall. I'm the Secretary of the Barker's Creek Hall Committee, and we're trying to think of ways to fundraise to give it a spruce up.'

'Okay, I will,' Isla said. She vaguely recalled the hall from her youth as the place that Brownies and other kids' activities had been held. That it was old with lots of wood was what she remembered of it. She also remembered the stories her gran had told her about the dances held there back in the days before she got married. Isla always fancied she caught a glimpse of her gran as a girl on the cusp of womanhood when she talked about those days because her eyes always sparkled as she relived them.

'Now go on with you,' Bridget said waving her away, but Isla saw her smile.

Oh bugger, she thought a few minutes later, shutting the front door behind her. She didn't have a water bottle. The Four Square was still open she saw, glancing up the road in that direction and spying lights. She opened the passenger door of her mum's idling car and climbing in kissed her on the cheek. 'Hi Mum, good day?'

'So, so. I sold a bottle of Revlon Age Defying foundation to Mrs Flintoff this afternoon, but I had to explain to her that once she's opened it, she can't bring it back if she doesn't look like Elle McPherson after five days.'

Isla laughed at the trial and tribulations of the beauty biz.

'Got your dancing shoes on ready to go?'

'Uh-huh, but can I just run into the Four Square and grab a bottle of water?'

'Alright, but don't mess about, I want to get there while the lights are still on. We don't want to trip over and injure ourselves before we even get in the door.'

Isla walked through the door of the little supermarket where she had toiled away many a Saturday afternoon, and as she headed over to the fridge, she spotted Annie. She was conferring with a tall man. He had an impressive head of shiny, swishy hair and didn't look Greek in the slightest. She had a bottle of wine in her hand which appeared to be the object of intense discussion between them.

She debated going over, Mum had told her to get a move on.

'Hello again!' Annie said spotting her, her face breaking into a grin and Isla felt a twinge of guilt at having even tossed up on whether or not to say hi. *Mum could wait*.

'Carl, this is my new friend, Isla. She's an interior designer who's just got back from the UK. She's going to put together some ideas for jazzing up the Kea.'

Carl stepped forward and held out his hand. His grasp was strong which belied the soft skin. Actually, Isla looked up and him and realized his skin was beautiful. She wondered what his secret was. His nails were well-shaped unlike her own which were a mess thanks to all that veggie gardening at Break-Free. He dropped her hand and ran his fingers through his hair which swished satisfyingly back into place. Isla observed this and turned a shade of green. Oh, to have hair that did that.

'Carl's staying with Kris and me for a few nights. He decided to escape the big smoke and make a long weekend of it,' Annie informed her.

The penny dropped. 'Ah, so you're the Carl that Annie travelled to Greece with?'

'The one and the same, and knowing Annie she's told the unfortunate Acropolis story. Travel tip darling, never leave home without a box of Diastop.'

Isla laughed, and Annie shook her head. She spied the water bottle. 'Where are you off to looking all sporty?'

'No Lights, No Lycra at the Barker's Creek Community Hall.'

Two blank faces gazed back at her.

'Apparently, the idea stemmed from a bunch of dance students in Melbourne. They wanted the freedom to express themselves outside the conformity of their classes,' she repeated the spiel her mother had given her. 'Sounds great in theory but I'm dubious as to what it's like in practice. I'm keeping an open mind, though. The alternative was sitting at home with my gran who was getting het up over Skipping the Light Fan-Tango.'

Annie and Carl listened in amusement.

'Hey, why don't you guys come with me for moral support? Annie, you've met my mum, there's room in the car.'

Carl was the first to answer. 'I like the sound of that, it's my kind of exercise, and I seriously need to destress thanks to David. What do you think Annie?'

'Kris has a tonne of marking to get through; he won't mind if we eat dinner later. I'm not dressed for it though.' Annie gestured to her floaty tunic dress and boots. The boots were gorgeous, Isla loved the red colour – she'd ask her later where she'd bought them.

'Listen here, Annie my sweet. I've seen you doing a Beyoncé dance in a little black dress that barely covered your bum and killer heels that could rival Queen B's herself. You'll manage an hour in a pair of boots, yes?' Carl said grabbing another three bottles of the same wine Annie had in her hand.

He was dressed in a blue and white checked cotton shirt that he had tucked into a pair of jeans. The brown cowboy boots were not dissimilar to the pair Isla had just bought her dad. Annie caught her gaze as they followed him up to the till. 'It's his down home country boy look. He thinks it makes him look like one of the local lads. I tried to tell him he just looks conspicuously gay, but he wouldn't have a bar of it,' she whispered.

Isla laughed.

They exited the shop with their wine and water. Isla saw her mother's hand was hovering over the horn and saving her the trouble, she opened the passenger door and leaned in.

'Mum, you know Annie from the Kea, and this is her friend Carl. They're going to come with us if that's okay?'

'Get in – the more, the merrier,' Mary trilled.

'Carl meet Mary Newton-John,' Isla said twisting in her seat after she'd done her belt up.

Mary looked back over her shoulder. 'Ha ha, she's very funny my daughter. Mary Brookes and it's nice to meet you, Carl. Are you staying in Bibury long?' she asked pulling out of the carpark before heading off down the main road.

'I've run away actually. My partner David's being a prat and I needed some time out, so I've landed on Annie and Kris for a few days to get my head straight.' He laughed. 'Well, you know what I mean.'

The three women smiled in the darkened car interior and then Mary gave a sympathetic tut. 'Bibury's a good place to get your head straight ... um, I mean in order. It's got a peaceful aura.'

They all ignored the boy-racer who chose that very minute to overtake them with his sound system thumping and muffler backfiring.

'What is it you do with yourself work wise Carl?' Mary carried on.

'I am a fashion photographer.'

'Really?'

'Mum, eyes on the road!'

'Well, that's a coincidence. I'm in the industry too.'

'I thought you looked familiar; I haven't photographed you have I?'

Mary's laugh was high and girlish. 'Oh no, I'm far too old for modelling but I am in the business, I'm a Revlon Consultant at Mitchells Pharmacy on the High Street.'

'I love Revlon. It's one of my favourite brands. I photographed Stella Rockhampton last year for them. She was a real sweetie, not like some of the girls out there. I blame the attitude on a lack of food. Who can be nice when you're permanently peckish?'

'I agree, better to have that cheeseburger and burn it off with a bit of NLNL.'

'Amen to that, Mary.'

Isla was trying not to laugh at the banter between them, and she didn't have to look back to know that Annie was too.

The hall sat in the middle of a field and Mary pulled into a parking space off to the side of the building. Dusk had settled in, but it was still light enough for Isla to see that the building was indeed looking tired. She hoped no one's exuberant dance steps would cause them to go through the floorboards inside, which no doubt would be riddled with woodworm.

'Okay, gang – let's get our groove on!' Mary cut a move

and clapped her hands in a way that made Isla cringe and Annie and Carl laugh. At least she'd had the sense not to wear anything too inappropriate for a woman her age, and there was not a leg warmer in sight. Isla inspected her mum's lycra pants and singlet top. She'd had to do the headband thing, she noticed, shaking her head as she followed her lead into the hall.

A few women, none of whom Isla recognized at first glance, were standing on pews pegging sheets over the windows. A stereo system was perched on the raised wooden stage near the entrance, and an alcove to the right of the stage indicated the facilities. It hadn't changed in the twenty years since Isla had last been inside it. She'd be willing to bet it hadn't changed in the one hundred odd years since it had been built.

'Evening Mary love, I see you've brought some newbies with you.'

'Linda, you remember my daughter, Isla?'

'Oh Isla of course, gosh look at you! You're all grown up.'

Isla nodded and smiled biting back that she had, in fact, been grown up for some time now. She vaguely recalled the big woman in the resplendent lightweight black and silver active wear ensemble from somewhere in her formative years.

'And these are her new friends. Carl, he's a fashion photographer by the way.' There was a collective oohing and mass sucking in of tummies. 'And Annie, you've probably seen her around town, she's hard to miss with all that gorgeous red hair, is related to Noeline somehow or other. She's working at the Kea.'

'Welcome, welcome all, we'll get started in a jiffy,' Linda said.

Carl emitted a low whistle as he looked around him. 'They don't build them like this anymore. All that timber is to die for.'

Isla nodded, testing the floor with her foot. It felt solid, and there were no squiggly telltale signs of Bora eating away it. 'It's Kauri,' she said referring to the native wood. 'My grandmother's the chairperson for the hall's committee, and apparently, they want to give it a long overdue overhaul. It all looks pretty sound inside, but I'm guessing the toilet and kitchen facilities would struggle to pass a council inspection these days.'

Annie was standing at the far end of the hall next to the stuffed stag's head staring up at two varnished war memorial plaques. A Roll of Honour on each depicted in gold lettering the names of the young men who had lost their lives fighting for their country in both the Great War and the Second World War. Carl and Isla joined her.

'Sad, isn't it?' Annie said.

'Yeah, I don't know what I'd have done at eighteen if I'd been made to go off and fight for my country. I'm a lover, not a fighter, but if those men hadn't gone, then our country would be very different to the one we live in today,' Carl ventured sagely.

'That's very wise of you Carl,' Annie said touching his arm.

'I can be sometimes, I'll have you know. Especially now that I'm officially a middle-aged man.'

Isla guessed him to be in his early forties although his brow was suspiciously smooth. She turned her attention back to the plaque. 'It's hard to imagine what it would've done to a small community like Bibury, losing all those men.'

They were spared dwelling on it further by Linda calling out. 'Hit the lights, Karen, here we go ladies and gentlemen!'

Chapter 9

They were plunged into darkness, almost.

'I can still see you,' Annie hissed.

'I suppose it can't be pitch black, or we could hurt ourselves,' Isla said.

'How? There's nothing to trip over?'

'I don't know, do a hip or something.'

Annie's snigger was drowned out by the sudden blaring out of Macklemore and Ryan's Downtown. It was not what Isla had expected. She didn't know what she'd expected really, she'd been open-minded, up to a point. She began to move a little awkwardly to the beat.

The floorboards began to vibrate as everybody thundered into action. They didn't believe in a gentle warm up then, Isla thought, as her eyes adjusted to the dark. Her mouth fell open at the sight of her mother doing an impressively high leg kick. Annie seemed to have relaxed and was grooving away, sedately, but grooving nonetheless. Isla did a little side-step. Oh, this was not good, her legs felt like lead. The last time she had danced like nobody was watching was not when she was stone cold sober in a community hall on a Thursday night.

As the song wound up and another equally danceable beat boomed out, she found herself relaxing a little. Nobody was watching her, she realized. They were all just doing their own thing and letting loose. She picked up her pace a little and found herself enjoying moving to the music. By the time the opening chords of *Sweet Child O' Mine* sounded, she was twirling with the best of them.

'I love G'n'R!' Carl yelled in her ear, and she laughed as he began playing air guitar. This was fun.

The hour whizzed by and they all blinked like possums caught in headlights when the lights were flicked back on.

'Wa-hoo! Good workout people,' Linda called out like a nineties relic from a step aerobics class. Everyone clapped the way you would in a step aerobics class and somebody, Isla had a suspicion it was Mary, shouted, 'Yeah! Right on!'

Isla drained her water bottle. She was hot, she was knackered and her Achilles was giving her grief from all that thumping around. She needed the loo too.

The toilets were clean on inspection, but there was no wheelchair accessible loo, and it was very '50s utilitarian-style. When she was done, she poked her head around the kitchen door; it was the same in there. It was a functional homage to Formica and stainless steel. She walked back to the hall.

'We're heading back home for moussaka if you want to join us?' Annie asked, folding one of the sheets that had been pegged over the window with Carl. 'You can meet Kris.'

'I'd like that if you're sure you've got enough?'

'Kris' moussaka is to die for, and he makes so much of it he could feed a small nation,' Carl interjected.

'I'll drop you all off,' Mary said, having overheard the conversation. She was pleased that her daughter was settling in and making friends. She'd worried about her over in London, mooning around after Tim. She'd not warmed to him, there was something off about him but she'd never quite been able to put her finger on what it was.

'That'd be great thanks, Mary, and you're welcome to join us too.'

'No, but thanks. I'd best be getting home to check on Joe.'

'Good job we stocked up Annie. I feel a red wine evening coming on,' Carl said rubbing his hands together.

'Our place is only small but it's been modernized inside and being through the school, the rent's peanuts,' Annie said pushing the front door open, and giving Mary a wave as she reversed off. 'We're back!' she called heading up the hall.

There was light at the end of the hall, and Isla could smell the wonderful aroma of garlic, onions, and tomatoes. 'Yum,' she said. She'd had some of her gran's bangers and mash earlier, but after all that exercise she was hungry again. Nobody needed to know it was her second dinner. She followed Annie into the kitchen, Carl bringing up the rear, wine bottles at the ready, 'I've got the vino, get the glasses, Kris!'

'We've brought one more for dinner,' Annie said walking into what Isla saw was a surprisingly modern and compact kitchen given the age of the house. 'Kris, meet Isla. I told you we met at the Kea the other day. Isla's an interior designer.'

Kris took his glasses off and placed them next to the stack

of exercise books piled on the table in front of him. He got up from his seat and stepped forward with his hand outstretched in greeting. Isla shook it, and looking up at him, she decided she was going to like this man. He had an endearing dimple in his left cheek that made him look younger than he probably was, and the kindest of brown eyes. His nose was pretty acceptable by Grecian standards too, she thought as she finished her appraisal. He released her hand. 'You've just got back from living in London, is that right?' His accent was gentle, and his English clear and precise.

'Yes, I was away for quite a while. It's good to be home.'

Carl busied himself opening the wine. 'Right we've earned a vino. Move those books Kris, my friend; your work's done for today.'

Over dinner, Isla shared her story, leaving out the parts she wasn't willing to tell. Then it was her turn to listen to Carl, Annie and Kris tell theirs, and all the while Carl ensured their glasses were never empty. She had a second helping of the moussaka. She couldn't help herself, it just melted in the mouth. Everybody had a backstory, she realized, spooning it onto her plate as she listened to the reason behind Annie's and Carl's trip to the Greek Islands. It had been a pilgrimage of sorts for Annie's older sister, Roz, who'd passed away when Annie was a young girl. She hadn't gone into details but reading between the lines, Isla surmised it had been the result of a car accident.

It had been Roz's dream to travel to the Greek Islands, Annie told her. Carl and Roz had been best friends until she drifted away doing her own thing, and he'd taken Annie under his wing after her death. It had been natural for him to want to join her on her quest to fulfill her big sister's dream.

Annie got up while Carl was talking and unwrapped an apple pie that had been defrosting on the bench. She popped it into the oven, and when she sat back down, she informed Isla that Kris had a chronic sweet tooth. 'He goes into shock if he doesn't get something sugary after dinner. I think his mama well and truly spoiled him as a boy.'

'You are right,' Kris dimpled. 'It is my mama's fault she fed me too much baklava as a baby.'

Isla laughed, and while they waited for the pie to heat through, he told the story of how on a school trip he'd seen this beautiful girl with flaming hair and a sad face sitting on a rock at the Acropolis. It was Annie, and he'd just had to talk to her. She'd told him why she was in Greece while his students took notes on their historical surrounds nearby.

'After meeting her that day I couldn't get her out of my mind, and so when my teaching year finished, I sailed to Crete, where I knew she'd gone. I had to see her again.'

'How romantic! That's like something from a film,' Isla said, but Annie and Kris were gazing at each other over the table in their own wee world.

'Just like Shirley Valentine, I found much more than I ever dreamed I would,' Annie said.

Isla was about to ask who Shirley Valentine was but Carl cleared his throat and filled her in, 'It's a late eighties film about a Liverpool housewife who heads off to Greece on a package holiday and rediscovers her lust for life. Get a room, you two. Make you sick, don't they?'

Isla smiled. If she didn't like them both so much, she'd be envious.

Annie poked her tongue out. 'It's a brilliant film, a classic.' She got up to dish the pie out.

'Not too much cream on mine, thanks, Annie.'

'I apologize for it being store bought, but by the time I knocked off today, I was over baking. So, voila, the humble Four Square apple pie is as far as I got.'

'Tastes good to me,' Isla mumbled through a mouthful. 'Sara Lee knows her pies.'

'Saralee is the name of the new secretary at the school,' Kris said digging in. 'It's an unusual name, yes? She's going out with Ben, from the garage. He's a nice guy.' He popped his spoon in his mouth, missing the look Annie shot Isla. Isla's stomach had done an involuntary twist at the mention of Ben's name, and it wasn't down to all the moussaka currently jostling for room inside it.

Carl held his hand out to collect the empty bowls a short while later, and Isla saw Kris stifle a yawn. She remembered he'd be dealing with a classroom full of teenagers in the morning. It was time to make tracks. 'I can honestly say that's the best moussaka I've ever had and a pretty darn delish apple pie too. Thanks so much for inviting me tonight, it's been lovely to meet you, Kris and Carl.'

'I like this new friend of ours,' Kris said with a grin.

For the first time in a long while, Isla felt a sense of belonging. It had been a lovely evening.

The next morning, Isla woke with a dry mouth and a niggling headache that told her she had over indulged the night before. She lay in bed for a few more minutes, with a vague plan forming that today would be a good day to go and look at cars. She stretched, hearing Gran moving about in the kitchen. *Time to get up and face the world, Isla Brookes!* Or a certain someone would be in ripping the curtains open, and demanding to know why her granddaughter was sleeping her life away.

Twenty minutes later she'd showered, dressed and was sitting down to a breakfast of scrambled eggs on toast. Bridget had plopped it down on the table as soon as Isla stuck her foot in through the kitchen door.

'You don't have to make me breakfast, you know. Although, it does look good, thanks.' Isla began to dig in. She loved a cooked brekkie and a brekkie cooked by someone else was even better!

'I don't trust you to eat properly left to your own devices,' Bridget replied bluntly, picking up her teacup and placing it on the bench. She was dressed in black pants and a pretty short-short sleeved blue top, a matching cardi slung over her arm in case the weather chose to misbehave.

'You look lovely in that shade of blue, Gran. Where are you off to today?' She was hardly ever home – Isla was sure that it was all her committees and clubs that kept her fit as a fiddle for the most part. It had been a comfort for her to see for herself that Gran was alright after her fall, apart from her hip which obviously gave her a bit of grief here and there.

Bridget wasn't one for compliments, but still, she was

pleased. The top was organic bamboo cotton and had cost a fortune. The cotton was breathable with long wearing properties, the enthusiastic sales girl in Greymouth had promised, before appealing to her conscience by telling her it wasn't made in a sweat shop either.

'Margaret's picking me up shortly. We're off to your stomping ground last night, Barker's Creek Hall, for a committee meeting to discuss fundraising ideas.' She sighed and rested her hands on the back of the chair opposite Isla.

She no longer wore her wedding ring, Isla noticed in surprise, although the indentation from all the years was plain to see beneath her knuckle, which looked swollen and knobbly.

'The Hall's getting in a bit of a sorry state as you'd have seen for yourself. We're very much teetering on the fence with the Council's list of requirements for a public space these days. It's bloody ridiculous the number of things they expect us to comply with.' She made a tutting sound. 'I won't see the hall shut down, not in my lifetime. And what about you? What're you going to do with yourself today then, miss?'

'Well, I'm going to borrow Mum's car, if she'll let me that is, and drive into Greymouth. I thought I'd nab Dad while he's on his lunch break and see if he can help me find a car.'

'Oh Isla, don't be silly, you know you'll come home with a petrol guzzling monster if you enlist your father's services. Joe's motto is the bigger and noisier the better.'

'Too true, and I want something economical that preferably doesn't require a heavy vehicle operator's license for me to get behind the wheel,' Isla said, sighing. 'The problem is I don't know anything about cars other than whether I like the colour or not.'

'Well, I'm not much help to you.'

'I haven't owned a car in years, not since the wee, Honda I got when I moved to Christchurch. There was no need for a car in London, not with the Underground, and there'd have been nowhere to park it anyway.'

Bridget's eyes gleamed. 'Listen, why don't you pop over to the garage and ask Ben's advice? He'd see you on the right track.'

Isla slopped her tea into the saucer. 'Oh, I couldn't do that!'

'Why not?' Bridget was warming to her theme, and from the look on her face, Isla knew she wasn't going to get out of this one easily. She couldn't think of an answer either. She was sure his girlfriend wouldn't like it, but Gran would pooh-pooh that as a silly excuse. They were grown-ups, weren't they?

Chapter 10

So it was, half an hour later Isla found herself walking self-consciously across the forecourt of the Shell garage to stand in the workshop. 'Er, morning Ben.' She wished those butterflies currently going berserk in her stomach would flipping well migrate. This was ridiculous, she thought. She had not been that teenage girl who'd fallen head over heels in love with Ben Robson in a decade and then some.

He looked up at her from where he was standing in the pit, fiddling around with the underneath of a hatchback parked over the top of it.

'Isla ... hi, how's it going?'

'Good, thanks, yeah um what it is, well what it is—' *Spit it out Isla for God's sake*. 'It was Gran's idea actually. She suggested I come and see you for a bit of advice with regards to buying a car. I want something economical that doesn't cost the earth. I was thinking of heading into Greymouth and asking Dad to come to a couple of yards with me today but Gran put me off the idea, she reckoned I'd come home with a monster truck.'

Ben laughed. 'She wouldn't be far wrong! Look I'll be

finished working on this in around five minutes and Vanessa's running the shop today. I don't have anything urgent booked in for the rest of the day, so why don't I take you over to Greymouth?'

Isla felt her face flush at the idea and hoped she didn't resemble a tomato as she said, 'I wouldn't want to put you out.'

'Hey, it's no bother, it'll be good to escape for a couple of hours, to be honest.'

'Well, if you're sure, that'd be fantastic, thank you.'

'I'll swing by and pick you up in say ...' he glanced at his watch. 'Twenty minutes? That'll give me time to get washed up.' He turned away and got back to whatever it was he doing under the car. Isla headed off, feeling inexplicably pleased with how things had panned out.

It was amazing the state she'd worked herself into in such a short space of time. She applied and then reapplied her lipstick before blotting it off. She didn't want to look like she'd gone to any special bother. Shrugging into her favourite top, she froze upon appraising her reflection. It was pale pink; Ben had always loved her in pink, said she was pretty in pink. He'd think she'd dressed to impress! She hastily yanked the top back over her head opting for a green shirt instead. It was as far removed from pink as she could find. By the time Ben pulled into the driveway, she'd decided she'd have to do. She pulled the front door shut behind her and clambered into the passenger seat of his mud-splattered Toyota truck, kicking at an empty McDonald's bag with her foot.

'Sorry about the mess.'

Isla smiled, noticing he'd changed into jeans and a t-shirt that hugged his broad shoulders as she buckled in. A jacket was slung over his seat. 'You never were a tidy Kiwi.' As he reversed out of the drive and onto the High Street, she felt a frisson of panic. What if they had nothing to say to each other? It was a forty-minute drive to Greymouth, she hoped it wouldn't feel much longer. Conversation was never a problem between them in the past, they used to talk about anything and everything, and he always made her laugh. That was years ago though, and so much had happened since. She cast a furtive glance at him. He looked relaxed as they drove past the pharmacy and the Four Square. His big hands, which he'd obviously just scrubbed clean, were holding the steering wheel loosely, his fingers tapping out the beat of the song playing on the radio.

Isla leaned back into her seat as they left Bibury behind and gazed out of the window up at the hills cloaked in bush, rearing up on either side of the road. The ground would be thick with ferns and mosses she knew, thanks to many a school tramp. Glancing up at the Nikau palms she could visualize the climbing vines dangling from them, giving the bush a Jurassic feel. She hadn't appreciated the beauty of it all when she was a kid, dragging her heels and moaning along with the rest of her classmates. She hadn't appreciated a lot of things when she was younger, she thought with a sideways glance at Ben.

'How was life in London?' He kept his eyes on the road ahead.

Isla felt her nerves dissipate as she began to talk slipping back into the easy feeling of being in the company of someone you'd once known well. 'I guess it became home for a while.'

'Ten years.'

'Yeah, ten years,' she echoed. 'I had some good times and some not so good times towards the end.' She shrugged. 'There'll be things I am going to miss and some things not so much.'

'Like what?'

'Well, my good friend, Maura, for starters. I miss her already, but we won't lose touch, Skype's a beautiful thing. Then there's the theatre and the museums, all the cultural stuff. But I won't miss the queues and disgruntled commuters.'

'Not much call for a queue in Bibury but what's wrong with the Bibury Players and their annual show at the Town Hall or the Miners' Museum if it's a bit of culture you are after?' He raised an eyebrow and smirked.

'Have you been overseas?'

'Yeah, I have. I had a glance round Australia and a good look at Asia. I love Vietnam. The food there's great, and the people are fantastic but home's home, you know?'

'I'm beginning to know, yes.'

He shot her a quizzical look.

'So, Dad told me you're dating the school's new secretary.' It shot out of her mouth before she could stop it, and she squirmed in her seat. Now he'd think she had been asking after him. The fact that she had was neither here nor there.

He kept his eyes on the road, but Isla thought she detected a slight flush to his cheeks. 'Yeah, I am. Her name's Saralee. She's a nice girl, you'd like her.'

No, I wouldn't, Isla thought. Her name had instantly conjured up the apple pie she'd dug into the night. She managed to unclench her teeth. 'Yeah, I'd like to meet her sometime.'

That quizzical look again. 'I'm sure you will, Bibury's not exactly a metropolis.'

The silence stretched out, and Isla wished he'd turn the volume up on the stereo or something but he didn't. 'What about you? Were you, or are you still with someone over in London?'

It was a fair enough question, tit for tat. Isla took a moment before she replied, 'I was, it was serious, but then it all went rather pear-shaped.'

'Is that why you came back?'

'It's not the whole reason, but it was a contributing factor. I suppose I'd just got to a point where I wondered what I was doing it all for.'

'Your job you mean?'

'My job, my relationship, none of it seemed that important anymore.' Isla looked out the window seeing but not seeing as she found herself back with Rita in that light and airy room with the picture of the peace lily and the giant sequoias.

Break-Free Haven Lodge

Isla rolled off the beanbag onto all fours, feeling her knees protest at the hard floorboards beneath them. She blinked the tears, sitting, waiting to fall away and imagined what Toad would say if he could see her now with her leisure-pants-clad bum sticking up in the air. It pleased her to know that she didn't care what he thought anymore. The relationship had been over for a long time, she'd realized since coming here, and she'd grieved for it while she was still in it. She'd come to Break-Free and had broken free from him. She was also rapidly concluding that there was a lot to be said for leading one's life in leisure pants and being out of the corporate rat race. Optimum stress-free comfort at all times, for one thing. She got to her feet and stretched. 'I've just got to get a drink of water, Rita. Would you like one?'

'No, I'm fine thanks.' She gave a wave of her hand. They both knew Isla was stalling.

Isla poured herself a drink from the cooler and sipped it slowly. She'd known she would get to this part in her story eventually. The part where she had to be honest with herself. That, after all, was why she was here, sitting on a beanbag in California. She drained the contents of the plastic cup, dropping it in the wastepaper basket before flopping back down into her familiar seat.

'Better?'

'Yes thanks, I'm not used to talking this much.'

Rita smiled gently. 'I think you've got a bit more to do yet. Why don't you tell me why you were frightened at the intensity of those feelings you had for Ben?'

Isla squirmed on the beanbag. She'd never told anybody about all the complicated emotions she'd had swirling around inside her back then. Not even Ben, it would've felt far too disloyal.

'It's okay, take your time honey.'

Rita, Isla fancied, looked the way an older and much wiser sister might. She'd be the sort of big sister who wouldn't steal her stuff or make fun of her, she could trust her, she decided. So she began to talk.

'I used to look in the mirror sometimes, and I'd see my gran looking back at me. I take after her with my olive colouring. People say we're peas in a pod. Mum's the complete opposite. She got her looks from Granddad's side of the family. They're both amazing women, my mum and my gran. I can see that now but as a teenager their lives, well, they just seemed so small and confined.' Isla's voice trembled and Rita passed her the box of tissues she kept to hand on the chunky wooden coffee table.

She accepted the box and blew her nose before continuing, 'Gran grew up in Bibury. She got married young, had her family and joined lots of committees and well, that's it. Then, my mum grew up and got married, had two kids and when we were old enough, she started work at the local pharmacy. She's still there, and Gran's still on loads of committees. When I'd look in the mirror back then, I could see my life playing out the same way as theirs if Ben and I stayed together. I didn't want what I saw then as a little life like theirs. I wanted a big, exciting, high-flying life.'

Isla exhaled, she'd admitted how she felt out loud, but this wasn't how she'd expected to feel having finally owned up to a fear of following in her grandmother's and mother's footsteps. She'd thought she would feel unburdened, cleansed maybe or at the very least validated over the way she'd felt. Apart from feeling knackered though, she felt no different whatsoever. No, that wasn't quite true. Talking about how naïve she'd been and knowing how her own so-called big life had worked out for her, she realized she felt sadder than she had before.

'So, your relationship with Ben made you feel trapped?'

'Pardon?' She blinked to try and dispel the trance-like feeling that had settled over her.

'I asked you if your relationship with Ben made you feel trapped.'

'Oh, sorry.' She rubbed her temples. 'My brain feels all weird and mushy.'

'That's quite normal.' Rita smiled serenely, clasping her hands in her lap and Isla couldn't help but think that she would be just as at home in a new age Yurt keeping an eye out for UFOs somewhere in Arizona.

'Yes, and no. It was a case of push me, pull me. I knew that while he was in my life, I would have felt the pull to go back to Bibury, no matter how big the push to get away was. Ben's life was already mapped out for him. He wanted to work for his dad in their family business and eventually take it over. Everything he wanted was already there in Bibury, and it was everything I didn't want.'

Rita's expression did not flicker, and Isla wondered if learning how to control your facial muscles was part of the training you had to undertake to become a counsellor. 'Did you ever talk to him about how you felt?'

'No.' Isla looked down at her hands and began to pick at a hangnail by her thumb. 'Mostly because it felt so bloody selfish to feel like that. Him, all our friends, they were all happy with their lot it was just me that had this incredible need for more.' The skin around her thumbnail was an angry red now, and it had begun to throb, but at least she could feel it hurting.

Isla frowned as she stared out at the sequoia trees outside standing tall and proud. Common sense told her now that leaving Bibury was all part of growing up and finding her way in the world. It was a rite of passage she'd had to undertake, and for the most part, it had been fantastic. She'd worked in a business she loved; she'd travelled and gotten to see and do fabulous things. She'd met some fantastic people along the way too. Of course, she'd met some not so fantastic people along the way as well. The shine too, had been slowly rubbed off her love of design with the pressures of deadlines always looming.

'So, you moved to Christchurch.' Rita interrupted her train of thought.

'Yes, Art was always my thing. I enrolled in Polytechnic and graduated with a Diploma in Interior Design after which I began working in the city. I threw myself into my job, and I was good at it too, really good at it because I loved what I did. To take a blank space and transform it into someone's dream home was such a buzz. I even won an award for one of my home design ideas.' Her visits home during this time had gone from fortnightly to monthly, and even that felt too frequent. It was hard going back. No one got the new Isla; she'd moved on from her friends who'd left high school but hadn't left Bibury. Worst of all she couldn't get to her gran's house without passing by the Robsons' garage either, where

Ben had done what he'd always planned on doing and joined the family business. Try as she might to not look, her eyes would always slip towards the forecourt in the hope of a glimpse of him.

She'd hear things from time to time too. Things like what he had got up to at the Pit on a Saturday night with the girl who was there with a group of city friends on a hen's night and her stomach would twist. It was like a form of torture. Okay, yes, it was her that broke it off, but it didn't make it any easier to hear that in her absence he hadn't entered the priesthood. What she needed was to get far, far away and then opportunity had knocked.

'I was doing well on the local and international design scene, and I came to the attention of the company I work for now. They offered me a great package to relocate, and so I got on a plane and flew to London.'

Oh yes, she'd embraced living in one of the world's foremost cities wholeheartedly and the years had simply rolled over one after the other until suddenly they totalled ten. It was the anonymity of the crowds she loved. The seamless blending into the to-ing and fro-ing of people leading their lives without worrying about what it was she was up to in hers. She didn't even mind the daily tube ride that her colleagues always griped and moaned about. Okay, so she hadn't been all that enamoured by the heavy breather she'd been wedged in front of that time. Or the leerer who'd just about nosedived into her top when the train had stopped suddenly. It was street theatre or rather tube theatre. It was all part of being somewhere bigger than, well, Bibury. She'd felt, as she rode that tube each morning, as if her real life, the one she was meant to be leading, had finally started.

'And you know the rest of the story.'

Rita nodded. 'So we've come full circle Isla.'

'Yes, I suppose we have.'

'So I'm going to ask you again, where do you see yourself going from here?'

Isla thought about how she'd been living this last year. She'd lost her zest so to speak and sitting here now, she felt empty and rather alone. It had been a long time since she felt connected and part of the lives of the people around her. Faces floated before her, familiar faces, lovely faces that she missed desperately and suddenly she knew with absolute clarity where she needed to go. 'I'm going home Rita; it's time for me to go back to Bibury.'

Isla rubbed at the steamy patch her breath had left behind on the passenger window and then turned her attention to the left-hand side where she saw the Tasman Sea thrashing ashore the pebbled beach. They were heading into Greymouth, passing by the well-tended gardens of the old weatherboard houses. 'That's new,' she said placing her mind firmly back in the here and now as she pointed to the Aquatic Centre with a blue hydro-slide snaking out of the side to her right.

Ben grinned over at her. 'Yeah, it'd be a few degrees warmer than Bibury Area's old pool. Do you remember that time we scaled the school fence and went for a midnight dip?'

Isla laughed. 'And Mr Hannigan from across the road marched over in his pajamas waving his flashlight around, telling us he'd ring both our parents if we didn't get out and go home pronto!'

'It was down to your squealing we got busted.'

'It was freezing!'

They smiled at the shared memory and then she recalled what had come next when Ben had warmed her up with his kisses as they sat in his old Ford. She turned her attention to the passing panorama of houses lest he read where her mind had wandered.

A few beats later, before the silence between them could get uncomfortable, Ben flicked the indicator and said, 'There's a good yard near the Monteith's Brewery, I thought we could check that out first.' He swung the truck off the state highway.

'Sounds like a plan. I'm in your hands.' Oh dear, why had she said that, she thought as she received another of his quizzical glances.

Chapter 11

An hour later, Isla was the proud owner of an '06 red Mini Cooper; it cost her far more than she'd planned on spending, but she was smitten. 'I've always wanted a Mini, especially a red one,' she declared spying it in the carpark and making a beeline for it. She hadn't known this was her dream car until she spotted Delilah as she'd already named her and a magnetic yearning dragged her in for a closer look.

Ben was frowning, he'd been about to steer her in the direction of a much more practical, in his opinion, and price friendly Toyota Auris. Once Isla had gotten behind the wheel of the Mini though, he'd known by the look on her face that she wasn't going to budge. He'd managed to get the price down for her though, and made sure the smooth young sales guy had known that he knew a bit about cars. She'd always been a girl who knew her mind, he'd thought, exasperatedly watching as she headed off to the office to put the finance into place.

Swinging her keys, she came out of the office ten minutes later all smiles. Ben was leaning up against the bonnet of his wagon. 'Have you got time for a bite of lunch before we head back? My treat,' she called out.

'I never pass up a free lunch.'

They wound up in a funky café that had, to Isla's delight, whitebait patties on the menu despite the season not being until mid-year. August was when the long serving whitebaiters would stake out their territory in the local rivers to catch the tiny silvery, baby fish as they made their dash up the river. She'd steered well clear of Tainui Street, where the pizza restaurant she and Ben had gone to on their first date was. It was probably long gone by now anyway, but she wasn't running the risk of driving down that particular memory lane.

'Yum, whitebait patties in buttered white bread with a squeeze of lemon is the best,' she mumbled with her mouth full. 'Is your steak okay?'

'Yeah, it's great thanks, medium-rare just how I like it. You know I never really got the whitebait thing. I mean they look like tadpoles.'

'Thanks for that, I'd forgotten you didn't like them.'

He grinned. 'I liked going whitebaiting with Grandad when I was a kid though; it was my job to pick out the ones that were too big to make good eating. He used to tell me stories and he told me once his father came out from Scotland in search of the gold he'd heard could be found here on a ticket he won at the horse races. Imagine the course of your life hanging on a horse race? If the horse he put money on hadn't won that race then the generations that followed, including me, wouldn't have existed. Weird thought aye?'

Isla nodded. 'I remember that horse race story. I grew up

hearing from Gran about how hard a life it was when she was young with everything being done by hand. Ugh, and they had an outside dunny. It wasn't for the faint-hearted. But Ben, I said it years ago and I'm saying it now, you can't call yourself a Coaster if you don't like whitebait. It's programmed into our DNA to love the stuff.'

'Not mine, and I can if you don't tell anyone.'

She grinned. 'What's in it for me?'

'I won't tell anyone, meaning your dad, what you paid for Delilah out there.' He indicated to where she'd pulled up outside the café. He'd parked his truck a few cars down from hers. 'That's a terrible park by the way, any further out and you'd be stopping traffic.'

'What can I say? It's been a while, and I was never good at the parallel park. Can I steal a chip?'

He laughed. 'Go for it, and you didn't have to buy me lunch. I didn't do anything, not really.'

'Yes you did, you drove me over here, and you made sure the sales guy didn't take me for a ride once I'd made my mind up.'

'Yeah, he saw a pretty girl coming alright, and I'd forgotten how stubborn you can be.'

Isla blushed. He still thought she was pretty. He used to gaze down at her with those bottomless eyes of his and tell her she was beautiful. *Stop it Isla, you're far too young for all this nostalgia.* 'I get the stubborn streak from Gran, or so Mum says.'

Ben nodded. 'I'd agree with that, having seen both you and Bridget demonstrate that particular personality trait more than once over the years. Do you remember when the council wanted to paint the no-parking yellow lines out in front of her house? She got me and your dad to plonk her armchair in the middle of the road, and she sat in it refusing to move until the roadworks truck moved on.'

Isla laughed. 'I'd forgotten about that! It didn't take the council long to concede, and she made the six o'clock news. Good for her I say.'

He pointed his fork in her direction. 'Exactly, you two operate on the same wavelength. If you can't get your way, you dig your heels in.'

Isla made to protest, but Ben got in first with a raised eyebrow. 'May I remind you of the placards and the protest you organized outside Bibury Area's intermediate block about not being allowed to use their play area at lunchtime!'

'Oh yeah.' Isla's smile was sheepish as the headline in the *Bibury Times* sprang to mind – *Bibury Area School Pupil Argues Ageism Rife in School System*. 'But I wouldn't have done it if I hadn't believed whole-heartedly that I was right. The junior playground was way too tame.'

'You were ten years old; I rest my case.' His phone began to ring, and he put down his knife and fork. 'Bugger, it's Vanessa, I'd better take it.' He got up from the table and headed outside. When he came back in Isla could tell by his peeved expression that it was time to go.

'There's an emergency repair job that's just come in for a couple of tourists. Bloody kea brds pecked the rubber off the windscreen wipers of their campervan while they had a coffee in the tearoom.'

The native parrot-like kea birds were prone to being naughty, and Isla recalled the time they'd left friendly deposits all over her father's freshly polished whatever it was he was driving back then. He'd gone mad, shooing them away and threatening them with far worse. The birds hadn't cared though; they were like naughty toddlers.

'I'm going to have to make tracks,' Ben interrupted the flashback. 'I'm sorry to cut lunch short; it's been great catching up with you.' He shifted from foot to foot in front of her.

Isla stuffed down her last mouthful, pleased that Ben had managed to finish the best part of his lunch. She got to her feet too. 'Look, it's fine, it's work. I get it. Thanks for coming with me. I'll follow you back, though, if that's okay? Just in case Delilah doesn't behave on her first outing.' Isla didn't want to admit to him she was nervous at the thought of the drive back to Bibury. It had been a long time since she'd been behind a wheel and the little test run she'd done tootling around the streets of Greymouth was not the same as one hundred kilometres on the open road.

Ben headed for the door, and Isla followed. 'She's pretty roadworthy, but it's still a good idea to tail me while you get used to driving her.' He held the café's door open for her, and she slipped past him. A shiver of delight shot through her, and she wasn't sure if it was due to the sight of her shiny new red car, or the fact that Ben had rested his hand on the small of her back to steer her towards it.

'Come on Gran, I'll take you for a spin.' Isla took her hand off the horn and called out the window as Bridget appeared on the front doorstep, frowning in consternation as she wondered what all the noise was about.

'Isla Brookes, what have you bought?' she called out.

'A Mini Cooper, and she's called Delilah. Isn't she gorgeous?'

Bridget shook her head, closing the front door before she made her way down the steps. Isla noticed her movements were careful; it was another sign that her seemingly invincible Gran, was slowing down. She got into the passenger seat, and Isla helped her buckle in before reversing down the drive and cruising down High Street. Bridget ran her hands over the dashboard, and Isla could tell she was a little bit smitten too. She pulled up outside Mitchell's Pharmacy, jumped out and raced inside to fetch her mum.

Mary was unpacking a box of stock when her daughter ordered her to come and meet the newest addition to the family. There was only one customer in the shop; he was inspecting the pretty display of soaps. Looking for a present for his wife, Isla guessed.

'Will you be alright for a minute just looking, Mr Butler?' Mary said loudly. 'My daughter's just bought a new car, and she wants me to go outside and have a look at it.'

Mr Butler held a block up to his nose and sniffed. He glanced at Isla who was hopping from one foot to the other, before nodding. 'Off you go Mary dear, she looks like she'll have an accident if you don't get out there quick smart.'

'You could be right. I'll be back in a jiffy.' Mary followed her daughter outside and spying her mother sitting in the passenger seat of a red Mini Cooper, she waved. Bridget gave her a Queen's wave back and listened in amusement as Mary made all the right noises while running a hand over Delilah's sharp looking paint job.

'You'll break your dad's heart when he finds out you bought a Mini, lovely as Delilah is, you know Isla?' She shook her head. 'But good for you. I can't wait to go for a spin in her. We can pretend to be Thelma and Louise off on our grand adventure. I want to be Louise, please. Susan Sarandon is fabulous, and she's done her bit for Revlon too.'

Isla couldn't help but laugh. 'Of course, Mum, because if I get to be Thelma then I get to you know what with Brad Pitt.' She winked.

'Oh, I hadn't thought of that. We'll talk about it later. I'd better get back. Have fun you two and don't do anything I wouldn't do!' She headed back inside the pharmacy to help Mr Butler. Perhaps she'd be able to convince him that Mrs Butler would much prefer the latest in Revlon anti-aging innovation to a bar of lavender soap!

Isla didn't see Ben peering around the side of the camper he'd been called back to fix. He was watching her showing Delilah off with amusement. She did, however, spot Carl emerging from the Kea Tearooms, as she pulled away from the curb. She tooted, checking in the rear-view mirror to see if any cars were behind her. The road was empty, so she stopped in the middle of it and wound her window down.

'Who on earth's that?' Gran said peering past Isla to where Carl was striding towards them dressed once again in his trusty down home on the farm outfit.

'That's Carl, Annie from the Kea's friend. I had dinner with them last night.'

'You had a lot of wine with them last night you mean.' Bridget had heard Isla banging around before all had gone quiet and she'd crashed out in bed.

Carl peered in the window to say hello. 'I just had the most divine slice of gluten free tan-square. Annie made it specially; I'm intolerant.' He made a whistling noise between his teeth. 'Nice wheels, I'm liking the red, you're sitting pretty sister!'

'Carl, meet Delilah. I bought her today, and I'm just taking my gran, Bridget—' she gestured to the passenger seat, and Bridget gave another tight little wave of her hand, 'for a spin – would you like to join us and sample the delights on offer in Bibury?'

'Will there be wine?'

A tsking sound emitted from the passenger seat.

'We could stop at the Pit at some point to celebrate my new addition, yes.'

'Well, I don't mind if I do ladies, but Isla you might want to pull over to the side of the road. There's a logging truck heading your way, and it's a lot bigger than Delilah here.'

'You could hitch a ride on it; you'd be right at home in that outfit,' Gran muttered as Isla got out of the truck's way, choking back a giggle.

A few ticks later, Carl held his hand out to help Bridget from the car, and as she got to her feet, he admired her choice of top. 'I have to say that colour works an absolute treat on you, Bridget.' Overhearing, Isla leaned across the seat and called out, 'Carl's a fashion photographer, Gran – he knows his stuff.'

And, by the time Carl had found the lever that sent the passenger seat lurching forward, he had won Bridget over with his extensive knowledge of organic bamboo cotton and its miraculous long-wearing properties.

Chapter 12

'Come on you two,' Isla urged revving the engine.

Carl ducked down and clambered into Delilah, arranging himself on the backseat, his knees nearly up to his ears.

'Alright in the back there?' Isla glanced up into her rear-view mirror.

He gave her a thumbs-up. 'Houston, we are ready for lift off.'

'Gran, are you buckled in?'

'Affirmative,' she answered, giggling along with Carl.

Isla rolled her eyes. These two were going to be trouble together. Then they were off, cruising through the streets of Bibury. They drove down the High Street while Bridget chatted away. 'When I was a girl, all of the roads right through to Greymouth were unmade and a trip to the big town as we used to call it was almost unbearable. The car was forever stalling from overheating, and I'd always feel sick.'

'Yes, I can be prone to carsickness, it's not fun.'

Isla and Bridget looked at each other in alarm.

'Are you sure you'll be alright in the back?'

'Oh yes, it's only on windy journeys. I tell you ladies, I think

I lost half my body weight on some of those roads Annie and I experienced in the Greek Islands.' He filled Bridget in on his and Annie's trip.

'Well, I don't know how Bibury's historical points of interest will stack up against those of ancient Greece, but we'll do our best. How about the Historic Cemetery? The museum's only open on a Saturday and Sunday. Oh, that's the house where I grew up.' Bridget pointed out the window to a house that looked rather unloved. 'It's long since been sold on and is rented out now but when I was a girl, it was immaculate. Keeping up appearances meant a lot to my parents, it's the way it was back then.'

There was something in her gran's tone that made Isla glance over at her curiously, but her expression gave nothing away.

'The school where Kris teaches is just up here isn't it?' Carl asked leaning forward in his seat.

'Yep, that's my old stomping ground, Bibury Area. Who votes for a drive up to the Historic Cemetery then?' Isla said.

'Sounds intriguing.'

'It is, and I tell you what Carl, if those headstones could talk there'd be some stories told,' Bridget added.

Isla began heading up the winding road to the old cemetery, grateful Delilah was automatic, and she didn't have to faff around with the gears. The cemetery nestled on a flat green field at the top of the hill that was at odds with the rest of the rugged landscape around it.

'My parents, grandparents and great-grandparents are buried up here,' Bridget said.

Isla smiled as Bridget launched into the familiar story. It had been a while since she'd last heard the tale be told, but she'd always loved it.

'How my great-grandparents met is quite a story you know, Carl.'

'I'm all ears Bridget, my love.'

It was all the invitation Bridget needed. 'Well, they left West Cork in Ireland and sailed on the Adamant, a ship that docked in Nelson in eighteen seventy-four. It would have been a horrendous trip.' She shook her head at the thought of it. 'Their fellow passengers by all accounts were a mixed bag. There were families and couples seeking a brighter future along with ruffians after making their fortune with their gold pans. It's how my great-grandparents were paired that always intrigued me, it was through a professional Matchmaker.'

Carl's well-shaped brows shot up. 'A matchmaker? Do you mean like an olden day version of Tinder?'

'What's Tinder?' Bridget frowned.

'It's a dating app,' he said as if that explained everything.

She'd heard the word app before. Margaret thought she was a bit of a technology whiz, and she bandied it about a lot. But Bridget was sure *she* didn't actually know what one was either.

'I've never used it personally of course. I never needed to, having been with David forever, but here, have a look.' Carl produced his phone and got the site up before passing his phone over.

'I haven't got my glasses with me,' Bridget said, squinting and holding the phone a fair distance from her face. 'Nine hundred matches,' she read out slowly. 'Well, I never! Isla why don't you sign up for this.'

Isla shot Carl a look in the rear-view mirror.

'Sorry,' he mouthed.

Bridget passed the phone back. 'The old Matchmakers of West Cork would be out of work with the likes of that Tender.'

'Tinder,' Isla said.

'That's what I said. Every locality in the county had a Matchmaker back in the day you know?'

'I've never heard of a professional matchmaker before, it's fascinating.'

'Oh yes, it is indeed, and it was an important job back in the day. The Matchmaker responsible for my great-grandparents pairing off came out on the boat to New Zealand with them. The tradition didn't survive here though. It died with him.'

Isla was all ears too, even though she could almost recite the story by rote.

'The farmers of Cork led isolated existences and if a daughter was getting to the wrong end of being a marriageable age, then it was the Matchmaker who would bring news of this to another farmer whose son was in the same boat. He, and it was always a he, the role handed down from father to son, would suggest the match but the arrangement ultimately was finalized between the parents.'

'So it was an arranged marriage?' Carl asked.

'They called them "must" marriages, so Great-Granny Kate told me, but I suppose it was. I like to think it was a bit more romantic than that, but either way, my grandparents made a good match. They were happy despite the hard times they had at the beginning of their married life. You know we had it tough when I was growing up, nothing came easy. We had to work hard to put food on the table, and learning to grow your own vegetables was part of the school curriculum. I often wonder how Great-Granny Kate coped in those first few years here.'

'They were made of hardy stuff, those settlers,' Carl said clutching onto the headrest in front of him as Isla hit a pothole.

'Ooh, sorry about that, didn't see it. Are you alright Gran?'

'I'm fine. I used to bicycle around these roads as a girl, and there were far more potholes then so don't fuss Isla.'

Isla exchanged an amused glance with Carl in the rear-view mirror as Bridget carried on with her story.

'They were real pioneers Carl, the youth of today would never cope – not with their incessant need to know what everybody else is up to every single minute of the day.'

Chastened, Carl slipped his smartphone back in his pocket.

'Great-Granny Kate camped in a tent near the Greymouth Beach after they'd sailed down from Nelson on a boat they chartered with their four children, while my Grandfather went on ahead to Bibury. He found work at the Bibury Mine. That closed down a long time ago, well before Barker's Ridge did, but it saw him through his working life. My great-grandmother and the children, including my grandmother who was the baby, followed him here six weeks later. It was the Maori who brought them down the river by canoe when he'd finished building their first home. It wasn't much more than a mud hut.' She shook her head at the thought of it.

Carl was listening to the tale raptly. 'Wow, your roots really are buried here then, Bridget.'

'They are. I can't imagine living anywhere else.' Her eyes misted as she recalled the past. 'The thing I remember most about my great-grandmother though, Carl, and Isla has heard this story many a time, was that she had the most beautiful silverware. It survived the journey from Ireland tucked away in the pockets of silk inside its wooden case. She'd been given the set by her mother when she wed my great-grandfather, and apparently Kate had come from quite a well to do family but in the eyes of her family, she'd married down.'

They had arrived, and Isla pulled over onto the grass verge at the side of the road at the sight of the familiar gates. She stilled the engine and listened while Bridget finished telling her tale.

'Great-Granny Kate always insisted the table be laid out properly for dinner, no matter what the family's living conditions were. I suppose it gave her a sense of order, in times that were anything but. I was only a tiny tot, but I can remember helping her polish the silver from time to time. She had such a lovely sing-song accent, and I can still hear her as she'd say to me, "Home is where the hearth is, Bridget. Be it ever so humble there's no place like home."'

'That's lovely Bridget, did you inherit the family silver.'

Her lips pursed. 'No, it went to my elder sister Jean.'

None of them saw the way the tall tree with the silvery leaves began to sway, its branches bent towards the sudden gust of wind as it presided over the gate to the little cemetery.

The trio piled out of Delilah, and Carl linked arms with

his new BFF while Isla fiddled with the link chain keeping the main gate shut. 'It's like Fort Knox this place, you'd never know it's a public cemetery,' she grunted.

Carl clutched Bridget's arm a little tighter as he looked beyond the gate. There were fields surrounding the little row of headstones he could see to the left of the path. 'There aren't any animals around here are there? I mean a bull's not likely to come stampeding down that hillside is it?' He pointed up to where the tree-lined path disappeared over a rolling dip in the otherwise flat field.

Isla paused in her fiddling. 'No, not likely but a ram on heat could.'

'What!'

'I'm joking! We're not likely to see anything other than a couple of horses grazing. Yes that's it.' The gate squeaked its protest as Isla pushed it open and she waited until Bridget and Carl were through before shutting it behind them once more. 'Watch your step on these stones Gran.' The path's shingle was loose underfoot. A sign that read 'Church of England' hung from the smaller gate to their left, and behind the low wire and post fencing was a grassy area laid out in four neat rows of graves. Bridget pointed up to where you could no longer see the path. 'Up the top, that's where the Presbyterian and Methodist cemeteries are.'

'What's the difference?' Carl asked, following Isla who had unlatched this second, smaller gate with no great difficulty.

She shrugged. 'I don't know. Gran?'

'I gave up trying to figure it all out a long time ago,' Bridget said sighing. 'Religion's got a lot to answer for in my book.'

Carl looked at her curiously.

'My parents were Presbyterian, quite devout too. I was a bit of a black sheep in that respect.' Her lips formed a thin line that told them she would say no more on the subject.

The grass surrounding the graves was long and tickled their ankles. A few of the heavier headstones were beginning to lean precariously, a large stone cross in particular looked like one good storm would topple it. Carl leaned forward to peer at the inscription on a headstone, the urn having fallen from the top of it, now lying by the side of the solid slab of stone, 'Look! This man died in 1893 at the age of eighty-five. That's not a bad innings for back then. He must've eaten his porridge for breakfast.'

The grave was surrounded by a spiked iron fence that was orange with rust and covered in loose pebbles through which clumps of grass were beginning to grow. The headstone, like the others in the small cemetery, had lichen threatening to overwhelm it. Isla was aware of there being no sound at all except for their voices and the chirruping of birds. Surprisingly, it wasn't an eerie place to be, she thought. It did have a feeling of calm and the inscription on the headstone her eyes had alighted on seemed fitting. *Peace Perfect Peace*.

'Are you alright to walk up there, Gran?' She pointed to the top of the hill.

'Don't fuss, Isla,' Bridget said for the second time that day. 'It's hardly Everest.'

Chapter 13

They wandered up the path past a wooden caretaker's hut and as Isla had predicted they saw a few horses grazing in the fields beyond the gaps in the trees. At the top, the view afforded them a glimpse of the rocky tips of the Southern Alps, their sharp angles peeking through the gaps in the surrounding bush range. They had a mooch around the Methodist Cemetery first, with Carl exclaiming over the old-fashioned names. 'Look, Eliza and Abraham! Ooh, doesn't it make you think of a fierce looking man with a tophat and tails, thumping his bible and a woman in a plain dress with a white bonnet, baking bread or something?'

'Hang on, wasn't that a scene in that old Harrison Ford movie about the Amish?' Isla laughed.

'You might be right. I do love a good Harrison flick. Now he's a man who's aging well even if it is dubious as to whether he should still be allowed to fly that plane of his.'

Bridget had gone on ahead to the Presbyterian plots, Carl and Isla decided to hang back to give her a few minutes. She was standing in front of her parents' double grave reading the inscription they'd chosen; *in my father's house are many mansions*. She was lost in her memories.

Bridget's parents had lived through the Great War and had both lost several brothers to it. They'd also survived the 1918 flu epidemic and the Depression of the late twenties and early thirties. She'd heard her father talk about how he and his brother had been given the grim task of removing the bodies from homes at the end of each day when the flu epidemic was at its peak. Miraculously neither brother had succumbed to the dreaded virus.

Yes, like their parents before them, her mother and father had known what it was to suffer loss and go hungry. That was why she'd forgiven them for the hard line they took with her from time to time as a child. That steely determination or stubbornness she'd been accused of more times than she cared to remember had been inherited. It had caused her to butt heads with her parents, time and time again throughout her childhood.

Bridget herself had fleetingly, vague recollections of the shortages the Second World War brought with it. She did, however have a vivid memory of sitting on the floor by her mother's knee hearing the voice of the BBC radio announcer crackling over the car battery powered radio in the evening. 'This is London calling.' In the mornings it was the now iconic Aunt Daisy who graced the airwaves, encouraging women with her household tips and to cook their way through the war. It was her mum who taught her how to cook though, not Aunt Daisy. It was a necessary skill back then in the days before anything frozen was available. It was a skill she lamented not being able to pass down to Mary despite her best efforts; she'd had more success with Isla.

It was washing day that Bridget had found the biggest headache of all, especially when the rain didn't let up, as it often didn't for days on end in their part of the world. Their house had a large, back porch where the washing could be hung until it was almost dry. Then it would be brought in and aired out in the kitchen, hung from a contraption dangling from the ceiling. To this day she couldn't stand the smell of damp washing in a house, and her one winter luxury was using the clothes dryer instead of stringing her whatnots about the house. She shuddered thinking that while life was harder, it was also simpler in some respects. She wished though that she'd found it easier to forget the hard line her parents had taken with Charlie. She could still hear her mother's voice in her head. 'Nothing is perfect Bridget, so it's a waste of time crying to the moon.'

With her mother's voice echoing in her ears she moved slowly, almost reluctantly down the row of graves, coming to a stop in front of a simple headstone. There were no flowers adorning it because there was no one left to bring any. The family, Bridget knew, had moved away, unable to stay in Bibury after the tragedy. Most, if not all of them, would be long gone now. She shivered despite the sunshine. 'I would've brought you some flowers Clara, but I didn't know I was coming to see you today.'

'Alright, Gran?' Isla ventured resting her hand on her arm, perturbed by the strange look on her face.

Bridget blinked. She hadn't heard Carl and Isla approaching.

'I was just remembering the way things used to be that's all. This is where my friend, Clara, was laid to rest.'

Isla looked at the inscription; she had died in 1957 at the age of seventeen. It was a year shy of the age she'd been when she'd moved to Christchurch to begin her design course. 'Gosh she was young, Gran.' She wondered why she'd never mentioned her before. It was odd given that they'd visited the cemetery every year when she and Ryan were small, to put flowers on their great-grandparents' graves.

Carl reiterated the sentiment.

'Too young to die, far too young,' Bridget murmured making her way back to where her parents lay before Isla could ask her anymore. She wasn't sure whether she heard her say, 'she's been on my mind a lot lately,' or not.

Carl continued to walk around the small Presbyterian cemetery, but Isla trailed behind her gran. Her eyes settled on the plastic pot sitting on top of the familiar double grave where Bridget had been standing a few minutes earlier. The cloth roses it housed were faded, and she made a promise to bring her great-grandparents some fresh flowers before following her gran back down the hill.

'Have we got time to pop by Barker's Creek Hall, Isla?' Bridget asked once they were all back in the car.

'I thought you were there this morning for a meeting Gran?'

'I was, but I want to show you what I was talking about when I said it's been let go. You wouldn't have had time to have a good look at the exterior when you went along to your dance thing-a-me-jig.'

'No Lights, No Lycra,' Isla offered up by way of explanation for Carl.

He shrugged. 'I'm in no rush ladies, just so long as there's a glass of something nice on offer afterward.'

Isla started the car and drove back down the hill towards the hall.

A rusty sign at the entrance with a missing letter 'H' from the word 'Hall' told them they were there and Isla pulled into the carpark. One lonely cabbage tree presided over the overgrown front garden area, and even from here in the light of day, she could see that the building's paintwork was beginning to flake and peel.

'Oh, I had some good times at the dances here back in the day,' Bridget said, as much to herself as to Isla and Carl. She closed her eyes and could see the carpark as it had been the night of the Valentine's Day dance when she first met Charlie. All the lads milling around alongside vehicles that were mostly borrowed from their fathers. Cigarettes dangling from their mouths in a practised, cool fashion, cat-calling as they smoothed their quiffs and eyed the girls in their full skirts heading towards the hall.

'Gran met my granddad at a dance here. He was from down Haast way but came to Bibury to work in the Barker's Creek Mine,' she explained to Carl.

Isla didn't notice her gran's expression cloud as she opened her eyes. 'Clara and I met him here at the Valentine's Day Dance in 1957. It was Clara, who went out with him first. She was a lovely girl, such fun,' she said giving a small smile. 'Everybody loved Clara. You couldn't not.'

'Was she sick, is that why she died?' Isla hadn't known her grandfather had been out with someone else that he'd met here too. It made her feel odd, and she felt a prickling on the back of her neck. It instinctively told her she was about to hear was an important story from her gran's life.

'No, an illness might have been easier to bear. Clara fell down an abandoned mine shaft in the hills up there.' She waved towards the hillside with its felled logs and scrubby bush. 'She hit her head and that was that. It was dreadful, for all of us, for the whole town. She was only seventeen.' Bridget shook her head. 'Death's such a hard lesson to learn when you're young and think you'll live forever.'

'Oh, Gran! I'm sorry, that would've been tough.'

Bridget nodded. 'It was, but it all happened a long time ago now.' At times though it still felt like yesterday. Memories were funny like that.

'Yes, that's awful.' Carl recalled the impact his dear friend Roz's death had had on him. 'But how did it happen? I mean to fall down an old mine shaft, surely it would have been boarded up?' He did that funny thing with his face that Isla had come to recognize as a frown.

'Oh, it wasn't like it is nowadays with Oscars breathing down everyone's neck.'

Carl looked puzzled and then the penny dropped. 'Oh, you mean Occupational Safety and Health, OSH.'

'Yes, that's what I said.'

He decided not to argue the point.

'The area was an accident waiting to happen, and then it did. The men searched through the night for her and found her at first light. The womenfolk were all holding a candlelight vigil in the town hall waiting for news.' Her sigh was heavy. 'And when it came, it was the worst possible outcome.'

'I can imagine how it must've affected the town,' Carl said.

'It did, her death touched everyone. Bibury's had more than its share of tragedies. Mining towns are like that.'

Isla rubbed her arms which were covered in goosebumps.

'She'd gone to meet Tom up there.' Bridget gestured up towards Barker's Ridge, where the defunct mine was hidden by an overgrown tangle of greenery. A lone rain cloud hovered low over the ridge, spectre-like. 'He was pulling a double shift and Clara's father, Mr Brodie, dropped her off at the bottom of the hill. He was on his way to a meeting in Greymouth, and it was out of his way as it was. I suppose Clara thought one of the other lads clocking off would give her a ride back to town later. Her poor father never got over the fact he hadn't driven her the whole way up to the mine, but he'd been running late, and Clara insisted she'd be fine walking. She was taking Tom a meal. He'd been working all the hours under the sun, and she was missing him. At some point she decided to take a short cut across the valley,' Bridget said shrugging. 'The shaft wasn't boarded up properly, and she fell through it.'

This backstory to her grandparents' romance made Isla feel peculiar. She shivered, a chill settling over her from the story her gran had just told. Bridget wasn't finished yet though.

'It was grief over Clara's death that brought Tom and me together eventually.' She didn't mention the grief she'd already been experiencing thanks to a broken heart. What she'd just told Isla and Carl was more than she'd ever told anyone and it was enough.

'How come you have never talked about any of this before, Gran?'

'It wasn't time.'

'And it is now?' Isla was puzzled.

Bridget nodded. 'It is. Clara told me once that the Valentine's Day Dance here was the best night of her life. It was such a short life, for someone who was so full of the joy of it all and there's nobody left here anymore who remembers her except me.'

Isla reached out and rested her hand briefly on her gran's arm.

'The thing is you see, I don't want my friend forgotten. I'd like to hold a memorial of some sort for her here at the hall, but it wouldn't be fair, and more to the point the council wouldn't allow it in its current state.'

'Oh, I think that's a lovely idea, Gran,' Isla breathed.

'Me too,' Carl echoed.

'I'm the secretary of the hall's committee,' Bridget told him. 'We had a meeting to brainstorm fundraising ideas this morning, but it wasn't very fruitful. The problem is everything's been done before and well, people just don't get behind community projects like they used to.'

'The interior was a real slice of kiwi history too,' Carl said as they strolled around the outside of the building. 'It'd be sad to lose that.'

It was easy to spot the rotting boards amidst the flaking

paintwork and as Isla poked at a timber sill, the wood crumbled to dust beneath her fingers.

A circuit completed, Carl clapped his hands. 'Come on. I think it must be wine o'clock. We'll put our thinking caps on for some fundraising ideas over a nice glass of mulled red. It's good for the brain, red wine, it's do with all the antioxidants.'

'Mulled red wine? Carl, it's summertime and have you been to the Pit yet?' Isla feared his illusion of a warm and welcoming West Coast pub with a roaring fire and the ghosts of weary gold miners past still holding up the bar, would be shattered when he stepped over its threshold.

'No, and I'm looking forward to checking it out. Come on girls we've earned a drink.'

Bridget quite like being called a girl, but she wasn't feeling like a girl. She was tired with all the things weighing heavily on her mind these days. Still, a drink with her granddaughter and their new friend would be a nice way to finish the day. She exchanged a glance with Isla, knowing they were both thinking the same thing. Carl was in for a surprise when he got to the Pit.

Chapter 14

Carl side-stepped the collection of muddy boots as he pushed the door of the pub open and held it for Isla and Bridget. Isla walked in first, and the small group of men propping up the bar, clad in black singlets and shorts, all sat to attention.

Her eyes moved on to the array of jugs lined up in front of them. It must be happy hour; she thought catching a waft of stale beer. It transported her back to her barely legal pub days. A quick glance around at the decor on her way up to the bar confirmed what she had suspected. Nothing had changed in over twelve years, apart from the publican. She didn't recognize him.

Bridget followed behind her, shooting one of the singlet men a sour look. It was a look that spoke volumes; stop leering at my granddaughter because you're old enough to be her father. Carl let the door close behind him and sauntered inside, eager for a taste of an authentic West Coast pub.

His step faltered as with a sweeping gaze he took in the scene. It was a drinker's hall, not a cosy wee pub. Down the middle of the room was a row of lean-to tables with stools and around its periphery were a smattering of tables with blue cushioned seats. He knew without looking that they would be stained. The cigarette burns decorating them would be a nostalgic reminder of the good old days for those who were slaves to nicotine. There were two pool tables on the far right of the lounge bar area with a door leading to an outside courtyard. One lonely smoker, stood out there chuffing away.

Up ahead and to the left of Carl was the bar itself. A television set adorned the wall at the far end of the room, and the channel was set to the horse racing, although mercifully the sound was off. A jukebox was pushed up against the wall near an empty stage area. His eyes swiveled to his immediate left where two men were playing darts near the door leading to the toilets. He hoped their aim was good or one could get more than what one bargained for on a visit to the little boys' room!

He reached the conclusion that a classy joint, it was not. Isla had tried to warn him, he supposed, seeing her beckon him over to the bar. Looking at the group of drinkers standing next to her, he was glad he'd worn his checked shirt and jeans because at least he'd look the part. In keeping with his Southern Man role, he attempted a swagger. It was how he imagined a cowboy who'd been riding hard all day and had earned a beer would move towards the bar. Bridget and Isla watched in bemusement.

'Do you think we should call in on Mary and ask her for something to help with that chafing of his?' Bridget asked, wondering why Isla giggled, but she was distracted by the publican clearing his throat.

'Afternoon all.' He nodded at Bridget. 'Mrs Collins, we don't see you in here often.'

He had a dimply red nose and cheeks that were road mapped with the spider veins of a serious drinker.

'Mick.' Bridget nodded back. The last time she'd been in the pub was for a birthday drink for Joe's fiftieth birthday bash, and that was more than a few years ago now. 'This is my granddaughter, Isla; she's not long back from the UK.'

'Alright, guv'nor?' He addressed Isla in a shocking faux Cockney accent for which he received a weak smile.

'Yes, good thanks.'

'And I'm Carl, originally from the UK but a Kiwi boy through and through these days. Now, lovely ladies, it's my treat, so what'll it be?'

To Isla's amazement, there was a bottle of perfectly acceptable Marlborough Sauvignon in the fridge. *Things were looking up at the Pit!* She ordered a glass of the wine and received a generous country pour and not the precisely expensive measure she'd been used to in the London bars. Bridget settled for a whiskey and coke. 'Single, mind,' she tutted at Mick. Carl, with a glance over at the men with their jugs, ordered a handle of Speights.

'Do you like that stuff or did you just order it because you thought you should?' Isla asked as they made their way across the room to a table near the pool table.

'The latter if I'm honest, I'm not much of an ale man. I much prefer a cheeky cocktail but ...' he shrugged. 'You know, when in Rome and all that.'

'I wouldn't compare Bibury to Rome,' Isla said, setting her

drink down on the table as Carl fussed around, pulling a chair out for Bridget and settling her in it. She smiled to herself. Gran would slap her away were she to fuss her like that, but she was lapping up the attention from Carl.

'Now then, Bridget, what are we going to do about this hall of yours?' he said, finally sitting down himself. 'How about a Pub Quiz Night? They always go down well. An eighties music theme, perhaps? It's my strong point, eighties music, lived and breathed it.' He looked at the two black t-shirt boys who were playing pool with their jeans halfway down their backsides. 'Perhaps not, ACDC trivia might be more the ticket in Bibury, yes?'

'A pub quiz has been done,' Bridget said. 'The PTA's got that one covered.'

'Well, what about ... oh I don't know, a karaoke night?' Isla suggested.

'The Bibury Line Dancers Association have already nabbed that to fundraise for their trip to the championships down in Gore.'

Dear God, she was serious, Isla realized, but there was worse to come.

'Margaret suggested we hold a barn dance, but the Bibury Scottish Dancers pipped us to the post with their successful Haggis and Hoedown evening. They were fundraising for new kilts.'

Carl was looking at her, his eyes wide. 'Never a dull minute in Bibury then.' He fished around in his pocket and produced a few coins. 'We need a spot of music, come on Bridget, what do you fancy?'

'I've only just sat down.' She took his hand though, letting him help her to her feet and followed him over to the jukebox. A few seconds later the sounds of the Everly Brothers' *Unchained Melody* came on.

'I thought about Elvis, but it's a bit too early for *Jailhouse Rock*,' Bridget said sitting back down, leaving Carl over by the box.

'Are you alright Gran? You seemed a bit lost in thought at the cemetery this afternoon.' Isla rested her hand atop her gran's soft crinkly one.

Bridget didn't answer straight away and Isla wondered if she'd even heard her, but then she sighed. 'Ah, don't worry about me. As you get older you tend to dwell on the past a bit more, and I was just thinking about how things used to be and how things could have been.'

It was a cryptic reply, Isla thought, sitting back in her chair.

'Are you hungry girls?' Carl interrupted, sitting back down. 'Because I just about helped myself to a chip from that basket over there.' He waved over to the two pool playing lads. A bowl of chips had been placed down on a nearby table, and they were snaffling them in between shots. 'Didn't think they'd appreciate it though.'

'Mm yeah, I could have a few chips.'

'I've got the crockpot on. There's a nice bowl of stew waiting for me at home, there's enough for you too Isla if you want it? Otherwise, I'll pop it in the freezer.'

'Thanks, Gran, but I've got room for both chippies and your yummy stew.'

'What does it say on that blackboard?' Carl asked peering at the bar. 'Steak pie, steak'n'cheese pie, mince'n'vegetable pie and, ah, chips in a basket. Don't mind if I do.' As he got up, he said, 'I might text Annie and see if she and Kris can be persuaded to join us for a tipple. It would be rude not to being a Friday night and all. It's nearly 5.30, that's officially the weekend!'

'He's got ants in his pants that one,' Bridget muttered.

They watched as he placed his order and Mick disappeared out the back to tackle the deep fryer.

'He's good fun, isn't he?' Isla ventured.

Bridget nodded. 'It's a crying shame, I have to say, that he bats for the other team because you could do a lot worse.'

'Gran, I'm not looking to meet anyone. After Tim, I just want to be on my own for a bit,' Isla stated emphatically as the door swung open and Ben walked in.

Bridget raised an eyebrow at the expression on her granddaughter's face as she saw the pretty blonde girl whose hand he was holding come in behind him.

Isla waved over but only because Ben had seen her as soon as he stepped inside the pub. Bridget didn't miss the scowl that flashed across his face as Carl re-joined them and leaned in close to Isla to say something.

Isla hoped he wouldn't come over and say hi, she didn't want to meet this Barbie doll of his no matter how nice she was. Thankfully, she saw out the corner of her eye that he'd gotten talking to one of the singlet men. Carl watched her watching Ben with amusement.

'Fancy him, do you?'

'No! I mean who? What're you on about?'

'Mechanic Man up at the bar, I recognize him from the garage. Looks spoken for, I'm sorry to say sweetheart.'

'Oh him.' Isla knew her attempts at feigning innocence weren't fooling anyone. 'I've known him for years – most of my life in fact. I was just curious as to who he's wound up dating that's all.'

'They were an item, these two, before Isla moved away. They made a good couple too, but she broke it off, more fool her.' Bridget pointed at her granddaughter as she put her ten cents' worth in.

'Gran, do you mind! It was over twelve years ago, Carl. Obviously, we've both moved on.'

'You haven't, I can tell by your face you still have a soft spot for him,' Bridget said.

'Unfinished business.' Carl nodded knowledgeably.

'You two are incorrigible. I can't win this conversation, can I? There's absolutely no point in my telling you that I'm not interested in Ben Robson and that I wish him a wonderful future with his lady friend.'

'No,' Bridget and Carl chimed as Mick plonked a bowl of chips down in front of them and grunted. 'Sauce?'

Annie and Kris arrived at the pub as Isla was licking the last of the salt from her fingers. The fries had been just the ticket to soak up the oversized glass of wine she'd partaken of. Not that she was complaining and she fully intended to have another. She didn't want to miss out on the happy hour discount. She noticed Gran yawn after Carl had done the introductions. He was filling Annie and Kris in on what they'd done that afternoon. 'Are you ready for the off Gran?' she asked.

Bridget had finished her drink and didn't want another. 'I wouldn't mind, Isla. I'd like to get home in time to watch the news.'

Isla knew her gran liked to keep abreast of what was happening in the world, though, sometimes when she caught up with current events she wondered why she'd bothered. It seemed there was hardly ever any cheerful news about the goings on in the world.

'I'll drop you home then. Are you guys going to stay on for a bit?' She directed to the others.

'The night's young,' Carl said raising his glass. 'And, the second pint tastes better.'

Annie and Kris were sharing a jug of beer and didn't look like they were in any rush. 'Well, I might drop Gran home and come back down then.'

'That's a good plan.' Carl got up and planted a kiss on Bridget's cheek. 'I'm going to rack my brains for ideas for your hall, darling.'

Bridget looked pleased as she nodded at Annie and Kris. 'Enjoy yourselves but don't overdo it. I know what you young ones are like.'

She linked her arm through Isla's and nodded at Mick on the way out.

'It's been a good day Gran,' Isla said, feeling happy. She'd bought a car and made some lovely new friends.

Bridget rested her hand on her granddaughter's forearm, her whiskey and coke making her feel misty-eyed. 'It has.'

Annie and Kris were nice people, she could tell. She was a good judge of character. As for Carl, he was an absolute delight. Isla was settling in at home again, and it warmed her heart to see it.

Chapter 15

The pub had begun to fill up in the short time Isla had been away and there was a fairly evenly mixed batch of both sexes compared to the earlier odds. It was busy but then it was Friday night, so she shouldn't be surprised. She found a space to squeeze into, that was a safe distance away from where Ben was still standing with his girlfriend. It made no difference, though, he'd seen her come back in. Out the corner of her eye, she saw him lean down and say something to his lady friend before they both headed over in her direction. Bugger, she thought, while smiling at Mick and ordering.

'Hey Isla,' he said clutching his handle of beer. 'This is Saralee Talbot.'

'Hi Ben. Saralee, it's nice to meet you.' *Not*, she thought affecting what she hoped was a genuine looking smile.

Saralee smiled back at her, and her cheek dimpled. She had a pretty, open face with an upturned nose. Yes, as much as it pained her, she knew Ben was probably right, and she was going to like her. Why couldn't she have been a hard-faced, mouth of the South type? That would have been much easier to stomach.

'Hi Isla, Ben was just telling me he goes way back with your brother.'

Isla wondered if that was all he had told her. 'Yes, they got up to all sorts when they were younger.'

'And, I hear you've just got back from the UK is that right?'

'Uh-huh. I've spent the last ten years living in London.'

'I spent a year in London in my early twenties, it was great fun. Are you settling back in okay? It must be a culture shock – I mean London to Bibury.'

Isla noticed Ben looking at her intently and she felt uncomfortable under his scrutiny. 'I am, actually. It was time to come home.'

'Ben told me he helped you find a car today.'

Isla felt her face heat up; she should have mentioned it earlier in the conversation because it wasn't as though there was anything to hide. 'Yes, he was a great help keeping the smarmy sales guy in check, although I'm not sure he's sold on my choice. I bought a red Mini Cooper, and I've called her Delilah. It's love.'

Saralee giggled. 'Good for you.'

'Are you staying on for the band?' Ben asked.

'I didn't know there was one.'

'Yeah, that's why there's a good turn-out down here tonight. They've played here before. They do covers mostly, but they're pretty good. We thought we'd stick around for a bit.'

Saralee nodded in agreement as Mick interrupted them by placing Isla's drink down in front of her.

'I'd like to, but I'll see what those guys are up to.' She pointed over to where Annie and Kris were laughing. Carl was in his element holding court and looking for all the world like he was doing semaphore as he flapped his hands around embellishing his tale.

'Well, if Annie, Kris and your friend over there aren't keen then you're welcome to join us,' Ben said. Isla got the impression from the way Saralee's smile faltered ever so slightly that she wasn't quite so enthralled with the possibility of a third wheel rolling in on her date.

'Thanks. You guys enjoy your night. It was nice to meet you Saralee.' She raised her wine glass at them both before making her way back over to the others.

'Hi!' Annie beamed as Isla sat back down. 'Carl's been telling us about your day. He's quite smitten with your gran you know. He wants to be her honorary grandson.'

'It's true. I do.'

'Well, I think the feeling's mutual.'

'He was saying that she's wanting to come up with a fund-raising idea to restore the old hall where we went dancing last night.'

'Yes. There's a lot of memories for her there.' Isla traced her fingertip around the rim of her glass. 'Did he tell you what happened to her friend Clara when they were teenagers?'

'No.'

Isla looked at Carl quizzically, and he shrugged. 'It wasn't my story to tell.' He took a sip of his beer, the froth on top leaving behind a foam moustache.

Isla pointed to his lip before relaying the sad tale.

Kris and Annie made sympathetic noises. 'How awful,' Annie said. 'I think it's lovely your gran wants to remember her friend in a place where she was happy. We'll have to put our heads together and see what ideas we can come up with.' She shivered. 'You know, it was the names of all the young servicemen listed on that plaque inside the hall that got to me, and now there's Clara' story linked to it too. That's a lot of sadness for a small town.'

'The ancient Greeks believed that the key to immortality for the dead lay in the living remembering the deceased,' Kris said.

You could tell he was a history teacher, Isla thought, noticing the way his eyes lit up when he mentioned the ancient Greeks. 'What's your family like Kris?' she asked curiously.

His smile was wide. 'We're a typical Greek family. My pateras does what he is told, and I have a bossy mama and three equally bossy sisters.'

'Did you meet them while you were over there, Annie?'

'No, we'll head back over to Greece when Kris' contract finishes here, and I'll meet them then.' She studied the contents of her glass. 'I don't know what they'll think of me.'

Kris draped his arm around her shoulder and pulled her close. 'They'll love you like I do, of course.'

Annie didn't look convinced, and Isla filed the exchange away to ask her about later.

'And you Carl? Your parents emigrated I take it.'

Carl's face lost its jocular veneer. 'Yes, when I was twelve, and I tell you Isla, it was not easy being a gay boy in New Zealand back in the late eighties. It was illegal until the mid-eighties for one thing which just seems mad in the world we live in today. Anyway, that's where Annie's big sis came in.

She rescued me, made me popular. It was like something from a Molly Ringwald film except neither of us had braces.' Isla was still a twinkle in her father's eye for the best part of the eighties, but she got the gist of what he was saying. 'Mum and Dad are in their late sixties now. They've mellowed, but it took them a long time to accept my lifestyle and David.' He ran his fingers through his hair and it swished back into place, as Isla watched on enviously. 'No siblings you see, so I think that made my sexuality all the harder for them to accept.'

Isla wanted to get up and hug him, but Annie reached over and patted his arm. 'Carl, stop being a stubborn fool and text David, you know you want to.'

'But he hasn't texted me.' His bottom lip protruded.

'That's because he's as stubborn as you are.'

'Should I?' He looked over at Annie hopefully.

'Yes!' All three of them chimed as Carl got his phone and tapped a message out. He put it down on the table when he'd finished, and they all sat staring at it, mentally willing a message to bounce back. It did within seconds, and Carl snatched up the phone, the corners of his mouth twitching.

'Well?' Annie asked.

'He's having a microwave ready meal in front of the telly and says he's sorry he behaved like a Neanderthal. I'm going to let him sweat it out a few more days though; I'm not telling him I'm coming home on Sunday.'

'That's the Carl we know and love. Hey, look, a band's setting up.' Annie pointed over to the stage area before gazing up at Kris and squeezing his arm. 'I'm in the mood for a bit of a boogie. I'd forgotten how much I love to dance until last night.'

'It's a good job there's four of us then,' Carl sniffed. 'Otherwise, I'd be left sitting here on my own like a right Neville No Mates. Isla, you'll do me the honour won't you?'

'But of course.'

'You better hope they don't do any Michael Jackson then because he'll break out his moonwalk and robot moves,' Annie muttered, and Carl poked his tongue out at her.

Isla grinned and waved over at Annie and Kris who were stamping their feet and clapping their hands on the crowded dance floor to Van Morrison's Gloria. Carl had danced with her until he'd had enough and gone off to find someone to play pool with. She'd just been accosted on the edge of the dance floor by a singlet man with hairy shoulders who was out for a good night. She'd made her escape by claiming she was dying of thirst. Her excuse didn't faze him in the slightest, and he sidled on up to a huddle of girls instead. With an abundance of tattoos and piercings on show, they looked more than able to handle themselves, and Isla watched on with amusement from a safe distance.

The evening was flying by, and she glanced up at the clock behind the bar. It was next to the Southern Man Poster. She smiled at the familiar picture of the hardy Southerner in his Drizabone oilskin coat and hat as she pushed her way through the crowd. It was already half past nine. She put the back of her hand to her cheek – it was hot. She knew it wasn't down to all the dancing, though she had a definite glow on. She'd have to watch her drinking, or she'd be feeling a tad sorry for herself again tomorrow morning. It was time to order a glass of water. But first the call of nature needed to be answered.

Isla dodged past the lads who had been playing pool when they'd first arrived at the pub. They'd moved on to darts and she resisted the urge to yank their pants up for them as she pushed the door to the restrooms open. She was getting old. There was a corridor with the ladies' room off to the left, the men's to the right, and a smoke stop door with a large red exit sign over top of it at the end. She double checked the sign on the ladies' room to be sure. It wouldn't be the first time she'd accidentally barged in on the wrong gender.

A few minutes later Isla shook the water from her hands before holding them under the hand-dryer. Apart from the tell-tale bleary eyes of someone who'd been indulging since early evening she didn't look too bad, she decided, glancing over at the mirror. Hands dry, she ran her fingers through her hair fluffing it out and satisfied that she would do, pushed the door open. Ben exited the men's at the same time, and they both hesitated. Isla was aware there was nobody else there in the corridor. A dulled beat could be heard coming through the door that led back into the pub.

Ben spoke first. 'You look like you're having fun out there. I told you the band's good, they always get everyone up on the floor.'

'Yeah, they are, but I haven't seen you and Saralee have a dance yet?' She raised a questioning brow.

He shrugged. 'I'm not much of a dancer you know that.'

It was a phrase he'd uttered many times during the year they'd been together.

'Will you dance with me because I'm wearing pink?' The words slipped from her lips, and her hand flew to her mouth. 'Sorry!' That had been their catchphrase; it was his cue to reply, 'I will because you look so pretty in pink.'

But he didn't. He stared at her hard for a moment before indicating towards the door with his head. 'Is that the new boyfriend then?'

'Carl?' Isla managed to laugh. She was relieved to move on, to pretend she hadn't just said what she'd said. 'No, he's already got a boyfriend, and even if he didn't, I could never go out with a man whose skin and hair is in better condition than my own.'

Ben raised a smile and ran his hand over the stubble on his chin. 'Oh right.' He shifted from foot to foot, his hands thrust into his jean pockets. Isla was aware of the smell of him; it was subtle but fresh like the native forest around these parts after the rain.

'Right well, we'd better get out there and see what everyone's up to,' she said making no move to break the stand-off between them. She could almost feel the tension crackling in the air and she gasped when he took a step towards her. Her arms seemed to take on a life of their own as they wrapped themselves around his neck. She felt almost disembodied as her fingers entwined and locked behind his neck while he wrapped his strong arms around her waist. He lifted her up to him as his mouth crushed down on top of hers. Oh God, what was she doing? That was her last thought before his lips bruised hers urgently. She wanted more than anything to back up towards the toilets and drag him into a cubicle so they could finish what he'd just started. She moaned, and his hands slipped lower as he held onto her buttocks and pulled her into him.

'He has a girlfriend, Isla. A nice, pretty girlfriend with dimples,' her conscience whispered.

'Oh shut up and let me just enjoy this,' she whispered back, pushing her body hard up against Ben's.

'Isla Brookes, this isn't you. You are not a boyfriend stealer.'

'Oh crap,' she said aloud disentangling herself from Ben's embrace just as a bloke pushed open the door from the pub area. The noise from the band and voices shouting over the music brought them crashing back to reality. They stepped apart awkwardly and the man, who looked like he could do with a hot bath and a shave, winked knowingly at them. 'Don't stop on my behalf.' He leered before swaying into the men's room.

'Shit.' Ben ran his fingers through his hair. 'Shit, I shouldn't have done that.'

'It takes two, don't beat yourself up. Let's forget about it and just put it down to too much alcohol and old times, okay?' Isla said.

She couldn't read his expression as he muttered, 'Yeah, old times. I'm sorry.' He didn't look back as he strode off through the pub. Isla headed for the sanctuary of the ladies' room; she needed to splash some cold water on her face.

She looked like a startled rabbit caught in headlights when

she saw her reflection in the mirror. Other than that, she was relieved to see she did not look like a woman who had just been snogging the face off someone she shouldn't have been. A minute later, having cooled her face off and reapplied her lipstick, she took a steadying breath. She told herself to get back out there before Carl took it upon himself to check if she was okay. A mental picture of him running in clutching his trusty pack of Diastop, in the false assumption a tummy upset was what was holding her up, flashed before her, but she couldn't raise a smile.

The shine had gone off the evening, and she sat down at an empty table with a glass of water vowing there would be no more wine for her tonight. Annie and Kris were still on the dancefloor, and Carl had waved over from where he was in the last throes of his pool match. She was aware that Ben was standing on the edges of the dancefloor with Saralee, but she couldn't bring herself to look in his direction. She was beginning to feel very bad about what had just happened and she realized she was starving too. All she wanted was to go home, scoff her Gran's stew and crawl into bed. Sleep would help her forget about Ben and whatever it was that had just happened.

It was time to call it a night. She got to her feet and made her way up to the bar to enquire about a courtesy wagon. She assumed the pub still operated one. She was in luck, Mick informed her. It was leaving in fifteen minutes. Isla thanked him, hoping Delilah would be alright parked up overnight in the car park. It didn't feel right leaving her on their first night together, she felt like she was abandoning her baby, but she didn't have a choice. She headed over to tell Carl that she was going to call it a night. The band announced they were going to take a short break as she felt a tap on her shoulder – it was Annie. Even in the dimmed light, Isla could see that her fair skin was pink and glowing, and she was holding her hair back from her neck in a ponytail. 'That was fun! I'm boiling, though.'

Kris grinned down at her, he had his arm around her waist, and Isla felt a pang at their uncomplicated, easy way with each other.

'Yeah, the music's great guys, but I'm done in and the courtesy wagon's leaving in ten or so minutes, I'm going to grab a ride home in that.'

Kris looked at Annie who nodded her agreement. 'I think we will too. I'm not going to be able to move tomorrow morning after two nights in a row of dancing. Let's see what Carl wants to do.'

Carl wound his game up and bade his new friends good-night. He promised to bring them an autographed photograph of a Victoria's Secret Model he had photographed last time he was in New York, next time he popped by for a pint. Carl was a man who knew how to win friends and influence people, Isla thought.

Chapter 16

'Hey Gran, I thought you'd be in bed,' Isla said, popping her head around the lounge door and spying her gran stretched out in the recliner.

'I do on occasion push the boat out and stay up past nine thirty, Isla. Did you have a nice time?' Bridget yawned and stretched.

'Yes ta, it was fun, lots and lots of dancing.' And snogging of an ex-boyfriend, Isla thought, hoping Super Gran with her special powers of deduction wouldn't guess she'd been up to something untoward. She stepped into the room. 'What's that you are looking at?'

Bridget had spent her evening tripping down memory lane leafing through photographs.

'Oh, just some old pictures.'

'You dropped something.' Isla bent down and picked up what she saw was an old newspaper clipping and glanced at the headline curiously, *Presbyterian Women's Guild Valentine's Day Dance a Success!* There was a picture of two grinning girls with their arms linked dressed in all their '50s finery, Barker's Creek Hall in the background. 'Gran is that you and—'

'Yes, it's Clara and me.' Her gran's expression was sad. 'I remember that night like it was yesterday.'

Isla sat down on the floor by Bridget pulling her feet to her chest. 'Tell me about it, Gran; I love listening to your stories.'

Bridget looked at the top of her granddaughter's dark head. She was in the mood to talk, she realized. She wanted to tell her how it had all once been. 'It was 1957, and I was sixteen years old,' she began.

Isla closed her eyes and the more her gran talked, the more she felt she was there with her, a fly on the wall observing a snapshot in time.

1957

The carpark in the Barker's Creek Hall grounds was nearly full as Colin steered the Holden FJ and its three passengers through the gates. Jean pointed to a gap between a shiny Ford Fairlane and a more sedate Morris Minor, and he carefully nosed his father's car into it. Jean sat waiting for Colin to come around and open her door but Bridget and Clara clambered out the back, far too excited to wait. They adjusted their skirts, gave each other the once over and, satisfied that all was at it should be, they linked arms and headed in the direction of the hall.

Several groups of lads were leaning up against their cars, a study of coolness as they bantered with one another. One of them clad in jeans and winkle pickers with his hair coiffed, a cigarette dangling out the corner of his mouth, whistled as the girls passed by. Bridget and Clara did their best to ignore him and saunter nonchalantly in the direction of the hall, their chests thrust proudly forth. But Clara still squeezed Bridget's arm in eagerness of the night ahead.

'Hey there girls, let me take your picture?' It was a reporter from the *Bibury Times* in an ill-fitting suit and with far too much hair cream slicking his hair back. Nevertheless, the two girls paused to smile wide for his camera, chuffed to be immortalized on the pages of the local rag.

The Valentine's Day Dance had been organized as a fund-raiser by the Presbyterian Women's Guild with monies raised to go towards a planned extension for St Andrew's, their parish church. It cost one shilling to get in, and the girls handed their money over to Mrs Taylor who was sitting at a table in the foyer. A cash tin was open in front of her while her youngest daughter checked coats into the adjacent cloakroom.

'You can put your plates in the kitchen, girls,' Mrs Taylor trilled. 'Next.' She shooed them towards the hall with one hand and beckoned to the two lads behind Bridget and Clara with her other. Groups of girls were huddled around near the entrance off the hall to the kitchen and Bridget, and Clara pushed their way through to deposit their plates.

Inside the small kitchen, which was kitted out with the bare necessities, it was a hive of activity. Three women, one of whom was a biggish lady with horn-rimmed glasses that Bridget recognized as Mrs Staunton, a friend of her mother's, sorted the plates into the food that could be served as it was and food that would need to be heated. She bustled forward and held her hands out to take Clara's plate of fish paste sandwiches. 'Thank you, dear. I shall put a damp tea towel over them to stop them drying out.'

She placed it on the table and looked at Bridget's offering, 'Now ... pikelets, jam and cream. Let me guess Bridget, your mother made those.'

'She did, yes.'

'Her specialty. How is your mother?'

'She's good, thank you.'

'Well, be sure to tell her Irene Staunton was asking after her, won't you?'

'I will pass it on, Mrs Staunton.'

Clara tugged at her arm.

'First dance, is it girls?' Mrs Staunton looked amused.

They both nodded.

'Well, behave yourselves and have a good time.' She waved them both out of the kitchen with a flap of her tea towel.

Bridget followed Clara through the door, pausing to soak up the festive atmosphere. Balloons were strewn from the ceiling beams along with streamers, and there was a low buzzing of excited chatter. The air felt hot and heavy with the tension of youth. At the far end of the rectangular room with its polished floorboards was the raised stage. The band were all dressed in matching blue suits and were busy warming up. To their left, up against the wall, a long trestle table covered with a white tablecloth had been set up for the supper that would be served at the end of the night. Bridget and Clara headed over to join the other girls waiting with an impatient excitement for the evening to begin.

Clara jostled her way through the gaggles of giggling girls until she was satisfied she had a good position in which to check out the lads, who were lining up on the other side of the hall. They were milling about jocularly in their sports jackets and long-sleeved shirts.

Clara, who had a soft spot for her older brother's new friend Tom Collins, was scanning the crowd for him. 'He's here! And, oh Isla, he looks so handsome all dressed up. I told you he was gorgeous.' She clutched Bridget's arm. 'Oh no! He saw me looking.' Her face was puce. 'He'll think I'm sweet on him. Quick, look like you're talking to me and I'm super interesting!'

'I am talking to you, and you are sweet on him, you've told me so at least a hundred times and I can see why. Mmm, he's very dashing and yes, Clara sometimes you are interesting.' Bridget laughed rubbing at her arm.

Clara gave a little jump of excitement and clapped her hands. This caused several of the fellas across the way to elbow one another as her well-endowed chest jiggled with the effort. 'Oh, I hope he asks me to dance and not spotty chin Jim. I'll die if he does.'

'Well, you know Jim's keen on you because it wasn't my order he put an extra scoop of chips in.'

Both girls knew enough from listening to Jean talk about past dances to know that when the band started to play the rush would be on. The lads would stampede over in their haste to ask the girl they liked the look of to dance. The fear on the girls' part was that if you were picky and said no to the first chap to ask you, then you ran the risk of being left on the sidelines, while everybody else filled the dancefloor. That was a mortifying thought indeed. Bridget spied the short, squat figure of George Donaldson and remembered Jean's advice to her that afternoon, in a rare show of big sisterly concern.

'I just remembered that Jean said we're to be careful if George from the butcher's asks either of us to dance. He's quite likely to, given that we're new blood, Jean's words not mine. Apparently, he's a member of the WHS and Jean reckons his nose only comes up to here.' She pointed to the dip in her blouse, where her chest jutted forth on either side thanks to the special powers of her bullet bra. It would take a brave member of the Wandering Hands Society to attempt anything even vaguely inappropriate on the dancefloor, Bridget thought, her gaze swinging over to the back wall by the entrance.

Three older members of the Presbyterian Ladies Guild were seated in a prim row, hands folded in their laps, ankles crossed. They were positioned strategically so that they were as far away as possible from the band, but could still keep their beady eyes on any shenanigans the young ones might get up to. A tongue lashing from Biddy Johnson was not something you would live down easily, Bridget thought, taking in Biddy's pushed in jam tin expression and lemony lips.

She turned her attention back to the lads milling about with nervous energy across the hall, equally eager for the dance to get underway. Her eyes met those of a leanly built, tall chap she'd never seen before. She smiled at him, having forgotten the plan hatched with Clara to act coy and shy around members of the opposite sex. He had a lovely smile.

Bridget found herself unable to tear her gaze away from his. His hair was so dark it looked to be black, but that could be the dim lighting in the hall, and he wore his suit jacket and trousers with ease. She put this down to his being older than most of the other boys she knew. He looked to be around twenty, at a guess. The local lads looked awkward by comparison, like they were playing at dress up.

She was the first to look away, turning to Clara and whispering that she'd spotted who she hoped would ask her to dance. 'You can look over at him but don't make it obvious, alright?'

Clara nodded.

'He's one but right from spotty chin Jim. I think he's new in town because I've never seen him before.'

Clara did her best to look over while surreptitiously informing Bridget of her findings. 'Well, given he's talking to the man of my dreams, I'd say your fellow must have started work up at the mine too. And yes, he's rather dreamy but not as dreamy as my Tom.'

Bridget flashed her friend a grateful smile for the information.

'Ooh the band's about to start, wish me luck,' Clara screeched excitedly as the boys swarmed forth like bison stampeding the American plains to the first notes of Shake, Rattle, and Roll.

'May I have this dance?'

Bridget blinked to make sure it was him. He was even more handsome up close, and she looked up into his dark, dancing eyes. And yes, his hair was black. With his olive colouring and dark features, he looked Italian. Bridget was already conjuring up romantic images of them whizzing around Rome on a scooter like Joe and Anya in the film she'd seen last year, Roman Holiday. He smelt of soap, fresh and clean, and she let him lead her by the hand out onto the dance floor that was already thronging.

A thrill ricocheted through her as his hands settled on the sides of her waist and he lifted her effortlessly high up into the air. She felt like she was flying. She suppressed a smile as she came back down to earth and spotted a less than pleased Clara being twirled about the floor by Jim. She bet her friend was willing the song to finish, but she never wanted it to end. There was nobody else that she wanted to dance with.

She needn't have worried because Charlie (she'd managed to make his name out over the music) shook his head at anyone who tried to cut in telling them she was taken. This included Clara's Tom who Bridget surmised must be waiting for Jim to deposit her back to the side of the dancefloor.

'Do you mind?' he shouted, leaning down to be heard.

'No.' This time her smile was genuinely shy and coy.

It wasn't until intermission when Bridget, having gratefully gulped down a glass of lemonade Charlie had fetched for her, joined the line of girls queuing for the Ladies' that she caught up with Clara again.

'I'm having the best night of my life.' Clara bounced up and threw her arms around her friend, causing some of the girls in the line to smile at her enthusiasm. 'Tom stepped in at the end of the second dance, and he hasn't left my side since. He said it was only fair to let Jim have a turn or two around the dance floor with me first. And as for you, well I've seen you and your fellow making eyes at each other. You'd better watch out or Biddy Johnson will hobble over and tap you on the shoulder with her stick!'

They both giggled.

'His name's Charlie, that's all I know about him, and I think I might be in love,' Bridget declared with the absolute certainty of a sixteen-year-old encountering her first breath of romance.

Present day

Isla realized her gran had stopped talking. She'd been so caught up in the story, feeling as though she too had been taking a turn on the dancefloor all those years ago. 'What happened to you and Charlie, Gran?'

'That's a story for another night.' Bridget's tone was firm, and she tucked the newspaper cutting back in the sleeve of the album resting on her lap. She cocked her head to one side as the rose bush's thorny branches tapped on the windowpane, like it was asking to come in. 'Where on earth did that wind come from? It was as still as anything an hour ago. Go and get yourself something to eat, Isla. I'm off to bed; it's been a long day.'

Isla knew there was no point pushing it and besides her stomach had started to rumble at the thought of the simmering stew in the crockpot.

Chapter 17

Isla headed across the road to the Kea with her iPad tucked under her arm. It was a damp, sticky Tuesday morning, and she'd spent the last few days working on her concept for the tearoom's makeover. She hoped Annie liked what she'd come up with. Not that Noeline would be open to making any changes by the sounds of things, and it was her business after all, but still it had kept her busy. It had felt good to be productive again, to put her creative cap back on. The thing that had become clear to her as she played around with different ideas was that the café, given a bit of TLC and with not too much money spent, really could be something special. Isla found her eyes straying to the garage, but there was no sign of Ben in the forecourt today.

She pushed open the door of the tearoom and saw there was an older lady sitting in the corner. She was with a woman who, given the resemblance between them, had to be her daughter and they were sharing a pot of tea. The smell of roasted Blue Mountain coffee hung in the air and Annie's head was bent over a book up at the counter. She looked up on hearing the door close.

'Isla hi! Good timing, I've just made a fresh pot of coffee. Ooh you brought your iPad, does that mean what I hope it means?'

'Yep, I've spent the last couple of days playing around with some ideas for this place.'

'Great, can't wait to see them. I love the top by the way. The colour's you.' Annie set about making their drinks.

'Oh, thanks.' Isla glanced down at the lemon top with its sparkly detailing. She'd bought it in a shop at Los Angeles Airport. It had been spur of the moment and very different to her usual un-frilly style, but it had felt right somehow to buy something out of her comfort zone. 'I got it in the States on my way home. What're you looking at?' Isla turned the open recipe book around and peered at the glossy picture. 'Yum, that looks good.'

'I know, and it's good for you – sort of. It's a sugar-free brownie, and it uses dates for sweetness. Aunty Noeline's not interested in anything that's not good old plain fare, though. She says there's no call for fancy tastes here. It frustrates me, especially when so many people have food intolerances these days. She really should have a couple of gluten-free options available at the very least.'

'Mm, you're right. Would you like to own a café?'

'Nah, I don't think so. The responsibility of running a business would scare me, and I couldn't commit to it because at some point Kris and I will head back to Greece, but I'd like more of a managerial say in things here. The first thing I'd do is invest in a coffee machine.' She laughed opening the fridge behind her to get the milk out.

'Oh, I don't know, the Blue Mountain's growing on me. Did Carl get off alright? He popped by on Sunday to pick up some scones Gran had baked for him to take home, but I missed him. I'd gone around to my parents' for lunch.'

'He sure did. He reckons he'll come back soon but with David this time.'

'That'd be great. I'd like to meet him.'

'David's a sweetie, you'll love him too.' Annie slid Isla's coffee towards her. 'Actually you just saying you had lunch with your parents made me realize I'm long overdue to go and catch up with mine. I'd like to buy some ingredients for that chocolate brownie recipe too, and I doubt I'll find mesquite powder in Bibury. Do you fancy a trip to Christchurch one of these days? I'd have to fit in around Aunty Noeline, but we could catch up with the boys then?'

'I think you're probably right regarding the mesquite whatever it is and yes, I'd love to go with you, thanks. Just say the word, I'm pretty flexible with my time these days.' She smiled ruefully.

'I will. Why don't you go and grab a seat and I'll be with you in a sec.'

Isla picked up her drink and went and sat down while Annie checked the mother and daughter duo were happy before joining her. She switched the iPad on and held the screen so they could both see and to her surprise, she felt nervous. She needn't have been because Annie clapped her hands in delight as her ideas lit up the screen.

'The countertop looks fab and, oh wow! I love the miner's oil lamps; they look fantastic hanging from that exposed beam. The railway sleepers framing the fireplace look amazing too, and is that a gas fire?'

Isla nodded. The theme she'd gone with tied in with the area's mining history. She'd stripped the interior of the café back to its bare bones and worked with what was already here but also added more functional, modern items like the gas fire. Existing features, like the ceiling beam which had been painted in the same cream as the walls, would look incredible taken back to their original timber. The flooring too was currently a pale speckled lino, but Isla was sure, given the age of the building, beneath it, they'd find original floorboards. Polished up they would lend a truly rustic atmosphere to the interior that was more in keeping with the cottage exterior.

There was more that she'd put into her visual presentation. Beside the fireplace was an oval antique miner's lunch box pail filled with pinecones. One of the walls was decorated with framed photographic memorabilia which would, of course, all be of Bibury. Against this wall was an overstuffed couch with a hand-stitched quilt draped over it, inviting customers to sit down and relax. The tables and chairs she visualized were chunky, made of solid wood and iron. They'd be durable just like the hardworking miners whose backs upon which Bibury had been founded.

'If Aunty Noeline doesn't take this on board, she's mad,' Annie said as the tearoom's door opened. Both women glanced up to see a tall, good-looking man dressed in a suit walk in followed by Saralee. As she dimpled up and waved over-enthusiastically at her and Annie, Isla felt her face heat up as though someone had just turned the gas element to high. It was the first time she'd seen her since the Friday night debacle with Ben.

'Hey Callum, Saralee. Morning tea time, is it? Excuse me a mo, Isla.' Annie got up and went back around the counter. They placed their order, and while she busied herself putting it together for them, Saralee came over to say hi. The man in the suit followed her, and Isla found herself sitting a little straighter in her seat as she smoothed her hair back behind her ears.

'Isla, this is Callum Packer. Callum started this term as the Deputy Head of Bibury Area School. Isla's just got back from living in the UK.'

Isla held her hand out. 'Hi, Callum, nice to meet you.' He took her hand in his with a smile, it felt warm and dry, and his grip was strong but not too much so.

'Nice to meet you too.'

He released her hand, and to her surprise, she found herself almost batting her lashes, 'Well, Deputy Packer, you've got a tough act to follow. I went to Bibury and back in my day Miss Seastrand was an absolute terror.'

Callum chuckled. 'I met her when I applied for the position. But I can be quite tough too when I want to be.'

'It's true,' Saralee chirped. 'He can seem very scary if you're five. This morning these two little boys were marched into the office by the new entrants teacher, Ms Brightman. Go on, Callum you do it so well.'

Callum grinned and affected a high-pitched, prim voice. '*Deputy Packer, I just caught George and Leo using some very bad words in the playground.*'

Saralee giggled. 'He sounds just like her. Anyway, personally, I think George has got a bit of a weasel look about him, but that might be down to his shaved head. Leo, the other one, well he's a sweet looking cherub with blonde curls. Both of them were busy dobbing the other one in, and I had already decided my money was on the weasel-faced George being the culprit when Leo looked at Callum with his big blue eyes and said, "It fucking well was him, Mr Packer."'

Isla's eyes widened and then she burst out laughing. 'Oh dear, you can't judge a book by its cover.' *That could apply to you Isla; poor Saralee has no idea what a Judas you are.*

She was relieved when Annie presented them both with a brown paper bag.

'Thanks, this will fill the gap. Right, I need to get back and check young Leo's still hard at it picking up the playground litter.' Callum lingered. 'It was nice meeting you Isla. I hope I'll see you around.'

Once the door was closed behind them, Annie sat back down and raised her eyebrows. 'I think he liked you.'

'Don't be silly.' Isla drained her coffee and grinned. 'He was pretty cute though.'

'And single.' Annie tapped the side of her nose. 'I have that on good authority because Kris told me all the women at school have been going silly over him.'

'Well, I won't be. I've sworn off the opposite sex,' Isla stated with what she hoped was conviction. She remembered what she'd made a note of to talk to Annie about. 'Hey, while I think of it, I noticed you seemed a little uptight at the mention of meeting Kris' family when it came up the other night. You can tell me to mind my own business if you like.'

Annie gave a little laugh. 'It's okay, and if I seemed uptight, then that's because I am. Honestly, Isla, if his mama's true to type she won't approve of me.'

'Why not?'

'Because Greek women are tiger mamas when it comes to their sons. I know, I've seen it first-hand. Trust me, Kris' mama will have a nice Greek Orthodox girl in mind for him, and I won't fit the bill.'

Isla frowned. 'I find that hard to believe. You and Kris are perfect together; you make each other happy. I don't think any mother could ask for more than that. Plus, you're gorgeous, she couldn't not love you.'

'I'm not so sure, but thank you.' Annie's smile was shy. 'I suppose it's just that I love him so much. I don't want anything to spoil what we have, and family is everything to the Greeks. Their opinion matters to each other. So yes, the thought of meeting his mama and even his sisters terrifies me.'

'Well, I think you're worrying about nothing. When they meet you, they'll see exactly what Kris sees in you. You guys are a perfect match.'

'Aw, you're sweet.'

She didn't look convinced, though, and then she changed the subject. 'My turn now. What's the story with you and Ben from the garage? You promised to tell me when you knew me better.'

Isla did feel like she was beginning to get to know Annie and she trusted her. 'Oh, there's not much to tell really. We dated each other for a while when we were teenagers, then

I moved to Christchurch, and it got too hard. That's all.'

'Then why have you gone bright red?' Annie raised a knowing eyebrow.

Isla put her hands to her cheeks. They were hot, and she squirmed.

'Something happened the other night, didn't it?' Annie looked at her face. 'I knew it!'

'Shush.' Isla looked around as though the walls had ears. From what she remembered of growing up in Bibury, more often than not they did. Satisfied the mother and daughter, who were getting up from their seats and picking up their handbags, would not give a toss what she'd gotten up to on Friday night, she filled Annie in. 'The thing is, it didn't mean anything, it was just a nostalgic snog after we'd both had too much to drink. I feel awful about it though because I like Saralee. That's not the type of woman I am either. I don't do stuff like that, well not normally anyway.'

'It takes two to tango Isla. It's not all down to you,' Annie reiterated Isla's sentiment to Ben the other night. 'He's the one with a girlfriend remember.'

'I know.'

'So, what are you going to do?'

Isla shrugged. 'I don't know, pretend nothing happened I guess.'

'Can I make a suggestion? It might take that glum look off your face.'

'Please do.'

'Since its gone quiet why don't you come out the back and help me with a recipe I've wanted to try?'

'Here you go.' Annie handed Isla an apron once she'd finished washing her hands. She put it on and saluted her, announcing she was reporting for duty.

Annie laughed and pointed to a magazine folded over on the stainless steel bench. 'Do you think we can do it?'

Isla frowned as she gazed down at the complicated but deliciously rich sounding three-layer Black Forest cake. She took a deep breath. 'Definitely. There are a couple of fancy ingredients in this though, Kirsch, Morello cherries. I don't fancy your chances of finding them down at the Four Square.'

'All bought on my last trip into Christchurch. Here, have a sniff of this.' Annie opened a bottle, and Isla inhaled. It brought tears to her eyes.

'Whoa, that's got a kick to it.'

Annie grinned. 'I know, it's good, isn't it? Can't make a Black Forest cake without Kirsch. Come on, let's get baking.'

Isla was the mixer, Annie was the measurer, and they worked away companionably in the small space until they heard the tearoom's door open. Annie went to serve the customer while Isla carried on, her finger tracing the recipes steps. She was enjoying herself. It was time to open the jar of cherries and drain them. She moved on to thickening the juice and the cherries in sugared water over a low temperature, and by the time Annie returned she'd just gotten the sponge out of the oven and was testing it to see if it was springy to the touch.

'That looks great. We need to let it cool before we slice it into three.' Annie checked her phone. 'It's all quiet out there now, and it's nearly two o'clock. I think we've earned ourselves some lunch.'

They sat down to a ham sandwich each, with Annie apologizing that it was nothing more salubrious but at this time of the day if they were still sitting in the cabinet, they were not likely to sell. Isla didn't mind in the least. She was quite partial to a ham sandwich; it reminded her of being a kid when she and Ryan would call into the Kea for a treat with their mum. A ham sandwich and an afghan biscuit. The menu hadn't changed much in twenty-five years.

They had just gotten up to clear their plates when the door opened. Their noses were assailed with a waft of an oppressive fragrance, that Isla recognized as Christian Dior. If she'd closed her eyes, she would've still known instantly who it was. Poison was Noeline's signature perfume. Her eyes, however, were open, and she saw that the lady herself was as loud and large as Isla remembered, with her emerald coloured sleeveless pantsuit ensemble and her red hair piled high on her head.

'Isla Brookes as I live and breathe! Come and give me a hug. Your grandmother told me you were back and that you and Annie were friendly.'

Isla felt herself pulled into a suffocating hug and, once released, managed to answer Noeline's twenty questions as to what she'd been doing and where she'd been and whom she'd been doing it all with. When she'd heard enough, she held up her hand blinding Isla with the sparkly flashes from her bejewelled fingers. 'Well, it's been lovely seeing you, dear.' She turned her attention to Annie. 'Busy day?' The gushy tone had disappeared and been replaced by that of a woman who meant business.

'Steady,' Annie reported before filling her in on what they were up to out in the kitchen.

'Black Forest cake?' She raised her pencilled in eyebrows. 'Annie, we're not German.'

Annie ignored her. 'Aunty Noeline, you know how I've said a few times now that the Kea could do with a bit of a revamp?'

The hand went up again. 'Darling, stop right there.' Isla couldn't help but think she looked like a pensioner version of Geri Halliwell back in her Spice Girl Days as she swept Annie through the tearoom to the kitchen. 'That's why I'm here. I need to have a word. Isla, do you mind if I drag Annie off to the kitchen for a bit of a chat?' She tossed over her shoulder.

Isla felt deflated. She'd been looking forward to showing Noeline her design ideas. It wasn't as though she'd expected her to give her an open cheque and say, 'go for your life', but she hadn't expected to be completely dismissed either. Still, you didn't cross a woman in an emerald green pantsuit. 'Of course not, Noeline.' She sat back down at the table and slid her iPad into her tote bag. 'I can keep an eye on things out here for you both if you like?'

'Thanks, Isla.' Annie threw her an apologetic smile, but Isla could see she was worried as to what it was Noeline wanted to talk to her about. She watched them until they'd disappeared out the back. The only familial similarity Isla could see between them was their hair, but for one of them that colour definitely wasn't natural.

Chapter 18

Isla wasn't on her own in the tearoom for long, and her face broke into a wide grin upon recognizing the customer who'd just closed the door behind her. 'Miss McDougall! How are you?' It was Bibury Area School's former secretary. Isla had a soft spot for her; she'd always been kind to Isla whenever she'd wound up in the school's sick bay or needed a plaster after a grievous playground injury. Even when she'd been marched into the office by a jubilant Miss Seastrand, Isla had always felt Violet McDougall was secretly on her side.

She was dressed in the same style she always dressed in when Isla was still a pupil at the school. A plain blouse with the skirt just below the knee, and flat, sensible shoes. If the weather were not so muggy, Isla knew she would also be wearing her trusty cardigan. Isla and her friends had used to joke that she had a different coloured cardigan for each day of the week in winter. Her hair was cut in the same blunt, ash blonde bob style, and her eyes shone a familiar, bright and twinkly blue.

'Oh goodness! Isla dear, call me Violet, you're not a child anymore.'

Isla wasn't sure she wanted to. It was a bit like calling one of your mum's friends, who you'd always addressed as Aunty so and so, by their first name. It never seemed to trip off the tongue easily. 'Er, alright then, Violet. How's retirement suiting you?'

'Retirement, what's that? I'm busier than I ever was. Have you met my replacement, Saralee yet? She's stepping out with your old flame, Ben Robson.'

Isla bit her bottom lip in an attempt to keep her expression neutral. 'I have yes, she's a nice girl.'

'Say it like you mean it dear.'

Isla flashed her an apologetic grin and wondered if Miss McDougall still hankered after the school's Principal. It had been entertaining when sitting in the office, waiting for whatever punishment was about to be bestowed to witness her and Miss Seastrand try to outdo one another as they vied for his attention. They were both desperate to catch the widower's eye, but he'd always seemed oblivious to their carry on.

'All I meant was that you'd be a hard act to follow.'

'I know *exactly* what you meant dear. Now, what about you, what are you doing with yourself?'

Isla explained that she was in limbo with regards to work but that she was manning the tearoom while Annie and Noeline were out the back.

'Well, there's no need to disturb them. I'm sure you can manage to make me a pot of tea, and I'll have one of those Belgium biscuits please.' Violet fossicked in her purse and thrust a note at Isla who did as she was told, and went behind the counter.

'Righty-ho. Just bear with me while I figure the till out.' She flexed her fingers and was proud of herself when the drawer pinged open, and she managed to count out the correct change. She set about making the tea, and as she put Violet's order down in front of her without slopping any milk from the jug, the ex-secretary patted the empty seat next to her. 'Sit down for a bit Isla, and tell me all about that glamorous life of yours in London. I do love hearing how our old pupils are getting on.'

Isla was happy to oblige, and the two women soon found common ground when Isla, knowing of Violet's passion for the Scottish Society mentioned a trip she'd made to Edinburgh. Violet had gotten so excited hearing of this visit to her ancestral home that Isla had thought she might leap up from her seat and demonstrate a highland fling. They'd moved on to the Scottish Society's use of the Barker's Ridge Hall once a month. Violet was busy telling Isla her concerns that if Bridget got her way and the hall was done up then the society might not be able to afford the increase in rent it would no doubt bring. Isla got the distinct impression she was hoping she'd have a word in her gran's ear but before Violet could attempt a bribe, Noeline reappeared.

'Violet! How are you, my dear? I haven't seen you since you retired. You're looking well on it. Being a lady of leisure obviously suits you.'

Violet snorted. 'I've hardly had time to catch my breath, I've been so busy since I left the school. I was just telling Isla that the Scottish Society keeps me busier than ever. We've just been enjoying a cup of tea and a catch up. And, you dear, how are you keeping?'

'Oh, I'm very well Violet, very well indeed. Watch this space.' She tapped the side of her nose with a red fingernail. 'Exciting things are afoot.'

Violet opened her mouth to inquire as to what those exciting things might be, but Noeline was already at the door. 'Must run, places to be and people to see. You know how it is ladies. Toodle-oo.'

'Well, I wonder what that was all about,' Violet said putting her teacup back in the saucer. 'I'd best be getting on my way too. It's been lovely seeing you again dear.'

'You too Miss Mc—er Violet.'

'And perhaps you could have a word in your gran's ear?'

Isla smiled. 'Will do.' Violet nodded her thanks and left.

'Is the coast clear?' Annie asked, poking her head around the kitchen door as the door banged shut. She looked very down in the mouth to Isla.

'Yes, it's just me here. Come on out and tell me what that was all about.'

Annie mooched in and slouched over the counter her chin resting in her hands. 'Aunty Noeline's selling up. She's going home to ring my dad; he's an estate agent, and she wants him to list the tearoom. Apparently, she's fed up with everybody else having all the fun.'

'What fun?' Isla was unaware of copious amounts of fun being had in Bibury.

'Oh, my folks are big on cruising, and they're always on about what a great time they had on the last one they did and now the Robsons from the garage are into it too. Aunty Noeline's decided she wants to see a buffet for herself and sip cocktails while the sun sets. She said the Kea is becoming a noose around her neck. I can't say I blame her for wanting to sell up and set sail; she is nearly seventy.'

'But what about you? You are related after all. What're you supposed to do if she sells?'

'She was sorry about the timing, but she said that she's hopeful whoever buys the place will keep me on. She asked me if I was interested in buying it.'

'And are you?'

'No. As I said to you earlier I don't want to make that kind of commitment. Hopefully, it will take a while to sell, but I think Aunty Noeline just wants to be rid so she'll take what she can get.'

'Oh, what a bummer, Annie.'

'I know, but them's the breaks I guess. Come on, let's go cream our Black Forest cake. The sooner it's finished, the sooner I can have a bloody great big piece of it.'

'Comfort eating, good plan.'

Isla beat the cream while Annie spread frosting on the layers. They worked in silence. Annie wasn't in the mood to chat, and Isla's brain was buzzing. Annie had just begun piping the thickened cream onto the top of the cake when Isla whipped off her apron. She paused with the piping bag in mid-air, a blob of cream dangling from the nozzle.

'What's up?' Annie asked, startled.

Isla knew she looked a little manic, and she probably was, but there was someplace she needed to be. 'I can't explain it just yet but promise me you'll save me a piece of cake. I'm hoping we're going to have something to celebrate. I'll be back soon.'

Annie watched with open-mouthed bewilderment as Isla called out before haring out of the tearoom, 'Wish me luck!'

Isla raced across the road towards home, hoping that her gran was out as she didn't want to talk to anyone, not yet. She didn't want to give anyone the chance to tell her what she was about to do was a mad idea. She wanted to throw caution to the wind. Her luck was in, and within minutes she'd retrieved Delilah's keys and was reversing down the driveway. So intent was she on her mission that she didn't see Ben watching her from over the road at the garage with a perplexed expression on his face.

As she drove, she weighed up the pros and cons of what she was planning. Was it mad? Probably, she had no experience after all, but then that was what was so appealing. *Right Isla, if my memory serves me properly, this is it.* She pulled over to the side of the road not bothering to lock Delilah as she strode up to the front door of a tidy, cream Summerhill stone house. She rapped on the bevelled glass pane of the door a little more forcibly than she'd intended, but it had the desired effect as she spied a shadow moving towards it. The door swung open, and the woman standing there in her emerald green pantsuit looked taken aback at seeing her on her doorstep.

'Isla? Twice in one day, goodness dear is everything alright?'

'Everything's great Noeline, or at least it will be if you let me buy the Kea from you.'

'You've done what?'

'I've bought the Kea, well almost, I need to get a valuation done because that's what Noeline and I have agreed I'll pay, market value. We shook on it. You've got cream on your nose by the way.'

Annie wiped at her nose impatiently. 'I don't know what to say. I'm blown away.'

'So am I to be honest. It was all very spur of the moment, but it feels right.' Isla shrugged. 'Bloody terrifying but right all the same. I want something new to sink my teeth into, and I'm not ready to buy a house just yet, but I do want to make a commitment.'

'Well, I think it is fanbloodytastic!'

Isla beamed. 'You'll carry on managing the day to day running of the place with me, won't you?'

'I'd love to.'

'We can work through new menu ideas together. I was thinking about my dad's garden. He always has so much extra produce that maybe we could buy our veggies from him and use seasonal produce. And I'll have to sort out the renovation.' She looked panicked. 'There's so much to think about.'

'Oh, Isla it all sounds brilliant.' Annie squealed and clapped her hands. 'It's so exciting!' This time it was Annie who whipped her apron off. 'Wait here; I'll be back in a jiffy.'

As she headed to the door, Isla called after her, 'Don't tell anyone, Annie, not yet. Not until it's a done deal.' She'd sworn Noeline to secrecy too.

Isla took the opportunity of being alone in the café to wander around looking at the dated, characterless furnishings and she felt a frisson of excitement. It was going to be hers, her very own project to put her stamp on.

'Let's have a toast.' Annie burst back through the door waving a bottle of fizzy grape juice. 'It was all I could find with bubbles – to Isla Brookes, the soon to be new owner of Bibury's Kea Tearooms.'

'Ooh, say it again!' Isla grinned as Annie popped the cork and poured them each a mug of the sweet fizz.

Chapter 19

'Mum!' Isla called pushing open the front door. 'We're here.'

'Come in, come in, I'm in the kitchen beating the egg whites for my lemon meringue pie.'

Bridget and Isla wandered down the hall through to the living area where the open plan layout gave way to the kitchen. The air was warm with the smell of roast chicken clinging heavily to it, and the windows shut to keep the pesky flies at bay. Isla spied the foil covered roasting tin sitting on the bench with the chicken resting beneath it. Next to it was a bubbling pot of veggies on the stovetop. Mary looked up from the breakfast bar where she was giving the hand beater a work out.

'Hi Mum, Isla love. You two are the first to arrive. Joe's in the garage tinkering on that bike of his.'

Isla kissed her mum, leaving a glossy mark on her cheek. She peered over her shoulder at the open copy of the *Edmonds Cookery Book*, calling out, 'She's on page two hundred and eleven, Gran.'

It made Bridget smile.

Mary batted her daughter away with her free hand. 'Go and make yourself useful. Pour some drinks. There's a bottle of wine in the fridge, or juice, whatever you fancy. Oh, I've lost my place now.' She traced her finger along the recipe peering over the top of her reading glasses. 'Okay, so I'm done beating next I spoon my meringue topping over the lemon filling.'

Bridget shook her head at her daughter's culinary skills. 'I'll just have a juice please, Isla.' Then she remembered her daughter-in-law, bossy boots Ruth would be arriving shortly. 'Actually, on second thoughts I'll have a wine, thank you.'

'Oh good, I'm not drinking alone then,' Mary said picking up her glass and raising it as she saw Isla open the fridge and reach for the orange juice. 'Bit early in the day for me under normal circumstances but I needed some Dutch courage for dealing with Ruth. Cheers,' she said taking a sip.

'Oh, she's not that bad Mum.'

'Yes, she is,' Mary and Bridget chimed, grinning at each other and presenting a united mother-daughter front.

Isla's hand shook slightly as she poured her gran's wine. Over lunch, she planned on announcing her news. It'd been so hard not breathing a word of what she was up to and she'd sworn Annie and Noeline to secrecy too, but now that the contract had been signed the tearoom's purchase was a done deal. The thing was she hadn't wanted advice, and she knew that if it had become public knowledge that she was buying the tearoom, she would have received plenty. It wasn't that she was pig-headed, well, maybe just a little, but this was something that felt so right. She didn't want anybody trying to talk her out of it or being negative – not when, for the first time in a very long while, she was feeling so positive.

'What time are you expecting them?' Bridget asked, sitting down at the table that was already laid for lunch. Good grief, you'd need your sunglasses on with all the shiny topped surfaces in this room, she thought. Isla was behaving peculiarly too. The tremble in her hand as she poured the drinks didn't escape Bridget's eagle eye. She'd been like a cat on a hot tin roof these past couple of weeks. Too much energy, in her opinion, and it was high time she began to show some signs of finding employment. It was all well and good helping Annie over at the Kea but Noeline, Bridget knew, was as tight as a cat's arse and would not be dipping into her purse to pay her granddaughter as well as Annie.

'They shouldn't be too far away,' Mary replied.

'Mum.' Isla looked at her mother's glowing face. 'I've been meaning to ask you, why is your skin lending itself towards a shade of orange these days?'

Bridget snickered.

'It's not orange, it's a sun-kissed natural glow. You've just lived with all those pasty-faced Brits for far too long. It's all the go now, self-tanners and bronzers. Foundation's a thing of the past.' Mary was not in the least bit offended as she popped her pie in the oven. 'Ten minutes, girls and we'll have a dessert fit for a king.'

Bridget was glad she was feeling so confident because, having sampled many of Mary's desserts over the years, she wasn't so sure.

Isla perched on a stool at the breakfast bar with her OJ in

front of her trying to quell her nerves as her mum chatted. Her ears pricked up hearing Ben's name mentioned.

'Actually, speaking of dessert, Ben's lady friend came in to collect a prescription the other day and I couldn't stop thinking about cheesecake after I saw her name on it, Saralee. I had to go to the Kea to see what was on offer and there wasn't any cheesecake but there was the most delicious Black Forest cake in the cabinet. I have to say the food's gone up a notch there since your friend Annie's been on board, Isla.'

The sound of car doors slamming in the driveway outside saved Isla from having to comment.

Ruth finished air kissing Mary's cheeks and exclaimed, 'Jack's outside talking to Joe. Gosh you're looking well Mary. Don't tell me you and Joe snuck off to Fiji or Raro for a wee holiday and didn't tell us? You didn't get that glowing tan here on the Coast that's for sure.'

Isla snorted, and Mary shot her a warning glance but Ruth had already moved on, her arms outstretched towards her niece.

'Isla, sweetie-pie is it you?'

'Yep, it's me, Aunty Ruth.' She was enveloped in a cloud of floral top notes as she was squashed into her aunt's ample bosom. 'How's Theresa and Tom?' she whispered into her aunt's chest, feeling strangled.

'Oh, they're both doing ever so well.'

Isla felt her inhale, a sure sign she was about to launch into a lengthy update, when she spotted her mother-in-law.

'Bridget, how are you dear?' Ruth enunciated loudly and

clearly having released Isla who was gasping for air. 'Why don't you sit in one of the comfy chairs over by the window, dear?'

Bridget opened her mouth about to tell her daughter-in-law that she was neither deaf nor decrepit and to stop calling her dear, thank you very much, when a hollering from outside interrupted her.

'Isla! I've told you not to park that red hair dryer in the drive way!'

'My Mini Cooper, Delilah, ruins Dad's image apparently,' Isla muttered in Ruth's direction as she headed over to the window. Her father, his face hidden beneath his Stetson was stalking around her car in his cowboy boots, while her Uncle Jack looked on with amusement. She opened the window and leaned out. 'If I have to put up with a dad who thinks he's flipping Clint Eastwood then you can put up with a daughter who drives a Mini.' She shut the window before he had a chance to reply.

'Bridget, dear would you like me to cut you another piece of Mary's lovely lemon meringue pie? Top up anyone?' Ruth asked. She was getting a definite glow on, Isla thought, noticing her refill her glass yet again.

Bridget chewed her bottom lip. What she really felt like doing was flicking a piece of the pie across the table at her daughter in law, but she wouldn't. No, she'd content herself with a rude finger sign in her direction under the table. They'd all just suffered through Ruth's monologue of how wonderfully Theresa and Thomas were doing, and how they were setting the world alight in their respective jobs.

Thomas was a plumber and Theresa managed a women's clothing store. Both lived in Christchurch and hardly ever came to see their gran. It was par for the course with Ruth. If poor Mary mentioned Ryan was doing well then Ruth jumped in with how Tom had just had a promotion at work. Likewise, if Isla was making a name for herself in the world of interior design then Theresa had just been told by her boss that her eye for knowing the latest fashion trend was uncanny. Honestly there was singing one's children's praises and then there was being plain obnoxious about it.

All the same they were her grandchildren and she loved them. After all, they couldn't help their mother's behaviour. She shook the thoughts away, eyeing Isla suspiciously. She'd hardly touched her food.

'No thank you Ruth,' Bridget managed to reply civilly. 'I've had plenty to eat. Well done, Mary that was a lovely meal and dessert. Sara Lee, eat your hat out.' The roast chicken had been dry and stringy and thank the lord for dental floss, but she'd had worse.

Mary and Isla got the private joke and laughed. 'Actually Gran, it's eat your heart out,' Isla corrected her.

'That's what I said.'

'Um, I've got an announcement to make,' Isla said deciding it was best to move things along. She tapped her glass with her spoon wanting to say her piece before anybody got up to leave the table, her cheeks flushed pink with building excitement. Everybody turned their attention to her. 'And you can take that bloody look off your faces I'm not pregnant! I've bought the Kea Tearooms.'

Aunty Ruth and Uncle Jack left not long after Isla announced her news. The atmosphere had gotten very strained. Aunty Ruth didn't help matters either when she slurred that Theresa was looking into buying her own clothes shop. Isla was surprised that Bridget didn't tell her to put a cork in it. Jack sensing his mother was close to losing her rag with his wife quickly got up from the table and made his excuses that they must be on their way. Ruth, who was onto her fourth glass of wine, not that anybody was counting, didn't take the hint until her husband took her by the arm and hauled her to her feet. Mary just sat there at the table still laden with the lunch-time detritus, with a hurt expression on her face. From time to time she'd shake her head like a bewildered sheep. 'Did you not to think to mention it Isla? I am your mother,' she said, not really expecting a reply.

Joe's face was puce as he muttered on about Isla throwing good money after bad. Bridget was the only one at the table who seemed pleased with the news. She gave Isla's hand a supportive squeeze under the table. 'Well, I for one think its great news that Isla's home and she's putting down roots,' she said receiving a withering look from her daughter.

'A house would have been a more sensible idea,' Joe said.

Isla felt her blood beginning to boil and she bit back the retort on the tip of her tongue. Common sense prevailed. She knew they needed a bit of space to get used to the fact she was soon to be in the food business, and if she didn't leave right now she might say something she'd regret later. She got up from her chair being careful not to scrape it back over the shiny floor and elicit more angst from her mother. 'I'm sorry, maybe I should have spoken to you both first before I went ahead and signed the contract but your reaction is exactly why I didn't. I'm going to go for a walk and let you get your heads around it.'

'Good idea, Isla dear, off you go,' Bridget said. 'I'll make a start on the clearing up.'

The air outside had an autumnal bite, and the ground was wet thanks to the rain shower that had been and gone while they'd eaten lunch. The leaves were red and gold, piling their pretty colours into the gutter and Isla fancied the air actually smelt like green would if it had a scent. It was the scent of the bush and it was a smell she'd missed. She inhaled deeply and felt herself calm down. Her mum and dad would come round to her way of thinking, especially once she proved she could make a success of the business.

She was striding along, arms-swinging, lost in her plans for the Kea one minute and the next she'd crashed down on the pavement in a heap. Her foot, thanks to her choice of impractical ballet flats had slipped out from under her on the slick asphalt.

'Isla!'

It took her a beat to comprehend her name was being called and to register that there was a truck idling in the road. Ben was leaning out the open window his face creased in concern. 'Hey, are you okay?'

'I'm fine.' She lied still on her knees.

'Hang on a sec.'

He pulled over and got out of his wagon. Striding over to her, he held his hand out. She put her hand in his. It was warm and dry and she could feel his strength as he helped her to her feet.

'You've ripped your jeans and you're bleeding.'

She glanced down. So she was, but it was nothing a spot of Dettol and a band-aid wouldn't fix. The jeans were her favourite pair, though, that was a bummer.

'Come on, I'll give you a ride home.'

'No, it's okay, really. I'm alright now.'

She didn't want to be alone with him in his truck, not after what happened at the Pit.

'You can't walk home like that, that knee's gotta hurt. How would I explain leaving you in this state to your gran, she'd string me up?'

She raised a smile at that. 'Oh, alright then, thanks. I hope I'm not holding you up or anything.' Now the shock of slipping over was wearing off, she was beginning to feel embarrassed at the spectacle she'd made.

'Nope it's all good. You heading home?' He held the passenger door open for her and she clambered in carefully.

'Mum and Dad's please.'

Ben nodded and got in. He turned the radio down, flashing her an apologetic smile before indicating right and driving off. 'Hey, uh, about what happened the other night, Isla I—'

Isla did not want to go there, not now. 'You don't have to say anything Ben, it was one of those silly drunken mistakes. I've forgotten about it already and you don't have to worry about me saying anything to Saralee either, okay?'

'That's not what I was going to say.' He slapped the steering wheel. 'Man, you are hard work sometimes Isla, do you know that?'

Isla was taken aback and felt tears spring to her eyes. Everybody was annoyed with her and her knee was beginning to sting. 'Yes, actually I do know. You're the third person to tell me that in not so many words this afternoon.'

He looked at her and seeing her face, loosened his grip on the steering wheel. 'Why, what've you been up to?'

'I told Mum and Dad that I've bought the Kea off Noeline at lunch today, and it went down like a lead balloon. They're annoyed because I didn't talk to them about my plans first but I'm thirty years old for goodness' sake and I've been making decisions on my own for a long time. Ben, watch it, you nearly took out the Four Square sign!'

'Shit, sorry. What did you say?'

Isla filled him in. 'I said I've bought the Kea. Gran was on my side. Hopefully she'll have talked them round a bit and they're over their snit,' she said as he pulled into her parents' driveway behind Delilah. 'It just kind of took the shine off it all though. Hey, thanks for the ride. I'll see you around.' She climbed down from the wagon.

'Sure, look after that knee.' Before she closed the door, he spoke again. 'And Isla, I for one think its great news.

Chapter 20

By the time the keys to the Kea were officially handed over late on a Friday afternoon with the first hint of winter nipping at its' heels, Isla had her parents on side. She'd swayed her dad around to the idea of his daughter being the owner of the town's tearoom by asking whether he would consider providing her with seasonal produce to use in the daily menu. She'd promise to pay him a fair price for it. His chest had puffed up, and he'd stuck his fingers in the loops of the waist-band of his jeans before swaggering home to plant out another row of leeks. As for Mary, well she'd been easy. The offer of a free cake on Fridays had done the trick. Her only request was that it please be Black Forest.

Now, Isla sat in the empty tearoom with the keys to her new kingdom on the table in front of her. She'd already put a sign in the window proclaiming the business to be under new ownership and apologizing for the inconvenience of it being closed for renovations. She'd placed an advert in the *Bibury Times* which would run in the next edition advising the same thing too. It would help quell the small town stories going around as to what was happening with the Kea. Gran told her that when she'd popped into the Four Square, Ellie, the girl whose pants always looked like they needed to be surgically removed, had asked her if it was true. Was Isla planning on opening a wine bar? Then there was Ted from the butcher's who'd asked if it was going to be a TAB and Frances from the craft shop who'd heard it was going to be an artisan cheese shop. The change of ownership seemed to have given locals the opportunity to lend voice to their dream retail outlet.

A truck thundered down the road, and Isla felt the floor tremble slightly as she looked at the surrounds she now owned. She'd bought the plant as well as the building, and her dad was going to store what she wasn't keeping in his garage while she listed the surplus plant for sale on Trade Me. She didn't expect much for the furnishings but whatever she got would go towards the new coffee machine she'd already ordered online.

Annie had been elated at the news and kept going on about how she could officially call herself a barista once it arrived. Isla didn't like to point out that there were courses one had to attend before graduating as a qualified master of coffee making, there was plenty of time for that. In the meantime, so long as she got the hang of how to work the thing everyone would be happy. The kitchen would stay as it was, it was functional and passed all council requirements. It was the dining area that was to be her project and once she got the furnishings out it would be a blank canvas with which to work with.

For a second she felt overwhelmed at the prospect of what

lay ahead. Oh, the design part of the tearoom was easy, it was her forte after all. No, it was the practical stuff that would be hard. The project managing of the actual building work, never mind the finishing touches. She might be an interior decorator, but she'd never actually wielded a paint brush and didn't plan on starting now. She'd have to ask around for advice regarding tradespeople.

The realization that whether or not this new business venture succeeded was down to her began to sink in. To quell the building panic, Isla rummaged in her bag until she found her book of affirmations. She flicked through its pages looking for words that felt appropriate until her eyes settled on, *I am in charge of my own happiness and responsible for filling my own needs*. Exhaling slowly, Isla began repeating the phrase aloud, closing her eyes as she did so.

She was on her fourth repetition when the door to the tearoom burst open, and Annie appeared with an enormous smile and a bouquet of flowers. Carl brought up the rear waving a bottle of wine in each hand, followed by Bridget, Mary, and Joe.

'You didn't think we'd let you celebrate the fact that you're now officially a woman of independent means on your own did you?' Carl beamed. 'Now where will I find a corkscrew?'

The next morning, Isla was glad she hadn't overindulged as she began the task of clearing up. The empty bottles of wine and the greasy fish and chip papers were leftovers from last night's impromptu celebration. It had been such a lovely surprise, though. She'd been touched that Carl too, had made the journey from Christchurch. It was a shame David was away on business, but it had provided Carl with the perfect excuse to come and join in the celebration. She smiled. Gran had been especially chuffed to see him, behaving like a dowager duchess as he fussed around her.

Isla had risen early this morning, eager to get over to the tearoom, or café as she'd announced to everyone it was going to be referred to from now on, during last night's party. She'd wanted to roll up her sleeves and get to work. Her dad would be calling by in half an hour or so with his trailer to pick up the tables and chairs and any other bits and bobs she'd decided to sell. Annie, Carl, and Kris had headed home last night with promises of popping by to give her a hand too. If she'd thought that she'd be embarking on her new venture alone, then she'd been wrong. That was why when she heard the knock on the door and not her father's tell-tale General Lee horn she assumed it was the three of them reporting for duty, and flung the door open. 'How're the heads troops – oh! Hi, it's Callum, isn't it?'

He nodded and smiled.

Isla stared at him wondering what he was doing here. 'I'm not open yet, sorry.' She pointed to the sign.

'I know, but a little bird told me you might need a hand moving some stuff out today.' He was dressed in a sweatshirt that had seen better days, a pair of jeans with holes in the knees, and sneakers. It was a complete contrast to the smooth looking man in a suit she'd met when he'd come into the café with Saralee.

Isla frowned. She knew who the little bird, or rather birdies, were. She'd put money on Annie having been in Kris' ear getting him to play cupid in the staffroom at Bibury Area School.

'Don't look so dubious, I might be in the teaching profession, but I can assure you I'm a man of many skills, and I'm here at your service,' he said winking.

Isla thought once again how cute he was and hoped her nostrils weren't flaring as she tried to pinpoint the name of his aftershave. She was sure it was Davidoff, Cool Water – one of her favourites. 'Well, I can't turn down an offer like that, now can I? I was just about to have a coffee before I get stuck in,' she replied lying through her teeth. 'Would you like one?'

'I wouldn't say no.' He closed the door behind them.

He was easy to talk to, Isla thought, sipping her hot drink; and he'd asked her about herself first too, not launched straight into a 'me, me, me' monologue. He'd scored brownie points for that. Plus he had gorgeous eyes. They were an unusual hazel colour and contrasted strikingly with his dark hair. He knew a bit of her backstory now so it was only fair he shared his. 'Where are you from originally?'

'I'm a born and bred Christchurch boy.'

'My old playground. How're you settling into life in Bibury?'

'It's a great little town.'

She raised an eyebrow over the rim of her mug.

'What? It is. The kids are awesome. They're different to city kids.'

'Really?'

'Oh yeah definitely, they're not in such a rush to grow up

in the country. But I'll admit it's been kind of hard to get to know people. I suppose it'd be different if I were married and had kids. That would open doors but hey,' he said shrugging. 'It is what it is.'

'Do you live by yourself?'

'No, I share a house near the school with Jeremy Cramer who's the high school PE teacher. It works pretty well, but socially he's more into planning his next marathon than getting out on the town. Most weekends I head back to Christchurch and stay with friends.'

'Ooh, I see. You're a party boy then?'

'I'll admit to having a "stuck at home on a Saturday night with nothing to do" phobia. What about you, what do you do for fun *in these here parts*?'

She smiled at the Southern drawl he'd affected. 'Well, I go to the Pit occasionally.'

This time it was Callum who raised an eyebrow.

'I know it sounds sad, but a pub is a pub. It's the company you're there with that counts. You should come down and see for yourself.'

'If that's an invitation to join you and your friends at the salubrious Pit the next time you decide to go, then I'd love to take you up on it.'

Isla grasped that he was flirting with her. She was so rusty she hoped she didn't squeak, but two could play at that game. 'Deputy Packer, you would be more than welcome to join us at said salubrious drinking establishment, the Pit tonight. That's if you haven't already made plans?'

'Nothing I can't change.'

Isla smiled shyly across the table at him. They would have held each other's gaze in silent, pleased acknowledgment of just having made a date had the Dixie tune not gate-crashed the moment.

'Come on, I'll introduce you to my dad.'

Callum helped carry the tables outside with Joe, lifting them onto the back of the trailer, while Isla stacked the chairs and carried the boxes over to them to load up. Isla was grateful the weather although cold was clear.

'That's it for this run,' Joe said closing the back of the trailer a short while later.

'Do you want a hand unloading it at the other end, Joe?'

'No thanks, you carry on here. My mate's around home doing some engine work on the Harley for me; he'll help.' Joe kissed Isla on the cheek before climbing behind the wheel. 'Back soon love.'

Isla could have kicked him as he winked and said far too loudly, 'Don't blow this one aye?'

He sounded the horn again as he drove off and she cringed. 'I wish his mate would disable that bloody thing. Oh, look!' With her dad's Toyota no longer blocking her view she saw a tiny black kitten sitting in the middle of the road. At the same time, she registered Ben's tow truck travelling towards it. She waited for a beat, but he wasn't slowing, and instinctively she stepped out into the road as Callum hollered at her to watch out. Isla was oblivious as she swooped down and scooped the kitten up. There was the smell of burning rubber and the sound of screeching brakes, but the kitten purred in her arms, not in the least bit phased by the unfolding drama.

'What're you doing, you madwoman?' A familiar, furious voice yelled.

Isla went over to the open window of the tow truck. 'I was worried you might hit this wee fellow.' She showed him the little black bundle in her arms.

'So you'd rather I knock you down instead?' Ben shook his head. 'Unfrigginbelievable!'

'Don't shout at me Ben Robson, you were driving too bloody fast!'

Callum, hearing the shouting, came and stood protectively beside her. 'I tried to stop her, but she was on a rescue mission.'

Ben frowned. 'It's Callum Packer, isn't it? The new Deputy Principal.'

'Yeah, not so new now though. I've been there since the start of the year.'

'Oh right.'

He was acting like a surly prat, Isla thought and not doing his bit to sell how friendly the locals were to Callum.

'You're Saralee's boyfriend, right?'

'We're friends yeah. I'm Ben,' he added reluctantly with a nod at Callum. 'I've got a job to get too. I'll see you around. And have a look before you run out into the middle of the road next time, Isla.' He closed the window before Isla could say a word and drove off. If her hands hadn't been full holding the kitten, she'd have flicked him the birdy.

'He's a bit of an oddball.'

'No, Ben's all right. It was my fault. I gave him a fright, that's all.'

'You gave me a fright too.'

'Sorry.' She gave him a sheepish grin. 'I wonder where this little chap lives.'

'*He* might be a girl.'

'Only a boy would play chicken like that.' Isla tickled him under her chin. 'You're a silly boy, yes you are.'

'Well, he's got no collar on him. Put him down on the pavement, he might make his way home.'

Isla did so. 'Off you go, homey-home.'

The kitten blinked at her with its blue eyes and mewed, but she turned her back and headed back to the café.

Callum watched with bemusement. 'I think you've made a friend.'

Isla looked back over her shoulder to find the kitten trotting along behind her.

Chapter 21

Isla cradled in one arm the kitten she'd begun calling Coal, having decided that was an appropriate interim name, and locked the door of the café with her other. It had been a productive day, she thought with satisfaction as she crossed the road and headed home. Annie, Kris, and Carl had shown up at lunchtime with sandwiches Annie had made, and Callum had stayed on sharing in the picnic. The café was now an empty, scrubbed shell of its former self. The magic could begin, once she'd organized somebody to wave their wand and do it. 'Oh, Coal, there's so much to do.' Isla tickled him under his chin and smiled as he arched his little neck enjoying the fuss. 'First things first, though, we need to see if Gran will let you stay until we can find out where you came from.'

'Gran, I'm home, and I've got someone I want you to meet.' Isla popped her head around the living-room door. Bridget peered over the top of her glasses, from where she was sitting in her recliner reading a magazine.

'Good day, dear?'

'A great day, Gran and this ...' she said coming into the room and holding Coal out towards Bridget, '... is Coal.'

The kitten cried hello, and Bridget's eyes widened. 'He's tiny. Where on earth did you find him?'

Isla relayed the story of how they'd met, leaving out Ben's churlish behaviour.

'Well, you should go and check the community notices board at the Four Square to see if anybody's missing him and if there's nothing there, put a notice on the board yourself with our telephone number on it. I suppose he can stay with us for a few days if there's no sign of anyone looking for him but you'll need to pick up a bag of kitty litter and some food for him.'

'Aw thanks, Gran, you're the best. Will you keep an eye on him while I zip over there now?'

'Oh alright, bring him here.'

Her brusque tone didn't fool Isla – she was itching for a cuddle, and she smiled as Bridget tickled behind his ear and said, 'You'd better behave yourself, young man. I'm too old for any nonsense, and if you so much as think of climbing the furniture there will be bother.'

Coal promptly shot off her lap and scampered up the arm of the settee. Isla beat a hasty retreat.

Lugging the bag of kitty litter and other supplies in through the front door twenty minutes later, Isla heard a shout from the living room and cringed. Coal had probably just made a deposit of some description. There had been no lost pet notice on the board at the supermarket, and so she'd penned a brief description of the little black kitten along with their phone number, pinning it to the board. She already knew as she trawled the aisles looking for kitten accessories, that she was hoping no-one would claim him and that she could convince Gran to let her keep him. Now she dropped her bags and opened the living room door in trepidation hoping he hadn't just marked his card, or the carpet, permanently.

'Sorry Gran, I'll clean it up.'

'What are you on about?'

Coal was curled up on Bridget's lap looking like butter wouldn't melt. Spying Isla, he jumped down and ran to her, mewling. Bridget looked decidedly agitated, and Isla wondered what had happened. 'Are you alright?'

She waved her hand impatiently. 'I'm fine. When you've sorted him out with some dinner can you fetch your computer? I need you to gurgle something for me.'

Despite her concern, Isla laughed. 'Google something you mean?' She bent down and scooped Coal up.

'That's what I said. I've had an idea, and I think it's rather a good one. I take it there was nothing on the notice board then?'

Isla shook her head. 'Nope and I put a notice up with our number on it. Come on Coal, lets' get you fed. I'll be back in a sec with my laptop, Gran.'

Coal wasted no time diving into the bowl of food Isla put down on a sheet of newspaper for him by the back door. He was obviously famished, poor wee fellow. Isla finished shaking out kitty litter into the plastic tray she'd purchased. She'd put it in the laundry and would introduce him to it properly once she'd figured out what had gotten Gran so hot under the collar.

'Right Gran, ready when you are,' Isla said a few minutes later when the laptop was open on the coffee table.

'I want you to gurgle Lisdoonvarna,' Bridget said.

Isla decided to let the mispronunciation go this time as she typed in the letters Bridget was spelling out for her. 'Okay hang on a sec, ah right, here we go. According to Wikipedia, it's a spa town in County Clare with eight hundred and twenty-two people living in it as of the 2002 census. What about it?'

'Let me have a read of that, and you can have a read of this.' Bridget held her hands out for the computer and balancing it on her lap, she passed Isla her magazine folded over to the page she'd been reading. 'It's my *Ireland Today* magazine, it comes quarterly. Why's the screen gone black?'

Isla retrieved the search and showed Bridget how to use the laptop's arrow keys. Once she had the hang of scrolling down, Isla turned her attention to the magazine frowning as she read the headline. 'Gran, I've been back from the UK less than four months, and you're already dropping hints about me heading off to some Matchmaking Festival over in Ireland.'

'No, no, you silly girl. Nobody's going to Ireland. I want us to organize a Matchmaking Festival right here in Bibury, at Barker's Creek Hall. We'll hold it on Valentine's Day, and the proceeds of the advance ticket sales will pay for the hall's renovation.'

'Pardon me?' Isla frowned, Bridget had a maniacal gleam in her eye.

'A Matchmaking Festival dear,' she explained patiently. 'It will run throughout the day on the grounds of the hall, and come the evening we'll hold a dance the likes of which Bibury hasn't seen since Clara, and I took a turn on the floor all those years ago. What better way in which to remember her?'

'Ah Gran, it's a novel idea and a lovely one too,' Isla said, but she was dubious. She began to skim over the article. It talked about how the tradition of matchmaking had been taking place in Lisdoonvarna for the last few hundred years. She looked up and said, 'It says here that the Irish festival runs over the course of six weeks beginning in September and that they have a genuine Matchmaker in attendance called Willie Daly. He says he is the one true Matchmaker left in Ireland. Oh, and he's a horse whisperer too.' She held the magazine up and pointed to the picture of an affable, grey-haired man sitting on a log with a string bound old book under his arm. Isla thought that he looked like someone you'd trust with the important business of finding you a spouse. 'But he's not likely to come here now, is he? The closest thing to a Matchmaker we have in Bibury would be Mick from the pub, and it's not his skills that get people together, it's the amount of beer he plies them with.'

'True enough and yes, I suppose this Mr Daly would be a busy man in his neck of the woods. We could advertise, though, couldn't we?'

'Advertise a six-week position as Bibury's official Matchmaker?'

'No, you're missing the point Isla, not six weeks, one day.

We'd hold the festival in the day and the dance in the evening, and I don't see why we couldn't advertise.'

'I'll tell you why not, because you'll be inundated with weirdos.'

Bridget conceded Isla's point, brightening as she had a thought. 'What about asking Samuel West? Do you remember him? He does a lovely Father Christmas at the Four Square each year.'

'Good grief! He's not still dressing up in that red suit, is he? He was prancing around in that when I was a kid, and he seemed ancient then.' He'd made a very dodgy Santa in Isla's opinion because everybody knew the real Father Christmas didn't have red whiskers nor an eye for the young ladies.

'Yes he is, and he's younger than me. I'm sure he'd be up for the craic, as the Irish say.'

Isla decided to humour her. 'Alright then, but who do you think will come to this one-day festival? Are you planning on rounding up all the pig hunters and getting them to come down from the hills in search of a bride?'

'Sarcasm is the lowest form of wit, young lady.'

'I wasn't being sarcastic.' Isla thought of the black singlet and shorts crew who regularly propped up the bar of the Pit.

'Yes well, every pig hunter needs a bride and preferably one who is not a boar.'

'Oh, Gran that's terrible.' Isla had to join in her laughter, though.

'I'm thinking more globally than Bibury. Well, at least as far as Christchurch. Carl must know lots of glamorous single ladies in his line of work?'

'I'm sure he does but what would be the lure to get them to come here to meet their match? We'd need lots of eligible bachelors to entice them, and I don't think there are that many to go around on the Coast.'

Bridget frowned, wracking her brains. She was determined not to be thwarted where her festival idea was concerned.

'Although, Carl did say his boyfriend David spends lots of time at the gym. I bet there are lots of buff chaps looking to meet their match there.' Isla felt a frisson of excitement; perhaps Gran was onto something. It could be fun, and if they could pull it off, it'd bring a lot of people to Bibury. As a new business owner in the town that could only be a good thing! 'I have to say the idea is growing on me Gran, and I'd love to sit here and plot, but I need to show Coal where his litter tray is before it's too late. Then, I've got to get ready for my date. I'm going to the Pit and meeting up with Callum, Annie, Kris and Carl, so I'll mention this festival idea to Carl and the others tonight, see what they think.'

'Right, back up a moment. Just who exactly is this Callum fellow when he's at home?'

The pub was busy. Isla scanned the room and spotted Callum up at the bar. She didn't appreciate until then that she'd been feeling uptight in case he'd changed his mind. Her stomach gave an involuntary flutter. He was rather attractive, she thought, making her way over.

The black singlet brigade had swapped their singlets for Swanndri bush shirts worn over the top of their shorts, she noticed, ignoring their leers. Isla hadn't seen one of those in a long time. Their tartan design should have been put forward when all that hoo-ha was going on about a new flag design for New Zealand, because the Swanndri was as Kiwi as, well, as the Kiwi.

She grinned up at Callum. 'You made it.'

'I wouldn't miss it.' He leaned down and gave her a kiss on the cheek. 'You look lovely by the way. What would you like to drink?'

'Thanks.' Isla realized it had been a long time since she'd been given a straightforward compliment, one that wasn't followed up with a 'but' and left her feeling that somehow she'd gotten it wrong once again. It felt good, and she smiled brightly at him. She'd come a long way in a short time. Rita would be proud of her. 'Um, I'm a Sauvignon girl please.'

She scanned the room to try and spot a free table with enough seats for the others to join them too and saw a familiar face beaming over at her. Saralee was waving madly trying to catch her eye. She was sitting at a table with Ben near the pool tables, and there was no possible polite way in which she could ignore her. 'Callum, you'd know Saralee from school. I think she wants us to go over and say hi.'

She knew Callum was thinking about their encounter with Ben that afternoon, but she admired him all the more for smiling and saying, 'Great, lead the way.'

'Hi guys, pull up a seat and join us,' Saralee dimpled up at them both. Isla felt decidedly two-faced as Callum fetched a seat for her and she found herself sitting next to the pretty blonde. This was going to be uncomfortable, she thought, attempting a smile over at Ben. To her surprise, he seemed to have gotten over his pique with her because he smiled back. Perhaps this wouldn't be so bad after all; she took a tentative sip of her wine. Callum and Saralee were already chatting away about one of the little chaps in the juniors and his penchant for pinching food out of the other kids' lunch boxes. Isla looked at Ben. His hair was damp, he must have come out straight from a shower. She wondered if he still used the same shampoo, and fought the urge to lean over to see if he smelt like apples. *Cut it out Isla*; she cast around for something to say. 'I took the kitten I saved home, and I've called him Coal. I'm hoping no one claims him because he's such a sweetie.'

'So, he was worth nearly being flattened for then.'

His smile softened his words, and Isla smiled back at him. 'Definitely.' She spotted three familiar faces walking in and waved over at them before turning her attention back to Ben. 'You wouldn't happen to know of any good builders, would you?' She explained the changes she had in mind for the café's interior.

'What about Hayden?'

'Hayden, as in your brother Hayden?'

'The one and only.'

'I'd forgotten he's a builder. How's he getting on these days?'

'Yeah, he's great. He wound up marrying Joanne Coombes, do you remember her?'

Isla nodded. 'Oh yeah, Joanne was one of the cool girls a few years ahead of me that I used to idolize. I so wanted to get my fringe permed like hers.'

Ben laughed. 'Yeah well, she keeps her hair pretty short

these days, they've got two kids now. A boy, Harry who's five and three-year-old Amelie. They live over in Greymouth. I'll give him a call if you want and see how he's placed. You might be in luck because this time of year's not usually mad busy. I assume you want to crack on with it as soon as possible?'

'That'd be great, and yeah I want to get things moving along. It's all happened so fast, I don't know where to begin.'

'It'll work out, and if Hayden has got too much on, he'll know of someone else who can fit it in. From what you've said to me it doesn't sound too big a job. Leave it to me, I'll sort it.'

'Thanks, Ben, I appreciate it,' Isla enthused feeling warm under his gaze as he smiled back at her.

Chapter 22

'Hello, all,' Carl said announcing his arrival while Annie and Kris looked around for a couple more chairs. Nabbing one each, they dragged them over to the table. When everybody had been introduced and was settled with their drink in front of them, Isla relayed Bridget's grand plan.

Blank faces looked back at her when she finished talking, but Carl's eyes lit up. 'Okay, so this is how I've got it straight in my head.' He tittered, and Annie rolled her eyes. 'Stay with me people, and think Tinder before technology. Back in the day in certain parts of Ireland, the business of matchmaking was pretty much an arranged marriage. Isla's great-great-grandparents met through a Matchmaker in Cork.' The way he crossed his legs and sat back in his chair said he was enjoying being in the know.

'It's a bit different nowadays but what Carl says is true. Here, have a look.' Isla fished Bridget's *Ireland Today* magazine out of her bag and flicking to the right page, passed it to Annie who was sitting beside her. It went around the table, and Kris was the first to speak in his accented and careful English. 'I think this festival sounds like it could be fun.'

Annie shot him a look. 'You've already found your match, Mister.'

He grinned back at her and gave her hand a squeeze.

'I agree, it does sound fun but how would it work?' Callum asked.

'Well, my gran's thinking is that it'd be a one-day extravaganza. A festival and dance. She figures the money raised from pre-ticket sales would go towards bringing the hall up to date in time for Valentine's Day. The festival part would run during the day with a Matchmaker in residence and then in the evening a Valentine's Day Dance would be held for those who've made matches to get to know one another better. Gran wants the dance to be dedicated to the memory of her friend, Clara.'

'Who's Clara?' Ben asked frowning.

Carl, Kris, and Annie listened again as Isla told the other three squished around the table Clara's story. They all agreed it was a tragic ending to a short life.

'I've never heard that story before.' Ben was bemused. 'It's weird because I thought I knew most of the mining folklore from around here.'

'I know, I thought it was strange Gran had never mentioned it to me before too,' Isla said shrugging. 'Maybe she found it too painful to talk about it until now. I don't know but either way, I could tell by the look on her face tonight, she's determined to hold this festival in Clara's name.'

'Well, if Bridget's got a bee in her bonnet then it'll happen,' Ben said.

'I told her I'd put the idea out there and see what you all

thought. Personally, I think it'd breathe a bit of life back into Bibury and I, for one, could do with all the help I can get in that department what with the café.'

'I think it's a fantastic idea,' Saralee ventured. 'I was a secretary at an events management company in Christchurch when I first left school. I picked up plenty of pointers, and I'd love to help organize the festival ... that's if you want some help?' Her voice trailed off shyly.

Isla's eyes widened, but before she could reply Carl announced that Bridget could count him in on her plan.

'I shall spread the word amongst the skinny gals of the modelling world. I think a few of them could do with snaffling some proper food like the wild boar on the back of the truck out there.' He gestured at the exit and car park beyond, his eyes taking on a glazed look. 'Grilled over a campfire by a real Southern man.'

'He's been watching Bear Grylls again,' Annie muttered.

For Isla's part, she was assailed by a mental picture of the Barker's Creek Hall full of super models and pig hunters; it made her mouth twitch. She remembered her conversation with her gran earlier. 'Carl, I wondered whether David might get some excitement going amongst the single men at the gym. You mentioned he spends a lot of time there.'

'Lives there, you mean and oh yes, he's good at doing that all right.' Carl pursed his lips. 'I shall tell him to start putting it about.'

Isla choked back a laugh because he was quite serious.

'You could call it Project Matchmaker,' Kris said looking pleased with himself before his forehead creased into a frown.

'But there is a problem I think. Who will be the Matchmaker?'

'Ah well, Gran mentioned Sam West.'

'Who's Sam West?' Annie piped up.

'The dodgy Four Square Santa,' Isla replied glumly.

Ben smirked putting his pint glass down on the table before patting his knee. 'Come and sit on my knee, young lady and tell Santa what it is you're after for Christmas,' he leered.

'Ugh don't! You do that a bit too well!' Isla laughed. 'Oh well, at least it's ages away. Someone else more suitable might turn up between now and next Valentine's Day.'

'Believe me; we're going to need all that time if we're going to do this thing properly,' Saralee stated, counting the months off on her fingers. 'We've got just under nine months to put together the biggest festival ever to hit Bibury.'

Isla smiled at her enthusiasm and looked round the table at the excited faces; it would seem that Project Matchmaker had just got the green light.

Isla came out of the toilet cubicle and saw Saralee was at the mirror reapplying her lip gloss. 'Hi,' she said squirting soap on her hands. 'Are you enjoying your night?'

'Yes thanks, I'm glad you guys could join us and congratulations on the café by the way. I meant to say that earlier, but then we got side-tracked with Project Matchmaker. Good on you. It must be exciting being the owner of your very own business.'

'Thanks.' The genuine sentiment touched Isla. 'It is. It's scary too but it helps to have Annie on board. And thanks for volunteering your services for the festival. My gran's going to be so excited when I tell her it's going full steam ahead. We're going to need all the help we can get, especially as I'm going to be snowed under for a bit getting the café up and running too.' Isla still couldn't quite believe everything that had happened since she'd got home. 'Ben's going to talk to his brother about the building work that needs doing. I've got my fingers crossed he's available.'

'That's good.' Saralee put the cap back on her gloss and slid it into her denim jacket pocket.

Isla shook the water from her hands and headed over to the hand dryer. 'I'm curious as to what brought you to Bibury, Saralee? You said you worked in Christchurch when you left school. Is that where you're from?'

'Uh-huh, I grew up just outside of the city and moved in closer when I left school. I went to London for a year, and when I came back, I found it hard to settle down.'

It echoed her journey in a roundabout way, Isla thought, glancing over to where the other girl was leaning against the sink.

'My boyfriend at the time got work in Greymouth, and I followed him there. I liked the Coast it felt like home. It's a special part of the world I think. The people are friendly and so laid back. Anyway, he wasn't so enamoured with the Coast or me because he broke things off between us and went back to Christchurch. I didn't know what I wanted to do but then the job at Bibury Area School came up, and I decided to give it a go here,' she explained with a grin. 'I'm a small-town girl at heart; I love it here.'

'And then you met Ben.'

'Yeah, he's a nice guy. And hey, speaking of nice guy's, I was surprised to see you here with Callum.' Her eyes were alight with curiosity.

Isla shrugged. 'He told me he spends most weekends back in Christchurch, but he's keen to get to know more people in Bibury. That's not going to happen if he never ventures out here, so I invited him along tonight.'

'I asked him to join Ben and I for a drink here not long after I started seeing him, but I think he thought he'd be a third wheel. He's a catch, great at his job too, the older kids have a real respect for him. Maybe it's his age; they feel they can relate to him or something.'

'You're probably right. When I was at school, the deputy head Miss Seastrand always seemed ancient, and her mission in life was to eradicate all usage of mascara between the hours of nine am and three pm; that and to catch all smokers red-handed. I don't think she had any interest in our education as such, she'd have been far better off taking on a dictatorship in a small foreign country.'

Saralee giggled. 'You're funny. I can see why Ben thinks you're great.'

Isla flushed, and it wasn't down to the heat of the hand-dryer. 'Does he?'

'Yeah, but then you two go way back.' It was said without guile.

'I guess we do. He's pretty taken with you, I can tell.'

'Do you think? We're not serious. He's a lovely guy, but I don't see it going much further, to be honest.' This time Saralee shrugged and smiled. 'Hey, and that's okay. He's not bad in the sack, and Mr Right will come along when he's good and ready. Who knows? Maybe I'll meet him at the Matchmaker Festival. In the meantime, we enjoy each other's company amongst other things.' She winked. 'You ready?'

Isla followed the other girl back inside the pub with an open mouth. She was taken aback both by the revelation that the relationship between Saralee and Ben wasn't serious and the fact she'd just told her the sex was good. For one thing, the thought of the latter made her feel very peculiar and for another Saralee simply did not look like a woman who would say stuff like that. She looked like a children's television presenter, not somebody who would enjoy casual sex. She shook her head; it was true that you couldn't judge a book by its cover, she thought.

The courtesy wagon took Annie and Kris home despite Kris having sat on a couple of pints all evening. It wasn't worth getting behind the wheel, he said, not with the drink driving limits being so low. Isla felt the same way. She'd sat on a lemon, lime & bitters for the last hour but Mick's pours were generous, and she'd not long had Delilah. She didn't want to run the risk of not being able to drive her.

The Bibury cop, Tep, was very zealous Ben had told them all as he and Saralee had shrugged into their puffer jackets and set off home on foot. Isla watched them head out the door with a pang. *They're probably going back to his place for some good sex.* Callum distracted her from this line of thought by puffing up chivalrously and offering to walk her home; she didn't object even though she knew it would be freezing outside. She didn't object either when he draped an arm around her shoulder as they set off.

They chatted companionably under the street lights. One lone boy racer did a wheelie up ahead of them. 'Where's Mr Zealous Cop when you need him?' Isla muttered as a dog barked in one of the gardens they walked past, causing her to jump.

'So much for peaceful country living,' Callum said with a grin.

When they got to her gate, she paused. 'Well, this is me.' She hovered, uncertain as to what she was supposed to do next. It had been a long time since she'd been in the predicament of standing at the front gate with a man at the end of the evening.

'Thanks for inviting me tonight. It was good to get to know my colleagues a bit better, and you were right, Ben's an okay guy when you get talking to him.'

'I'm glad you enjoyed it.' The atmosphere turned awkward as Isla's hand rested on the gate latch. *Would he try and kiss her or wouldn't he?* And then his lips were on hers, and his arms snaked around her waist as he pulled her close. He was a nice kisser; she thought losing herself in the sensation. He broke away first, and his voice was hoarse as he said, 'Goodnight Isla.'

'Night,' she said smiling all the way to the front door, knowing he would stand there at the gate until she was safely inside. He was a gentleman. She gave him one last wave before closing the front door and still had a silly grin on her face when she felt something squish beneath her foot. She didn't have to look to know what it was; she could smell it. The culprit was peering around the kitchen door at the end of the hall and mewling a greeting.

Chapter 23

'Are you going to sleep with him? You've been seeing him for a while now. I slept with Kris the second time I met him,' Annie said from Delilah's passenger seat.

'Trollop!' Isla grinned. 'And I will when the time is right.'

'What was the movie like last night?'

'It was a laugh, but I laughed more when I told Gran what we'd been to see. She said, and I quote, "She's a good actress that Sandra Bollock." I said "it's Bullock, not Bollock, Gran" and she looked at me and said, "don't lower the tone Isla, that's what I said."' Isla kept her eyes fastened on the curves of the road ahead of her as Annie chuckled. They were driving into Christchurch for supplies for the café. It was less than a week until showtime. The time had flown by since Ben's builder brother, Hayden, had come on board and taken things in hand. He'd been fantastic, and she made a note to drop a bottle of something nice into the garage for Ben as a thank you for teeing him up to do the refurb.

It hadn't been a big job, but she'd have been lost without him. The new chunky wooden counter he'd fitted along with the fireplace looked wonderful. He'd taken all the stress out of organizing a painter too, roping in a guy he could vouch for at short notice. The floor sander he'd booked had done a brilliant, albeit messy, job of bringing the original boards back to life too. She was over the moon with the result. Annie had spent her time devising menus and helping source all the finishing touches of memorabilia and furnishings, as well as cleaning up the dust and debris left behind from the works in progress. She'd refused to take any pay until the café reopened, insisting it was a labour of love. Isla was planning on springing for a luxury weekend getaway for her and Kris as a thank you. It would have to wait until she was up and running and able to cope without her right-hand woman for a few days, though!

Finding the perfect name for the café had been a mission in itself. Isla wanted to put her stamp on it, and there had been a wastepaper basket full of discarded paper with lists of potential names scribbled out. She'd wanted to steer away from mining themes, despite having the photographs of the old days in Bibury and other mining memorabilia on display. She felt that with the Coalminer Tavern already up the road, it would have been overkill. Names like Isla's Inn and the Coaster's Café had all been vetoed, and it had been a relief when Isla had looked up from the foodie magazine she was reading and said, 'What about Nectar?'

'Nectar,' Annie repeated. 'I like it. Where did you get that from?'

'An advert for honey, see?' She grinned and showed Annie the picture of the tub of honey proclaiming itself to be *nectar* from the Gods.

It fitted the delicious food they had in mind to serve in the café, although Annie reckoned it was probably a good thing Noeline was currently on a ship floating about on the Pacific Ocean. She'd most certainly have had something to say about the change of name.

Isla was having a party to say thank you for all the support she'd received, next Friday afternoon. The café would officially open for business the following morning. She'd advertised a free slice with every hot drink purchased as an opening day special, everywhere she could think of, and was hopeful for a successful day. Friday night would also be the big reveal because in the last couple of weeks anyone who wasn't Annie or a tradesperson hadn't been allowed through the front door.

Today though, the girls planned on hitting the gourmet food stores once they reached the city followed by a lunch date at Annie's parents' home. After lunch, there was a whole-foods shop over the on the Rivers' side of town that they needed to visit. They planned on having dinner with Carl and David. Isla was looking forward to meeting up with them all. They'd been invited to stay the night and she'd accepted the offer gratefully, not keen to navigate these twisty pass roads in the dark. Kris had opted to stay well away from this girls' day out, and besides, Annie said he would be grateful for the peace. He had end-of-term school reports to be getting on with.

The girls crossed the road from Piko's where they'd had a very successful shopping trip sourcing a lot of their specialty ingredients, and Isla placed the box of food onto Delilah's backseat.

A few minutes later the red Mini waited to join the flow of traffic down Kilmore Street.

'Gosh, it all seems chaotic after Bibury doesn't it? I can't believe I used to live here,' Annie muttered. 'You're clear,' she said looking back over her shoulder.

'I know, it's amazing how quickly you can get used to living in the country,' Isla agreed.

Annie was chief navigator as Isla found herself unable to recognize a lot of the city streets, post-quake. 'All my old landmarks are gone,' she said looking sadly over to where the old Saggio di Vino Tuscan-styled building used to be.

They pulled up outside the Rivers' house just after 1.30. It was a brick home in a tree-lined suburb. Isla glanced around at the neighbourhood. It was well-kept, but the trees without their foliage looked a little forlorn this time of year.

She was distracted by Annie's mum flinging the front door open as she stood waiting to greet them. Liz was softly padded, cuddly. She was like a watercolour version of Annie, Isla thought, before she was caught up in a hello hug. She'd seen the deep sadness lurking in her soft green eyes, or at least she thought she had. Perhaps Isla was being fanciful because she knew Mrs Rivers had had a daughter that died. The loss of your child wasn't something Isla could imagine. She knew, though, it would be something you never got over but rather had to learn to live alongside. Annie's dad, the larger than life Pete dropped the fact he worked in real estate into the conversation straight off the bat, and his wife told him off.

'He's always working the room, looking for angles.'

'It's all part of the job, Liz, it's called networking. Besides, this young lady owes me; she pipped me to the post by buying Aunty Noeline's tearoom before she could list it with me.' He winked at Isla. 'And if I don't mention what I do for a living then I could miss out on a potential client. For all I know, Isla here might have come back from London all cashed up and looking for a city pad investment as well as a business.'

'Are you looking for a city pad dear?'

'No, I'm not, the café has stretched me to my limit but thank you anyway.' Isla's eyes swung between the pair.

'There you go, now leave the poor girl alone Pete.'

Pete, Isla could tell by the time she was halfway through her quiche, was a man of opinions. He had opinions on the Christchurch City Council and how they were handling the city's rebuild. He had opinions on the neighbours' proposed extension and he had opinions on the cost of living. He also had a good sense of humour, glimpses of which came through when he veered from informing them that the price of lamb in this country was an abomination to tales of his clients' unreasonable demands, making them all laugh.

Liz fluttered around them all making sure everybody had enough to eat and drink, but Annie seemed a little out of sorts, Isla noticed. She wasn't tucking into her lunch with much relish given that it was delicious and they hadn't eaten since they left Bibury. She'd ask her about it later.

The girls helped to clear up and then sat chatting while Liz rustled up coffee in a spacious but dated sitting room, with echoes of the eighties resounding in its pink and grey colour scheme. A framed portrait of two girls on the wall beside the log burner caught Isla's eye. Annie was instantly recognizable with her red hair hanging in two plaits on either side of a sweet, freckled face. Her two front teeth were missing, and she looked to be around five or six years old. The girl next to her must be Roz, Isla realized. She was a blonde, teenage beauty forever frozen in time. There was obviously a sizable age gap between the sisters but then that made sense given that Carl was a good nine or ten years older than Annie.

Liz came into the room carrying a tray of steaming mugs and followed her gaze.

'They were very different, your girls,' Isla said flushing at being caught, but Liz smiled and glanced up at the picture before putting the tray down on the coffee table.

'They were, chalk and cheese, but Annie absolutely idolized her sister when she was little. She was like her shadow, following her everywhere. Roz never minded,' she said with a gentle smile.

'I was so jealous of Roz's blonde hair. I mean look,' Annie pointed at the portrait. 'It's like looking at a photograph of Pippi Longstocking and Barbie.'

Isla couldn't help but laugh at the analogy.

'Annie got her colouring from my side of the family. My great-grandmother Maggie was a true redhead,' Liz explained.

'She's got a lot to answer for, that Maggie,' Annie muttered.

Liz smiled fondly at her daughter, and Isla was once more taken aback at the resemblance between the two of them.

A plate of caramel slice was offered around, which Isla was only too happy to help herself to. She had a weakness for anything gooey made with condensed milk.

'Yum,' Annie mumbled with her mouth full. 'You remembered it's my favourite. I'm glad to see you're not on one of your diets, Mum.'

'Come Monday, I shall be going Paleo. I put on four kilograms on our last cruise and I can't shift it. I wonder how Noeline's managing on the Pacific Pearl. She can't say no to a cream cake at the best of times, let alone when they're there for the taking morning, noon and night.'

Annie smirked. 'Poor you Dad, caveman fodder on the menu for the foreseeable future.'

Over her coffee, Isla brought up the subject of the Matchmaker Festival. Her gran and Saralee had said it wasn't too soon to start spreading the word and with the date being Valentine's Day, it was an easy one to remember even if it was months away. Liz listened with her head cocked to one side while Pete made a few snorting noises. Nevertheless, he promised to put a bundle of tickets at the front desk of his real estate office when they'd been printed up. Never one to miss a chance, it was in exchange for a stack of his business cards and a promise that should either girl hear of anybody thinking of moving, they pass on one of his cards. Liz thought the girls at the supermarket where she worked part-time would think it was a fabulous idea. 'They're always lamenting the lack of single men around the city over their morning tea,' she informed them.

'So you like cruising?' Isla asked recalling Liz's comment about the weight she'd gained on the last trip they had done.

That was all the invitation needed and a photo album showing an airbrushed version of Pete and Liz in evening dress on the cover with a starry night and a cruise ship behind them was produced.

'These are the pics from the last one we did, ten days around Australia. It was fabulous, wasn't it Pete?'

He nodded and echoed the sentiment. 'Fabulous.'

Isla smiled recalling her conversation with Ben about how his parents were mad on cruising. She wondered if it was something to do with all those years spent raising a family and pondering what to make for dinner. Ten days of not having to do groceries or plan an evening meal would seem blissful.

Annie announced they should be making tracks when Liz asked if anybody would like another cup of coffee.

'Thanks, Mum, but Carl and David are expecting us around five, and we've still got a few more places to call in on.'

Isla got to her feet and followed her friend out to the kitchen to put their coffee cups next to the sink before heading to the front door.

'Thanks so much for lunch, it was lovely to meet you both.' Isla hugged Liz.

Pete came over and gave her a kiss on the cheek. 'And don't forget if any of your friends are thinking of buying or selling then Pete Rivers is the man for the job.'

'Dad!'

'Pete!'

'It's called networking, ladies.'

Chapter 24

'My feet are killing me. I hope Carl hasn't got any wild plans for tonight because I won't be able to stand the pace.' Annie said, getting out of the car.

'Me neither,' Isla agreed opening the boot to retrieve their overnight bags. The door to the sharply-angled, modern townhouse they'd just pulled up in front of swung open. Carl appeared in the wide entrance alongside a jaw-droppingly handsome man. Isla closed her mouth. That had to be David; she was instantly smitten.

'Welcome to Casa Carl, and David's,' Carl called before rushing forward and grabbing the bags from Isla and kissing her on both cheeks at the same time. He turned his attention to Annie, and Isla found herself sucking in her tummy and simpering a breathy 'hello' to David.

Carl rolled his eyes, announcing to no one in particular, 'He always has that effect on women.'

David laughed. 'Stop embarrassing her Carl. It's lovely to meet you, Isla. I've heard so much about you. You're every bit as stunning as Carl said you were. He told me you reminded him of a young Cindy Crawford and I think he's right, minus the mole of course.'

Isla preened and managed to say thank you.

'Annie Rivers, you gorgeous girl, come here.' David wrapped his gym-honed arms around Annie's small frame, and Isla wished she could swap places. Carl carted the bags into the house, urging them all to come inside and to stop standing out on the street putting a show on for the neighbours.

He continued to lead the charge ushering the girls through his and David's stylish and very white abode. Isla thought he was rather like a flight attendant doing his safety demonstration as he directed them towards the main points of interest. The kitchen, the living room, the bathroom, along with his and David's bedroom, before finally dropping their bags in the guest room. There was a double bed in the centre of the room with a plain white coverlet and an assortment of gorgeous looking cushions that blended in with the artwork on the wall behind the bed. It was all very tasteful, and exactly as she had imagined it would be, Isla thought with a happy sigh. Stylish, sleek and modern, Carl to a tee.

'You two will be top and tailing,' Carl informed them before clapping his hands. 'Chop, chop ladies, David's shaking up his famous margaritas as we speak.'

'Mm, this is good. You are a man of many talents, David.'

'Isla, your flirting is wasted on him,' Carl stated before draining his glass.

'Ignore him, he's just jealous,' David said with a wink at her. 'Now then girls, I've been mentioning the Matchmaker

Festival at the gym, and there's been a lot of interest. Partly because I've been telling the boys what Carl does for a living and that there's bound to be lots of models looking to make a match there. I've put an email sign-up list on the front desk too, and so far over fifty guys and a fair few gals have registered. So Isla, be sure to let me know when the tickets go on sale and I can send a mass email out to them.'

'Oh wow, that's fantastic thanks, David. Gran and Saralee will be so impressed when I tell them.'

Carl wasn't to be outdone. 'Well, be sure to tell them that I've not been resting on my proverbial either. I've been telling the girls there's bound to be a lot of buff bods from the gym making their way to Bibury next Valentine's Day.'

'Teamwork!' David and Carl cried high-fiving each other.

Isla couldn't help but giggle.

'I suppose you and Annie have been busy, busy, busy with Nectar, and not had much time for Project Matchmaker,' Carl lamented.

Isla nodded. 'I don't think Gran had any idea as to what a massive undertaking it would be. Saralee's been a godsend.'

Carl turned to David. 'Right, to keep you in the loop, this is the low down. Saralee is dating Ben who owns the local garage, but there's lots of simmering sexual tension between him and Isla. They've got history. In the meantime though, Isla's begun dating Callum who is the school's hot Deputy Principal.'

Isla opened her mouth to protest but then closed it. What was the point? She glanced over at Annie who looked highly amused at Carl's soap opera summary.

David raised an eyebrow. 'My, my there's more drama in Bibury than in an episode of Revenge.'

'Right guys and gals, where to for dinner? I thought we could try the new Italian on St Asaph Street,' Carl asked in an abrupt change of subject.

Annie and Isla looked at each other and shrugged. 'No good asking us. I don't know where anywhere is in Christchurch anymore,' Annie said.

'Me neither.' Isla agreed.

'I'm back on the high protein tomorrow as you know Carl, so I quite fancy an Italian blowout of epic proportions.' David drained his margarita. 'All those in favour of another round say aye?'

'Aye!' Came the chorused reply.

They rolled home from the restaurant, which had been a great pick on Carl's part, stuffed full of rich tomato-based pasta, garlic bread and tiramisu. It was sloshing around nicely with the bottles of red that had been knocked back with gusto. Their plans of hitting the newly emerging city's nightlife had been scuppered due to severe bloating.

'I don't even have enough room for a nightcap but girls, feel free.' Carl gestured to the liquor cabinet a bottle of Mylanta antacid in his other hand. Annie and Isla looked at each other and groaned.

'I think I'll go for a cuppa.'

'Ooh, a cup of tea bliss.'

'I'm off to the gym first thing, so I shall love you and leave you until the big reveal next Friday.' David said referring to

Nectar's grand opening in a week as he leant in and gave them both a garlicky kiss goodnight on the cheek before disappearing down the hall.

Carl yawned before saying, 'I'm with him. You know where everything is Annie. Our home is your home girls. Night, night, lovely ladies.'

Isla and Annie sat at opposite ends of the couch, feet curled under them, each clutching a mug of tea. On the mantle over the gas fire was a vase and couple of other expensive looking ornaments, but it was the framed photo of David and Carl that made Isla smile. It was a selfie by the look of it, and they both looked so happy. 'That's a lovely picture.'

'It is. They're like family to me, those two.'

'I've had a lovely day today.' Isla blew on her drink before taking a tentative sip.

'Me too.'

'Your folks are great. You seemed a little edgy while we were there though, is everything okay?'

'Yeah, Mum and Dad are great, although Dad has far too much to say for himself sometimes. He can be a little overpowering, but you'd have seen that for yourself,' she said with a half-smile. 'If I seemed a little out of sorts I suppose it's because as much as I love them both, I get a little claustrophobic around them sometimes. It's hard to explain, but there's this weight of responsibility I feel when I'm with them for still being here. Oh, I don't know, that probably doesn't make sense.' She shook her head. 'It's just there's this need I sense, especially from Mum, and it's a need I know I can never fill.'

'Your sister's death must have been so hard on you all.'

'Roz alive was hard on us all.'

Isla looked at her startled over the rim of her mug.

'She was into drugs, we never really understood why she went down that road, not when she had everything going for her.' Annie shrugged. 'Carl thinks it was the crowd she worked with, they were a party hard lot but at the end of the day, the how's and why's don't matter. She made her choices, and we lived with them for years. Her addiction nearly tore Mum and Dad apart. They tried everything to get her off the stuff, but she never met them halfway.' She chewed her bottom lip. 'Unless you've been through it, you can't understand what it's like to live on the edge all the time, waiting for something to happen. Then it finally did. She crashed her car after an all-night session. It was a blessing nobody else was hurt. She killed herself but she damned well nearly killed me, Carl Mum and Dad too.'

'I'm so sorry Annie.'

Annie raised a smile. 'You don't have to be sorry. It took me a long time to put the resentment and hurt aside but one day I understood that nobody gets a smooth run, it's not the way life rolls. It is messy and it is short and the only thing I could do was get on with the business of living. Carl's been a rock too.'

Isla put her tea down on the coffee table and reached over to give her friend a hug. Annie returned it but then pulled away with a sniff. 'It's fine. I'm okay. I made my peace with Roz when I ran away to Greece, and in a roundabout way, I have her to thank for my having met Kris.'

Isla reflected on what she'd just heard. Annie was right. Life was messy. 'I ran away once too, but for very different reasons,' she said telling Annie the story of her journey home.

'Oh wow, that all sounds so, so ...' Annie cast around for the right word as Isla's voice trailed off.

'Californian?'

'Yes, Californian. It obviously helped you though.'

'It did, it really did. I don't know if I'd have realized home was where I needed to be without those beanbag sessions with Rita.'

'Well I'm glad you're here and that you saw the light where that horrible Tim was concerned. He sounds a right prick.'

'Yeah he was, in hindsight, and a bullying one at that.'

'You really loved Ben, didn't you?'

'I did, and I didn't handle the break-up with him very well, Annie. I'm not proud of how I behaved.'

'It's ancient history.'

'I hope so.'

'Hug?'

'I'd love one.'

The two girls embraced once more, squeezing each other hard, and smiling as they separated. 'It's exhausting offloading.' Annie yawned before draining what was left of her cold tea.

'It is,' Isla agreed standing up and stretching. 'Time for bed I think.'

Chapter 25

David, as he'd told them he'd do the night before, had gone to the gym by the time Isla and Annie made an appearance the next morning. Carl suggested a café just a few minutes' walk down the road for breakfast, and it was after bagels and coffee that they said their goodbyes until Friday. It didn't take long to leave the city behind, and soon Delilah was sharing the road with numerous four-wheel drives. Each seemed to be filled with families no doubt making the trek to one of the lakes for the day or to explore Castle Hill's lunar landscape. A blue-skied day in winter brought the outdoorsy types out in droves.

Her eyes were gritty from lack of sleep; it had been well after two in the morning by the time she and Annie had crawled into bed. Now, she felt small and vulnerable in the Mini, as the oversized vehicles overtook them, one after the other. 'Nobody drives at the speed limit in this country,' she muttered with a scowl up at the driver of an overtaking big, shiny Jeep. 'Tosser!' she threw up at him, gripping the steering wheel. 'Sorry,' she said glancing over at Annie, but she was oblivious, her head lolling as she snoozed.

She elbowed Annie as they drove into Bibury. 'We're nearly home, wakey-wakey. I'll swing by the café first and drop the stuff in the back off, then I'll drop you home, okay?'

Annie yawned and nodded. 'Thanks, sorry I made such a lousy co-pilot.'

The main street in Bibury was quiet, Isla noticed as she drove to the café. It was so quiet she could visualize tumble-weed blowing down the road like in the cowboy flicks. It was Sunday, but still, it didn't bode well for business. She pulled over outside Nectar and, getting out of the car, she told herself to cast the negative thoughts aside. Rita would tell her she had to think positively and that was what she planned on doing. She pushed the seat down and passed a box out to Annie. Once people had somewhere worth stopping by on a Sunday, things would be different.

She put the box full of organic goodies she was carrying down and unlocked the door. All was as it had been left on Friday night and they carried the boxes through to the kitchen, 'We can put this lot away tomorrow morning,' Isla said setting the box down on the bench and shaking her arms out. It weighed a tonne! She cast one more look round Nectar and felt a burst of pride. She still had to pinch herself sometimes to believe it was hers.

'Coming?' Annie stood at the door, no doubt eager to get home to Kris, Isla thought with a smile as she nodded and followed her out. They made plans to meet at the café bright and early in the morning for what promised to be a hectic week getting ready for Friday and the grand opening. Isla waited until Annie disappeared inside her house, and then with a toot and a wave drove off. There was someone waiting for her at home that she couldn't wait to see too.

As she walked through the front door, Coal scampered down the hall, crying his pleasure at her homecoming. She picked him up and gave him a big fuss; he'd grown tubby in the weeks since he'd come to live with them. Nobody had contacted them to say he belonged to them and Isla knew if they did now it would break her heart to have to hand him over. Bridget appeared in the kitchen doorway wiping floury hands on her apron. 'Hi Gran, ooh something smells good.'

She smiled. 'Scones are in the oven, and I'll put the kettle on. Oh, and there's two big cartons in the living room that arrived here for you by courier yesterday.'

Had Customs finally seen fit to release her stuff? Isla stuck her head around the living room door. They had – there was her life in London, all boxed up neatly, over and done with. Isla realized that was how she felt now too. It was as though that part of her life fitted into another compartment and she had put the lid firmly on it and moved forward. Coal nuzzled her neck in agreement.

'Annie, are the vegetable tartlets done?' Isla called from the dining room as she rearranged the platters laden with food for the umpteenth time in the last hour. The star attraction in the middle of the table was the triple-layer Black Forest cake. The two women had trawled through recipe ideas online for tonight's party and had saved the winners on Pinterest. Annie had been in charge of the café's opening weekend menu and their culinary adventure when they opened officially for business tomorrow was going to be a baptism by fire, but sometimes, Isla reflected with a tweak of the tablecloth, that was the best way to learn. Besides, she and Annie were keeping good company. The Domestic Goddess herself, Nigella Lawson, was a self-professed cook and not a trained chef.

'Yes, and the garlic and pesto share-and-tear loaf is in the oven, it smells divine too. I'll put the sausage rolls in shortly.'

'Thanks,' Isla managed to call back. The sausage roll recipe had come from Gran and the secret ingredient, she divulged to the two women in a whisper, was the homemade relish in the sausage meat. Thankfully she had also supplied the home-made ingredient, made with Joe's late summer oversupply of tomatoes preserved last year. Isla narrowed her eyes, fancying she spied a smudge on one of the wine glasses sitting on the tray on the counter waiting to be filled. *There'll be no smudges on my watch*. She picked up her tea towel and honed in on it. 'Prosperity and success is my natural state of mind,' she murmured not for the first time that day. Her nerves were in overdrive, and she fumbled the wine glass as she picked it up to polish.

'What're you on about?' Annie appeared from the kitchen, her hair tied back in a ponytail and her face pink from leaning over the oven. In her hands, she held two fizzing champagne flutes. 'Isla, that glass is fine put it down before you drop it.' Annie's tone held no room for argument and Isla did as she was told, grateful to be taken in hand.

'We've got twenty minutes until show time so come and sit down and compose yourself. You need to take a load off those feet; you haven't stopped since this morning.'

Isla was full to brimming over with nervous energy, but she followed Annie's lead and sat down opposite her. The reclaimed timber table top worked a treat with the wrought iron chairs; she ran her hand over the wood. They'd been worth every penny she'd bid at auction. She cast her eyes around the room trying to see it through a customer's eye. She'd never felt uncertain about her design choices in the past, but then she'd never had any input on a project so close to her own heart before either.

The fireplace with its railway sleeper mantle and surround looked great. The gas fire below with its flickering flames might have cost a bomb to install, but it did add cheer and warmth to the room as well as lift the last of the winter chill. Did the couch in the corner beckon you over with its over-stuffed cushions and quilt draped over its arm, though? She hoped the exposed timber ceiling beam and floors along with the mining memorabilia lent the space a rustic, countrified air. Her aim was for people to feel they'd walked into a place that was cosy and comfortable. A space where they could relax and enjoy the wholesome food and drink on offer.

Perhaps she should have gotten a liquor licence too? There was so much red tape involved with that though, something Gran and Saralee were already coming up against with Project Matchmaker, not to mention the expense. She'd fretted over the decision but in the end had opted to leave that corner of the market to the Pit up the road – had she made a mistake?

'Isla, it looks amazing. You should be proud of yourself.' Annie seemed to have read her mind.

'I couldn't have done any of it without you.'

'To us then.'

'To us,' they chorused.

Isla felt the tension slowly leave her body and her shoulders relaxed as the bubbles tickled the tip of her nose. This was her big night, and she was going to enjoy it. There was no need to be a bundle of nerves, not when everybody who was coming tonight wished her well. The two friends sipped their champers in contemplative silence, which was broken by a knock on the door. They looked at each other and smiled with the anticipation of everyone's reactions to all their hard work.

An orange face peered around the door. 'Can we come in?'

'Of course Mum, welcome to Nectar,' Isla declared, quickly untying her apron and smoothing the fabric of the plum-coloured wrap dress she wore beneath it.

Mary stepped inside the refurbished café, her heavily mascaraed eyes wide as she took in her surrounds. 'Oh Isla, Annie it's wonderful, and you both look lovely.' She promptly burst into tears.

'Your makeup will run, and you'll look like one of those ring-tailed lemurs,' Bridget tutted at her daughter but her eyes too, Isla noticed, were suspiciously shiny. 'Well done girls, you've done a marvellous job, and I agree with Mary, you both look very smart,' she said.

As for Joe, well Isla only knew it was her father bringing up the rear by the cowboy hat and boots at either end. His face and midriff were completely hidden by two huge bunches of red-stemmed silver beet and leeks that he pronounced were freshly picked for use in the café over the weekend. Isla's mind was already whirring; *the leeks could be used in the base of the French Lentil soup being served over the weekend, and the silverbeet would go well in the vegetarian quiches.* A glance at Annie told her she was thinking the same thing as she took the vegetables from Joe and carried them through to the kitchen. She too had discarded her apron and looked lovely in the rust-coloured shift dress that set off her colouring a treat. Isla coveted those gorgeous red leather boots of hers. Yip, she decided, for a pair of country bumpkins they scrubbed up pretty well!

'You've done us proud, Isla,' Joe said, once he could see where he was, and he pulled her into a bear hug. That was when Isla felt her own eyes well up. As she broke free of his embrace, she spied Saralee, in a pretty floral top and black jeans, with Ben and Hayden hovering near the door and she went over to welcome them.

'Did Joanne and the children come?' she asked looking over Hayden's shoulder.

'No, she sent her best wishes and apologies, but Jo didn't trust the kids not to trash the joint.'

Isla laughed. 'They can't be that bad.'

'Yes, they can,' Ben muttered receiving a sharp look and elbow in the ribs from Saralee.

Annie appeared offering to fetch them all a drink, and they moved over to the counter. Isla watched in amusement as her friend's face lit up at the sight of Kris walking in through the door.

She was distracted by a tap on her shoulder.

'I hope I'm not late. I had a meeting with this kid's parents about their son who's a total bully, only they refuse to acknowledge it,' Callum grinned apologetically. 'The joys of teaching in a PC world gone mad.'

'Oh, poor you, and you're not late,' Isla said smiling back at him.

He produced a bunch of flowers from behind his back. 'These are for you, and you look gorgeous by the way.'

'Oh, Callum they're beautiful, thank you.' Isla knew it would have taken some organizing on his part. The closest florists were in Greymouth, and this beautiful colourful bunch hadn't come from the bucket of water inside the Four Square's entrance.

'You're beautiful,' he whispered, kissing her on the cheek.

'Thanks, I'll take all the compliments I can get. I feel frazzled – like I've run a marathon and just about reached the finish line.'

Isla didn't see Ben watching her from across the room as she headed through to the kitchen to put them in water, but Bridget noticed. The older woman shook her head. Saralee was a lovely girl, and she was doing a wonderful job on Project Matchmaker, it was just that she wasn't the girl for Ben. Just as Callum wasn't right for Isla. The four of them needed their heads banging together, but she knew it was a conclusion they would have to reach in their own time. She eyed the pumpkin seeds sprinkled on top of her vegetable tartlet with suspicion before taking a bite. Outside, the wind began to blow.

Carl and David were the last to arrive, making a grand entrance as always. Carl announced to all and sundry that he felt as though he'd just been blow-dried within an inch of his life thanks to that God-awful, unseasonal nor'wester blowing outside. Running his fingers through his hair, he made a beeline for Bridget, eager to introduce his honorary grandmother to David.

Isla mingled around the room, at the opposite end to Annie, as they made sure everybody had something to eat and that their drinks were topped up. She hadn't planned on making a speech but looking around at everyone gathered, she felt an overwhelming urge to say thank you. The excitement and enthusiasm they were all displaying for her venture brought a lump to her throat as she went and stood alongside the countertop.

'Excuse me,' she said in her loudest voice tapping her wine glass with a spoon and waiting until all eyes had swivelled towards her.

'Hi everyone, I'd like to take a minute to welcome you all officially to Nectar.'

There was a general murmuring response and raising of glasses.

'Everybody in this room has been instrumental in some way or other, whether it's been hands-on help or giving moral support with getting this café looking as gorgeous as I hope you all think it does.'

'Hear, hear,' Carl called, and Isla smiled.

'I've had to pinch myself several times today to make sure this is all real. I can't say it's a dream come true because I didn't know it was. It just happened. But a dream come true is how it feels standing here tonight, and I feel so blessed to be sharing it with you all. Annie, none of this would have happened without you, and I'm so glad I met you although, I have to say I'm going to miss the Blue Mountain coffee.'

Annie raised a watery smile, and Kris pulled her close to him.

'I am so excited about this wonderful adventure we're embarking on as of tonight, and I couldn't do it without all of you. So, thank you, everybody, for coming. To Nectar.' She raised her glass.

'To Nectar.'

She felt warmed by the round of applause. Her speech was completely off the cuff, but it was also heartfelt.

Isla said goodnight to the last of the revellers, but Callum lingered. 'Early start tomorrow?'

'Uh-huh, Annie and I'll be in at five prepping anything we haven't been able to make ahead of time today.'

'I suppose I should see you home then.'

Isla's eyes twinkled, she was still celebrating. 'Or we could go to your home.'

Chapter 26

By closing time on Saturday, Isla was a wreck, and she had to do it all over again tomorrow, she thought, squeezing the sponge out before wiping the kitchen bench down. She wasn't complaining though. If it were as busy everyday as it had been today, then she'd be doing very nicely thank you very much. The vacuum cleaner droned from where Annie was clearing up, front of house. The day had been a big success with the locals turning up in force to take them up on the offer of a free slice with any hot drink purchased. The consensus was that Annie's Neenish slice was a hit and should be a Nectar staple.

Isla had seen so many familiar faces, all come to wish her well and to see what it was she'd done with the place. The feedback, Annie told her as she whizzed out the back to collect the soup that Isla was ladling from the simmering pot on the stove, was all good. Principal Bishop, or Jim as he insisted Isla call him now that she was an adult and would no longer be sent to his office for a slap on the hand, had popped in. He was followed closely behind by Violet McDougall, and Isla smiled seeing his former secretary's face turn puce with pleasure as he offered to buy her a cup of coffee. She wished she could bang their heads together and make them see that they were made for each other, but you couldn't do that. People had to come to that conclusion in their own time, she mused as Annie frothed up a storm behind her with her new baby, the coffee machine.

She appeared now, dragging the vacuum cleaner behind her. 'I'm shagged,' she said before giggling and adding, 'But then you'd know all about that.'

Isla groaned. 'Ha, ha.'

'Well?'

'Well, what?'

'Was it good?'

'It was nice.'

Annie glanced at her quizzically as she wrapped the vacuum's cord up before shoving it back in the cupboard, 'Nice?'

'Alright then, very nice.'

'Oh, dear the "nice" word.' She made an inverted commas sign with her fingers.

'What's wrong with that?'

'I think the problem with sex with Callum being *nice* is obvious.'

'Actually I said very nice, and what do you mean?'

'I mean the person you're mad about is Ben. I saw you looking at him last night.'

'I was not!'

'Ah, yes you were, and I caught him looking your way too more than once.'

'Nope, no way.'

'She who doth protest too much.'

'Oh alright, maybe I do still have feelings for him but it's a waste of time, he's with Saralee, and I do really like Callum.'

'So what're you going to do about Ben?'

'There's not much I can do. You can't revisit the past, and like I told you I hurt him. I doubt he'd ever trust me in a romantic way again. It's a moot point anyway because he's obviously happy with Saralee even if she did say things weren't serious between them. And, I want to give things a chance with Callum.'

The days turned into weeks and ticked over into months. Time was whizzing by and Isla wouldn't have believed summer was nearly here had she not spotted a cluster of vibrant poppies in the front garden as she'd headed to Nectar that morning. The apple tree too was in full blossom. It was evening now though, and outside the wind had begun howling like a banshee. The petals on those poppies and the apple tree's blossom were probably headed to Christchurch by now, she thought as she folded the washing in the clothes basket.

Coal had claimed his spot on the rug by the fire, which they'd laid despite the lateness of the month, and the air was rich with the smell of roasting meat drifting in from the kitchen where Bridget had taken charge. Isla smiled, watching his little nose twitch as he caught a whiff. 'Sorry buddy, it's a tough life being a cat. Gran and I are having a roast dinner, but it's a cordon bleu meal of Friskies and Jelly-meat for you.' His ears twitched at the sound of his beloved's voice, but he was too warm and cosy to bother opening an eye and looking at her.

She must remember to give Carl a call later regarding the meeting for Project Matchmaker that Gran wanted to hold next month. It was only four months until Valentine's Day now, and things were progressing nicely in that department, with the tickets having officially gone on sale this week. Isla had put a stack on the counter today, and between her and Annie they'd already sold fifteen, mostly to locals.

She'd owned the café for nearly six whole months and business was certainly brisker than it had been under Noeline's ownership, with Nectar gaining a reputation for wholesome, delicious food that brought people back. Her dad was a star, keeping them well supplied with fresh produce, and Isla and Annie had settled into an easy-going daily routine. Those first few weeks of mayhem as they found their feet were a distant memory that they would shake their heads over now, looking back and wondering how they ever got through.

Isla had wondered if she'd done the right thing initially. Rita from Break-Free had said she'd been suffering from Rushing Woman's Syndrome and that she needed to slow down and be kinder to herself. So, what had she gone and done? She'd sped up. But she and Annie had got through it, and Isla was happy. She was enjoying rising to the challenge of building up the café and slowly word had spread that it was a place worth stopping by on the tourist trail. They'd established a weekday clientele of regulars too.

One of Isla's favourites was the town's policeman. Tepene, or Tep as he was known to the locals, was a big burly Maori fellow. He called in most mornings for a coffee and something sweet. There was no lady at home filling the tins with sweet treats, he'd lament leaning on the counter, adding that it was his bad luck that the two most beautiful ladies in Bibury were taken.

Marie, who owned the town's only hair salon was a regular for her morning latte too. She'd confided in Isla that she was lonely as she waited for her coffee one morning. It was three years since her husband had left her and she was ready to move on. There wasn't much on offer in Bibury, and those that were available weren't keen to take on the baggage that came with three kids under sixteen, she said eyeing the chocolate brownie. The same routine played out most mornings, with Marie insisting that she was going to be good today. It was swiftly followed by, 'Ah, no go on Isla. Life's too short to be good, I'll have a piece of that brownie please.'

Principal Bishop had taken to having his lunch at the café on Friday, his treat to mark the end of the working week. It made Isla sad to think of him going home to an empty house for the weekend, and she'd always give him an extra piece of toasted bread with his soup. As for Violet McDougall, well, she'd negotiated a discount for her and her Scottish Society ladies who held their meetings at Nectar on a Wednesday morning over tea and cake. The pinched set to her mouth these days hinted at an underlying unhappiness, and Isla knew she was lonely. Then there was young Beau, the butcher's apprentice. Isla had an unspoken arrangement with him whereby he gave her the choicest meat cuts, and she gave him the largest sausage roll for his morning tea. He'd always appear in the café at the same time as Ellie from the Four Square and Isla, would will him to just talk to the girl, but the one time Ellie had tried to spark up a conversation he'd gotten all red in the face and tongue-tied.

Isla knew there were some lonely hearts in Bibury and she hoped the Matchmaking Festival might weave some much-needed magic through the town. She wasn't one of them though because to her surprise she was still seeing Callum. Their relationship was easy and uncomplicated; she could relax around him. They had a lot of fun together too, but it didn't go much deeper than that. Neither of them seemed to have an inclination to take things to the next level either, and that suited her just fine. For once in her life, Isla was going with the flow.

Ben and Saralee were still growing strong and from time to time she'd feel a pang of something she could only label as jealousy when she saw them together. She'd shake the feeling off though and concentrate on happy, positive thoughts like Rita had told her to do. Saralee was a lovely girl; the couple were well suited. She and Ben had never been meant to be, she'd tell herself, drawing a line under it.

Now, she picked up her pile of folded washing. She put her things away first, saying hello to Caroline as she always did when she walked into her room after a day at work. She liked to think the doll was pleased to see her despite her unblinking gaze. Normally she left Gran's things on her bed but hearing her pottering away in the kitchen she decided she'd save her the job. She found where she kept her tops in the third dresser drawer down, hung up a pair of trousers and then she opened one of the drawers in the top of the dresser to pop her smalls into. Well, they weren't so small actually, she thought with a wry smile.

It wasn't an underwear drawer she'd opened, though. It was filled with old receipts, clothing tags and odd buttons but they weren't what caught her eye. On top of the detritus was a pile of cards. The top one, Isla saw was a Valentine's Day card, it wasn't old either by the looks of it. The bundle was tied together with a ribbon. She stood looking down at it, her fingers twitching to pull the ribbon. She knew she shouldn't untie it, because if her gran had a secret admirer she didn't want to talk about then that was her business. She hovered uncertainly as her conscience went to battle with curiosity.

Curiosity won out, and she pulled the ribbon. There were six cards in total she counted before opening the one that had initially caught her eye. She scanned the text. The card was from a chap called Charlie Callahan. Isla's eyes widened. Was it the Charlie her gran had met at the dance with Clara? If so, he lived in Australia these days and very much wanted to come and visit Bridget. It was him, Isla was sure of it, but she didn't get the chance to ponder the card any longer because Bridget snatched it from her hand. Isla jumped, she'd been so engrossed in what she had been reading she never heard her coming.

'What do you think you're doing?'

She knew she'd gone beetroot at being caught. 'I'm sorry Gran, I know I shouldn't have opened them but I was putting your washing away and, well, I saw the cards, and I couldn't help myself. I am sorry.' She attempted to lighten the situation.

'I know it's none of my business, but it's not every day you discover your gran is getting Valentine's cards.'

Bridget sat down heavily on the edge of her bed still clutching the card to her as though she were frightened Isla might try to take it off her. 'You're right, it is none of your business.' Her expression was conflicted as she debated whether or not to tell her more. She knew her granddaughter only too well, and once her curiosity was piqued, as it was now, she would be like a dog with a bone until she got an answer. She sighed and patted the bed beside her. 'Sit down and I'll you about Charlie and me.'

Isla did as she was told and listened as the story unfolded.

Chapter 27

1957

Bridget knew that supper, when the band was packing up and the tea and coffee being served, would be the only opportunity she would have to talk to Charlie properly. She was in two minds. In one respect she wanted the night to hurry up so she could find out more about him, and in the other she never wanted it to end. She wanted to dance with him forever. Eventually, though, when she thought her feet would surely drop off, the band finished and supper was announced.

Charlie told her, while she balanced her cup of tea and afghan biscuit in her right hand, that he was from further up the coast, Westport. It was work that had brought him to Bibury and he had started a fortnight ago at the Barker's Ridge Mine, just as Clara had guessed.

'It's not a bad wee place, Bibury, so far as small towns go. I've lived in worse.' Charlie gave her a rueful smile before popping his biscuit in his mouth.

Bridget didn't know what to say to that, she'd lived here

her whole life and sometimes felt she lived in a hick town where nothing much ever happened. The magazines she read gave her glimpses of the big wide world and she felt trapped, or at least she had until tonight. At this moment in time under the glare of the hall lights, she thought Bibury was the best place on earth to live.

It was only last Saturday afternoon, though, that she'd been convinced Bibury was the dullest place in the whole of New Zealand. She and Clara had taken themselves off down to the local Milk Bar. They sat sipping at their chocolate shakes wondering where all these Milk Bar Cowboys they kept reading about in the papers were. How come they never roared up to the Bibury Milk Bar on their motorbikes, with their slicked-back hair and rebellious attitude that made the staid townsfolk frown at what was becoming of the young people of today?

The two girls sighed with frustrated boredom and began to plan their escape to the Big Smoke, where things actually happened. They sat there in their booth, the red vinyl seats carved with the initials of teens who had gone before them and lamented their lot. What they would do for accommodation or work when they got to Christchurch they didn't know, but the very thought of running away livened up what had been amounting to a dull Saturday afternoon.

Now, Bridget thought nibbling daintily on her chocolate iced biscuit as she looked up at Charlie from beneath her lashes, the small world she occupied was suddenly full of thrilling possibilities.

'I'm boarding just off the High Street on River Road, with

a Mrs Jessop. She runs a clean house and the lad I share with keeps himself to himself, so it suits me fine.'

Bridget knew Mrs Jessop. She was a widow who was well thought of in the community and her establishment respectable. 'Do you get your meals included then?'

'I do, yes, and my washing. She's not a bad cook either. Her steak and kidney pudding is almost as good as my mum's.'

Bridget smiled.

'What's it like working at the mine?'

'Ah, its dirty work alright, and it's not for the claustrophobic but it's the lads who make the job. They're a good bunch. Tom Collins, who's been giving your friend a turn around the floor, has been a good mate to me and taken me under his wing. What is it you do with yourself?'

Bridget filled him in on her job and was telling him about her family when Clara came over with a plate heaped full of sandwiches and sausage rolls. They would not be going home hungry. She introduced Tom to her. Bridget recalled having already met him at Clara's house a while back now when he'd called round to pick her brother up. After her brother and Tom had left, Clara had flopped down on her bed with her hand on her heart and a daft look on her face and refused to move for half an hour. She smiled at the memory as she said hello.

The two men grinned at each other in silent acknowledgement that they were both having a good night, as Clara offered the plate round. The sausage rolls smelt yummy but Bridget was not going to run the risk of pastry sticking to her lipstick so she opted for an egg triangle sandwich instead. The foursome stood chatting amicably about the latest Marilyn Monroe film coming to the Town Hall next week, until Bridget spotted Jean tapping at her wristwatch. She then held her fingers up to demonstrate five minutes before pointing in the direction of the carpark. Bridget knew if she didn't do as she was told, it might be the last time she got to attend a dance or even leave the house after 6pm for a very long time.

'We have to go, Clara.'

Clara's face fell, but she looked up at the clock and saw that Bridget was right. She too had no intention of breaking her curfew and spoiling her chances of going on a date with Tom.

Charlie pulled Bridget aside. 'I've really enjoyed myself tonight, Bridget, and I'd like to see you again.'

'I'd like that too.'

'Perhaps I could call for you one night in the week, we could have a fish and chip supper?'

Bridget wanted to say tomorrow night was as good a night as any but she didn't want to appear too forward. 'Tuesday would be good.' She knew it would feel like eons between now and Tuesday but after church in the morning, she would spend the afternoon rehashing the night's events with Clara. Then it would be time to iron her clothes for work in the week. So, at least tomorrow would whizz by, and Monday she'd be at work so the day would pass fast enough. 'I live on School Road, it's the road the schoolhouse is on, no surprises there! You just follow River Road where you are staying to the turn off and we are at number twelve.'

'Tuesday night at six o'clock then?'

'It's a date.' She smiled hoping she didn't look too eager but if she did, well, she simply couldn't help it. He was wonderful, he was everything she had ever dreamed about on those long boring afternoons when she wondered what would become of her, living here in Bibury.

'Happy Valentine's Day.' Charlie leaned forward and kissed her on the cheek. She desperately wanted to turn her head so that his lips could meet hers instead, but she was sure she could feel Biddy Johnson's disapproving eyes upon her.

'You do know that Charlie you were mooning over is Catholic, don't you?' Jean said as Colin held the door of the Holden open for Bridget and Clara. Until then, Bridget had felt like Cinderella must have felt, having to leave the dance and her Prince Charming behind. Around them, the carpark was a cacophonous noise of horns honking, laughter and shouts of goodnight, the pungent smoke of cigarettes floating heavily past on the cool night air. At her sister's words, though, Bridget's stomach plummeted because if what she was saying was true then unlike Cinderella, she might not get her happy ever after.

She hadn't known Charlie was Catholic and nor did she care in the slightest as to what denomination he was. She knew however, it would be a different story where her parents were concerned. She could recall her older brother showing interest in Fiona Mulligan when she was home from boarding school one holiday. Bridget had only been ten at the time, but she still remembered her brother's romance had been squashed like an ant underfoot before it had a chance to begin. Thus, she did not rate her chances with Charlie were her parents to get wind of the fact that he too was Catholic. She sent up a silent prayer in the hope it wasn't true and that Jean was just being spiteful.

Even if it were true, it wouldn't stop her seeing him, she thought, feeling a flare of rebellion for the second time that evening. And there was no way she would give her sister the satisfaction of thinking that she had something over her.

'Does it matter what religion he is?' she asked affecting an air of coolness.

Jean shrugged. 'Not to me, I couldn't give a fig who you date, but Mum and Dad will, mark my words.' She turned to her boyfriend. 'Colin, you said he's a nice enough chap, honest and a hard worker.'

He nodded.

'But they won't give a monkey's, Bridget. All they'll see when they look at him is that he's not one of ours. If he has any plans to call for you, then you'd better hope Dad decides he must be alright because he's working in the mine and doesn't ask which church it is his family attends.'

Ah, so Colin knew of him through work even though he was a pencil pusher and not a miner. He would know then, it must be true – Charlie was Catholic. It had never entered her head to ask him. In the darkened back seat Clara reached over and picked up her hand giving it a squeeze, as she mouthed, 'It'll be alright.'

Bridget hoped more than anything that she was right.

Tuesday night could not come fast enough and the minutes

of each hour seemed to drag until at last six o'clock rolled around and Charlie knocked on the door as he'd promised he would. Bridget's heart leaped, she'd been chewing her nails, running through a thousand possible reasons as to why he might stand her up. As she got up from her seat, her father waved at her to sit back down while he went to open the front door. She'd mentioned to him more than once what a hard worker Charlie was, and how Colin had said that he was very well thought of by the lads at the mine. She was praying that that would be enough to win her dad over. He might have worked in the mine's accounts department, but he had a deep-seated respect for the men who ventured underground. He knew the peril they were placed in on a daily basis.

Bridget sat on her hands to stop her biting her nails right down to the quick. She could see her mother untying her apron in the kitchen. She flashed her a reassuring smile, as she too went to greet this potential beau of her daughter's.

A voice hollered down the stairs, 'Bridget, I can smell Arpege! If you have been helping yourself, I won't be responsible for my actions.'

Bridget squirmed, she'd had a teensy squirt, not that she would ever own up to it. Besides, Jean had no right to get shirty with her, not after what she'd done on Sunday night. Her sister had only gone and tiptoed into her bedroom when she was sound asleep and unwound one of her hair rollers because she was short one. Bridget had had to go to work on Monday morning with a straight piece of hair in amongst her waves. She'd not been happy but Jean was unrepentant.

Now, she didn't reply and hoped her sister wouldn't come down the stairs and see that she'd borrowed her cardigan and shoes without asking too! If she did, there really would be fireworks.

'Bridget! Don't keep Charlie waiting.' Her mother called and Bridget shot out of her seat, quickly smoothing her skirt before she rushed to the front door. She was glad to be making her escape before Jean got hold of her, and she was pleased that Charlie had obviously passed muster. No way would she stick around and give her parents a chance to change their mind. Her father was standing in the doorway pipe in hand, 'Don't be late back.' He directed to Charlie who was not looking as self-assured as he had at the dance. Bridget's heart went out to him.

'No sir, I'll have her home by ten o'clock. You have my word.'

This was met with a nod.

Oh, how embarrassing, Bridget fumed, she was sixteen, very nearly seventeen, and she had to be home by ten o'clock! It was ridiculous especially now she was working and contributing to the household. Still, she knew now was not the time to debate her archaic curfew because she'd be the one who'd come off worse for it.

'Have a nice time.' Her mother smiled. 'Oh! I can smell burning.' She shot back in the house to sort out the chops she'd left sizzling in the pan.

'It was nice to meet you Mr Upton – goodbye Mrs Upton,' Charlie called over her father's shoulder.

They set off down the path and Bridget resisted the urge

to seek his hand, because she knew her father would stand and watch them from the doorway until they were out of sight.

'Phew, thank goodness that's over and done with.'

Charlie laughed. 'They're fine people, your parents. They just want to make sure their daughter is stepping out with a fellow whose worth her while.'

'What did they ask you?' Obviously not where he went to church, Bridget thought, relieved.

'Oh, this and that, they wanted to know what had brought me here to Bibury and where my family came from.'

'Well, you obviously won them over.' Bridget smiled up at him.

Spotty chin Jim was working in the fish and chippy which was busy. It always was at this time of night thanks to the six o'clock swill at the local pub which saw the men knock their drinks back as fast as they could before closing. Jim asked after Clara, and Bridget felt sorry for him as she told him Clara was fine before asking if they could have a can of tomato sauce too.

The chips were salty, crispy and delicious but Bridget wouldn't have cared if they were soggy. She was just happy to be sitting on the grassy banks of the Ahaura on a balmy February evening sharing a scoop with Charlie as they watched the ducks being carried along by the current. They'd talked about anything and everything and she had listened as he told her what it was like growing up in a large family of seven children.

'There wasn't a lot to go around in the Callahan household but we never went without either. It was just that the food had to be worked for, and we all had a task to make sure there was something to put on the table of an evening. Mum's got a veggie patch the size of a football pitch.'

His family were not Italian as Bridget had romanticized on Saturday night, but rather a second-generation Irish Catholic family. They had put down roots first in Greymouth and then Westport, lured to New Zealand, like so many others, by the promise of a better life and the possibility of a fortune to be made. His father and his brothers, except for one who'd gone into the police force, all worked for the Westport Coal Company. Charlie though, as the self-confessed awkward, somewhere in the middle son, planned on working his way up the mining hierarchy until he got himself into a managerial role. That was what had brought him to Bibury, the whiff of opportunity.

'Mum was disappointed when I left school. She had high hopes of me being the scholar in the family because I won a scholarship to board at St Kevin's in Oamaru for my high schooling. I was bright enough, but it wasn't for me. I hated being sat in a classroom all day when I could see all this life happening outside through the windows. I wanted to be out there amongst it all.' He swatted a pesky sand-fly away. 'I got bored and I caused many a Brother to lose his hair with my antics as a result.'

Bridget smiled at the mental picture of a short fat, bald Brother, and of Charlie as a lad in shorts, a blazer and long socks getting up to high-jinx.

'What about you then? I know that your dad is an accounts worker for the company and that you have an older sister but that's about all. I want to know everything.'

'Well, it's not very exciting I'm afraid.'

'Let me be the judge of that.'

'I don't know where to start.'

'Okay, where do you come in the family, are you the middle child, youngest?'

'I'm the baby of the family, I've two older brothers, who left a few years ago now and live in Christchurch with their wives and children. Mum misses them all something terrible and there's only myself and Jean at home now. We fight like cats and dogs but there's high hopes it will just be me hogging the bathroom soon. Jean's angling to get Colin to put a ring on her finger before the year is out.'

'She could do worse than Colin, he's a nice enough chap if not a little—'

'Full of himself,' Bridget finished for him with a smile. 'Just a tad.'

They both laughed, and Bridget plucked at a piece of grass. 'It scares me, the thought of Jean leaving because then it will just be me. I sometimes feel like I am suffocating here,' she confided.

'There's worse places than Bibury you know, and you've your whole life ahead of you to go and explore,' Charlie said with a smile.

'I know it sounds silly and it's hard to put into words, but there are times when I feel trapped and I don't see a way out. It's like deep down I know that I will never leave, my whole life will be played out here from start to finish with nothing very exciting in between.'

'Okay, so where would you go, if you could go anywhere in the world right now, where would it be?'

'That's easy. I'd go to Ireland, I want to see the rainbows around every corner that my Great-Granny Kate used to talk about.'

'I'll take you there one day.' He fished a pack of Pall Malls out of his pocket and offered the pack to Bridget, but she shook her head.

'No thanks, but I'll have a puff of yours if I may.'

'Sure.' Tapping a cigarette out of the pack, he produced a gold zippo from his pants pocket. 'My father gave me this on my eighteenth birthday.' It was mumbled, with the cigarette dangling from between his lips, as he flipped the lid striking the flint until he had a flame. Lighting the cigarette, he inhaled deeply before passing it to Bridget. She took a little puff, aiming the smoke she exhaled up into the sky before handing the cigarette back.

'How will we get there? By sea?'

'We could fly.'

'An aeroplane going all that way, imagine.'

'It will happen one day, you'll see, and it won't just be for the rich either.'

Bridget smiled up at him. The early evening light was bathing everything in gold and she was mesmerized by the way it played with his hair turning the black tips a shade of rich chocolate.

'What?' he asked.

'Nothing,' Bridget said, embarrassed at being caught staring.

'You're beautiful, do you know that?' He ground his cigarette out into the ground next to him and Bridget didn't get a chance to reply, nor would she have known what to say to his compliment because he leaned over and she felt his lips settle over the top of hers. He tasted salty and smoky, and his lips were soft. She felt his tongue begin to seek hers and she opened her mouth hesitantly, unsure as his arms entwined around her and he pulled her closer. As his hands roamed her back, feelings flared up inside her, feelings she'd never experienced before and soon she was kissing him back with a passion that almost frightened her. Charlie pulled away first, running his fingers through his hair.

'Did I do something wrong?' Bridget asked in a small voice feeling slightly bereft with longing.

He laughed. 'Oh no, you did everything right but I promised your father I wouldn't behave inappropriately, and I'm afraid that if I don't stop now I won't be responsible for my actions.'

'Oh.' She blushed.

He reached over and stroked her cheek before getting to his feet, brushing the grass from his trousers. 'Come on, I'll get you home. Better to be a few minutes early because I don't want to mark my card on our first date.' He held his hand out and she took it letting him help her to her feet. They followed the path along the river, Charlie's hand warm and strong as it clasped hers.

'What are you thinking about?' He looked down at her

concerned as they strolled along. 'Have I overstepped the mark, I didn't mean to launch myself on you it's just that—'

'It's not that. It's nothing.'

'I can see it's something, please tell me?'

'It's my parents. They won't approve of you being a Catholic.' She blurted it out. He was right, it was worrying her, niggling away at the back of her mind and casting a shadow over the golden evening.

'Oh, will they not?'

'No. My brother was sweet on a Catholic girl once but my father wouldn't hear of him taking her out once he found out what church she went to. It's ridiculous but it's just the way it is and it won't matter what I say to him.'

'Well then, do we need to tell them? Because it's been a long time since I set foot in a church.'

Bridget wasn't sure if that would be deemed as worse or not. 'I won't say anything but Bibury is a small town. Things just have a way of getting around.' She felt a sinking in the pit of her stomach as she said the words, knowing how true they were.

'Well, let's not spoil tonight by worrying about something that's out of our hands anyway. We'll cross that bridge when we need to, deal?'

'Deal.' Bridget nodded and he squeezed her hand dropping a kiss onto the top of her head.

'It'll be alright you'll see.'

Chapter 28

1957

Jean's revelation was made out of malice. It was over a matter so trivial that Bridget really and truly could have pulled her sister's hair out had she been able to get into her room after she had chased her up the stairs. Jean was not silly; she'd seen the look on her younger sister's face and had barricaded herself in by moving her chest of drawers in front of her bedroom door. She wouldn't shift it back no matter how many times Bridget hammered on the door. In the end, her father had threatened to come up the stairs with his slipper if she didn't stop her carrying on.

'You're sixteen years of age, as you keep reminding us Bridget, so stop behaving like a child!'

She peered over the landing to where he was stood in the hall looking up at her with displeasure. 'I'm acting like one because you're treating me like one.'

'Don't talk back to me young lady.' He waved the slipper at her in a way that meant business.

'I'm going to Clara's,' she stated having decided it was

best to put some distance between herself and her family.

'Ah no, you're not. You're not going anywhere today after that carry-on, and that's my final word on the matter.'

She'd gone and thrown herself across her bed then. The tears were unstoppable with the frustration of knowing that in a few hours, Charlie would be waiting for her outside the Town Hall. They were supposed to be going to see the seven o'clock showing of the Seven Year Itch. When she didn't come, he'd think she'd stood him up, and that was simply unbearable. The walls of her boxy room were closing in on her, and she contemplated climbing out her window and escaping to Clara's that way. Even as she was tempted by the thought of escape, she knew she wouldn't do it. For one thing, she was on the second storey and the rose bushes below would in no way cushion her fall, and for another, she knew life would not be worth living were she to disobey her parents.

Jean had ruined everything and, she'd done so because Bridget had gotten the teensiest of cigarette burns in her new cardigan. Bridget had retaliated by telling her parents what it was her sister had gotten up to in her boyfriend's car the other week. As Colin had been around on bended knee to ask their father for Jean's hand in marriage a day or two earlier, this misdemeanour was swept under the carpet.

'You won't be seeing him again, Bridget. He's not suitable, and that's the end of that,' her father had said in a voice low and firm enough for her to know he meant business. There was no point in trying to argue or make him see reason.

'I should have known, with a name like Callahan,' she heard him mutter to her mother, and she could see him in her mind's eye, shaking his head in that way he did before taking a puff of his pipe. Her mother, she knew, would be hovering in the doorway of the kitchen, apron tied around her waist. She would be twisting the rings on her finger in that nervous manner she adopted when her husband was upset.

'Nothing is perfect Bridget, so it's a waste of time crying to the moon,' she said later that day, popping her head around her daughter's bedroom door. The shadows were beginning to stretch long across the floor. She found her youngest child lying prone on her bed, the candlewick cover ruffled as she sobbed into her pillow. The clock on her dressing table taunted her with its ticking away of the minutes until seven o'clock. Her mother had softened enough to come over and rub her back gently.

'Come on now, don't be a big silly. You've only been out with the lad once. There's plenty more fish in the sea, Bridget. You've your whole life ahead of you, and the right man will come along, you'll see.'

Bridget shook her mother off. At that beat in time she hated her. The right man had come along, and they'd ruined things for her. She hated them all and their petty prejudice.

Bridget passed a restless night but Sunday morning eventually rolled round, dawning with a heavy grey sky that befitted her mood. She ate her breakfast quietly and spoke when spoken to but no more. She got herself ready for church and joined her mother and father in the short walk to St Andrew's. Jean was waiting on Colin, eager to share her engagement news with the congregation after the service. The service dragged as the minister intoned, his words not registering as she met Clara's questioning gaze across the pews to where she was sitting with her parents. She was desperate to tell her what had happened yesterday but it would have to wait. At last, the minister finished, and with a snap of closing bibles the congregation formed an orderly line and began making their way outside to the courtyard. They milled around there with the wooden white church a backdrop behind them.

It was customary to stand about chatting and catching up on the news of the week, weather permitting. Clara raced over to where Bridget and her parents were standing near the church's arched entrance. 'Good morning, Mr and Mrs Upton.'

'Good morning Clara, how are you dear?' Bridget's mother smiled in the hope that Clara might perk her daughter up. Her father doffed his hat at her, but his face remained stern.

'Fine thank you, Mrs Upton.'

Her parents moved off to talk to Mr and Mrs Pettigrew, fellow bridge players and Clara pulled Bridget away, out of earshot of any nosy parishioners.

'What happened?' Her eyes were wide. 'Tom and I waited with Charlie outside the pictures, but in the end, we went in ahead. Charlie said he was going to call around to your house to see what had kept you. He was dreadfully upset.'

'My poor Charlie.' Bridge was torn between wanting to run to him and wanting to scratch her sister's eyes out. 'Jean, that's what happened,' she spat her sister's name. 'She told Mum and Dad that Charlie was Catholic because she was annoyed that I got a wee hole in her new cardigan. Dad told me I should've known better than to go out with him in the first place. I wasn't allowed out, not even to pop around to your house and leave a message as to why I wouldn't be meeting you all. Can you believe it? Look at her over there, thinking she's the Queen Bee.' She pointed to where her sister, with her arm linked through Colin's, was holding court with a group of friends. She was waggling her hand under their noses as they all exclaimed over the ring on her finger. 'It's a tiny diamond, positively miserable. I don't know what all the fuss is about. If she comes near us, I swear I'll stick my foot out and send her flying. That'd take her highness down a peg or two.'

Clara giggled. 'Now that I would like to see. I thought that must've been what'd happened. I knew she'd spill the beans. She wouldn't have been able to help herself, it's in her nature to be nasty.'

'It is,' Bridget concurred and with a defiant toss of her head and flick of her ponytail she declared, 'I don't want to talk about her anymore. She'll get her comeuppance one day.

'I didn't enjoy the film at all, even though everybody was saying it was hilarious afterwards. I was far too worried about you and what was going on.'

'It was awful, Clara honestly you can't imagine how awful. I tried everything to make them see some sense and let me go out, but it was a waste of time. Dad's mind was set. I don't understand this silly prejudice of theirs anyway. We all believe in God, don't we? What does it matter how we go about worshipping?'

'You're right but it's always been that way, and it goes both ways. Mum told me she overheard the kids at St Michael's referring to us as proddy-dogs when we walked past this morning!'

'I still don't understand it, and it's not as though Charlie or I care what church either of us attends. The worst of it all is that I heard him last night when he came to the door. There was no point trying to talk to him as much as I wanted to because Dad would've gone mad. It's just so unbelievably unfair.' Bridget stamped her foot on the damp grass. 'They keep saying I'm still a child who doesn't know her own mind and in the next breath they tell me to stop behaving like a child and to act my age.'

Clara nodded in sympathy. 'Parents are illogical. It's just the way it is. What're you going to do though? If they won't let you see him, that will make things pretty tough. Will you try and forget about him?'

Bridget looked at her friend aghast. 'Would you forget about Tom if your parents decided he wasn't suitable just because of the church his family attend?'

'No.' Clara was contrite, her blue eyes wide. Neither girl had any idea what a pretty contrast they made to onlookers, one fair and one dark. 'I'm sorry, that was a stupid thing to say.'

'I can't just forget about him. I'd run away with him before I'd stop seeing him. Will you pass a message to him from me? Please, Clara.'

'Of course I will, but you do know there'll be hell to pay if you get caught.'

'It's a chance I'll have to take because if I don't see him again, I'll die anyway,' Bridget stated with all the passion of first love.

Present day

'But you didn't die, you married Granddad and had Mum and Uncle Jack,' Isla said as she sat on the bed next to her grandmother and squeezed her hand seeking reassurance herself. She'd loved her granddad, and it was unsettling to think there had been someone who'd played such a pivotal role in her gran's life before him. She'd always looked at them both with the mentality of a child. They were her grandparents. They weren't individuals as such and certainly not individuals who had experienced grand passions in their lifetime.

'I did, and I loved him, we had a good life together for the most part.' Bridget wouldn't change her life with Tom. They'd hurt each other along the way, but even if she could go back and somehow reverse the events of the past, she knew she wouldn't. She would stop him doing what he'd done though, and she'd erase what he'd told her in those last days at the hospital in a heartbeat. But, to reverse the past with Charlie would be to reverse the present and she couldn't imagine her life without Mary, Joe, Jack and even bossy boots Ruth. As for not having her grandchildren in her life, well that was simply unimaginable.

'Did Charlie move away after your parents stopped you seeing each other?'

'Not straight away, no.' She drifted back into her memories.

Chapter 29

1957

He behaved like a gentleman and Bridget did her best to behave like a lady. He told her that he loved her each time they sat on the wavering grasses, with the long summer evenings beginning to give way to autumn. It was a sentiment she returned with all her heart as the water rushed past them with an urgency. It was a sentiment that was wished with a heavy heart though because it was inevitable that they'd be found out. Still, though, when it happened neither of them was prepared for the fallout.

Bridget knew as she stood outside church talking to Clara, two weeks later that she was in very hot water. It was the way in which her mother and father turned simultaneously from the conversation they were having with Mrs Taylor who was also looking very lemon-lipped in her direction. The sky was an ominous grey, and the air smelled of freshly mowed grass and the faint scent of the bush readying itself for the deluge to come. She saw the set of her father's jaw as he made his way over to where she was stood. He ignored Clara as he ordered Bridget home in a voice that was edged with steel before turning on his heel to re-join his wife. Bridget knew he would not cause a scene here; that would come later at home. Clara looked at her friend alarmed and unsure as to what she should do, and Bridget mouthed, 'Tell Charlie they know,' before doing what she was told because there was nothing else she could do.

She readied her arguments in her head as she sat on her bed waiting to hear the door open and close downstairs, signalling her parents' return. She fully expected footsteps to pound up the stairs and she moved to the edge of her bed, in readiness for the fight that was sure to ensue. She felt like a gazelle taking water down at the waterhole, ears up and poised to take flight when she came into the lion's line of sight.

Her breath came out in short puffs as at last, she heard the front door, but footfall did not follow on the stairs, and the fight went out of her as the minutes ticked by. In the end, she could stand it no longer, and she took herself down the stairs, heart pounding. She was hoping that Jean had not come back from church with their parents, Colin in tow for Sunday dinner as had become their habit. She was in luck in so much as it was just her mother pottering about the kitchen. She stood in the doorway waiting for her to say something but she carried on switching on the elements on which the pots were sat. The set of her small rounded shoulders was the only clue that she knew Bridget was there. The vegetables had been sitting in salted water since Bridget had prepped them for the roast earlier that morning. 'Where's Dad, Mum?'

she asked her voice wobbling and giving away her uncertainty as to how they were behaving as she broke the silent stand-off. She wanted to get her punishment over and done with.

Her mother looked up then, and Bridget saw the disappointment etched on a face that age was only just beginning to catch up with. Then she turned away and opened the oven door to check on the joint she had slow roasting. The aroma would usually make Bridget's mouth water in anticipation of the meal to come. Normally she would pester her mum to make Yorkshire puddings too, but today she had no appetite.

'He's in the garden,' she said. 'Best you go and face the music young lady. You've let us both down badly, but worst of all you've broken our trust, Bridget.'

Bridget nodded, feeling the tears well up at the sting of her usually mild-mannered mother's words. Doing as she'd been told, she opened the door from the kitchen through to the laundry, her hand hovering on the back door handle. She felt sick, and swallowing hard, she opened the door.

Her father was standing with his back to the house alongside the rows of staked peas that were on their last legs now as they got nipped nightly be the cooler evenings.

'Dad?' She stood on the back porch waiting there uncertainly.

He didn't turn around, so she spoke louder, but her voice betrayed her once more. 'Dad?'

This time he turned, his hands in his pockets as he began to walk towards the house, pausing as he drew level with her. 'You'll not leave the house other than to go to church or work for one month. And you won't see that fellow again Bridget because so help me God if you do, you can pack your bags and leave. I won't have a daughter of mine sneaking around and lying to me. Understood?'

'Yes.' She stood with her head down unable to look him in the eye for fear of what she would see there. This was far worse than being ranted and raved at, at least then she could have countered with an argument. She knew too, from the cold tone in his voice, that she could expect to see him waiting outside the Farmer's building to escort her home from work each day at five o'clock until he felt she had regained their trust.

She spent the rest of the afternoon in her room wondering how she could get word to Charlie. There would be no chance of meeting Clara in the foreseeable future. In the end, though, it was Charlie who got word to her, by passing a note to a sympathetic colleague to give to her at work before he left town.

She'd read and re-read that note so many times, smoothing out the crumples. She knew it by heart. He'd been given his marching orders from the mine, he'd written, and Bridget had no doubt that her father had had a hand in that. He was going to Western Australia, to a place called Kalgoorlie where there was gold mining. He'd heard the lads at work talk about it and his plan was to keep his head down and save hard. Who knew? He might be the one to strike it big. Either way, he'd come back for her in two years' time with enough money saved for a deposit on a house. That way, he'd written, he would feel he was a sure enough bet to be able to approach her father again – this time, if she would have him, for her hand in marriage. Would she wait for him? She wanted more than anything to tell him to his face, that yes, she would wait forever for him. In the meantime, his cobber Tom would act as a go-between passing on the letters he promised he would write.

The words had smudged because of the countless times Bridget had run her fingers across the ink, imagining him writing it, her stomach aflutter at the thought of marriage.

Present day

Isla's arms beneath her jumper were covered in goosebumps. She looked at her gran lost in her memories, and in her she could see herself in years to come. Bridget turned and looked at Isla, seeing the younger woman she'd once been mirrored back at her.

'The letters never came, Isla. I never heard from Charlie again until the Valentine's Day cards started to arrive a year after Tom passed away. You know the rest of the story, what happened to Clara and how Tom and I turned to each other after she died.' Her sigh was heavy, but her voice when she spoke was clipped and to the point. 'You can't go back, Isla, the past is the past and that's where it should stay.'

Isla thought of Ben. Gran was right in some respects, but still, she couldn't help wondering what had happened and why Charlie didn't keep his promise.

'Come on, that's enough of all that, with any luck, the roast potatoes won't be burnt to a crisp,' Bridget said getting to her feet. She put the card she still clasped back where it had come from and closed the drawer on the past.

Isla finished washing the roasting pan. It had been a sod of a job as the potatoes had indeed been stuck to the bottom of it. Lashings of gravy had salvaged the overcooked dinner, and it had been a quiet meal time. She turned the pan over to drain on the bench and glanced at the oven clock. It was just after seven. Gran was a creature of habit, and Isla knew she'd be settled in her recliner watching her favourite current affairs show. It would be a good time to give Carl a call, to see if he was free for the date Gran had in mind for the Project Matchmaker meeting and she was dying to confide in someone. The more she'd thought about what she'd learned this evening, the more she felt she couldn't just leave things with Gran and Charlie the way they were. She was in need of advice, she decided, heading down to her room, phone in hand.

'Oh my goodness yes, Isla, you totally have to ring him. Gran has a long-lost lover! How fabulous,' Carl gushed down the phone after Isla had relayed Bridget and Charlie's story.

'Um, Carl would you mind not referring to Gran as ever having had a lover. It doesn't sound right.'

'Yes, I suppose when you word it like that, but Jane Fonda would disagree my lovely. Hold off on the telephoning him advice, because now the shock's wearing off ... I mean, my heart's saying "yes, go for it." It is hammering away, and each beat says you should get in touch with Charlie, and see how the land lies. My head, however, is shaking and saying if

Bridget was as adamant, as you say she was about the past staying in the past, you should respect that. Give me a minute to mull it over will you?'

'Sure.'

There was silence down the phone and Isla stretched out on her bed, the book she had been reading lying open on the bedside table. Isla stared up at the ceiling rose and decided she'd fetch the duster and flick the spider web off it when she finished this call – if she ever finished it. Carl was taking his time. She jumped, hearing him shout out.

'Sasha! What do you think you're doing?'

'Who's Sasha, and what's she doing?'

There was a beleaguered sigh down the phone.

'I'm in the former CBD doing a night time photo shoot, of which Sasha's the star. The brief was to photograph an ethereal vision rising in the moonlight from the post-quake rubble alongside the rebuild in a designer dress. You know, a Phoenix rising from the ashes sort of thing. The problem is Sasha's already split the seam of her Anna Stretton dress. She got herself in a right state over it too, so I told her to take a break. Guess what she goes and does?'

'I've no idea,' Isla said. She was finding this insight into the modeling world fascinating.

'Takes herself off to Burger King, that's what. She's shoveling a Whopper burger in as we speak. Bloody models! Listen, Isla I'm not an advocate of the emaciated look by any means, I love the fuller figure but honestly, you do have to fit the clothes supplied, and a size ten Sasha is not. No matter what she and her agency say.'

Isla could picture him running his fingers through his hair in frustration.

'Right enough about Sasha – oh no! Oh, my God, I don't believe it. She got fries too! I give up. Anyway, I've thought about the Char-Bridge situation, and I've never been one to listen to my head. The heart rules the roost, and I say this "*the past is the past*" business of Bridget's is code for, "*I am scared.*" I think she's frightened of the possibilities that meeting up with Charlie might bring.'

'I think you're right there.'

'And you know the way I see it is we all make mistakes along the way, I mean just look at bloody Sasha over there. But not many of us get a second chance. You need to hear what this Charlie chap has to say for himself, find out his version of events. Then you can make a decision as to whether or not you override Bridget and invite him to Bibury. She's not getting any younger and nor, I imagine, is this Charlie fellow. At their time of life, caution needs to be thrown to the wind. This could be their last chance at something wonderful and Isla my dear, life is too short for what ifs.'

'Phew, I was hoping you'd say that. Perhaps not in quite so many words but we are on the same page.'

'Oh my, I just had a rather spectacularly good idea.'

'What?'

'If you decide to ask Charlie to Bibury, why don't you invite him to come for the Matchmaker Festival?'

'Oh Carl, imagine—'

'I am, but we're getting ahead of ourselves, ring him. I've got to go, Sasha just spotted the Yogurt Story. Be sure and tell me how you get on and I'll see you in a couple of weeks at the meeting. Bye-eee.'

Isla hung up. She'd already decided to head round to Callum's shortly, and she sent off a quick text to that end. Not that she held out much hope of hearing back from him, he was hopeless at checking his phone. He was also as laid back as the hills, and she knew he wouldn't mind an unexpected visit. Especially, if there was the promise of it turning into a booty call. She'd play that one by ear she thought, yawning, but she would try and get hold of Charlie from his place. Sitting up, she swung her legs over the side of the bed and cocked an ear. The television was on, but she was betting Gran would have nodded off in her seat by now. She never lasted more than an hour when she hit that recliner of hers. She decided to check to see if the coast was clear.

She was indeed asleep. Her head was leaning back against the soft cushions of her chair, her feet crossed at the ankles on the footrest. Coal had managed to drag himself away from the fire she'd put a match to, to curl up on Bridget's lap. He too was sound asleep. Satisfied she wouldn't get caught a second time, she tiptoed across the hall and into her gran's bedroom. Opening the drawer, she took out the bundle of cards once more and undid the ribbon, skimming the last card's text until she spotted Charlie's telephone number. With one last look over her shoulder, she added him to her phone's contact list.

Chapter 30

'Gran, I'm heading round to Callum's. I'm not sure if I'll be back tonight or not,' Isla said hoping her face wasn't giving away the sudden attack of the guilt she felt at her skulduggery. The fire was dying down, she noticed, bending down and opening the door of the wood-burner before tossing another log into it. It was slow burning wood her father had gotten in for them through his work, and she knew it would burn for a while, keeping both her gran and Coal toasty. It was crazy lighting the fire this time of the year, but then that was the Coast for you.

Bridget opened her eyes, and despite being half asleep managed to give her a disapproving look. Isla felt another stab of guilt at her premarital sexual goings-on which was ridiculous given she was a woman of thirty. Still, if the shoe were on the other foot ... which, if this Charlie fellow kept his word and came over for the festival, it very well could be. She shuddered. *Enough of that Isla Brookes, you are getting way ahead of yourself.*

Jeremy opened the door; he was still clad in his PE uniform of shorts and a Nike singlet from which his muscles bulged.

He must be frozen, she thought. Or perhaps all that muscle mass kept him warm. Isla knew he was popular with the lady members of Bibury Area School's faculty, thanks to Saralee, but he was too pumped up for her and there was just something about him that hinted at the possibility of his being a medallion wearer. The hair that protruded from the neckline of his singlet, perhaps? Glad to be ushered in from the rain outside, she followed him through to the lounge where the boys had the fire roaring. Callum was engrossed in a game of basketball on the flatscreen, and he grinned his welcome, patting the seat next to him on the couch. His eyes never left the screen as she sat down. Jeremy picked up the bowl of nuts from the coffee table and flopped down in the armchair. Resuming his position before she'd interrupted, Isla thought.

Five minutes later, she was regretting having come over. It had been unplanned so she couldn't complain that Callum wasn't paying her attention. Still, the testosterone had just about knocked her out as the two men took on the shared role of armchair referees. It was not a night for venturing out really, but now that she was here, she could do what she'd come for and make the call to Charlie away from Gran's bionic ears.

On the pretext of making a cuppa, she left them to it. Instead of heading for the kitchen, though, she made a beeline for Callum's bedroom and shut the door behind her. She sat down on the double bed which she knew from experience had a squeaky mattress. It was cold in here. She pulled the blanket Callum had folded at the bottom of the bed over her legs. The room was nondescript, but he kept it tidy. His mother had housetrained him, he'd told her the first time she'd stayed over. Retrieving her phone from the carryall she'd stuck the bare necessities in, Isla took a deep breath. It's now or never, she decided as the phone began to ring and her stomach rolled over as a man's voice said 'hello.'

'Hello, is that Charlie?'

'It is, who is this please?'

'Um, hi Charlie, I'm Bridget Collins's granddaughter, Isla Brookes. Her daughter, Mary, is my mum.'

There was silence, and she hoped the shock hadn't seen him off. 'Are you there?' she asked.

'I am, but this has come a bit out of the blue. You're Bridget's granddaughter you say?' His understandable wariness took on an urgent tone. 'Is she alright?'

'Yes, yes, sorry. I should have said first off that this call's nothing to worry about, she's fine. She doesn't know I'm ringing you though.'

Isla explained how she'd come across the cards he had been sending these past years tucked away in a drawer. 'Gran, I mean Bridget, was very reluctant to tell me anything about you. She just said you broke her heart. I suppose I felt that there are two sides to every story and well, that's why I'm ringing you really, to hear your side of the story.'

There was a harrumphing sound. 'I broke her heart?' His voice had gone up a couple of notches. 'I wrote to that woman every week for a year, I'll have you know. I kept my promise to her, and she never wrote back, not once. It was my heart that was broken.'

Isla frowned, staring at Callum's suit hanging in readiness

for the next day on the back of the door. She hadn't expected this, and she pressed the phone closer to her ear in order not to miss a word he had to say.

'I left Bibury because her family didn't approve of my being Catholic. It was Bridget's father who put an end to us seeing each other. I lost my job because of him too, not that I blame him, it was the way things were back then. I decided to go to Australia because the money was good there, better than it ever was on the Coast. The plan was I'd come back in a year or two with enough money for us to be married if Bridget would have me. I thought if I were a man of means, her parents might see me in a different light.'

Isla tried to visualize the man at the other end of the phone but couldn't. The postmarks on the envelopes he'd sent were from Perth, and it would be late afternoon there. She might not have been able to form a mental picture of him, but that the disbelief in his voice at the way things had turned out was genuine, she was certain. He was agitated too, and she hoped she'd done the right thing in calling him, she didn't want to be responsible for any sudden heart attacks.

'I heard through one of the lads at the mine, who came to Kalgoorlie a year or so after me, that Bridget had gone and married my old mate, Tom Collins. I couldn't believe it. I couldn't believe either of them could have done that to me. Then when I heard what happened to poor Clara, has Bridget told you about her?'

'Yes, she has.'

'Well, I surmised it was the grief over her dying that brought them together. Tom was there, and I wasn't. Though, I never understood why she didn't reply to any of my letters, not a single one. It was cruel to leave me hanging like that.'

Isla bridled a bit at the mention of her granddad. Her grandparents had been happy together hadn't they? She recognized then that she didn't know, who knew for certain what went on inside a marriage? Her mum and dad were different, of course. Those two were transparent in their marital dealings. Her dad still struggled thirty-six years down the track to keep his hands to himself where her mother's derriere was concerned. Tom Collins might have been a gruff old man, but she could recall him pushing her on the swing down at Banbridge Park for what had felt like hours on end. Her five-year-old self calling, 'Higher Granddad, higher!' He never complained or said he'd had enough and she'd felt like she was flying high over the tops of the Punga trees.

'Perhaps your letters got lost. Gran told me she never heard from you again after you left Bibury. She assumed it was you who'd broken your promise to her.'

'She never heard from me?' He didn't sound convinced.

'It's true and if you don't mind my asking, if you feel so let down by her, why do you want to see her again?'

His sigh was weighted. 'When you get to my age you question things, choices you made, paths you took. I never stopped loving her, you know.'

'Loving the idea of her.'

'No, I loved Bridget Upton with everything I had. Nobody else has ever come close.'

Isla had goosebumps, and she pulled the blanket up around her knowing it wouldn't make any difference. 'Did you marry?'

'There was never anyone who could hold a candle to Bridget. She was a beauty. I wasn't a monk by any means, though. I've two fine sons to two fine ladies both of whom I'm on amiable terms with. My boys are both married with kids of their own and live here in Perth. They're good lads; they pop in on their old dad regularly.'

Isla found herself thawing towards this kindly sounding old gent. 'I've got a brother who lives over in Emerald.'

'Ah, he's in mining then.'

'Yes, my dad was too, but when Granddad got sick from the coal dust, my dad decided to get out of it. He's been working at a wood processing plant in Greymouth for the last eight years. Mum works in the local pharmacy and her brother, Jack, lives in Greymouth. He's something or other high up in the mining hierarchy.'

'I can hear Bridget in your voice.'

'Really?' Isla didn't think she sounded anything like her gran.

He laughed. 'Don't sound so surprised. You're her granddaughter, aren't you? Tell me about yourself Isla, what's your story?'

'Oh, it's nothing very exciting. I lived overseas for a long time and worked in interior design. I came home at the start of the year, and I've bought the local café. It's a complete career turnabout, but I love it.'

'No young man on the scene.'

'Kind of.'

'Ah, I see.'

There was silence.

Isla rushed in before she got cold feet. 'Listen, Charlie, we're having a Matchmaking Festival here in Bibury next February.'

'A what?'

She explained what it was all about and when he spoke his voice was thick. 'A dance to remember Clara, on the same date, in the same hall where I first met my Bridget you say?'

'Yes, would you like to come?' Isla chewed her bottom lip hoping she was doing the right thing.

'I'll be there.'

Chapter 31

Gran had promised to make a tray of her custard slice for the Project Matchmaker meeting which was just as well since the cabinet was nearly empty, Isla thought, glancing over at it. One sausage roll and a piece of caramel slice looked back at her, and she could guarantee Annie would snaffle that when she got here. Well, she could have it, Isla was saving her appetite for her all-time favourite, custard slice. Gran didn't make it nearly often enough. Mind you, she thought, glancing down at her midriff, it was probably a good thing. She bagged up the sausage roll for anyone who fancied it at the meeting.

She'd had a busy day here on her own at Nectar, Annie had taken a much-deserved Saturday off to spend with Kris. Although, she'd be calling in with him at five o'clock, when the café shut for the meeting. That gave her fifty minutes to get everything tidied up. *Get cracking girl.* She began to wipe the tables down, pausing only when the woman who'd ordered lunch and had moved outside to enjoy a pot of tea in the sun afterwards, popped her head in and asked if she could have a bit more hot water for her tea.

'Of course,' Isla said with a smile taking the jug from her.

'I was just about to come out and see if you were alright, I'll bring it out to you.' She was very glamorous, she thought, noting her glossy bobbed hair, her big black sunglasses pushed up onto the top of her head and the bold red lipstick. 'I love your dress, by the way; the colour really suits you.'

'Oh, thank you. It's nice to be able to give the summer wardrobe an airing at long last. Are you closing soon?' Her eyes flicked over to the cloth Isla had put down on the table when she'd popped inside.

'No, I'm just doing a spot of housekeeping, don't mind me.' Isla did not believe in rushing people. 'You enjoy soaking up that sun for as long as you like. I'll have this out to you in just a tick.' She headed through to the kitchen and waited for the jug to boil. The two-piece pavement setting she'd invested in for the warmer weather was proving popular, especially on days as gorgeous as today had been. She'd wanted to put a few more tables outside, there was plenty of room, but it had been a no-go. It was the horrible little council man who Gran was having all the bother with over the festival arrangements, who had put the kibosh on the idea. He'd insisted any more furniture outside the café would be hazardous to passers by. Isla had been highly annoyed; even with the two extra tables she'd wanted, a five berth motorised scooter would have been able to get past.

She took the pot outside, enjoying the feel of the sun on her face as she put it down on the table for the woman. 'Oh, I hope those kea birds are behaving,' she said gesturing to where the two parrots she'd nicknamed Dennis and Menace were strutting up and down the pavement.

'I'm enjoying watching them, they're funny.'

'They like an audience but they can be naughty, especially when it comes to windscreen wipers. They're part of the place too, though. In fact, the café used to be called The Kea,' she said with a smile. 'Enjoy your tea.' Isla turned to go, but the woman stopped her.

'You're the proprietor of Nectar aren't you?'

'Yes, I am. My name's Isla Brookes.'

'I'm Suzy Carmichael; I work for *Southern Gastronomy* magazine.' She held out her hand, and Isla shook it, feeling uncertain as to where this conversation was heading. *Southern Gastronomy*, she knew was a popular foodie magazine.

'I came here today to review Nectar for our Emerging Country Café Scene section. And look, I don't normally do this, but I wanted to tell you personally how much I've enjoyed both the food and the service today. Ten out of ten, Isla.'

'Oh! Oh wow, thanks.' Isla's smile was wide. Taken aback, she didn't know what else to say. She couldn't quite believe what she'd just heard.

'You're very welcome,' the woman said before turning back towards the sun and topping up her tea.

Isla felt like she was walking on air as she went back inside and continued the tidy-up she had fine-tuned over the months. Her mind, however, was racing, and she was desperate to share what had just happened with someone. It was still another half an hour before the others were due though.

'Bye, keep an eye out for next month's edition of the magazine, Isla,' Suzy Carmichael called ten minutes later, popping her head inside the door once more and adding, 'I probably shouldn't have had that last cup of tea, it's a long drive back to Christchurch.'

Isla laughed. 'Oh, I will. Thanks so much Suzy, drive safely.' She headed outside and watched as the woman got into her shiny black Jeep, waving her off.

She spied Ben bringing in the garage's sign and remembered the sausage roll she'd bagged up for whoever fancied it. Ben, was partial to a sausage roll. In fact, they were his favourite. She raced back inside, grabbed the bag and slamming the door behind her; she ran the short distance down the road to the garage.

He saw her coming and waited in the forecourt. 'Hey Isla, what's the panic?'

She held up the paper bag, puffing.

'You ran here to give me a—' he took the bag from her and opened it. 'A sausage roll. Were you worried it would get cold?' His eyes twinkled. 'Not that I don't appreciate such fine service of course. What do I owe you?'

She'd gotten her breath back and waved her hand. 'No, no, it was left over, and I know you like them and I had to tell someone what just happened,' Isla relayed what had transpired with Suzy Carmichael and when she'd finished Ben pulled her into a hug.

He stepped back quickly, looking at his overalls and then at her top. 'Shit, I hope I didn't get grease on you.'

Isla wouldn't have cared if he had. Gran would undoubtedly have a tip for removing grease from garments like she had a tip for most things laundry-related.

'Anyway, that's fantastic and well-earned, Isla.'

Isla grinned. 'Thanks. I can't wait to tell Annie.' She could see the genuine pleasure at her news in his eyes. They'd come a long way, her and Ben, she thought. From tiptoeing around each other awkwardly when she'd first come back, to that drunken encounter at the Pit. They'd both moved on from that, thank goodness! These days they quite often met up at the Pit for a drink at the weekend with Saralee and Callum, Annie and Kris making the numbers six.

'Speaking of Annie, I'd better get back,' she said.

'Ah, the big meeting. I tell you Saralee's been living and breathing this festival. I've sold a heap of tickets through the garage too. Mm, thanks for this,' he said biting into the sausage roll. 'It's good.'

'You're welcome. To be honest, I haven't had much to do with any of it, Nectar keeps my nose to the grindstone, but Gran said Saralee's been an absolute marvel. It wouldn't be happening but for her. I'm looking forward to hearing where everything's at. I'll see you.' She gave him a wave and felt his eyes on her as she walked back to the café. She still felt something for him, she'd be lying to herself if she didn't admit that. Who knew? Maybe she always would. It didn't matter now though. She'd come to a conclusion that where Ben was concerned Gran was right and the past was best left in the past. He was obviously happy with Saralee.

As for her and Callum, well, they were more like friends with benefits, she mused. Not for the first time she told herself she needed to sort out what it was they were doing. They'd slotted into this easy routine together, but it was becoming a habit. It wasn't that it was a bad habit, but it was a habit she probably should think about breaking if she didn't want to take things further. She doubted she'd be breaking his heart were she to call it a day because Callum hadn't shown any signs of being any more serious about her than she was about him. He was heading into the city for the weekend to catch up with some of his old mates, so that would give them a bit of breathing space. Her dad had asked her the other day what Callum's intentions towards her were when he'd turned up at the café with two bunches of radishes.

'Do you think you'll marry this one, Isla?' he'd said with a hopeful gleam. 'He's not a bad lad, Callum, much better than that Tim.'

'MYOB Dad,' she'd said relieving him of his radishes.

Gran still wasn't here, Isla registered, as she and Annie rustled up coffee and tea for the others who had joined two tables together and were chatting amongst themselves. Bridget's friend, Margaret, who was here in her Barker's Creek Hall Committee member capacity was looking very lemon-lipped at her tardiness. The other two members had bowed out, she'd announced as she arrived. The meeting had clashed with a Country and Western concert being held at the Bibury Retirement Village. Now she tutted. 'I have somewhere I have to be at six. I hope she fronts up soon.'

Isla was guessing she was chomping at the bit to join the others at the retirement village. Being late wasn't like Gran, she thought, frowning, and especially not as she was the one who had organized this meeting in the first place. She'd give her two more minutes and then she'd head over the road and make sure she was okay.

Bridget was sitting at her kitchen table; she'd pop over to the café in ten minutes, she thought, glancing up at the clock. She had one eye on the Saturday paper open in front of her and one eye on the custard squares she'd made earlier. Coal was partial to custard, and she didn't trust him not to launch himself on the tray given the opportunity. A knocking at the front door startled her. 'Hold your horses, I'm coming,' she said, getting up.

Her hip was a lot better these days. She picked up Coal, who was staring up at the bench trying to hypnotize the custard squares into falling within his greedy reach, and popped him in the laundry. Shutting the door on him, she muttered all the way down the hall that if it were the Jehovah's witnesses come to tell her the end of the world was nigh again, she would not be responsible for her actions. But it wasn't the Jehovah's witnesses she saw on opening the door but rather the oddest little man she'd ever seen.

His face was ruddy like he enjoyed a tipple and his eyes were button bright. The snowy white beard that hung to the middle of his chest made her think at once of her favourite of Snow White's Dwarves, Happy. But by golly gosh, he must be sweltering in that get-up of his, she thought, staring at his ill-fitting suit as he tipped his bowler hat and said, 'Rohan Sullivan, at your service madam.'

Gathering herself, Bridget replied, 'And what service might that be then?' She was wagering he was a mobile chimney sweep albeit an overdressed one.

'Matchmaking of course.'

Holding onto the door a little tighter, Bridget listened in disbelief as he told her that matchmaking was in his family. 'I'm a direct descendant of Cathal Sullivan,' he said thumping his chest proudly. 'The first Matchmaker to arrive in New Zealand. My grandfather sailed here from Ireland in the late eighteen hundreds, so he did.'

That she was gobsmacked was an understatement, but somehow, Bridget found her voice and revealed her family's connection to the matchmaking tradition.

Rohan smiled, revealing teeth that had seen better days. 'Well now, isn't that a coincidence.'

It was said in a way that left Bridget in no doubt that his being here now was no coincidence. For the first time since she'd opened the door to him, she noticed the leather-bound book he held under his arm. He followed her gaze and produced it for her to see. As he opened it, her nostrils were assailed by a musty smell, and she fancied she could see the dust motes fly up from the pages. 'You see,' he said. 'This is what I do.'

She put her glasses on and ran her fingers down the yellowing paper with its neatly written entries in search of her grandparents' paired names, but there were no entries dating so far back as Ireland. They began in New Zealand. Cathal Sullivan, Bridget knew, had to have been the man who matched her grandparents. Perhaps that was why she had the eerie feeling of already knowing Rohan even though she was certain they had never met. She shook her head; she was getting fanciful in her old age.

'How did you hear about the festival Mr Sullivan?' she asked deciding that being business-like was the best course of action.

'Call me Rohan, and I heard tell of it on the wind. There haven't been many calls for my services in a long while. I reckon it's down to that thing they call the internet. So, I was keen to come and offer them to you for your festival in exchange for a night's board and lodging in this fine town.'

Bridget assumed he meant he'd heard about it on the coastal grapevine and she simply could not believe her luck. A genuine Matchmaker standing on her doorstep offering his services for her festival! Hang on, she thought with dismay, she'd already given the job to somebody. But Rohan turning up like this well, it was fate, it was destiny. She didn't know how she would break the news to Samuel West that his services as Chief Matchmaker would no longer be required, but she would not look this gift horse in the mouth. Samuel West would just have to get over it.

'So tell me then, how would it all work on the day, Rohan?'

'Well now, I won't be needing much, just a table on which to rest my book and a chair for both myself and whomever I am talking to. Oh, and plenty of pens, please. I don't want to be running out of ink. The lonely hearts take it in turns to tell me a bit about themselves, and as the day goes on and my list grows long, I can begin the important business of comparing my notes and making the appropriate matches.'

'And then the people you match can get to know each other at the dance later that night. It sounds so simple.' Bridget clapped her hands delightedly.

'Ah now Bridget, you of all people should know the business of love is rarely simple. That's why I do what I do.'

How right he was, she mused, thinking back on her complicated life and wondering why he should assume that she knew all about the complications love wrought.

'Where do you live, Rohan?'

'Oh, here and there but mostly over there.'

Bridget was bemused, but she took his outstretched hand nevertheless, and they shook on their deal. He promised her he would be back in Bibury on the eve of the thirteenth of February to carry out his Valentine's Day matchmaking duties and Bridget promised she'd find someone who would provide suitable board and lodgings for him.

She shut the door, oblivious to the tiny green apples that fell from the tree in her front garden as a gust of wind suddenly blew through the town's main street. She was in too much of a hurry to collect her tray of squares and to release Coal. It didn't matter that she was running late for the meeting because what news she was bringing to it!

Chapter 32

With one minute to spare before Isla sent out a search party, Bridget appeared with her tray of custard squares in hand. She looked flustered, Isla thought, wondering what had held her up. Maybe her custard hadn't set, or she'd forgotten to add the all-important vanilla essence – that would have been catastrophic, indeed.

'I'm sorry I'm late everybody,' she announced as Isla took the tray from her. 'But I just had the strangest, most marvellous thing happen. You won't believe me when I tell you.'

'Well sit down for goodness' sake woman, and tell us about it,' Carl said, getting up and pulling a chair out for her. He'd arrived on the dot of five, informing Annie and Isla he had his overnight bag in the car.

Bridget did as she was told and when she was settled and satisfied all eyes were on her, she told them of her meeting with Rohan Sullivan.

This news was met with both disbelief and great excitement.

'Gran that's completely bizarre,' Isla said. 'And you reckon this Rohan's grandfather was the Matchmaker who paired your great-grandparents? My great-great-grandparents?' She shivered at the coincidence of it all.

'Yes, Cathal Sullivan, and destiny is what I'd call it.'

'He sounds odd if you ask me,' Margaret said. 'The Women's Forum group had a talk last month about pensioner safety and how elderly women living alone need to be wary of opening the doors to strangers.'

'Good point Margaret, but she doesn't live alone,' Carl piped up loyally. 'He does sound a bit different, though.'

'He was certainly very—' Bridget cast around for the right word. 'Eccentric.'

Isla wondered if nut-job might be a better turn of phrase. 'I suppose he'd have to be to do what he does in this day and age.'

'Well I think it's wonderful to have the services of a genuine Matchmaker for the Festival,' Saralee gushed, flashing her dimples at them all. 'The publicity we can generate with him on board will be priceless.'

'It'll certainly add to the magic,' Annie concurred. Kris was gazing at the custard squares in the middle of the table, much like Coal had been earlier. His girlfriend elbowed him, and he quickly looked up and added, 'Yes it'll be wonderful.'

'We're going to need more tickets, please Saralee,' Isla said getting up and retrieving the money tin from under the counter. She unlocked it and handed the contents over to her. Saralee had opened an account for the project and was in charge of the finances.

'You girls have done well,' she said adding up the wad of cash before jotting the amount down in her notebook.

'To be honest, I've been surprised how fast the tickets have sold.' Isla had expected the likes of the ever-hopeful Violet McDougall and young Beau from the butcher's to purchase tickets, but she'd been amazed at how many strangers passing through Bibury had too.

'David's had loads of interest through the gym, and he's directed them all to the Facebook page to buy their tickets. I've had a great response from the model frat too,' Carl said.

Margaret wasn't going to be left out. 'And I've sent the link to my daughter to share amongst any of her friends who fancy a weekend down South. She's in banking up in Auckland you know.'

Isla was careful not to make eye contact with her gran; she'd burst out laughing if she did.

'Thanks, guys, our online sales through Facebook are going really well, and nearly all the female staff at school have asked me if Jeremy the PE teacher is going. When I tell them he is, they're buying up large for themselves and their friends. Oh, and Principal Bishop bought a ticket too which surprised me, I didn't think it'd be his thing at all.'

Isla crossed her fingers under the table for Violet McDougall, you just never knew what could happen. After all, look what had just happened to Gran with this Rohan fellow landing on her doorstep, she thought.

Bridget spoke next. 'Margaret and I had an awful meeting with the horrid chap from the council at the hall this week. Honestly, the man has eyes like a ferret, and a comb over he could get arrested for. I've met his type before. If we'd dared so much as even glance in the direction of the hair, the list of specifications would have doubled.'

'As it was the list of works that need doing to comply with council regulations were the length of his arm,' Margaret said. 'And if they aren't completed in time then the festival won't go ahead.'

'Leave him to me,' Saralee said with a steely glint in her baby blues. 'I know how to deal with council rottweilers. First things first though, I need to go home and do the math, but I think we should just about be in a position financially to start work on the hall and begin tackling some of those specs. Ben's brother, Hayden, has kindly agreed to do the work for the cost of the materials only, and if we organize a community working bee, we should have that list of works knocked out in no time. In the meantime though, we've had a great response from interested stall holders which is more money in the kitty.'

The group listened, impressed, as she reeled off every sort of food truck imaginable from kebabs through to Chinese dumplings along with an assortment of Arts and Crafts stall holders that would be setting up their stalls in the grounds and lending a festive air to the day come rain or shine. Nectar too, of course, was on board to be showcase their wares.

'What about music for the dance later?' Annie asked.

'A friend of mine is into rock'n'roll dancing, and she recommended a band. I've seen them on YouTube, and they look great. Isla, you have wi-fi here don't you?' Saralee asked pulling her tablet out.

Isla nodded. She'd decided free wi-fi was an added service she could offer her customers. It had been a pain in the butt getting it connected, but she reckoned it had been worth it. Saralee keyed in her search and then held the device up angling it so they could all see. They certainly looked the part, Isla thought as the screen came to life, taking in their shiny '50s style suits, and they had a good sound. Carl got up midway through the number and pulled Bridget to her feet giving her a twirl around the café much to everyone's amusement.

'What do you think?' Saralee asked.

'They're brilliant. If they're available and not too expensive we should book them, Gran, Margaret the music was your era – what did you think?'

Bridget sat back down her face flushed and said they were 'very good.' Margaret agreed.

'Right then, I'll check them out,' Saralee said scribbling in her notebook. 'Oh, and I think we should use the Bibury PTA to do the catering for supper after the dance. What do you think?'

'Will they be able to cope with the numbers?' Annie asked.

'The PTA mothers are a force to be reckoned with,' Saralee said, and Kris nodded his agreement.

'You, Saralee are a force to be reckoned with,' Isla said smiling and reaching for a custard square. The greedy glint in Kris' eyes had not escaped her, and she was not going to miss out. First in, first served and all that. 'You've worked wonders organizing everything.'

Saralee, blushed prettily, as a murmuring of agreement sounded around the table.

It had been a week since the Project Matchmaker meeting, and Bridget was twitchy. Something was in the air, and it was making her irritable. She'd woken early and had given up on getting back to sleep. The wind that had started to blow up out of nowhere from time to time over these last few months had her feeling out of sorts. It was down to the wind that she'd woken up at this ungodly hour with the kowhai tree's branches tapping at her bedroom window. Coal didn't like it either, and she'd been tempted to put him out because he wouldn't settle. Lucky for him, she was getting soft in her old age.

Sighing, she got up and wrapped herself in her dressing gown before padding through to the kitchen.

'Alright, it's coming,' she told the mewling cat rubbing up against her legs. She fed him, then set about making herself a cup of tea, watching the swathes of pink emerging through the darkness from the kitchen window as she waited for the kettle to boil. It would be a nice day, she thought, if that blasted wind died off. As she'd passed by Isla's bedroom on her way to the kitchen, she'd given the door a gentle nudge with her foot. It opened enough for her to see that the bed was unslept in. She hadn't come home last night then. An eyebrow arched at the realization that she must have stayed at Callum's. She was never sure, as she hovered there in the hall, whether she approved or disapproved.

Yes, yes, she knew Isla was a grown woman entitled to do as she pleased but as her grandmother, she still felt it was her duty to disapprove. As a seventy-something-year-old woman, however, nothing the youngsters got up to these days shocked her anymore. Actually, that wasn't quite true she'd watched that show once out of curiosity, the one where those self-obsessed, dark-haired women spent all their time taking photographs of themselves. The Kardashians, that was them. The thought of the one with the big bottom being a role model for the young girls of today – now that had shocked her. What did upset her where Isla was concerned though, was that when it came to love she was getting it wrong again.

It was Isla and Ben who should be together. She'd seen it in the way they danced around each other emotionally these last months, both trying to act as though they had no feelings other than friendship for the other. Saralee was a wonderful girl whose talents were wasted in secretarial work, but she wasn't the girl for Ben. The same could be said for Callum. He was a perfectly nice lad, but that didn't mean he was the one for Isla. Neither couple seemed to be going anywhere. They were just meandering along, wasting time and when you got to Bridget's time of life, you finally grasped how precious that time was.

Oh, she knew right enough that Isla had been young when she'd first stepped out with Ben. Some would say she'd done the right thing in leaving Bibury. Bridget hadn't wanted to see her go but she'd understood her need. She'd escaped the small town and put her career first because she'd been far too young to settle down. Bridget could understand all this because she'd wanted a life of her own too until she met Charlie. After that, all she'd wanted was a life with him, but it wasn't meant to be. And then there was poor Clara, so alive and in love with Tom and then she was gone, just like that, she thought, sitting down at the table with her cup of tea letting her mind drifted back.

1957

'Bridget darling, you've a visitor.' Her mother's forced joviality drifted up the stairs and wound its way under the gap between Bridget's bedroom door and the floorboards, making her cringe. It had not escaped Bridget's notice that her mother had adopted this tone in the last week or so. It was borne of desperation, she knew, but she couldn't muster any sympathy. She had no room left inside her for that. Her mother's reasoning, Bridget figured, was that if she kept up the jolly façade of everything being alright then sooner or later it would be. Well, she was wrong. From where Bridget was perched on the edge of her bed, a wraith against the floral bedspread, she could not fathom how things could ever be alright again.

She didn't know how long she'd been sitting there. In her hand, she clutched the clipping she'd saved from the *Bibury Times* of her and Clara outside Barker's Creek Hall on the night of the Valentine's Day Dance. She'd been staring at it so hard and for so long that she no longer saw it. She didn't need to; she'd never forget that night, it would be forever imprinted on her mind.

It was Saturday morning, and outside her bedroom window she became aware of a lawnmower droning, Mr Field next door always mowed his lawn on a Saturday morning unless it was wet. This was what Bridget was finding so hard to comprehend. She had finished her third week back at work, going through the motions and clearing her in-tray day after day. This was the fourth Saturday morning she had lived through since Clara's funeral. The fourth Saturday that the day had stretched long and empty without Charlie and her friend to share it with. All around her, the business of life was marching on.

It seemed unbelievable somehow that despite what had happened, she still had a job that she went to Monday through to Friday. Mr Field was still mowing his lawn on a Saturday morning. The Milk Bar where she and Clara had whiled away so many Saturday afternoons was still opening. Spotty chin Jim was still frying chips. And yet Charlie was gone and had not sent her one single word to cling on to, and Clara was dead. How could that be? How could that have happened?

She hadn't written to send word to Charlie of what had happened to poor, darling Clara. He didn't deserve to know. Not if he could leave the way he had and not look back over his shoulder, not even once.

'Bridget!' Her mother's voice was more insistent this time.

Bridget blinked, she'd better go down and see who it was that had called for her. She cast a cursory glance in the mirror on her dressing table. She was pale, but she was presentable. She'd have to do. She smoothed her skirt and opened her bedroom door.

From the top of the stairs, she couldn't see who it was standing on the other side of their front door, her father's authoritarian form and her mother's nervous fluttering were blocking her view. For a second she floundered. The memory of Charlie standing there waiting for her the first night he had called hit her so hard she almost doubled over at its impact. She gripped the stair rail and paused, biting down hard on her lip to distract herself and as the pain registered and banished Charlie, she descended the stairs.

Her father moved aside, and Bridget saw Tom Collins standing there, his head slightly bowed in deference to her father as he twisted his cap around and around in his hands. He was nervous, she appreciated, feeling a pang, and he was hurting too. She saw it in his eyes as he looked past her parents at her. Clara's loss didn't belong to her family and friends alone; there was Tom too. Poor, poor Tom.

'Look who's come to see you Bridget dear; it's Tom.'

Her mother must think that grief made you simple, Bridget thought, as she gave a small smile and said hello. She was suddenly filled with a desperate need to get away from her parents and her home and was grateful when Tom spoke up.

'I wondered whether you might like to come for a walk with me?'

Her mother nodded encouragingly, and her father said that partaking of the fresh morning air would do her good. Both parents were eager for her to move on and put the goings on of the last while behind her.

So she'd gone, partly to escape them and partly to talk to someone who had loved Clara like she had.

One year later she married Tom, and Bridget Upton – who had once had a best friend she belly laughed with and a man called Charlie she had given her heart to – ceased to exist.

She became Bridget Collins, and soon after that, she became a mother. She was a grown woman with children of her own and the girl she'd been was locked away in a compartment of her mind that she only unlocked and set free on the rarest of occasions. She'd loved Tom, and they'd weathered their storms, come full circle she felt, as he lay dying. Until he decided to unburden himself and reveal that their whole life together had been based on a lie. Then Charlie had begun to send his cards, and the memories had kept flooding back ever since taking her by surprise like a rogue spring tide.

Bridget started as Coal began kneading her lap. 'Ooh, you've got sharp claws, cut that out,' she chided giving him a gentle push. He jumped off and stalked out of the room, and she knew he'd probably go and take up residence on Isla's bed, as was his morning routine.

A cat's life was so uncomplicated, she thought. Ever since Rohan Sullivan's visit she'd had this sense that things were going to change, that her life was about to get complicated. The morning light began to seep into the kitchen casting the room in a rosy pink glow. She should be feeling quietly proud at the way things were shaping up for the festival, she told herself. Not this fidgety unsettled feeling that something was about to happen.

Chapter 33

'Christmas is nearly upon us, and we need to talk turkey, Isla. They cost over sixty dollars these days you know for a decent sized bird. It'd be nothing short of sacrilege to let your mother get her hands on it.' Isla relayed what her gran had said to her the night before as she and Annie set about getting the food ready for the day's trade. It was going to be busy; they'd taken lots of luncheon bookings for this last week before Christmas. Isla had thought she'd never get used to the crack of dawn starts when she'd first taken over the café, but now she didn't even need to set her alarm. Of course, daylight savings helped. She hadn't particularly relished heading across the road in the dark in the depths of winter.

Annie chuckled as she beat eggs for the quiche she was making. 'Your poor mum, you and Bridget give her a hard time.'

'Ah, she's alright, it's just our way. Besides Mum's far too full of the joys of the Revlon Christmas Gift with Purchase promotion she's got running to worry about a turkey. I did feel a bit sorry for her when Ryan said he wasn't coming home for Christmas, though. He's spending it with his girlfriend's family in Sydney.' Isla recalled how her mother's orange face had turned red as she relayed the news to Isla. She'd brightened, or at least returned to her normal shade when Isla pointed out that Ryan wanting to spend Christmas with his girlfriend meant her philandering brother must be serious about her. She could tell by the look on her mum's face that she'd drifted off into a mother of the groom fantasy at this news.

'So who *is* doing the turkey then?'

'Gran is. I'm on roast potatoes, salads and veggies, Mum's on dessert and Dad's on booze. Everybody's happy, apart from Dad. He's fine with the booze bit, but he's been roped in for the self-tanning demonstration Mum's doing in-store this week. I don't know.' Isla shook her head. 'I would have thought one Oompa-Loompa in the family was enough.'

'Stop being horrid,' Annie said giggling. 'Hey, did you get the tree decorated last night?'

'Yep, Dad dropped it in as promised and Gran and I spent the evening decorating it. It smells gorgeous. It always feels like Christmas to me once the tree's up and the house smells of pine. Right, these are ready to go in.' Isla lifted the tray of Christmas mince pies up and carried them over to the oven.

'What about Callum, what's he doing for the day?'

'He's having breakfast with me and then heading off to Christchurch for a family lunch. And he did invite me,' she said in response to Annie's raised eyebrow. 'But I haven't had Christmas with my family in years. I'm looking forward to a good old Kiwi summer Christmas. What about you and Kris?

You're going to your parents, still aren't you?'

'Yeah, we'll stay over on Christmas Eve and come back on Boxing Day. I'm going to make Kataifi for breakfast. It's Kris' favourite. You make it with shredded filo pastry, almonds and cinnamon. Mum's doing lamb in a nod to Kris being Greek which is sweet of her. I have to say though, I'm green-eyed over Carl and David heading off to Hawaii for the silly season. Although, when I spoke to Carl last he was threatening to pull the pin on the whole trip if David doesn't buy appropriate swimwear. He says Speedos are just not on.'

Isla had to agree even if David would cut a fine figure of a man in them. 'While we've got a sec, I've got something for you.'

Annie looked at her friend expectantly as she rummaged in her handbag and produced a couple of sheets of paper. 'What's that?'

'See for yourself.' Isla handed her the papers with a smile and watched in delight as Annie's face broke into a big grin followed by a squeal.

'Flights to Queenstown and three nights at the Millennium Hotel! Oh, Isla I can't take this.'

'Yes, you can. You more than deserve it because I couldn't have taken this place on without you and Kris deserves it for all the hours he never sees you while you're busy toiling away here.'

Annie threw her arms around her friend.

The countdown to Christmas was a blur of functions, but Isla had enjoyed the festive bustling vibe even if she'd just about been on her knees by the time Christmas Day rolled around. Today, Boxing Day had dawned hot, without a cloud in the panorama of blue sky, and with the café shut she was going to lie in the sun and relax. Boxing Day was a day for doing nothing. Christmas Day had been a scorcher too, Isla thought, flapping her towel and spreading it out on the grass. It had been strange at first having Christmas dinner on her parent's deck under a sun umbrella after all those years in the UK, but the day had been lovely and the turkey had not been dry.

She smiled, flopping down on the towel, remembering her dad sitting across the table from her with an orange paper crown on his head from his Christmas cracker. It clashed dreadfully with his bronzed skin and made him look a little like the Wizard of Oz in the Judy Garland version. 'Loving the man tan Dad.' Isla hadn't been able to help herself, and Bridget had only encouraged her by sniggering.

'I only let Mary do it because she came to the Brass Monkey with me.'

'Under sufferance,' Mary said, but Isla knew her parents had had a ball doing whatever it was they'd done in the depths of winter on a muddy field with a bunch of bikers.

'And don't you go laughing too loudly,' Joe said pointing over at Bridget. 'She'll have you cornered next for the Gran Tan.'

They'd all done nicely on the present front too. Isla had bought Gran a year's subscription to her *Ireland Today* magazine. Gran had received a pair of possum lined slippers from Ryan that she was chuffed with and had insisted on wearing about the house ever since, despite the soaring temperatures. Isla had chosen a voucher for a day's fly fishing excursion for Callum, something he reckoned he'd always wanted to try. He, in turn, had given her a gorgeous pair of silver earrings, and she'd worn them Christmas Day pretending she hadn't heard her father mutter, 'shame it wasn't a ring.' Yes, she'd forgotten the simple pleasure of sitting around a table laden with food and the wine flowing with those she loved, even if they were all mad as hatters!

The best present ever as far as she was concerned though, had been the review for Nectar. It had appeared in the Christmas edition of *Southern Gastronomy* as Suzy Carmichael had promised and it had been glowing. Isla had cut it out and framed it. She hung it in pride of place on the café walls, and she and Annie had stood gazing at it, giving themselves a great big pat on the back. Now, feeling the sun warming her limbs she stretched out like Coal did when he was totally chilled which was ninety percent of the time.

Annie and Kris were flying down to Queenstown tomorrow. She hoped they loved every minute of their break away. They'd stayed on at her parents' in Christchurch so they could take them to the airport. It was an odd feeling knowing the friends she'd come to rely on so much weren't just around the corner even if it was only for a few days. Gran was pottering about in the kitchen, and the back garden was quiet apart from a resident Tui warbling over by the flax bushes. The day stretched long, and Isla planned on making the most of having absolutely nothing whatsoever to do except eat leftovers. Bliss, she thought picking her book up.

It had been quiet in the café in the days following Boxing Day as Isla had expected, with a few holiday makers calling in each day as they meandered through to their chosen camping spots. By the time New Year's Eve rolled around, she felt well rested and ready to take on whatever challenges came her way in 2018 Annie was back on board and full of the delights of the alpine town of Queenstown, as was Kris who had taken his life into his hands and done a bungee jump over the Skippers Canyon. Annie had not been keen to follow behind him saying that she wasn't going to pay good money to be terrified. Isla was with Annie on that one, adrenaline junkie she was not.

She was glad they were all together at the Pit tonight because she'd wanted to bring in the New Year with her wonderful friends and she was having a great night. She had a lot to celebrate; she thought as the countdown began.

Five, four, three, two, one, HAPPY NEW YEAR! The cheer went up, and Callum put his arms around her, kissing her softly on the lips before releasing her with a grin. He was looking a little unfocused, she noticed as she smiled up at him, but his eyes had already moved on. He was heading over in Annie's and Kris' direction. It wasn't that she was counting or anything, but he'd had quite a bit to drink, getting into the spirit of the New Year quite literally by ordering a few tequila slammers in between the beer he'd been tossing down his neck. School was definitely out for summer!

She watched as he shook Kris' hand. Kris' other arm was wrapped around Annie, and he looked reluctant to let her go as Callum honed in on her for a hug. He was feeling the love tonight, but he was also going to be feeling very sorry for himself at some point in the next twelve hours, Isla thought, with a fond rueful smile.

Kris smiled over at Isla and, releasing Annie, he opened his arms wide. 'Kali Xronia – Happy New Year.'

She hugged him back hard. Lovely, lovely Kris; he and Annie were a perfect match. He'd been telling them before the band started, when it was still possible to hold a conversation, that it was a tradition for presents to be exchanged on New Year's Day not Christmas in Greece. He'd told them how in the village he came from people gathered in the square on New Year's Eve to do last minute shopping or just to stroll around. It was all sounded so much more family-orientated and civilized.

Isla decided she'd send her mum and dad a text in a minute to wish them a happy new year. They were having a few friends around home for a Hawaiian themed barbeque. Isla had told them both that at least they had the tans to match their leis. Gran had gone to a Hogmanay night at Violet McDougall's house. She had tutted while she sat in the front room waiting for Margaret to pick her up. 'She only invited Margaret and me because she's under pressure from the Scottish Society to find out whether the Hall will still be free for them to use once the renovations are done. Typical Scots but they can go whistle and pay like everybody else is going to have to, Hogmanay or no Hogmanay.' She'd only drawn breath to add. 'I hope they don't do any of that awful haggis tonight and spend the entire night singing Auld Lang Syne.'

Bridget had missed Isla's smile as she picked up her

handbag, keen for the off despite her protesting when she heard Margaret pull up in the driveway and toot.

Isla's train of thought derailed as she spotted a black singlet man making a beeline towards her, and she blinked. Good grief, was he puckering up? Glancing around their group, she saw everyone was otherwise engaged apart from Ben who was standing a little off to one side. It was him or black singlet man, and she had yet to wish him a happy new year.

'Happy New Year, Ben,' she said venturing over.

'And to you, Isla,' he said raising his glass. They looked at each other both uncertain as to whether a hug and a cheek-to-cheek kiss were appropriate or not.

Oh, for goodness' sake, Isla thought. I've known him for years; it was one silly kiss. It didn't mean anything. Even as she awkwardly embraced him and felt his lips graze her cheek, she knew she was lying to herself. The very touch of him was making her stomach do some spectacular somersaults. Her face felt hot and flushed as she broke away from the embrace. 'You rescued me from been smooched by Mr Hairy Shoulder over there. He's determined to get a New Year's kiss in.' She inclined her head to where he'd diverted his attentions to some other lucky lady.

Ben grinned. 'Oh well, we couldn't have that now, could we?'

She met his gaze and wished the gymnastics in her stomach would stop, the band had started, and it was a welcome distraction. Isla recognized the opening beat of the Kiwi classic, Nature by Fourmyula. 'Oh, I love this song!'

'Dance?'

She looked at him in surprise. 'You don't like dancing.' She bit back the words, 'besides, I'm not wearing pink.'

'It's a new year's resolution of mine to put myself out of my comfort zone. Come on, or the song will be over.'

Isla looked around for Callum. He was deep in conversation with Saralee, so she followed Ben out onto the dancefloor area. It was barely big enough to swing a cat, let alone break out any radical moves so she should be safe. She knew from past experience that he was a surprisingly good dancer for somebody who claimed not to enjoy it; and she smiled up at him as she got into the swing of the song. She felt happy and carefree as he twirled her around, not caring about the disgruntled looks they got in the cramped space.

The song rolled into another, and another and then the beat agonizingly slowed. Isla saw couples come together on the dancefloor and her eyes locked with Ben's, but she couldn't read the expression in them. She knew that she desperately wanted to kiss him. Her body ached with the need to feel his lips on hers. She drew breath and looked down, glad when the song's slow rhythm that said they should be dancing as one came to a close.

'Another dance?'

She couldn't do this, it was torturous and she shook her head raising a smile. 'No, you wore me out. We should go back and join them.' She gestured vaguely at the crowd, and as she weaved her way back to where the others were standing, she made her resolution. New Year was a time of fresh starts, and if being near Ben made her knees go weak then it wasn't fair to keep on seeing Callum. She knew Ben wasn't available, but no one deserved to play second fiddle. She'd wait until he'd gotten over the hangover he had coming his way before having a chat though, that was only fair.

She felt her phone vibrate in her pocket and pulling it out saw a message from Carl. He and David were having a ball at Waikiki Beach, he texted, and he hoped hers was going off with a bang too. She had to smile as she showed the message to Annie. She grinned and produced her phone. Isla saw he'd sent the same sentiment to her and Kris. There was much more chance of theirs going off with a big bang than hers, she thought, glancing around and realizing Callum wasn't there.

'Have you seen Callum?' Isla asked over the music, sliding her phone back into the pocket of her jeans. Annie shook her head, but Kris leant down to be heard and said that he thought he had seen him heading outside. 'It's very hot in here, he probably needed some air.'

'Oh dear, maybe the tequila's caught up with him. I'd better go and check he's okay.' Isla wound her way back past the dancefloor to the entrance, getting her bottom pinched on the way. She swung round but given the three grinning lads, she couldn't be sure who was responsible so decided to let it go.

The air outside was welcomingly fresh with a light mist descending breaking the humidity of the day. She could see the droplets of moisture in the glow of the lights illuminating the carpark. Moths danced beneath them, and there was a group of guys clustered around a car with a haze of smoke hovering above their heads. Of Callum, there was no sign.

He'd probably gone down the side of the pub, she knew he wouldn't want an audience if he'd thrown up. She set off in that direction and braced herself to be greeted with his retching, hunched form. As she rounded the corner, she spotted him. Only he wasn't alone, and he certainly wasn't being sick. He was, Isla comprehended with a shock akin to a slap in the face, snogging the face off Saralee.

Chapter 34

Isla pushed her way back into the pub which felt oppressively hot. Callum trailed in after her, trying to get her to stop and talk to him. The band was packing up as he grabbed her arm. She swung around to square up to him. She could see no sign of Saralee.

'I'm sorry Isla,' he said shrugging and swaying slightly. 'It just happened.'

Isla didn't know what to do or say. That she felt humiliated was a given, that her heart was not broken she was certain. Still, he could have had the decency to give her the *'let's just be friends'* chat instead of sneaking off like a teenager behind her back. Mind you, the phrase pot calling the kettle black sprang to mind as she recalled her transgression with Ben. Poor Ben, she owed it to him to tell him what she'd just seen but then again she couldn't be sure if her motives were altruistic or selfish. She didn't want to spoil his night, and wasn't it up to Saralee to do the right thing and tell him what she'd been up to? *A-ha speak of the devil.* Isla spotted her walking back into the pub looking red-faced and dishevelled, not at all her usual sweetness and light.

'I'm so sorry Isla we—it, it just happened.'

It was the second time in the space of one minute she had heard that and this time Isla raised an eyebrow. 'What, you both just *happened* to find yourselves loitering down the side of the pub and had to have a snog?'

'What's going on?' Ben came over and clocked the look on Isla's face. 'Hey, I've been looking everywhere for you,' he said holding out a glass for Saralee. She thanked him and took it with a nervous glance over at Isla.

Isla narrowed her eyes to convey the message that it was up to her to tell her boyfriend what she had been outside doing before waving her hand dismissively. 'I'm going to say goodbye to Annie and Kris, then I'm off. Happy New Year everyone.' She turned away, leaving a red-faced Callum and Saralee and a bewildered Ben as she scanned the pub for her friends. The crowd was beginning to thin a little now and spying Annie, she headed in that direction. She had a pool cue in hand and was perched on Kris' knee waiting for the girl bending over the pool table to take her shot. Annie, Isla saw, was yawning. It wouldn't be long before those two made their way home either.

'We're playing doubles,' Annie offered up spotting her.

'Hi, listen, I've had enough, I'm going to head home.'

The look on Isla's face didn't escape Annie. 'Hey, are you okay? Where's Callum?'

'Yeah, I'm fine, don't worry about me. I'm just a bit over tonight that's all. Callum's staying on for a bit longer I think. I'll call you later.'

She gave them both a quick kiss on the cheek and said

goodnight, wishing them luck with their game and assuring Annie that she was sorted with the courtesy wagon for a ride home.

It was a sheepish Callum who called to see Isla that first afternoon of the year. She opened the door to find him standing there with a hangdog expression.

'Sore head?' she asked with a raised eyebrow.

'Yep, a doozy and a guilty conscience.'

Isla raised a smile and stepped onto the porch closing the door behind her. 'Come on, we'll go and sit in the garden out the back. Gran's pottering in the kitchen and her ears flap like an elephant's when she thinks something's up.' She led him down the path that followed the side of the house to the backyard to avoid any cross-examination on the way.

They sat down on the bench seat at the bottom of the garden, and Isla waved up at the house to where Gran was standing at the kitchen window. She waved back, before carrying on with whatever it was she doing.

'I'm sorry Isla, I behaved shockingly last night. I can't believe I did what I did,' he croaked.

'It was this morning actually and do you like her or was it just a kiss because you could?'

He rubbed his temples and winced. 'God, I wish the Panadol would kick in, and yeah I do like her. I like her a lot. We've been spending our lunch breaks together, going for a walk each day.' He looked at Isla registering the look on her face. 'But nothing ever happened until last night. I guess how I feel about her just snuck up on me, but I didn't mean to hurt you. I think you're great Isla, it's just—'

Isla held up her hand, she'd hashed it all over with Annie over the phone that morning and got how she felt straight in her head. 'Callum it's okay, you don't have to say it. I know what you mean. Our relationship hasn't exactly been love's young dream, and I'm not hurt.'

He looked a little taken aback. 'You're not?'

'No,' she said. 'I mean I was annoyed with the way you went about things with Saralee, and my pride took a bit of a nosedive. I'm glad you like her though, and it wasn't just a behind my back pash-fest on your part. If she feels the same way about you though, then the pair of you need to come clean with Ben.'

Callum nodded. 'Yeah, you're right. We will.' Now that was a conversation he was not looking forward to having.

'Go on. Go home and get some sleep, you look terrible.' Isla nudged him.

Callum wasn't about to argue, he'd done what he'd come here to do and that was apologize and clear the air. He got to his feet, and announced his new year's resolution was to never touch tequila again for as long as he lived.

'Isla, this is like the control tower of Grand Central station. Saralee is here to see you!'

Her gran's strident tones called down from the backdoor startling Isla from her cat nap in the sun. The events of the night before were catching up. She rubbed her eyes and called back. 'Send her down here, Gran, thanks.'

Saralee's ponytail didn't swing with its usual jauntiness as she made her way down the back steps and the sloping lawn to where Isla was sitting, shading her eyes with her hand watching her.

'Hi, I know I'm probably the last person you want to see, but I wondered if we could have a chat?' she asked looking uncertain. 'I want to clear the air.'

'Good idea,' Isla said smiling to put her at ease and patting the bench for her to sit down.

By the time Saralee left, with a generous slice of the ginger crunch Bridget had been busy baking, she was feeling much better. Instead of a woman scorned, she had encountered a very zen Isla who'd assured her there were no hard feelings. She hadn't launched into a tirade, she'd simply asked her if she was keen on Callum to which Saralee had told the truth; she was smitten. She just hadn't understood it until last night.

'I came clean with Ben.'

'Good.' Poor Ben, Isla thought getting dumped wasn't a great start to the New Year for him either.

'To be honest I don't think he was all that bothered. I mean I still feel awful about the way it happened because you and, well, Ben you're both so nice.'

Isla smiled and swatted a wasp away. 'I'll be fine, Saralee.'

Saralee gave her a tentative smile in return. 'Ben and I will be much better off as friends or at least I hope we will once he's over his wounded pride.'

The phone ringing was a timely distraction from peering out the kitchen window at the comings and goings, Bridget decided, wondering what was going on as she answered it.

She sat down at the table a second later and listened to Ian Fowler relay the news that work was underway on the bronze statue recently commissioned by the Barker's Creek Hall Committee. His assurance that despite the tight time frame, it would be completed in time for the festival was met with a sigh of relief. Things were coming together, Bridget thought as he thanked her for the prompt part-payment of his fee, before hanging up. The hall repairs were nearly finished, and the old girl would stand strong and proud for another hundred years. A jewel in the crown, or rather, field. It had brought a tear to Bridget's eye the day of the working bee. To see so many townsfolk get involved and get behind the project had been wonderful. All the voluntary labour meant there had been a considerable sum left in the fund-raising kitty, even after accounting for the final costings that Saralee had presented her with for the festival itself.

The idea for the statue had come to her after spotting a picture in one of Mary's glossy women's magazines that she was fond of leaving lying about. Perhaps there was something to be said for light reading, after all, she'd mused. The idea for the festival had been born out of her *Ireland Today* magazine and now this. Her eyes settled on the photograph of Copenhagen's Little Mermaid Statue. She'd torn the page from the magazine, not bothering to read the accompanying article on the delights of Denmark, before broaching her plan with the rest of the hall's committee members with trepidation.

What did they think of the idea of having a small bronze statue commissioned? Their statue would be of a young girl in the rock'n'roll attire of her day, Bridget could already see it in her mind's eye. A bronze girl with a ponytail whose gaze would forever be on the hall where she'd spent the best night of her short life. There was even a boulder upon which she could be affixed, by the path near the entrance to the hall. It would be a tribute to one of the town's own who was taken too soon, she told them, before explaining how Clara had died.

She had fully expected an argument as to how else the considerable sum involved could be better put to use. None of them knew what lay behind this need of Bridget's to have her friend remembered before it was too late and there was no one who'd known her left to do so. It was her way of atoning for something she could never make right. To her amazement, it was Margaret who had stood up and backed her by saying she thought it was a good way to showcase local talent.

'Ian Fowler's getting a bit of a reputation in artistic circles. And my Melanie – she's high up in banking, you know – well, she was saying just the other day that his name came up at a function she was at. He's a talent to be reckoned with, Melanie says.'

If Bridget weren't so desperate for the hall to give her statue the go ahead, she would have smirked at the about turn of opinion. Ian Fowler had a foundry he had built himself at the bottom of his garden and until his pieces had begun to take off, and in recent times sell for a pretty penny, most of the locals had him pegged as a bit of an artistic eccentric. Now he was someone to know if you were of a name-dropping disposition which Margaret was.

Margaret had ignored the muttering that, *yes Melanie who was in banking, would know of his work because you would need a bank loan to commission him to get out of bed these days*. 'Think of the publicity,' she'd declared loudly and passionately over the dissent. 'The festival, the unveiling of the statue and the touching story behind it, not to mention the fact it has been commissioned by a famous artist. The paparazzi will love it.'

Margaret may have been getting carried away but her enthusiasm was infectious and the vote to commission the statue was passed with a unanimous show of hands. Bridget had treated Margaret to coffee and cake at Nectar as a thank you for her support after the meeting. The cake she'd chosen had a sprinkling of toasted pumpkin seeds on the top, and as much as it pained her to admit it, they were growing on her. She was quite partial to their quinoa and kumara salad too, who would have thought? Annie and Isla had proven themselves to be marvellous wee cooks.

Now, Bridget got up and placed the phone back in the charger wincing at the sharp pain in her hip before saying out loud to the empty kitchen. 'I hope we do you proud, Clara.' She felt the hot sting of tears rush to her eyes. She was getting sentimental in her old age, a cup of tea was what she needed. As she looked out the kitchen window over the top of Isla's and Saralee's heads, beyond her back garden to the bush clad hills, she recalled the shock the town had been in in the aftermath of Clara's death.

It was as though an insidious and oppressive grey smog had descended and settled for months over Bibury. It crept into everyone's day-to-day lives, sneaking in through the cracks, a constant reminder that no one was immortal. They were all living on borrowed time. A young person passing on like that, unnaturally, did damage to a town the size of Bibury. It ruptured the sense of immunity to awful goings-on that those living in a small community took as their right. It should be in the small print of the rates paid quarterly to the council for the privilege of owning your home: *Nothing bad will ever happen in this small town.*

Bridget turned away from the window and flicked the switch on the kettle before setting about making a pot of tea. She hoped that by holding this festival and the dance in Clara's memory, she was ensuring that something good was going to happen in her small town.

Chapter 35

January was hot, and Isla was bothered. She was single and Ben was single, and this knowledge was going around and around in her head like a merry-go-round that she couldn't stop and get off from.

'Isla, get the pies in the oven.' Annie hollered from the front of house, shaking her head and apologizing to Jim Bishop for nearly deafening him as he drained his glass and got up to go.

'She was always a bit of a dreamer, that one,' he said with a smile and cheerio. The Principal had taken to popping in most days for an iced coffee and chat. He was lonely, Isla and Annie had surmised. The school holidays had dragged on for him.

In the kitchen, Isla cursed. She'd over beaten the cream because she'd been daydreaming of ways she could ask Ben out without seeming too obvious about it. As a result of this, she'd forgotten to get the pies in the oven. They wouldn't be ready in time for the lunchtime rush at this rate. She knew she was driving poor Annie to distraction with her absent-mindedness.

'Sorry, I know I'm hopeless, but he's all I can think about twenty-four seven,' she told Annie as she appeared in the kitchen to check her instructions were being followed.

'It's called love, and it's high time you did something about it.' Annie muttered, hearing the door jangle and going out to serve whoever it was that had just come in. Isla heard Saralee's familiar voice and ensuring she'd switched the oven on; she popped her head around the door to say hi.

'How're you Isla?'

'Great and you?'

'Yeah, good thanks. School's back Monday,' she said flashing her dimples. 'I thought I'd be organized for once and head in to check the school's email and clear the answer phone. It will be mad enough first day back without having a big backlog of messages to deal with as well. I need one of Annie's flat whites to go first. A shot of motivation, you know.'

'You're the most organized woman I know, Saralee. I mean look at the way you've handled Project Matchmaker.' It was true, Isla thought. All the renovations on the hall were finished, the working bee too was a huge success, and it was all down to Saralee. The Barker's Creek Hall had passed muster with the council and was good to go. 'Gran sings your praises constantly.'

'I'm organized when it comes to some things, and that's been loads of fun. I can't wait for the big day, not long to go now! Fifteen days and counting.'

Isla noticed as Saralee left that she'd bought two takeaway coffees and guessed the other was for Callum. There were no hard feelings on her part for either of them. They were a perfect match, she thought, leaving Annie to serve young Ellie from the Four Square. Beau from the butcher's was standing behind her feigning interest in the food cabinet. She headed back to the kitchen. There was a stack of dishes she could load in the dishwasher.

Her mum and dad were the ones taking her split from Callum the hardest. She'd told her dad to stop being so melodramatic when his response to the news was to tell her he felt like he'd just lost a son. Her mother too had gotten up from her seat and made a show of tossing her copy of *New Zealand Bride* in the bin. Annie had thought it hilarious when Isla relayed this to her, telling her about the time she'd gotten engaged.

'Really? You never told me that before.'

'Not much to tell. I think I liked the idea of the dress and the big day, but I had the wrong man. We both saw sense though, and the last I heard, Tony's settled down with someone far more suitable. Carl couldn't stand him; he used to call him Testosterone Tones.'

Isla smiled at that, typical Carl. Now, scraping off a plate into the food scraps bin they kept for Jed Brown's pigs, she felt slightly sick as the realization that her gran's ex, Charlie Callahan, could show up any day now hit her. Oh, she hoped she'd done the right thing. It could all so very easily blow up in her face.

'Isla, I can smell burning!'

Oh crap, the pies! She picked up the oven gloves and raced over to the oven – it was on grill.

As it happened, it was five days later when the opportunity to ask Ben out presented itself. It was all thanks to Delilah. She'd bunny-hopped her way down High Street and into the garage and Ben had downed tools to check under her bonnet, while Isla sat in her car. He'd proclaimed a few minutes later that it was nothing more serious than the spark plugs and he could replace them for her there and then.

He was true to his word and with Delilah's engine purring once more, Isla leaned her head out the window to ask what she owed him. He wouldn't accept any money from her waving the idea away with the suggestion that a sausage roll here and there would suffice. Isla had found herself saying, 'well, if you won't let me pay then at least let me cook you dinner tonight over at Nectar – and I think I can stretch to a few courses more than a sausage roll.'

Ben hesitated a beat, and her heart had lurched at the possibility he might say no, but he wiped his hands on a rag and grinned. 'You're on.'

She'd been walking on hot coals for the rest of the day. Annie had sent her home early to get ready saying she was no use to her in this state. She'd pushed her out the door making her promise to text an update the moment she got home from her date – if, in fact, she got home! Isla worked the menu out in her head as she set about putting her makeup on. She'd keep it simple but tasty. She was thinking bruschetta for an entrée. Her dad had brought in the first of his cherry tomatoes that very morning, and the basil on Nectar's kitchen windowsill was doing nicely. Jamie Oliver's Spring Chicken pie would prove not too heavy a main with its scrunched filo pastry topping, and she had all the ingredients she'd need for it. And the salted caramel cheesecake, Annie had whipped up for tomorrow would suffice for dessert. *Perfect!* She did not want to spend the evening slaving in the kitchen!

Isla had moved on to her hair by the time she had the courses sorted, and she tossed her hair straighteners aside in frustration. Her hair was misbehaving despite her just having sizzled it within an inch of its life, *and* nothing in her wardrobe was right. She took a deep breath and decided she'd just have to wear her hair up. As for what to wear, well the bed was strewn with just about everything housed in her wardrobe. She'd do what she always did when she didn't know what to wear, and that was go with the first outfit she'd tried on.

Right she thought a few ticks later – time to tackle her hair once more. At that moment Cole scampered into her room and ascended her leg as though she were a tree. She yelped and spying the thread he'd managed to pull in her white cotton pants, cursed loudly. She was not happy.

'What on earth's going on with you madam?' Bridget poked her head around the bedroom door as a black fur ball shot past her and skidded down the hallway. She'd left the six o'clock news to investigate, galvanized into action by hearing the shriek of a word she would not have used in her house.

'I've invited Ben to dinner at Nectar tonight.'

Bridget's mouth formed a round 'O'. The news that her granddaughter had a dinner date with Ben was enough for her to let the foul language slide. 'That's very progressive of you.'

Isla scowled. 'My hair's all wrong, and the bloody cat just did this to my pants.' She pointed to the rogue thread.

'Isla, calm down. There's nothing your old Gran can't fix, you know that. Get out of those pants and give them to me. I'll have them sorted as good as new in a jiffy while you get on with doing whatever it is you're trying to do to your hair.'

Isla did as she was told.

True to her word, five minutes later Bridget reappeared in the bedroom with the white pants. She decided to turn a blind eye to the bomb site that was her granddaughter's bed as she handed them to Isla for the once over.

'Oh thanks, Gran – you're a super star,' she said, inspecting the pants and finding no flaw.

'You're welcome. Your hair looks lovely up, by the way, you should tie it back more often. Enjoy your night dear.' Bridget's fingers were crossed behind her back.

The evening was going well, Isla thought, eyeing Ben as he tucked into the pie she'd just served up. The conversation between them as they'd laughed over shared memories, careful to skirt around those with intimate connotations, was easy. It flowed the way it did when you were in the company of someone you knew well. Ben hadn't changed she thought, but she had. She'd done a lot of growing up in the last decade.

'Man, you can cook Isla,' he mumbled. 'This is fantastic.'

'I'm glad you're enjoying it,' she smiled over the top of the flickering candle at him before forking up a mouthful herself. It was tasty she thought, wiping stray pastry crumbs from her lips.

Ben turned the conversation to that of the impending

festival and when he mentioned Bridget's name Isla felt a stab of guilt.

'Ben, I did something I'm not sure I should have.'

'Oh?' He placed his knife and fork down on his plate and leaned back in his chair, picking up his glass of beer. 'Come on then, 'fess up.'

She told him about finding the Valentine's Day cards and how Bridget thought Charlie hadn't kept his promise to write to her when he left Bibury. 'Somewhere along the line the letters got lost, and then when Gran's friend Clara died, she turned to Granddad for comfort. And well, they fell in love, you know the rest. The thing is though, I rang Charlie and told him Gran never got his cards.'

'Even though, Bridget specifically told you she didn't want any contact with him?'

Isla nodded, she didn't like the tone of Ben's voice, and she hadn't told him the worst of it yet.

'And I invited him to the Matchmaker Festival,' she blurted.

'What did he say to that?' Ben frowned.

'He's coming,' she rushed on explaining her actions. 'I liked him, Ben. If you'd heard him talk about Gran and the way he felt about her, you'd have felt really sad for him too at how things worked out. If nothing else it'll give him a sense of closure where she's concerned. I think that's important when you get to their time of life don't you?'

He shook his head.

'What?' she asked starting to feel annoyed by his obvious disapproval.

'You know nothing about him, that's what.'

'I trust his motives. He sounded lovely over the phone,' she defended herself. *Why was he being so difficult? She wished she hadn't started this conversation now but she'd wanted to confide in someone who knew her and Bridget well.*

'I just don't think Bridget will thank you for interfering that's all. It wasn't your business to go behind her back like that.'

Isla felt the shift in the atmosphere and knew this was not going to end well.

'You don't have to say it like that. I was only trying to help.'

'No, you weren't Isla. You didn't think it through. You just went ahead and did what *you* wanted to do, and that's typical.'

'I beg your pardon?'

'Sorry, I shouldn't have said that.' He held his hands up.

Isla wasn't going to let it go. 'Well, you did say it. And I take it what you mean is that you're still pissed at me for leaving Bibury twelve bloody years ago. For goodness' sake, Ben grow up. It was years ago, we were kids.'

'I didn't say that, but alright then, you could've handled things better back then. You bloody well hurt me Isla. And you could've handled this situation you've created for your gran better too. Think about how your actions are affecting others for once in your life, Isla it's not that hard.'

'Ben that's not fair! I was eighteen when I left. I didn't want to settle down, but if I had it would've been with you. I wanted a career and to see some of the world, what was so wrong with that?'

'You used to ignore me whenever you came back. How do you think that made me feel?'

'Only because breaking up hurt me as much as it hurt you. I had to make a clean break with you. I couldn't handle seeing you but not being with you,' her voice went up a notch.

'Then why the hell did you break up with me in the first place!' he yelled back.

'I wanted a bigger life than Bibury, and I was terrified I'd never leave if I stayed with you,' Isla's voice cracked.

'Ah right I see, I've just been wasting away in this little hick town living my little life. Is that it?'

'You're putting words in my mouth.'

He banged his beer down on the table. 'Look I don't know how we got here, but I've had a long day. I think it's time I went home.' He pushed his seat back and shrugged into his jacket muttering thanks for dinner. She heard the door bang shut behind him with a finality as she sat at the table with her head in her hands. It wasn't until she heard his truck drive off with a roar that she looked up. Her eyes settled on the space he'd filled a few minutes earlier, and she whispered the words she should have said to him a long time ago. 'I'm sorry.'

Isla got up from the table after an age. She eyed the half-eaten plates and knew she couldn't face clearing up tonight. She'd come in early in the morning and sort it out. Nor could she face the inquisition from Gran, not yet. She needed to clear her head. She felt around in her pocket, her hand closing over her keys. Perhaps a drive would help her gain some perspective on what had just unfolded.

Isla locked the café door behind her and looked up at the newly darkened sky. It was filled with stars and the promise of a sunny day to follow the night. The familiar outline of the Pit twinkled down at her, and she blinked back tears as a silver star streaked across the vast inkiness. She recalled wishing on a shooting star as a child, with her nose pressed to the window. She'd wished with all her heart that when she grew up, she would marry Prince Charming, like Cinderella. Well, she'd blown that, she thought crossing the road and clambering into Delilah.

Chapter 36

Bridget had woken early and was sitting at her kitchen table with her morning cup of tea in front of her. Coal was chomping his breakfast down, and as soon as he'd finished he'd want out, she thought, watching the black bundle fondly. He was a creature of habit just like she was. Isla wasn't home, and Bridget wondered if she'd spent the night at Ben's. She frowned. Given their history, it was safe to say Isla hadn't slept with him on their *first* date. The seven o'clock news had just finished on the radio when she registered a banging on the front door. Thinking perhaps Isla had forgotten her key she got up, tying the cord of her dressing gown tightly just in case it wasn't her. She didn't want to give the postman or whoever else it could be a fright. She made her way down the hall and opening the door.

'Ben, what is it?' She felt her legs wobble, she could tell by the look on his face he was not the bearer of good news.

'Bridget, listen she's okay, but Isla's been – oh shit, Bridget, there's been an accident, and it's all my fault.' He reached out to steady her. 'We had a stupid fight, I left her at the café, and she must've got it in her head to go for a drive. Shit. I assumed she'd lock up and come back here.' Seeing Bridget's stricken face, he hastily continued. 'When the call came in to tow her car, I rang Joe, she's going to be okay. She's at Christchurch Hospital, Mary and Joe are both with her, and they asked me to come and pick you up.'

Bridget just stared at him, trying to comprehend what she'd just been told before galvanizing herself. 'I'd better get dressed, can you give me a minute?'

Ben nodded, pulling his phone out of his pocket to check if he'd had any messages updating him on how Isla was doing while Bridget went back in the house. On automatic pilot, she threw on the first top she could lay her hands on along with a pair of cotton slacks. Not bothering with her morning ablutions she headed out the door to where Ben had the truck idling. They built those bloody wagons with high jumpers in mind, she thought as he helped her up into the passenger seat.

They didn't talk much on the journey, and it seemed interminable. Ben didn't know what had happened exactly or why she'd wound up in Christchurch hospital and not Grey Base on the Coast. The only thing that made any sense was that she'd decided to head into the city for the night after their row, maybe she'd been heading for Carl's. Oh God, he thought gripping the steering wheel, if he could turn back time, he would. He'd never have said the things he'd said. Isla only wanted what was best for Bridget, he knew that, and all that other stuff he'd gone on about – well, it was ancient history. Dredging up past hurts had only resulted in more hurt.

Joe had said something about a ditch and the car being upside down when it was found, but that, and the fact that she was at Christchurch Public and wasn't critical, was all he'd gleaned. At last, they reached the suburbs of Christchurch, and as they slowed to a virtual standstill in the rush hour traffic, Ben cursed, tapping the steering wheel as he willed the lights ahead to turn green.

'I'd better let Annie know what's happening.' He dug out his phone and made the call. She answered after a few short rings, and he filled her in, reassuring her that her friend was going to be okay. 'Yeah, I will do, and I'll let you know as soon as I know more. Hang on I'll pass you over to Bridget.'

Bridget pressed the phone to her ear. She hated the silly things as a rule, but at times like this, the cell phone was a blessing. Annie's worried voice asked her if she was doing okay, and she assured her that she was, but she'd be doing a whole lot better once she'd seen Isla with her own eyes. She said goodbye, promising as Ben had to let her know how Isla was once they'd seen her. 'How do I hang this thing up?' She asked thrusting the phone back to Ben. He switched it off and breathed a sigh of relief, as the leafy arbour that surrounded Hagley Park came into sight.

'We're nearly there, Bridget.'

Ben stopped outside the hospital's main doors and getting out of the truck he went round to the passenger side to help Bridget down. 'You go on in Bridget, and I'll send Joe a text to tell him to meet you inside.'

Bridget nodded and headed through the automatic doors leaving Ben to park his truck.

She'd only just got her bearings when he burst through the doors behind her.

'The Wilson's carpark is just across the road,' he said breathing heavily as though he'd been running. He was about to ask the woman at the front desk where Isla was when Joe appeared.

He looked understandably crumpled, Bridget thought, as he strode towards them.

'She's going to be fine Bridget, Ben. She'll be sore for a while, but she'll be fine.'

'I was so worried.' Ben rubbed at the stubble on his chin.

His agitation was apparent, and Bridget patted his arm, knowing the poor lad was still blaming himself and that she would be wasting her breath telling him again that it was an accident, no more, no less.

'Come on I'll take you both up to see her and Mary. She's in a right state,' Joe said putting his arm around his mother-in-law's shoulder. 'She needs her mum to sort her out.'

They walked past the café and pharmacy to the lifts, and Joe filled in the blanks for them as they went.

The town's local policeman Tep, had knocked on Mary's and Joe's door shortly after five o'clock this morning to tell them that Isla's car had been found upside down in a ditch near the town of Springfield. The accident, it had been ascertained, had happened shortly after 11pm. No one else was involved, she'd taken the corner too fast and lost control of the car. She'd drifted in and out of consciousness until a farmer had spotted Delilah as he set off on his early morning rounds. He'd stayed with her, talking to her and holding her hand until the Westpac chopper arrived to airlift her here, to the hospital. Joe listed off her injuries; slight concussion, three cracked ribs, and extensive bruising. 'She's going to be in pain with those ribs, but she'll mend.'

That she was alive was a blessing in itself. Despite having very good reason not to be religious in her opinion, this was an occasion when Bridget felt it appropriate to raise her eyes heavenward and send up a small thank you. They exited the lift and Mary made her way down the corridor towards them. She was, Bridget noticed as she stepped forward to hug her daughter, pale for the first time in months. She dissolved into tears as she felt her mother's arms enfold her and Bridget rubbed her back. Your children were always your babies, she thought, desperately wanting to comfort her. 'She's alright, Mary, it's the shock, that's all. It's been a terrible, terrible shock but she's going to be fine. There, there.'

Joe came over and kissed his wife's hair. 'I'll go and find you a cup of tea, love.' He disappeared back down the corridor.

Mary sat down on one of the seats and gestured to the room across the way. 'She's at the far end by the window, in the bed on the right. She's a bit out of it on the pain medication, but you can go and see her. It has to be one at a time for now though, the nurse said.'

'You go in first, Bridget, I don't know if she'll even want to see me after last night,' Ben said sitting down next Mary.

Bridget felt a rush of warmth for him; she knew how desperate he was to get in there himself. 'She'll want to see you love. I won't be long.' She patted Mary on her shoulder. 'Keep an eye on this one for me will you, Ben?'

He nodded and asked Mary if she'd rung the pharmacy and told them what had happened.

Bridget left them talking and walked quietly into the room trying not to stare at all the other patients as she walked to the last bed where Mary had told her she'd find Isla.

She inhaled sharply to stop the sob from escaping at the sight of her poor battered granddaughter lying on her bed in a hospital gown, with a sheet covering her legs. 'Hello Isla, my lovely,' she said sitting down in the chair by the bed and picking up her hand. She held it tightly. 'You've given us such a fright my girl.'

'Sorry Gran,' Isla croaked her eyes drifting towards the table.

Bridget followed their direction, 'Would you like a drink sweetheart?'

Isla managed a small nod and Bridget let go of her hand to pick up the plastic cup. She held it to her mouth and placed the straw between her lips to have a sip. When she'd finished, she put it back on the tray table and stroked her granddaughter's forehead gently. 'You've been in the wars.' She shook her head. 'I don't know what possessed you to go driving off like you did. Ben said you'd had a row. He's blaming himself for you winding up in here you know.'

Isla shook her head. 'Not his fault.' Her voice was slurred.

'Well, you be sure and tell him this isn't his fault and whatever it was the two of you fell out about put it behind you. He's a very special young man who loves you very much, he always has Isla Brookes. Don't make the same mistake twice and let that love slip from your grasp.'

Isla could sense the stern urgency in her gran's tone despite her befuddled state and she knew she needed to tell her what she and Ben had fought about but she was so tired.

'Gran, ask Ben, he'll tell you,' she rasped before her eyes fluttered shut.

Perplexed, Bridget kissed Isla on the cheek and got up to fetch Ben. Whatever it was she'd been talking about could wait.

Ben, sat down and picked up Isla's hand. His eyes smarted but he wouldn't let the sight of her bring him to tears, she needed him to be strong. 'I'm sorry I behaved like an arse,' he said quietly, and he knew even though her eyes were closed, she'd heard him by the way she gave his hand the gentlest of squeezes back.

Chapter 37

'Isla, my love, just look at the state of you.' Carl appeared from behind the ginormous colourful bouquet he was clutching.

It was Isla's third day in the hospital, and although she was still in a fair bit of discomfort, she was feeling much more with it. 'You didn't have to do that Carl,' she said her eyes flickering to the flowers. 'But I'm glad you did, they're gorgeous.'

'They're from David and me. He's in Sydney until Friday and sends his love. He says to get better soon. Oh, and he also said to tell you he'll give you a big hug at the festival – never mind the cracked ribs! Do you know when they're letting you go home?'

'Yes, the doctor came and saw me this morning, and they're discharging me tomorrow. I can't wait to get home. Not that the staff hasn't been wonderful.' Isla rustled up a smile mostly for the benefit of the nurse who was hovering over the patient in the bed next door.

'I hope Annie told you that I'd have been here yesterday, but I've been island hopping for *Her* magazine. Raro, Samoa, and Fiji. The weather was against us, so the shoot took twice as long as planned and I tell you, Isla if I see another coconut with a straw in it I will scream.' He drew breath long enough to bat his eyelashes at the nurse who'd finished with the woman in the next bed and was now checking Isla's clipboard. 'You've got fabulous cheekbones,' he said before asking her what he could put the flowers in.

Won over, the nurse retrieved the empty plastic jug sitting on the tray table next to Isla's bed and obligingly filled it up with water from the sink at the entrance to the room. She left him to arrange the stems, while continuing her rounds with a wiggle in her walk.

'They're stunning thank you.' Isla watched with as much amusement as she could muster given her current position, as he titivated them. 'So even if I'd made it to your place, you wouldn't have been there,' she said.

Carl shook his head. 'Nope, and promise me there'll be no more midnight flits from lover boy on the open road.'

'I promise, and he's not my lover boy.'

'Whatever you say, sweetheart. Have you spoken to Annie?'

Isla nodded, she felt so bad about having worried everyone half to death. 'Yes, she rang first thing this morning wanting to come in, and offered to bring Gran with her, but I told her not to worry.' She'd told her parents not to haul all the way in to see her today as well, telling them it was too far to come for the sake of one day. She was doing fine, and she'd be home tomorrow. 'I'm being discharged tomorrow, and besides, I need her to hold the fort at Nectar.' Annie had gotten Marie's oldest daughter, who was studying via the Open Polytechnic, in to help out while Isla was incapacitated. Isla had ended the call by asking her to pop around to Gran's to check she was doing okay and to cuddle Coal for her. She'd wished he was curled up with at the end of her bed. Annie had called her a big softie but promised she'd call in on Bridget and Coal.

Isla knew she'd be lost without her friend, without all of them. It wouldn't have looked good shutting the café this early in the piece, and once Annie knew Carl was popping up to see her, she'd been appeased, not wanting her friend to be on her own all day. The day *had* been stretching long, with only a green jelly, clear soup, and a sandwich to break it up. Still, what did she expect? She was in the hospital, not a five-star hotel, but then she'd heard Carl's breezy tones echoing through the ward and her spirits lifted.

Now, satisfied he had the arrangement just so, Carl placed the flowers on the deep window sill beside her bed. They brightened her little corner of the room up. He stood there leaning his back up against the sill.

'Gran knows about my call to Charlie,' Isla said plucking at the bedsheet.

'Oh, did you come clean?'

'Kind of ... I got Ben to tell her, or at least I think I did. That's part of what we fought about actually; he thought I'd overstepped the mark contacting Charlie when Gran told me she didn't want to see him and it just escalated from there. All this old crap got brought up. He's been to see me, and he apologized. Well, I'm pretty sure he did, but I was a bit out of it at the time. Besides it's me who owes him an apology for the way I behaved all those years ago.'

Carl shook his head, what was with those two? That they belonged together was obvious to everyone but themselves. Still, he shouldn't have stuck his big oar in where Bridget was concerned. He'd meddled there, or at least aided and abetted Isla. He would not make the same mistake twice. 'You were following my advice. I'm sorry if Char-Bridge is turning into a big mess.'

'I have a mind of my own, and I stand by what I did. I just hope it doesn't blow up in my face. I haven't seen Gran, but I'm hoping my being injured means she'll go easy on me. You know the way when something bad happens it puts other stuff into perspective?'

Carl nodded. 'I know what you mean. It's like when you're moaning about having to shave, and then you see an old woman in a terrible frock with whiskers and a mustache and think, what have I got to complain about?'

Isla wasn't sure if he was taking the mickey or not, his deadpan expression wasn't giving anything away.

'I'm joking, sweet! Trying to put a smile on your dial. Poor Bridget probably hasn't got the energy to work herself up into a state about seeing her man again after all these years, not after the shock of you winding up in here.' He came around the other side of her bed and sat down in the chair there.

'I know, I feel awful putting everybody through this especially given it's my stupid fault, I was driving too fast and then I swerved to avoid a pothole and I couldn't get the wheel under control. That's all I remember. Thank God I didn't hurt anyone else.' Tears pricked her eyes. They didn't escape Carl, and he launched into nurse mode.

'Right Miss, sit forward.'

She obliged carefully, easing herself forward to avoid jarring her ribs, and he plumped her pillow, settling her back against it.

'There you look more comfortable now, a sip of water?' He was already filling the plastic cup on the tray next to her bed with the water left in the jug. He held it to her lips, and Isla took a small sip.

'I would have made a good nurse you know, the only thing that'd let me down would be having to deal with bedpans and the like.' He shuddered. 'I couldn't be doing with that.'

Isla couldn't help but smile.

'Accidents happen, alright? The main thing is you're still with us.'

She nodded.

'Good, now how's Delilah doing?'

'She's at the panel beaters. Ben asked Annie to pass on that she'll be as good as new.'

'Well now, that is a relief.'

Isla giggled, he was such a tonic.

'You're lucky you've got a view of sorts, and a degree of privacy. Look at the poor sod down the end there,' he said turning and pointing.

Isla craned forward to see an older man, his mouth wide open as he snored for all and sundry to see.

She hadn't felt lucky when she'd woken that morning, she'd felt sore. The day had not got off to a good start when the woman in the bed next door to hers had gotten up to go to the toilet as Isla had been about to attempt breakfast. She'd had no knickers on, and the back of her gown was flapping open for all to see. Now though, as she relayed the tale to Carl in a whisper she could see the funny side of it.

Later that night lying in her bed with the curtain around her, she repeated the affirmation she'd found in Rita's book. *Loving myself heals my life, I nourish my mind, body, and soul.* Perhaps if she repeated it enough times, it would distract her from the breathtaking pain of her ribs every time she shifted to get comfortable and speed up her recovery. Mind over matter and all that, she thought. Isla was on her third repetition when she lost her train of thought thanks to the sound of her roomie next door breaking wind. Bugger mind over matter, roll on tomorrow and getting home to Gran's.

Bridget was kneeling by the fireplace holding an envelope containing a letter she hadn't read in a very long time in her hands. Even now the thought of taking out the piece of paper and unfolding it to read the words she knew had been written on it, words that once put down on paper could never be taken back, filled her with dread. It was a blessing, she thought, that Isla hadn't delved deeper into her flotsam and jetsam drawer as she called it. It had been stupid of her to hold on to it in the first place.

Annie had left ten minutes ago after popping in to tell her she'd been speaking to Isla and she was doing fine. She'd given her strict instructions to come and cuddle the cat for her, she said, making Bridget smile as she went to call Coal. He was curled up in a sunny spot in the garden and looked disgruntled at the realization no food was on offer after he'd obligingly trotted into the kitchen. He'd allowed Annie to hold him for a few beats before meowing and wriggling free. Normally Coal was anybody's when it came to fuss, but he wasn't his usual self. He was missing Isla, Bridget thought. Animals had a sense when all was not as it should be.

The day she and Ben had rushed into Christchurch, she'd stayed at the hospital until the end of visiting hours along with Mary, and Joe. She'd pulled an ashen-faced Ben aside when Mary went to say goodbye to Isla, and Joe who'd already said his goodbyes had gone to bring the car around to the front of the hospital to take the two women home. 'Isla told me to ask you, Ben. Ask you what? What did she mean?'

He looked uncomfortable as though wrestling with himself as to whether he should tell her or not.

'Spit it out, Ben.'

There was nothing else for it, Bridget Collins was not a woman you disobeyed. Ben felt about ten years old under her wily gaze. 'Isla and I fought about her taking things into her own hands and ringing someone she said you knew years ago, Charlie? And then it all kind of went from there.'

Bridget nodded. She wasn't surprised; she should have known Isla would never leave it be once she'd found those cards. 'Yes, Charlie.'

'She invited him to come to Bibury, to the Matchmaker Festival. I got mad at her because I didn't think it was any of her business to do that and then I went and dredged stuff up from the past.' Ben rubbed at his jawline, the six o'clock shadow threatening to turn into the beginnings of a beard. 'Bridget, you know Isla, she had your best interests at heart.'

Bridget was too shell-shocked by the events of the day to muster up much of a response. She laid a hand on Ben's arm; the poor lad looked petrified. 'It's alright. I think it's probably about time I put the past to rest once and for all.'

And here she was about to do so.

Chapter 38

It was the smell of the hospital, that peculiar mix of disinfectant and overcooked food that had brought the painful memories bubbling back to the surface, Bridget thought. That, and the news that Charlie was on his way here to see her to rake it all up again. She closed her eyes and could see Tom as he had been during his last hours waiting to die in his hospital bed. His head had looked shrunken against the pillow upon which it lay, and she'd been amazed at how such a big man could suddenly seem so small and wizened. It was as though she'd pushed 'play' on a rerun of a scene she wished she could wipe from her memory, and it began to unfold.

2010

'It began the night of the Valentine's Day dance.' Tom's voice had a rattle that came from deep within his ravaged lungs. 'I fell in love.'

Bridget looked at his ashen face, his hair damp and stringy. She rested her hand on top of his large gnarled one, a hand that had once been so strong but which now lay limply on the bed beneath hers. 'Shush, don't strain yourself, Tom. It's all in the past.' It was the night he'd begun courting Clara, and she met Charlie. But it wasn't Clara's name he wheezed next.

'It was you, Bridget, it was always you.'

Bridget didn't realize she'd removed her hand from his until she glanced down at her lap to where both were now tightly clasped. There was no sound but the clicking and whirring of the machinery to which he was connected. She sat there, ramrod straight in the chair next to his bed, as interspersed with fits of coughing, he rewrote their shared history.

'I looked across the dance floor and saw you there, Bridget. You were the most beautiful girl I'd ever seen. But then Charlie caught your eye, and there was no room for anybody else after that.' Tom tried to gather his breath and Bridget wanted to tell him to stop and just to rest. She knew instinctively that he was unburdening himself but that in doing so he would leave her to carry whatever that burden was alone. The words didn't form in her mouth, and he continued.

'She was a pretty lass alright, Clara, and I knew she liked me. Courting her was a way of being around you.'

She felt guilty then as if Tom's using her friend was her doing, and she had somehow betrayed Clara.

'But she was in love with you Tom, she thought you felt the same way. I had no idea.'

'I'm not proud of the way I behaved. We were all so young, but it was wrong what I d—' He erupted into a fit of coughing.

Bridget waited for a beat longer than she should have to pass him the glass of water. She held it up to his lips, and his rheumy eyes grasped onto hers. She could see the plea in them, that she understand what he was telling her, that she absolve him. He closed his eyes, and when his breathing had regulated a degree, he continued to speak in bursts that Bridget had to piece together.

'Charlie sent the letters he wrote to you care of my address at the boarding house. He asked me to pass them on to you because he knew there was no point sending them to your parents' house.'

'But he never wrote to me,' Bridget murmured. 'I wrote to him, and I never heard a word from him, not a single word.'

Tom's eyes fluttered open, and he tried to grab her arm, but she was out of reach. 'But he did write to you, that's what I'm trying to tell you.' His voice broke off again, and his frail, body convulsed and shuddered with the effort as it was wracked with coughing once more. A nurse came into the room and helped to settle him, and Bridget felt the urge to run. To leave now before he could finish telling her what was laying heavily on his heart because she knew it was going to change everything. But as she got up he cried out, and the nurse looked at her.

'He wants you to stay, will you sit with him awhile longer?' The look on her face said it wouldn't be much longer now.

She couldn't leave, and reluctantly she lowered herself back down on the seat. They sat in silence for a while, and she thought he must have drifted off to sleep because his eyes were shut. There was no sound in the room but that incessant whirring and clicking intermingling with the rattling of his breath, hollow and desperate in his chest.

He didn't open his eyes as his voice like sandpaper rasped. 'I never passed the letters onto you.'

Bridget wanted to put her hands over her ears to make him stop but he wouldn't, she knew that even before he continued to wheeze the words he wanted to say out.

'I thought I'd own up to what I'd done one day but then Clara died, and you finally saw me.'

It hit Bridget then what had happened, she just knew. 'Clara found the letters didn't she?'

A tear trickled down his cheek but Bridget made no move to wipe it away for him, and she watched it disappear under his chin pooling in the folds of his neck. He inclined his head in a nod.

'How?' Bridget's voice was barely a whisper now.

'In the Bible.' He moved his eyes to the bedside table, and Bridget got up moving around the bed. There was a photograph of the children when they were small and another of the grandchildren on the table and there was a bible too, though Tom wasn't a religious man. She picked it up and opened it. Inside the cover was an envelope. Her hands trembled as she tore the seal.

Present day

Now, Bridget took that same letter from the envelope once more, her hands trembling just as they had that terrible day in the hospital. The writing was the spidery scrawl of a dying man, and it was short and straight to the point. Tom was not a flowery man, nor was he a man given to too many words, not even on the brink of death. Her eyes flickered over what he'd so desperately needed to purge himself off. It was undated.

Dear Bridget,
I want to ask your forgiveness for what I did. I've lived with it for a long time, and I'm ready to go now and answer to my maker. It was love for you that made me do it, fear and love. I loved you from the minute I saw you, but I couldn't have you. It was Charlie you wanted, and it ate away at me seeing you with him. Looking back now I think it was a sickness I had. Clara was sweet on me and being with her meant I could be around you. I'm not proud of the way I treated her or of what I did. I've already said I've lived with it for too long.

After he had left for Australia, Charlie wrote to you. The letters arrived at the boarding house where I was living, only I didn't pass them on to you as I promised him I would. I burnt them. All except for one. So many times I've wished I could change what happened, but you can't go back. A lad from work called around for a drink before I had a chance to get rid of it and I put it in my jacket pocket meaning to burn it later. I was dead on my feet with the double shifts I'd been pulling, and I forgot it was there.

The day it happened, Clara told me she would bring my lunch to the mine as she hadn't seen much of me with the extra hours I was doing. I had a break between shifts, so I walked down the road to meet her. We decided to sit on the grass away from the road for a bit because I was hoping for more than lunch. I was a young man, Bridget, you understand, I had needs. The letter fell out of my pocket as I flapped my jacket out to lay on the ground for us to sit on. Clara snatched it before I could stop her. She must have seen something in my face because she wouldn't give it back and she saw that the postmark was from Australia. I don't know how she guessed, but she did, she ran from me and opened it then she threatened to tell you what I'd done. I could tell by the look on her face that she knew why it was I'd done what I'd done, and she started to scream at me.

I just wanted her to stop making all that noise. It got inside my head, and I wanted it to stop. I never meant to hurt her but when I pushed her she fell backward, and I panicked. It's no excuse, but it's the truth. She'd hit her head on a rock, and there was a pool of blood. She was gone just like that and I was so bloody frightened. It was as if I was somebody else that day. It's the only way I can explain what I did next because I picked her up and took her to the old mine shaft where she was found. I was going to confess to what I'd done, the guilt was terrible, but the days ticked by and it got harder and harder. Everybody believed she'd fallen in the shaft. I couldn't see how it would make things better by telling the truth as to what happened and then one day you looked my way. You needed me and I knew that if I tried hard enough I could make myself believe she really had fallen into that shaft.

Please forgive me, Bridget, for Clara, for not being faithful to you in our marriage and for all the hurt we have caused

each other. Only it was so hard you see, to love you and to know that you didn't love me back the same way.
Your husband, Tom

Bridget crumpled the paper, her husband's confession, and tossed it on the fire before striking a match. She watched the ball of paper erupt into flame and continued to kneel there until it was no more than a pile of ash. She had to hold onto the chair to haul herself upright. It was hard to believe now that she'd once been agile enough to do handstands, she thought, walking through to her bedroom, her hand supporting her hip. She paused in front of her dressing table to look at herself in the mirror trying to see what Charlie would see when he looked at her.

She couldn't believe that she was that old lady looking back at her. Where had that girl with the mane of dark hair, smooth skin and flashing eyes disappeared to? She caught glimpses of her from time to time in Isla and felt a pang for her lost youth. That was the cruel thing about aging, Bridget mused. Although your body gave the game away inside you never actually felt old. What was that saying? Something about a silk purse, that was it. 'You can't make a silk purse out of a sow's ear,' she said out loud to the old woman in the mirror. Well, she could bloody well try, she thought putting on her lipstick and fluffing her hair.

When the knock on the door came later that same day, Bridget knew it was Charlie. Even still, she clutched the door frame to steady herself when she opened the door, surprised her knees didn't give way seeing him standing there. He hadn't changed, she thought drinking in the sight of him. Oh, he'd gotten older of course, but he was still Charlie. It was in his eyes and the curve of his mouth as he smiled. She noticed his hand trembling as he held the bunch of red roses out towards her.

'These are for you, Bridget. I'm sorry if I've given you a fright. I would've telephoned but I wasn't sure you'd let me call on you, and I had to see you.' He studied her face. 'You're still my beautiful Bridget. I knew you would be.'

Bridget was conscious of her white hair and the age spots on the back of her hands as she took the flowers from him. Red roses were her favourite. He had remembered. She was too old to be coy and bury her nose in the sweet smell of the bouquet. She found her tongue at last. 'Isla told me you were coming. These are lovely Charlie, it's been a long time since I've had flowers, but you shouldn't have come back here.'

'They're still your favourite?'

'They are.'

'Do you know that I've lived a whole life since my time with you, but I never got over you, Bridget Upton. That's why I had no choice but to come when your granddaughter called.'

'She overstepped the mark there, and it's Bridget Collins these days. It has been for a very long time.'

'Yes, you married Tom.'

Bridget felt herself bristle at the accusatory tone. 'And you? Did you marry and have a family?'

'No. I had two significant others in my life though, and I have two sons who are both grown up with families of their own now. They're good lads.' His voice choked. 'We're too old to pussyfoot around each other. Why did you never write back to me? That's what I came here to find out, why you broke my heart the way you did. I thought you loved me as much as I loved you.'

'Charlie, I ...' The confusion and the hurt on his face even now so many years later was hard to bear witness to. She didn't know what to say. The truth would hurt him more, but he had waited a long time to hear as much of it as she had decided she would ever divulge. 'You broke my heart too, you know.'

'How? I would've waited for you, but you couldn't wait for me. I understood a little when I heard of Clara's death but still, to not write back and tell me that you didn't feel the same way anymore. That was the worst of it, Bridget, the not knowing what had happened.'

'Oh Charlie, I can't do this. You should have left things well alone.'

'Ah, but I can't, you and I have an unfinished history. You see Bridget, I reached a conclusion one day that I'm getting old, and I don't want to waste another day wondering. I had to come and see you again, but I can see it's been a shock to you and it's not my intention to upset you. I'll leave you to think things through.' He took a step backwards. 'I'm staying at Fern House, do you know it?'

Bridget nodded, it was the bed and breakfast near the river.

'I'll leave you be for now but please when you're ready, come and see me. We owe it to each other, don't we?'

She gave a small nod and turned away, shutting the door on him before he could see the tears that she knew were about to spill over. Leaning her head back against the solid timber of the door, she blinked hard to make them disappear but they escaped and streaked down her cheeks nevertheless. Hearing him go, and still clutching the blooms she went through to the living room, pulling the curtain back. His body was slightly stooped by age and his hair too was white like hers was – but he was still her Charlie, she thought watching him walk back down the path.

It was as though all the ensuing years had melted away at the sight of him. She let the curtain fall back and buried her nose in the roses, inhaling their pungent sweet scent wanting to hold onto something tangible and real. There was so much water that had gone under the bridge, too much and her mind began to trace the tracks back to that night in the hospital when Tom had wheezed and coughed his way through the story that she wished he'd never told her. A story that she could never share in its entirety because of the hurt it would inflict. She could never tell Charlie the truth of what happened all those years ago.

'I'm alright Mum, stop fussing, and for goodness' sake can you go a bit faster, you'll get a ticket at this rate.' Isla was seated next to Mary who was driving as though she'd reached an age when she should be considering relinquishing her license.

'I feel like I did when your brother was born and we brought him home from the hospital. It was windy that day too, I remember being frightened a tree might come down in it. I tell you Isla, you won't understand this until you have a baby of your own, but it's terrifying finding yourself in a car with a newborn and realizing that baby is now your responsibility.'

'Hmm.'

'I just don't want to hit any potholes, not with your ribs still healing.'

Isla shuddered at the mention of potholes. 'I'll be fine, Mum. I took some pain relief tablets before we left.' The hospital was getting further and further behind them. Mary put her foot on the accelerator.

'God, Mum it's all or nothing with you,' Isla said gripping the seat.

'Stop being a backseat driver and yes, I know you're in the front. Did Dad tell you I'm going to be his money girl at the festival? He's charging five dollars for a ride on his Harley, and he'll donate the proceeds to the Westpac Chopper Appeal.'

Isla was touched. She'd be forever grateful to the helicopter service, but she shuddered at the thought of her mother dressed up like Olivia Newton-John's bad girl in Grease as her father revved his engine nearby.

'Promise me, Mum that you won't wear those black spandex pants of yours and remember you haven't smoked in years.'

'You have your sense of humour back, that's a sign you're on the mend.

'I wasn't joking.' Isla leaned back in the seat. She closed her eyes and let her mother's voice wash over her, only tuning back in as they reached the turn off for Bibury.

'Nearly home love. Dad's meeting us at your gran's, and Annie and Kris said they were going to call in and say hello. I've made a nice shepherd's pie for tea, and there's plenty to go around if they want to stay for a bite. Your gran will be warming it in the oven as we speak.'

'Page one hundred and twenty-nine of the *Edmonds Cookery Book*.' Isla smiled at the mention of her mother's trusty recipe for feeding a tribe.

Chapter 39

The pie was a dinnertime hit, and Joe and Mary announced they would be heading off once the pavlova Bridget had made for pudding had been polished off. Joe said they wanted to get back and go for a ride on the bike to get into the swing of things for the festival. Isla watched in amusement as he piled the empty bowls together before swaggering to the sink and putting them down on the bench. She blamed his cowboy boots for this new walk of his; that, and all the time he spent sitting astride his bike. She shifted in her chair, trying to get comfortable and Annie flashed her a sympathetic smile before getting up to help Kris with the dishes.

'Be careful in that wind out there,' Bridget said to Joe and Mary. 'I've never known anything like it. These last few months it just seems to blow up out of nowhere.'

'Always am when I'm carrying precious cargo, Bridget,' Joe said hooking his thumbs through his jeans belt loops as Mary came over to where Isla was still sitting at the table to give her a careful hug.

She returned the embrace with as big a squeeze as she could muster. She was pleased to see her mother was looking more her usual orange self once again. 'Thanks for bringing me home today, Mum. I'm sorry for all the bother I've caused.'

'Don't be silly sweetheart, we're just glad to have you home.'

'You know if Delilah's too far gone I know of a Hilux going for a fair price,' Joe said with a naughty gleam in his eyes.

'She'll be good as new when the panel beater's finished with her thank you very much.'

'God, you sounded just like your grandmother then,' he muttered as his wife dragged him down the hall calling out good night to everybody.

Kris was wiping the bench down when Annie announced they should make tracks too.

'Rest up,' Annie said, giving Isla a kiss on the cheek. She'd made Isla promise not to show her face at Nectar for at least another day, bored or not, telling her she needed to be in form for the festival. It was only five days away after all. The girls were planning on the café being open on the big day and having a food stall where they could slip customers the café's calling card at the festival. Isla had organized a stack of coffee gratuity cards weeks ago, and the festival would be a fantastic opportunity to spread the word about Nectar and the good food on offer there.

They were going to split the day into two shifts. Isla was on the morning shift at the festival and Annie the afternoon. Isla had decided to take Marie's daughter Callie on permanently, on a part-time basis. Annie had said she worked like a trooper while Isla was in the hospital and the café was busy enough to warrant the extra pair of hands these days. It would ease the pressure off both of them from having to be on board seven days a week.

'Oh, and I'm with your mum, it's good to have you home.'

Isla smiled at her and Kris, feeling very lucky to have such lovely people in her life. 'Thanks for coming tonight, you two.'

Kris squeezed out the sponge and put it by the sink, smiling over at her before turning his attention to Bridget. 'The dessert was delicious, Bridget. I've never had this pavlova dish before; I think it's my new favourite.'

Bridget was already scooping some into an empty ice cream container for him to take home.

'Thanks for having everyone around tonight Gran, it was a lovely welcome home,' Isla said when her gran had seen the others off. She was putting the kettle on to make a pot of tea.

'My pleasure, but now it's just the two of us Isla, I think you have some explaining to do, don't you?'

Isla looked at her gran blankly, and then the penny dropped, *Charlie was here already*. 'Oh, right.'

'Yes, oh right indeed. A shock like the one I had today is not good for someone in their dusky years.'

'Twilight years Gran.'

'That's what I said.'

Isla knew better than to argue, besides she had some grovelling to do. 'Gran, I'm sorry. I hope I haven't caused too much upset, but I promise my intentions with Charlie were all good.' She picked at a dried bit of mince on the tablecloth. 'It was just that his cards read like there was unfinished business between the two of you and he sounded so lovely on the phone – and oh Gran, I just want you to be happy that's all.'

Bridget appreciated, as she looked at her granddaughter, that she shared the same sentiments where she was concerned.

If only Isla and Ben would look to the future and put their shared history behind them. It made her pause; the same could be said about her and Charlie. She couldn't change what had happened all those years ago, but she could change what would happen next in however many years she had left. She jumped as the back door blew open, and got up to shut it, sliding the lock across. 'Blasted, bloody wind.'

It was a relief to see the tendrils of pink lighten the sky, signalling morning had arrived at long last. Bridget wished she could erase the dark circles from beneath her eyes and was tempted to head across the road to see if Mary and her magic Revlon potions could undo the evidence of her sleepless night. She wasn't ready to tell her daughter about Charlie yet though, and so she'd done her best with a spot of pressed powder and blush. It would be unseemly to arrive on the doorstep of the Fern Bed & Breakfast before 10am, and she felt awash with tea by the time she closed the front door behind her and made her way around the road to the B&B.

'I never got your letters, Charlie, Tom kept them all and burned every one of them,' she said having decided to come right out with it. Charlie was right; they were too old to pussyfoot around. They were sitting in the front room of the B&B, having made sure the door was shut. Bridget knew of Jill Doyle the proprietor's gossipy tendencies. Still, she thought, her eyes skimming over the old homestead's high skirting boards as she waited for Charlie's reaction, she ran a clean house and that was the important thing.

Charlie was seated in the chintzy armchair opposite her, and she was momentarily mesmerized by the vein throbbing in his neck. 'What did you just say?'

'Tom never—'

He waved his hand impatiently. 'I know what you said. I just can't make sense of it.'

'That's just it, Charlie, there *is* no sense to it.' Bridget had thought long and hard about what she would tell him and what she would never tell a soul. Not just for herself but for the sake of her family and the memories they held of Tom too. He hadn't just been her husband; he'd been a father and a grandfather too. It would benefit no one to know the truth of how Clara died. 'He told me what he'd done with your letters when he was dying. It seems he was in love with me from the off and that poor Clara was merely a convenient distraction.'

Charlie made a choking sound and shook his head. 'All those years I thought you hadn't kept your word and here you thought I hadn't kept mine. I thought he was my friend, I trusted him. That bastard! I'm sorry Bridget I know you were married a long time but still—'

'I was angry when he told me what he'd done too, but then he died, and I knew it was a waste of energy because it was too late to change anything. Tom was gone, there was nobody to rail at, what was done, was done. Besides,' she said clasping her hands together, 'we'd lived a life together, raised a family together and seen our grandchildren come into this world. It wasn't all bad, Charlie, and I won't ever regret my children.'

He was silent, thoughtful for a few beats before speaking,

'I'd never expect that of you. I have sons of my own and grandchildren that I would never be without too. What I don't understand, is why you didn't contact me when you got my cards?'

'I was scared to.'

'Why Bridget?'

'I didn't want you to feel all that hurt and anger that I'd felt when I found out about the letters. It was almost too much to bear and look at me, for heaven's sake. I'm not that young girl you danced with and kissed down by the river anymore. Your head was always full of romantic notions, and I might be an old lady, but I'm also a proud lady.'

'You silly woman, don't you know I *was* hurt and angry for years? Can't you see? I needed to know what happened, why you never wrote to me. It didn't make sense to me because the girl I fell in love with wouldn't have behaved like that. That's why I've come back.' He got up from his seat, moving across the room towards her. 'And you'll never be old Bridget; it's not in your nature. You're still the most beautiful woman I've ever laid my eyes upon.'

He held out his hand to her, Bridget inhaled deeply. This was her chance. It would not come again, this second chance at happiness and so she took it, grabbing his hand with both of hers, knowing that this time she would not let go.

Bridget and Charlie were inseparable in the days leading up to the festival as they got to know one another again. They spent their time walking the familiar paths of bygone years, hand in hand. The years seemed to melt away, and she felt young and carefree in his company. She felt giddy with the joy of falling in love all over again. She'd have liked to have kept Charlie all to herself, but it wouldn't be fair for Mary to hear her mother had a beau from anybody else. She'd decided the best course of action where her family was concerned was to take the bull by the ears and invite them to lunch to meet him.

Now, as she sprinkled grated cheese over the top of the lasagne she'd made, her stomach fluttered at the prospect of how this luncheon would go. She was just as nervous as she'd been the first time Charlie had come calling for her. Back then though he'd had to pass her father's inspection. How ironic that today he needed her daughter's and son-in-law's stamp of approval. The difference this time around though, Bridget thought popping the dish in the oven, was that if Joe or Mary disapproved, they'd just have to get over themselves because she was not letting go of this man twice.

Charlie was the first to arrive, and she took the single red rose from him with a tsk telling him he shouldn't have. He was spoiling her.

'I'm making up for lost time,' he said leaning in to kiss her and Bridget responded with enthusiastic warmth. It was then that Joe's white Hilux roared up the drive. Bridget gasped breaking away from Charlie's embrace, as she watched Joe nearly take out the apple tree at the sight of his elderly mother-in-law kissing some old geezer on the front porch. Bridget couldn't help but think that the colour of Mary's complexion would be listed as Vermillion if it were to be described on a colour wheel, as she staggered towards them. They were not off to the best of starts and, she felt a surge of relief as Isla came to stand beside them in solidarity.

'Everybody, I'd like you to meet Charlie Callahan.'

Bridget ushered a gobsmacked Mary and Joe inside; Charlie hung back wanting a minute alone with Isla.

He took her hands in his. 'I was so sorry to hear of your accident my dear, but you look like you're on the mend.'

'I am, thank you.'

'You're the image of her,' he said.

Any doubt Isla felt at her actions in bringing Charlie to Bibury disappeared when she saw the genuine warmth in his smile as he said, 'I can't thank you enough for giving us both a second chance at happiness.'

At first, the conversation around the table was stilted. Bridget sympathized with her daughter, watching as she toyed with the lasagne on the plate in front of her. It must feel like one shock after another what with Isla's accident and now her mother's old beau arriving on the scene. Joe though, was behaving like a prized prat as he drilled Charlie like he was still that young man who'd called to her front door, cap in hand, all those years ago. She'd seen Isla elbow her father to try and get him to shut up as she valiantly tried to lighten the atmosphere by asking questions about Charlie's life in Perth.

It was as the coffee and jam tart came out that Charlie managed to win Joe and Mary over. Joe got up from the table excusing himself to pay a visit, and as he sauntered off in the direction of the bathroom, Charlie called after him. 'Great boots!' As for Mary, he appealed to her vanity. 'You know Mary if I hadn't known you were Isla's mother, I would've had you pegged as sisters.'

Isla made a note to change the tint of her foundation.

Chapter 40

The day of the festival dawned with a clear blue sky. 'Thank goodness that wind's finally dropped,' Bridget said, her hand firmly in Charlie's as she surveyed the scene around her with a sense of profound satisfaction. The Barker's Creek Hall stood smartly to attention with a line of people crowding the path to its entrance as they queued to see Rohan, the official Matchmaker. They'd just had the official unveiling of Clara's statue, and the beautiful bronze gleamed under the hot sun near where they stood.

The unveiling had been followed by Bridget giving a speech about Clara. She touched on the tragedy of her death but focused on the positive aspects of her short life. She'd said thank you to all those who had supported Project Matchmaker and the restorations of Barker's Creek Hall before asking Saralee to come and stand alongside her. She told the crowd the day simply would not have happened without her help and there was a generous round of applause. Her words had been well received by those that had come to see what all the fuss was about.

Clara's Last Dance as the statue had been called was everything Bridget had hoped for. It was the mark of a true artist that, despite never having known her, Ian had still managed to capture her friend's joie de vivre. It was the expression he had sculpted on her face. The full skirt and jauntily tied scarf denoted the era. He was indeed a talent to be reckoned with, she thought, spying him being ushered towards his latest masterpiece by a reporter from the *Bibury Times*. To the reporter's chagrin, however, an elderly woman leaped into his line of sight and photobombed the shot.

'Margaret, get out the way! What do you think you're doing? Come here, I've someone I want you to meet,' Bridget called over to her friend.

'So many memories,' Charlie said, quietly looking to the hall and then back at Clara's Last Dance oblivious to the silver-topped woman stampeding in their direction. 'That was such a lovely touch, Bridget. Clara would have loved it.'

She gripped his hand a little tighter before introducing him to her friend.

'Close your mouth Margaret; this is Charlie Callahan. We knew each other a long time ago, and I'm very pleased to tell you we have recently rekindled our friendship.' Against her better judgment Bridget left Margaret talking to Charlie and went in search of Isla. She wanted to introduce her to Rohan Sullivan before the official matchmaking proceedings got underway.

Rohan had kept his word and arrived in town the night before. As part of the fundraising effort, Mick Freeman had agreed to accommodate him at the Pit. Rohan had told Bridget that while not fancy, the lodgings were perfectly adequate and

Mick knew his way around a kitchen and how to handle a frying pan.

Isla's bruising was fading but her gait was still ginger, Bridget noticed, as her granddaughter walked carefully alongside her to meet the Matchmaker and man of the hour. But she was definitely on the mend.

'Gran, you're right he does look like one of Snow White's seven dwarfs,' Isla whispered as she followed Bridget over to where he'd set himself up at the stage end of the hall. He also looked familiar as though she knew him, had always known him. It was a most peculiar feeling, she thought, shaking the fanciful idea away.

'Rohan, this is my granddaughter, Isla.'

'I know.'

'Pardon me?'

He didn't reply, and Bridget decided she must have misheard him as he opened his old book, smoothing the tea-coloured pages with reverence. Isla inhaled, fancying she could smell the aged leather binding.

'So how does this all work then?' she asked, peering over at the book and seeing the pages he had it opened to were blank.

'Ah well now, it's a straightforward enough business. I have a bit of a chat with him or her, note down their age and their interests in here.' He tapped the book with his stubby index finger. 'And then as the day gets long, I begin to match him and her or him and him or her and her or whomever up.'

'The idea, of course, being that those paired off will use

the opportunity of the dance tonight to let romance blossom,' Bridget said.

Rohan nodded and picked up a pen from the pot full on the table top. Isla thought he would have been better suited to a feather quill and an ink pot. She watched him do a tiny doodle in the corner of the blank page before gazing up at them both with clear, piercing blue eyes and announcing that he was ready to begin. They left him to get on with what most of the crowd outside had come for, the business of finding their perfect match.

Isla waved Bridget off to rescue Charlie from Margaret. She had to get back to the stall. She'd left Callie manning it, but as proprietor of Nectar, she needed to show her face. They were doing a stellar trade with the boxes of chocolate truffles rolled in pink salt they'd made up in advance having been a morning tea time hit. She hoped the fresh ciabatta rolls they'd filled for the lunchtime rush were as successful. Isla caught a whiff of coffee beans as she passed by one of two coffee carts set up on the grounds. She was glad they'd opted out of doing coffee, there was too much competition for the sake of all the complicated logistics of having a machine on site.

Kris had helped set up a trestle table with a gazebo covering them for shade. Gran had done a fantastic job with the bunting she'd made, Isla thought, as she approached the stall with a cluster of people gathered around it chatting to Callie. They'd attached the bunting to the cloth covering the table, and the burst of colour looked pretty against the white fabric. She'd put a copy of *Southern Gastronomy*, open to Nectar's glowing review, on the table for customers to glance at. She and Callie had been handing out the coffee cards along with change and the promise of a free slice when the customer popped into the café and showed their card.

Kris was helping at the stall, and spotting her approaching, he finished serving a woman who, Isla noticed with amusement as she took her place behind the table, was batting her eyelashes at him. She was seemingly more interested in the man behind the ciabatta than the roll he was placing in a brown paper bag for her. Well, Annie needn't worry Isla thought. Kris only had eyes for her.

'It's going great.' Kris grinned oblivious to what had just played out.

Callie looked over at Isla. 'You'll have to text Annie and get her to fill more rolls.'

'Will do, we're due to swap over shortly so she can bring them down then. You're doing a great job, Callie.'

The younger girl stood a little taller.

Isla sent off a quick text to Annie and then gazed around the field. She guessed the café would be quiet. All of Bibury along with a good portion of the South Island population were here, judging by the thronging crowds. She'd seen David and Carl along with their enormous entourage of extraordinarily attractive people earlier. Carl had announced that he and David had been introduced to Charlie and that they'd given him their stamp of approval. His exact words had been. 'Go Bridget, I say. He's a silver fox, and I might be keen myself if it weren't for lover boy here.' The pair of them were off mingling now.

Isla smiled as she spied a familiar face weaving through

the crowd. It was the gumboot man who'd been after a New Year's Eve kiss, clad in his summer uniform of singlet and shorts. He was charging after the burger loving model Carl had introduced them to when he first arrived, Sasha.

The field surrounding the hall was a sight to behold. It was a sea of bobbing heads; there were food and drink caravans as well as an assortment of arts and crafts stalls. The smell of fried food intermingled with the scent of Asian and Middle-Eastern spices and there was a general sense of excitement at the possibilities today might bring, floating on the now gentle breeze. An impressive line of port-a-loos stood sentry at the far end of the field like troops lining up for battle. On a makeshift stage to the left of the field, the Scottish Society was demonstrating a highland fling while on the far right-hand side the Bibury Line Dancers in direct competition were taking a turn to the strains of 'Footloose'.

'Saralee has worked wonders,' Isla said to no one in particular. 'This is amazing.' Her heart swelled with pride at the sight of it all. It was a year to the day since she'd arrived home. So much had happened in that year that she'd had to pinch herself to make sure it was all real, or at least she'd had to until the painkillers began to wear off and the scorching pain of her ribs let her know that, no, this wasn't all a dream. Still, someone had been looking out for her that night because the accident could have been much worse. She was blessed to have the people she had in her life. Here in Bibury she'd re-established the bonds with her family, made wonderful new friends and opened her own business. There was still one unfinished bit of business though, but that would have to wait until later.

'Speaking of whom, there she goes,' Kris said gesturing with the tongs he was holding to where Saralee was marching along talking to a small group of Japanese tourists. She was wearing a vest that declared her to be an 'event organiser' and Callum trotted behind her like an adoring oversized puppy dog. She spied Isla looking over, and the couple gave her a thumbs-up. She grinned back at them.

A low rumbling distracted her and Isla craned her neck to see a Harley snaking slowly through the crowd. It came to a halt beside the stall. Joe took off his helmet. Her father looked like an aged gang member, Isla thought, choking back a laugh as her mother followed suit. Mary shook her hair out before retrieving a red bandana from the pocket of her leather jacket pocket and tying it around her hair, Axl Rose style.

'Just cruising by to say hi,' Joe said. 'I'll have a roll if there's one spare,' he called over to Kris.

'Sure thing Joe, looking good Mary,' Kris said bagging up a couple of rolls.

God, they were embarrassing, Isla thought watching as her dad, with a yoga-like move, reached around to pinch her mum on the bum.

Rohan had disappeared by the time the band got underway inside the hall that night. Bridget assumed he had taken himself back to the Pit, tired after his big day of making matches. She was grateful the wind that had begun to blow outside once more had held off until the last of the stall holders had packed up.

That the day had been a huge success, an unprecedented event for Bibury, everybody who had come up to talk to her over the course of the evening had agreed. Indeed, it had been everything that she'd hoped it would be and so much more, she thought with a fond glance at Charlie. She spotted Elsie scurrying importantly into the kitchen and told herself she must remember to go and check on the line dancing ladies and the Scottish Society volunteers who were beavering away in the newly refurbished kitchen getting the supper organized. Their services had been offered in exchange for one month's free use of the hall. Bibury Area's PTA had provided the food for the supper in exchange for a donation out of the funds the festival had raised, to go towards new laptops for the school. It had all worked out rather well.

New romances were blossoming on the dance floor, Bridget thought, as her eyes swept the hall. There was Violet McDougall taking a turn with Principal Bishop and the young lad from the butcher's was twirling the lass who worked at the Four Square. Really, she thought the doctor should have a word with the girl and tell her she was in danger of damaging her vitals wearing pants that tight. Oh, and there was the police officer everybody called Tep leading Marie the hairdresser out onto the floor.

There were lots of sights Bridget knew Biddy Johnson would have been aghast at, had she been there with them tonight. The first was Carl and David who were holding hands on the periphery of the dance floor and whispering in each other's ears. *Now that was something you would not have seen in Biddy's day*. Kris and Annie hadn't come up for air during the last three songs and Joe was dancing with his hands clamped firmly on his wife's bottom. All of them would have earned a sharp tap on the shoulder from Biddy Johnson's stick in her day.

It was Isla who caught her attention now though; she looked so lovely in her pink dress, Bridget thought, holding her breath as her granddaughter approached the bench where Ben sat.

Isla held her trembling hand out. 'Will you dance with me because I'm wearing pink.'

Ben smiled and, taking her hand, he got to his feet. 'I will because you look so pretty in pink.'

Bridget watched as Ben and Isla moved onto the dancefloor. She exhaled as she saw him bend his head and kiss Isla in a way that told her they would be fine from hereon in.

For Isla's part, there was nothing but that moment. The music faded, and the crowded dancefloor seemed to empty. She was aware of nothing but the feel of Ben's hands spanning her waist as his lips settled over hers and she was filled with profound joy. She was home and she planned on never leaving. She was exactly where she wanted to be for the rest of her days.

Bridget registered that Charlie was holding his hand out to her and taking it, she let him help her to her feet. He led her out onto the dancefloor, and she rested her head on his shoulder, grateful for a slow song. She looked up and caught a glimpse over his shoulder of a busty young woman with an infectious grin and a swinging ponytail, dressed in a rock'n'roll skirt. Bridget watched as Clara blew her a kiss and waved goodbye.

A Final Word If I May

I blew away that night having made many a successful match at the festival where old wrongs were righted. Life's journey can be an odd thing. Take Isla for instance; she was the one who ran away and came back to stay while Bridget who'd never left, flew far away. She went on a holiday to Ireland with Charlie, and I heard tell on the wind of a wedding in September. Oh, and in case you're wondering, Violet McDougall and Jim Bishop are now living in the proverbial sin next door to the young lad from the butcher's, Beau, who's playing house with his girlfriend Ellie from the Four Square. That nice policeman, Tep, and his hairdressing lady friend, Marie, are still stepping out together, and as for Callum and Saralee, they're like a pair of young kittens in each other's company, despite going strong for a good long while now. Carl and David are holidaying in the Maldives or some such place while Annie and Kris are packing their bags – there's a mother across the seas who says it's time for her to meet this woman her son loves so well.

All their stories are only just beginning but suffice to say that the two most stubborn women that I ever witnessed walk the West Coast, Isla Brookes and Bridget Collins, finally got their happy ending.

Acknowledgements

The seed for this book was planted after a family weekend spent on New Zealand's wild West Coast. We drove up to the inhospitable Denniston Plateau, a formerly flourishing mining settlement for only the most resilient that once visited is not forgotten. I would like to dedicate this story to those hardy souls and to those families of the Pike River Mine disaster whose grief just goes on. Your boys will never be forgotten, and I hope one day you can bring them home.

My awesome mother-in-law, Pam Vernal has wonderful tales of the dances she used to go to which I've used to pepper this story. I fell in love with the idea of the WHS society (the Wandering Hand Society), I hope you do too. Thanks, Pam. Thank you too, to Deirdre Kingdon. Our chat about what it was like being part of a Catholic family in New Zealand in the fifties was invaluable. I'd also like to say a massive thank you to Vicki Marsdon my agent at Wordlink literary agency for her continued input and faith in my abilities. Louise Thurtell for her helpful pointers as to the direction of this story. Charlotte, Eloisa and the wonderful team from Harper

Impulse, for your enthusiasm and vision that have shaped this book into one I am proud of. My lovely readers and their kind words that make the long hours on the laptop worthwhile. I'm truly blessed with my wonderful family and friends who are always interested and supportive; I love you all. Finally, to my three best boys Paul, Josh, and Daniel with whom life is an exciting adventure, you are my world x.

Printed in Great Britain
by Amazon

82569172R00233